Adventurers
⬥ Wanted ⬥

Other Books by M. L. Forman

ADVENTURERS WANTED, BOOK ONE:
Slathbog's Gold

ADVENTURERS WANTED, BOOK TWO:
The Horn of Moran

BOOK THREE

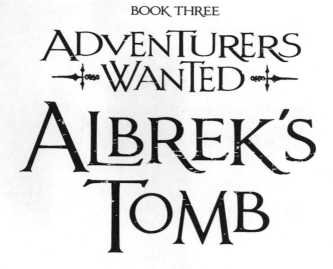

ADVENTURERS
⊷WANTED⊷
ALBREK'S
TOMB

M. L. FORMAN

SHADOW
MOUNTAIN

To my family, who is always there for me

Library of Congress Cataloging-in-Publication Data

Forman, Mark, 1964–
    Albrek's tomb / M. L. Forman.
        pages cm.—(Adventurers wanted, book 3)
        Summary: Newly-named wizard Alexander Taylor joins a familiar company of adventurers on a new quest to discover the fate of the legendary dwarf Albrek, find his mythical tomb, and locate the lost talisman that could be the key needed to save the entire dwarf realm.
        ISBN 978-1-60908-892-7 (hardbound : alk. paper)
      1. Young adult fiction, American. [1. Orphans—Fiction   2. Teenage boys—Fiction.   3. Wizards—Fiction.   4. Dwarves—Fiction.   5. Magic—Fiction.]
I. Title.   II. Series: Adventurers wanted ; bk 3.
    PZ7.F7653Alb 2012
    [Fic]—dc23   2011028997

Printed in the United States of America
R. R. Donnelley, Crawfordsville, IN

10 9 8 7 6 5 4 3 2

CONTENTS

CONTENTS

CONTENTS

ACKNOWLEDGMENTS

———◆———

Well, it's time for acknowledgments again, and I'm still not certain how this is supposed to work. How do you really thank so many people for everything they've done? Well, I'll give it a go, and if I leave someone out, I'm sorry.

Right up front I want to thank you, the reader. You are the people who make this all possible, and without you these stories would just sit in a computer file gathering . . . well, whatever the electronic equivalent of dust is. I thank you all and hope that the stories never let you down.

Special thanks to my editor, Lisa Mangum, who saves me from myself and makes people believe I know what I'm doing when I write. I should do more than just thank her, I should probably apologize for all the headaches I'm sure I've given her. Lisa, the next bottle of aspirin is on me.

Thanks to Chris Schoebinger, the big cheese at Shadow Mountain. I still don't know what his real title is, but he's still getting things done. Somehow he always finds time to answer my questions, read my work, and point out some of the bigger problems before the story ever gets to the editor. (Lisa, you might want to split that bottle of aspirin with Chris.)

Credit should also be given to Brandon Dorman, the illustrator. I'm always surprised and excited to see what the new cover looks like, and somehow it is always better than what I imagined.

Special thanks to Richard Erickson, Art Director. I'll be honest and say that I don't think I've ever met Richard, and I have to take other people's word that he's out there. I think Shadow Mountain must keep him locked in his office, working on projects all the time, but I'm glad he had time to work on mine.

And finally, a big thank-you to all the folks at Shadow Mountain who didn't get their names put into type. I know there are a lot of people doing a lot of hard work to make this happen, and I thank you.

CHAPTER ONE

A NEW QUEST

––––––◦◦◦◦∣◦◦◦––––––

The heat from the furnace was intense. Alex stood close, sweat dripping off his nose as he watched the small porcelain bowl filled with several lumps of true-silver ore. He was working in the smithy that his father had installed inside his magic bag, but no matter how hot the furnace got, the ore in the bowl simply would not melt. Alex moved back to the workbench, checking the book he'd been reading.

Alex had taken up working in the smithy as a hobby on the advice of his teacher, Whalen Vankin.

"Focusing on something nonmagical will give you a chance to work with your hands as well as relax your mind," Whalen had said. "If you think about magic all the time, you might not notice the normal things that are going on around you."

As Alex reread the page that explained how to work with true silver, he heard an odd tutting sound. He straightened up and looked around the room. The furnace hissed, the bellows pumped, and the true silver remained unchanged. He returned to the book, but he'd already read the information three times. He snapped it shut in frustration.

Another sound met his ears: a soft *humph*. He looked at the furnace again, but nothing had changed and the sound wasn't repeated. He moved closer, checked the status of the true silver again, and finally shut off the waterwheel that worked the bellows. The smithy was quiet, except for the furnace that continued to hiss and moan as it cooled.

Alex carefully removed the bowl from the furnace and poured the lumps of true silver onto the sand-covered table. He tried to bend the lumps or twist them—he even took one piece to the anvil and hit it with a hammer—but nothing he did made a dent.

The tutting sound came again, much louder now that the waterwheel and the bellows had stopped. Alex felt someone— or perhaps something—was watching him. Turning slowly, he scanned the smithy. He was alone, but the feeling of being watched remained.

"Who's there?" Alex asked out loud.

Silence.

"I know there's someone there," said Alex. "You might as well speak up because I *will* find you, one way or another."

He heard a soft *humph* from the far side of the room, a *humph* that said, "I doubt it."

"Come now, show yourself," said Alex. "I won't hurt you."

Again there was no reply.

Alex sent out a bit of magic to search the room as he tried once more to coax the hidden watcher out. "I'm being as nice as I can about this. Please, show yourself before I have to force you into the open."

The silence remained, but Alex's magic had found something. There was a small creature standing behind the books on the far side of the room. Alex had no idea what the creature was, but he didn't think it was dangerous.

"Very well, if you will not show yourself, I will have to use magic to force you into the open," said Alex.

Another loud *humph,* which Alex took to mean, "I don't believe you will succeed, but feel free to try."

"You asked for it," Alex muttered.

Alex remained still and silent, letting the magic he had used to find the creature form into a magical rope around the creature's legs. As the rope took shape, Alex added a little more magic to the spell, but the creature must have noticed what was happening because there was a gasp, followed by the sound of running feet. Alex was ready. The magic rope pulled tight, lifting the creature into the air and whisking it toward a large empty table in the middle of the room. Alex watched as his captive floated upside down above the tabletop; it looked like a nine-inch-tall dwarf.

"Gear offva me! Let go!" the creature shouted. "I've done nothing wrong. I claim the right of sanctuary in this bag!"

"The right of sanctuary? Who are you, and what are you doing here?" Alex questioned.

"I might ask you the same thing," answered the creature. "I'll answer to Master Joshua and none other."

"Joshua?"

"The master of the bag, Joshua Taylor," said the creature, looking at Alex suspiciously. "I demand to see the master of the bag."

"I'm the master of the bag," said Alex. "I'm Alexander Taylor, Joshua Taylor's heir."

"If you're the heir, then you should know who and what I am," said the creature hotly. "Master Joshua wouldn't have given his bag to an heir and not told him about us."

"My father didn't tell me anything about his bag," said Alex. "He died when I was just a baby."

"Died? What do you mean *died*? I don't believe it, not one word of it," shouted the creature.

"It's true—" said Alex.

"Prove it," the creature interrupted.

"Prove what?"

"I want proof that Master Joshua is dead and that you are, in fact, his heir."

"I can give you my word."

"Ha! A likely story. Just what a bag thief would say. 'Give you my word,' indeed. What's the word of a bag thief worth?"

"I'm no thief," said Alex angrily. "I give you my word that what I've said is true, and if you are foolish enough to doubt the word of a wizard then I'll have to expel you from my bag."

"A wizard you say? Ha! Oh, you've got some magic in you that's plain enough to see, but you're no wizard. You're far too young; you've no staff and no familiar. You're not even wearing one of those funny robes that so many wizards like to wear."

"Silence," Alex demanded. "I am Alexander Taylor, wizard and adventurer. I am the son and heir of Joshua Taylor, and I do have a staff."

"Oh, do you now? Well then, Mr. Wizard, be so good as to show me your staff."

"All right, I'll go and get it."

"Go and get it, he says," the creature sneered. "As if a wizard needs to go and get his staff. Ha!"

Alex frowned at the insult. He'd only been a wizard for a couple of months, and he didn't need his staff very often. Especially when he was home and not on an adventure.

He closed his eyes for a moment, remembering the spell that would summon his staff to his hand. Opening his eyes, he held out his right hand, releasing the magic at the same moment. There was a sound like a rushing wind, and Alex's staff appeared in his open hand.

The creature gasped, and Alex almost burst out laughing as its eyes grew large and its mouth tried to fall open but failed because he was still upside down.

"Oh, sir, a thousand apologies," the creature stammered as Alex finally turned him right side up and released him. "I had no idea, I mean, Master Joshua never said—"

"Yes, I'm sure my father didn't get a chance to say a lot of things," said Alex. "Now, will you tell me who and what you are?"

"I'm Bobkin," said the creature, snapping to attention. "Master smitty and keeper of the sanctuary."

"Master smitty?" Alex questioned.

"Yes, sir." Bobkin smiled with pride. "We're magical folk that work in smithies. I'm not surprised you've never heard of us—not many people have. You may have heard of our cousins, though, the cobblers."

"Cobblers? Oh, the little people who help make shoes," said Alex.

"Shoes are what they are most known for, but they do all

kinds of leather work. None better in the known lands," said Bobkin.

"So you do the same kind of thing, only with smithing work," said Alex.

"We do."

"And you live here in this bag?"

"As keeper of the sanctuary, I have to stay," answered Bobkin. "Of course, that could change now, what with Master Joshua gone."

"Why would that change?"

"Your father was a kind man, sir, and he allowed us to set up a sanctuary here in his magic bag," said Bobkin. "Smittys won't work just anywhere; we have to be invited. And the smith doin' the inviting has to have some talent for the work. He has to see the work as something more than just a job. It takes the right attitude to be a great smith, and if a smith doesn't have it, we won't stay. There are times when we have no place at all to live."

"They have to see smith work as an art," said Alex in a thoughtful tone.

"Yes, an art," Bobkin agreed. "Smith work can be one of the greatest arts, but so few smiths see it that way."

"I think I understand," said Alex. "So you had nowhere else to go and my father let you stay in his bag."

"Yes, sir, he did," said Bobkin. "Only now he's not here, and since the bag is yours, it's up to you if we stay or go."

"We?" Alex questioned. "How many of you are there?"

"There are only three of us here now, but there have been

as many as twenty in the past. We live in the room behind the secret door," said Bobkin, pointing to the far side of the room.

"What secret door?"

"The bookshelf in the far corner," said Bobkin. "I can show you if you wish."

"Maybe later," said Alex, not wanting to be distracted from the conversation.

"And the sanctuary?" Bobkin questioned.

"I suppose you'd better keep it," said Alex. "I'm sure my father had good reasons for letting you stay, and I won't go against his wishes."

"Oh, thank you, sir, thank you," said Bobkin. "We are forever in your debt, and . . ."

"And?"

"Well, beggin' your pardon, sir, but if you'd like some instruction or help with your smithing work, we'd be only too happy to assist you," Bobkin said in a slightly nervous tone.

"I could use some help," Alex said, glancing toward the true silver on the table.

"Not many know how to work the true silver," said Bobkin. "The trick is to heat it slowly. If you put too much heat on it too fast, it hardens even more than it was to start with."

"Really? That's not what the book said."

"I suspect that whoever wrote that book knew more about writing then they did about smithing," said Bobkin with a snort. "Let me introduce you to my cousins and then we can discuss the art of working true silver."

Alex nodded, and Bobkin puffed up and let out a long,

loud whistle. A moment later, the bookshelf at the back of the smithy moved slightly, and two small figures came hurrying out of the hidden room, one leading the other. They both stopped abruptly at the sight of Alex.

"It's all right," Bobkin said, gesturing them forward. "This is Master Joshua's son and heir. He said we can keep the sanctuary."

"Thank goodness for that," said the smitty in the lead.

"Master Alexander Taylor," said Bobkin. "Let me introduce you to my cousins, Belkin and Dobkin."

"A great honor," said Belkin with a bow.

"Dobkin!" Dobkin shouted at the wall.

"Um, well, don't mind Dobkin," Bobkin said quickly. "He had a bit of an accident and hasn't been himself for some time. 'Course, he's getting better. He remembers his name now."

"It's about the only thing he remembers, actually," Belkin said.

"What happened to him?" Alex questioned.

"We're not sure," said Bobkin. "Near as we can tell, he got hit on the head with an anvil."

"Or maybe a large hammer," Belkin added.

"Is he all right? I mean, is there anything I can do?" Alex asked.

"Ah, most kind, but Dobkin's fine, or he will be," said Bobkin.

"Dobkin!" Dobkin shouted at the table.

"Bobkin's right. If you set Dobkin to work on something simple, he'll make a proper job of it," said Belkin. "I just wish he'd stop shouting his name at everything."

"Maybe you'd better take Dobkin back to the sanctuary," Bobkin suggested.

"Do accidents like Dobkin's happen very often?" Alex questioned as Belkin guided the confused smitty toward the bookshelf.

"No, not often," Bobkin answered. "And I'm sure Dobkin will come out of it sooner or later."

"I hope so," said Alex. "He doesn't look like he can take care of himself."

"He'll be fine—especially under the protection of the sanctuary," said Bobkin. "Now, about working with true silver."

Alex was soon deep in discussion with Bobkin about working not only with true silver but also with all kinds of other metals. The smitty was a fountain of information, and Alex had to ask him to slow down once or twice while he got things straight in his mind. Their discussion went on for a long time, and only ended when Alex's stomach grumbled and he realized how hungry he was.

"I'll come back and practice as soon as I can," Alex promised as he prepared to leave.

"Whenever you have time, Master Alex," said Bobkin with a wave. "We'll be here, ready and willing to help."

As soon as Alex left the magic bag and returned to his room, he heard a loud dinging noise and saw a bottle-necked geeb waiting on his desk. The strange bowling-pin-shaped creature balanced on the edge of the table, tilting slightly to one side on its single birdlike leg.

"Oh, sorry, have you been waiting long?" Alex questioned.

"Ding."

"Couldn't you have delivered the message to me inside my bag?"

"Honk."

"You can't enter magic bags?"

"Ding. Honk."

Alex thought for a moment, trying to understand the conflicting answers. "You can enter a magic bag, but only if I give you permission to do so?" he ventured.

"Ding."

"Then I give all geebs permission to enter either of my magic bags to deliver and take messages from me," said Alex.

"Ding."

"Do you have a message for me today?"

"Ding."

"May I have it, please?"

"Ding." The geeb produced a large envelope.

Alex recognized Whalen Vankin's handwriting on the envelope, and he quickly tore it open to read the letter inside.

Dear Alex,

I've been invited to join a new adventure in Thraxon but find that I don't have the time. I've suggested to the leader of this adventure that you might be willing to take my place. If so, please meet the leader tomorrow morning at ten o'clock at Mr. Clutter's shop.

I don't know all the details of this adventure, so if, after your meeting, you don't like the sound of it, don't go. After all, it's an invitation and not a demand. I would, however, ask that you let me know what you

decide regarding the adventure, and, that, if you go,
you keep me updated as to your progress.

Yours in fellowship,

Whalen

P.S. The council was very impressed when I told
them about your staff. We are considering it as your
fifth great wizarding task.

P.P.S. I know we talked about your coming to live
in Alusia, and I've found a wonderful place for you,
if you are still interested. Think about it, and let me
know.

Excitement flooded through Alex. This was an opportunity
to go back to the magical lands that had become an important
part of his life—a chance to explore a new place, meet new
friends, and hopefully reunite with some of his old friends. He
felt honored that Whalen had suggested him as a replacement,
and he hoped the adventure would be an interesting one.

He had a different feeling, though, when he read the second P.S. The idea of living in Alusia made him nervous and
happy. Whalen had mentioned the possibility after Alex's last
adventure, but Alex had thought it would be some time before
anything actually happened.

The geeb dinged loudly, interrupting his thoughts.

"Sorry," said Alex, looking at the geeb. "Have you been
paid?"

"Ding."

"Waiting for an answer, then, are you?"

"Ding."

"All right, hang on a minute."

Grabbing some paper, Alex quickly wrote a note to Whalen. He said that he would be happy to meet the leader of this new adventure and at least listen to what he had to say. He also thanked Whalen for suggesting him and promised to send updates if he accepted the adventurer's bargain. He hesitated for a moment and then added that he would need to think about the move to Alusia but that he'd let Whalen know as soon as he'd decided.

"Can you take this to Whalen Vankin?" Alex asked, holding the letter out for the waiting geeb to take.

"Ding," the geeb answered and accepted the letter.

"And here is your payment for my reply," added Alex, tossing a fair-sized diamond in the air.

"Ding." The geeb caught the diamond in midair and then produced several gold and silver coins as change.

With a small popping sound, the geeb disappeared, leaving Alex alone to consider Whalen's letter. Alex wanted to tell his stepfather what was happening and ask for his advice about moving to Alusia, but it was already late, and Mr. Roberts was probably in bed. The conversation would have to wait until morning.

———◆———

"But you've only been back two months," said Mr. Roberts the next morning when Alex told him about the adventure.

"Most adventurers take at least three to six months off between adventures, sometimes even longer."

"Yes, but I'm not just an adventurer anymore," said Alex.

"True, true," said Mr. Roberts. "I suppose wizards aren't normal adventurers. I'm just worried you might be doing too much. Back-to-back adventures, and plans to move to Alusia? That's a lot to deal with, even for a wizard."

"I'm sure Whalen knows what he's doing," said Alex. "I feel ready for a new adventure, but if this adventure doesn't sound good, I won't go. I can wait awhile before deciding about Alusia."

"I don't want you thinking you have to move just because Vankin suggested it," said Mr. Roberts. "You've got a lot going on, Alex. Whatever you do, make sure it is something *you* want to do, and then make sure that you are ready to do it."

"I'll be fine," said Alex. "And I'll try not to overdo anything."

"All right, then," said Mr. Roberts. "And if you do decide to move to Alusia, you'll always be welcome here—even if you just need a place to rest for a time."

"Thank you," said Alex with more feeling than he'd ever said it before.

After breakfast, Alex left his stepfather's tavern and headed to Mr. Clutter's adventure shop. He knew he'd be early for his appointment, but he wanted some time to talk with Mr. Clutter before meeting the leader of this new adventure.

"Back so soon, Master Taylor?" questioned Mr. Clutter as Alex entered the shop.

"I was asked to come," said Alex. "Master Vankin has asked

me to stand in for him and at least listen to the leader of a new adventure."

"Oh, yes, of course," said Mr. Clutter. "But I'm sorry to say that the leader of that particular adventure has just gone in with someone else, so they might be awhile."

"I'm a bit early," said Alex, checking the clock on Mr. Clutter's wall. "I was hoping you might have a few minutes to tell me what other adventures are getting started right now."

"Other adventures?" Mr. Clutter questioned. "But if you've been asked to go on this one . . ."

"I've been asked, but I'm not sure I'll be going," said Alex. "I thought it would be a good idea to see what else is happening, just in case."

"Ah, sound wisdom, that," said Mr. Clutter. "I'll fix some tea and we can have a chat. Unless, of course, you'd like something besides tea?"

"Whatever you have will be fine," answered Alex.

Mr. Clutter hurried from the room, but was back almost immediately, carrying his large silver tea set. He started talking about adventures even before he'd seated himself behind the counter.

Alex was used to the way Mr. Clutter often carried on, and he sat back and listened to everything the adventure salesman had to say.

"Oh, now that's odd," Mr. Clutter said as he shuffled through some papers.

"What's that?" Alex questioned.

"Ah, well, an adventure has been requested, but with a high

level of secrecy attached to it," said Mr. Clutter in a slightly nervous tone. "Not that being secretive is so strange."

"No, I'm sure a lot of adventures are that way," said Alex.

"Exactly. No, the odd thing is that the requester is asking that no one from Thraxon be told about this adventure. Now that seems very odd to me, as Thraxon is where the adventure is going to take place."

"That *is* strange," said Alex. "But as I'm not from Thraxon, could you tell me as much as you can?"

But before Mr. Clutter could say much about the adventure, a familiar voice interrupted them.

"I'm sure you'll like the rest of our company," the voice said from the back of the shop. "A good group so far, and I have great hopes that our seventh member will be a wizard."

"I'm sure the group will be fine," answered a second voice.

Alex recognized the first voice as his friend Thrang, and he wondered why Whalen hadn't told him that the dwarf would be leading the adventure.

"All settled, then?" asked Mr. Clutter as Thrang emerged from behind the curtains. "Anything else you need?"

"We are all set, thank you," said Thrang, turning to look at Mr. Clutter and spotting Alex instead. "Alex! I mean, Master Taylor. So good to see you again."

"No need to be so formal," Alex laughed, moving forward to shake Thrang's hand but getting a bear hug instead.

"Well now, as you're here, allow me to introduce Mistress Katrina Dayyed," said Thrang, nodding to the young woman who'd followed him through the curtains. "She goes by Kat, and she comes from Barkia. Kat, allow me to present my friend, Master Alexander Taylor."

"The wizard," Kat said, bowing to Alex.

"A pleasure," said Alex, returning the bow. He couldn't help but notice the faint glow of magic around her.

"Well," said Thrang, looking quickly from Kat to Alex and back. "I suppose I should explain this adventure to Master Taylor, then."

"As you wish," said Alex.

"I will see you in Telous," Kat said to Thrang. "I have much to do before this adventure begins."

"Yes, yes, of course," said Thrang, bowing slightly as Kat left the shop. He turned to Alex. "Now then, Alex. Shall we?"

"After you."

Thrang led Alex to the hidden rooms at the back of the shop. They both settled into the comfortable chairs.

"So, tell me about your staff and everything that's happened since we parted company," Thrang said.

"The adventure first," said Alex. "We will have time to catch up after."

"As you wish," Thrang said, stroking his beard. He paused to gather his thoughts. "This adventure is a quest to recover the Ring of Searching, which has been lost for almost two thousand years."

"Two thousand years?" Alex repeated in surprise.

"I really shouldn't say lost," said Thrang. "The owner of the ring didn't lose it, after all. And two thousand years sounds like a long time, but to dwarfs it's only, oh, ten generations—more like two hundred years to humans."

"I never thought of it like that," said Alex. "So, why do we need to look for this ring if it isn't really lost?"

"A good question," said Thrang. "Albrek, the ring's owner, is who we are really searching for. Well, the *tomb* of Albrek would be even more correct. You see, Albrek was a great dwarf lord. In fact, because of the Ring of Searching and its ability to find new mines, Albrek was one of the richest dwarf lords."

"Find new mines?"

"Of course," said Thrang with a grunting laugh. "You can only mine in one place for so long before the mine runs out of whatever is in it. Albrek's ring was used to find new mines—the *best* mines. Albrek went looking for new mines about two thousand years ago and he hasn't been seen since. Now the primary mines of Thraxon are beginning to dry up, and King Thorgood—the ruler of the dwarf realm of Thraxon—wants the ring to find new mines."

"Surely your people can find mines without the ring," said Alex.

"Of course we can," said Thrang. "But it takes a lot of work and only about one in twenty mines found that way is a really good mine."

"I see," said Alex, considering everything Thrang had told him. "Do you have any idea where the tomb of Albrek might be?"

"Details are a bit sketchy, to be honest, but we know the three places that Albrek had planned to look for new mines. Of those three, we've narrowed it down to the best one. Of course, he may have looked somewhere else, but at least we have a starting point."

"How many adventurers are going on this quest?"

"Seven," Thrang answered. "Including our friend, Arconn. I've also talked King Osrik into letting young Thrain come with us. You've already met Kat, of course. And I believe you met Master Nellus on your last adventure."

"It seems there is only one adventurer left for me to meet," said Alex, laughing. "Though I don't know Nellus very well, and I only just met Kat."

"That may be," laughed Thrang, "but I'm guessing you know more about her than most would even after so short a meeting."

"Yes," said Alex, remembering the magical aura he'd sensed around her. "Kat is a seer. I think she will be very helpful on your adventure."

"You sound as if you're not coming along," said Thrang, worried.

"I haven't decided yet. I haven't heard about the agreement, yet, and Whalen advised me to think carefully before agreeing to anything."

"Master Vankin is most wise," said Thrang. "It was out of respect for him that I asked him to join our quest, but I am happy he passed the request on to you."

"Then the agreement, if you please," said Alex.

"Since you are a wizard *and* a warrior, I can offer you five shares in twenty-two," said Thrang, sounding concerned that Alex might not agree. "The primary treasure for this quest is not set. King Thorgood has promised one-tenth of all profits from all new mines found with the ring within the first five years."

"That could be a huge amount of treasure," said Alex, stunned by the generous offer.

"Yes, it could," said Thrang with a nod. "And there's a good chance of secondary treasure as well. Anything we find along the way or in Albrek's tomb is ours to keep. We will divide all secondary treasure equally between the company."

"And how will the primary treasure be paid?" Alex questioned. "I mean, how will Thorgood deliver so much treasure over five years?"

"That *is* a bit of a problem," Thrang admitted. "Thorgood has agreed to either deliver each member's share to Telous on a yearly basis or to hold their shares in Thraxon for them. And, remember, the payment isn't just for five years, it's for a share of all the mines found in the first five years after the Ring of Searching is returned. The mines will likely produce for several hundred years, probably much longer than that, so the shares will be delivered to named heirs for as long as the mines remain active."

Alex thought for a long time before speaking. The amount of treasure they were talking about was almost beyond reason. He didn't really need any more treasure, but he did wonder about Thorgood's arrangements. There was also something else about Thraxon he wanted to know, something to do with the secret adventure Mr. Clutter had mentioned, but he decided that now wasn't the right time to ask, and the thought slipped to the back of his mind.

"Very well," said Alex. "Before I agree, I must ask something of you."

"If it is in my power, I will do whatever you ask," said Thrang in a serious tone.

"I still carry five lost bags. One of the heirs lives in Thraxon, or so the bag maker told me. I would like to return the bag to the lost adventurer's heir if I can."

Thrang nodded solemnly. "We will make time for that noble deed. Do you know where the heir lives?"

"In the city of Kazad-Syn," said Alex. "Do you know it?"

"I do," said Thrang. "Kazad-Syn is one of the largest dwarf cities in Thraxon. We will almost certainly pass through it on our quest. You will easily be able to return the bag."

"Then you had best show me where to sign," said Alex. "Then we can go to Telous, and I can answer all your questions about my latest adventure."

"Wonderful," said Thrang. "I am pleased and proud that you'll be coming with us."

Alex signed the agreement. He was excited to be going on another adventure and happy that so many of his friends would be joining him. Thrang led Alex back to Mr. Clutter's office, handed Mr. Clutter the signed agreement, and asked him to file it for him.

"Another adventure is under way," Mr. Clutter said happily.

"Which way, then?" Thrang asked, cutting off Mr. Clutter before he could get going.

"The back door, I think. Unless, of course, you'd rather use the wardrobe."

"The back door will be fine," Thrang said quickly. "The wardrobe always ruins my appetite."

"Very well, then," said Mr. Clutter, moving to the back of his shop to open the door for them. "I wish you the best of luck. I'm sure you will find success."

"Thank you," said Thrang with a bow as he stepped through the doorway.

Alex didn't say anything, but simply smiled at Mr. Clutter before following Thrang. Almost instantly, he was standing in a green field just outside of Telous. He took a deep breath of fresh air and almost burst into laughter. It was time to start a new adventure.

CHAPTER TWO
REUNION

S o, you've taken your staff," said Thrang as he and Alex walked toward Telous.

"Whalen thought I should," Alex said with a shrug, "so I did, though I must admit, I wasn't as sure as Whalen was."

"If Whalen Vankin thinks you're ready for a staff, you're ready," Thrang said matter-of-factly. "Old Vankin knows more than most." He sighed. "Halfdan told me a little about your last adventure. I wish I'd been able to go with you."

"How is your cousin Halfdan?" Alex questioned. "Why isn't he coming along on this adventure?"

"Halfdan's taking my place as minister." Thrang laughed. "Somebody had to take over the trade agreements with Vargland, after all."

"And is he happy about that?" Alex asked, remembering how Halfdan had laughed at the thought of Thrang as a minister.

"Not really. He'll be in charge of the trade expedition and all the details, which he is nervous about. Still, the job will be good for him, I think—teach him a bit of responsibility. And he will get to travel to Vargland, which will make him happy."

Alex and Thrang talked as they continued to walk. Thrang seemed completely happy to discuss the business in the dwarf realms and didn't ask Alex about himself or his new status as a true wizard. Alex was relieved because that meant he could answer all of his friends' questions at one time when they reached the Golden Swan.

"Alex!" an excited voice called as Alex and Thrang approached the Swan.

Alex's young dwarf friend, Thrain, rushed down the tavern steps, but at the bottom, he suddenly skidded to a stop and looked completely unsure of what to do next. Alex could see that Thrain hadn't changed much since he'd last seen him in Vargland, and he had to smile at Thrain's boundless enthusiasm and excitement.

"I see that my friend the oracle told you what you wanted to hear," said Alex.

"Oh, yes," Thrain said happily. "I was going to tell you before, but the oracle said not to."

"You were wise to listen," said Alex. "And now you're off on your first adventure."

"Yes," said Thrain breathlessly. "Master Silversmith has been kind enough to accept me on this adventure. He's also been very generous by helping me prepare and buying all of my equipment."

"Spending more of your fortune on first-time adventurers, I see," said Alex, winking at Thrang. "Which reminds me, I still owe you for my first adventure."

"A debt you have repaid several times over," answered Thrang with a laugh, gently patting the magic bag at his side. "After all, we did collect a fair amount of treasure on our last adventure together. Most of it because of you, I might add. And I don't have you and Andy to help me spend my gold anymore."

The three of them climbed up the steps of the Golden Swan and entered the tavern. Alex looked around, hoping to see his elf friend Arconn, but the main room was empty.

"We'll meet the others for the midday meal," said Thrang, walking toward the bar. "And you can tell us about your last adventure once we're all together."

Alex relaxed next to Thrang at the bar and asked Thrain about the dwarf realm of Vargland and for news of the friends Alex had made there during his first adventure. Thrain told him that King Osrik, who was Thrain's grandfather, was still uncomfortable with all the ceremony that went along with being king, which didn't surprise Alex at all. Umbar and his family were doing well since Alex had returned his father's lost magic bag to him. Thrain also told Alex that hundreds of people had started moving east now that the evil dragon Slathbog had been destroyed.

"I met your friend, Sindar," said Thrain. "He told us a little about your last adventure. Did you really kill all those goblins?"

"We really should wait for the others," said Alex. "But, yes, we did kill quite a few goblins in Norsland."

Alex could see that waiting until midday before asking questions was going to be hard for Thrain. He fidgeted in his chair and kept looking toward the front door as if hoping the rest of the company would appear. Thrain's excitement reminded Alex of his own first adventure, and he smiled to himself.

Fortunately for Thrain, the wait was not a long one. The other members of the company soon arrived, and Thrang immediately led them all to a private dining room in the back.

"Master Taylor, I believe you know everyone here except Barnabus," said Thrang after introducing Kat to the rest of the company.

"Barnabus Martin," a man said, extending his hand. "I'm from Neska, and I am very honored to meet you."

"The honor is mine," said Alex, shaking Barnabus's outstretched hand.

Thrang seemed a little unhappy that Barnabus hadn't waited for the formal introduction, but didn't say anything. Instead, he simply rang the bell that would bring their meal.

"We'll talk about our upcoming adventure this evening," said Thrang. "For now, I think many of us would enjoy hearing about Alex's last adventure."

"And I have a few questions for all of you as well," said Alex.

Alex spent most of the meal answering questions and telling stories. Thrang and Arconn had the most questions because they had known him longest, but even Thrain and Nellus asked several questions. It wasn't until they had almost finished their meal that Alex managed to ask his friends about themselves.

"I wish I had been able to join your last adventure," said Arconn. "I would have liked to seen Skeld and Tayo tamed."

"As would I," Thrang added with a grunt. "Though Halfdan has told me all about the weddings and about what you did in Oslansk."

"I did only what was needed," said Alex with a laugh. "And I believe it has done some good."

"A great deal of good, I should think," Thrang agreed.

Alex stood from the table. "My apologies, but there is another friend I would like to see as well."

"Shahree is fine," said Arconn with a knowing smile.

"I'm sure she is, but I would like to see her all the same," said Alex, and he excused himself from the company.

Alex left the Golden Swan through the front doors and walked quickly to the stables. A soft whinny greeted him as he entered, and he smiled as he moved toward his horse.

"Ah, Shahree," Alex said to his silver-gray horse. "I hope you are well rested and ready for the road once more."

Shahree whinnied again and nuzzled his shoulder. Alex had missed his horse as much as he had missed his other friends, maybe even more. For several minutes, he stood stroking her neck and remembering their travels together. He was fond of Shahree, but he worried that she might be getting too old for adventures. She was a good horse, but Alex knew she couldn't go on forever.

After making sure Shahree had plenty of food and water, Alex returned to the Swan. The group had finished eating and were discussing some last-minute preparations for the adventure. Arconn needed some new clothes and invited Alex to join him. Thrang, Nellus, and Barnabus were heading for the blacksmith's shop so Thrain could buy his first weapon. Kat had already left, though she hadn't said where she was going.

"You are a true wizard now," Arconn said, walking beside Alex. "Whalen must be pleased."

"He is."

"And he asked you to take his place on this adventure?"

"He said he didn't have time right now," answered Alex. "He didn't say *why* he didn't have time, but that's not unusual."

"I'm sure he's busy with other matters."

"Whatever his reasons, I'm glad he asked me to fill in."

Alex and Arconn continued to talk while they were shopping for clothes. After buying several new sets of clothes and two new pairs of boots, Alex felt that he was ready to go. As he and Arconn left the clothing shop, however, he saw something that made him change his mind.

"I'd like to stop at the apothecary's shop and buy a few things," said Alex. "Just in case."

"Your study of potions has been progressing, then?" said Arconn. "Have you tried many of the potions from the book Iownan gave you?"

"A few. I haven't had the time or the ingredients to try most of them."

"Then might I suggest a stop at the bag maker's first?"

"Why? Do you need a new room?"

"No, but you will be able to keep fresh ingredients longer if you have a greenhouse," Arconn said with a smile.

"That's an excellent idea," said Alex.

"How is your dragon's bane plant doing?" Arconn questioned in a low voice.

"It's grown quite a bit. It seems to be thriving inside my bag."

"The magic in the bag is probably helping," said Arconn. "Though a greenhouse may allow it to bloom."

"That would be good," said Alex, remembering how useful the dragon's bane plant had been in the past.

Alex and Arconn made a detour to the bag maker's shop, talking as they went. The bag maker was pleased to see them both and quickly added a greenhouse and a second expanding room to Alex's bag, which now had ten rooms in all. Arconn asked Alex about the extra room as they left the shop.

"On my last adventure there were times when it would have been very useful to have a second expanding room," Alex said.

"Surely you haven't gathered that much treasure already," Arconn said, sounding serious, but smiling.

"No," Alex answered. "Though I have quite a bit more than you might guess. My father's bag already held a large amount of treasure, which I haven't had time to sort and move."

"Your father?" Arconn questioned, looking confused.

As they walked back to the apothecary's shop, Alex explained what had happened after his first adventure and what he had learned about his father and his stepfather both being adventurers.

"I see," said Arconn thoughtfully. "I do remember an adventurer named Taylor, though I never traveled with him."

"He went on many adventures," said Alex proudly. "Mr. Roberts told me about a few of them already."

"Mr. Roberts," Arconn repeated. "That name also sounds familiar. I'm sure I never traveled with him either, but still, they are both somehow familiar to me."

"They are common names," said Alex. "I'm sure there have been other adventurers with similar names."

"I'm sure," said Arconn, still looking thoughtful. "And, of course, there are many adventurers whom I have never met."

Alex entered the apothecary's shop and was amazed by what he saw. The shop was much larger than it looked from the outside, and it was filled with rows and rows of fascinating and magical items. Alex wandered up and down the aisles, collecting items that he'd only read about until now. It wasn't long before he had a massive pile of things sitting on the shop's counter, and the apothecary was looking happy, but a little troubled as well. Alex knew several of the items he wanted to buy could be dangerous, if not downright deadly. Fortunately, he knew how to use all of them—or at least most of them— and he wanted to have as many supplies available to him as possible on his adventure.

Once Alex had gathered his supplies, he asked the shopkeeper about live plants. The shopkeeper nodded and led Alex and Arconn through a back door into a huge greenhouse. It was warm and damp inside, and it smelled like springtime. With Arconn's help, Alex quickly found several plants for his own new greenhouse, and he added them to the items already on the counter.

"A strange selection," said the apothecary, looking over the items Alex had chosen. "I would say you are either a healer or a wizard."

"Both," said Alex.

The apothecary looked at Alex in disbelief. "Well then, you'll know I'll need to see your staff before I can sell you any of this."

"As you wish," said Alex, reaching for his magic bag.

He withdrew his black staff that had been woven with silver and gold patterns and showed it to the apothecary.

"Oh, my, yes, of course." The apothecary's face turned red. "My apologies, Master Taylor, I didn't know it was you."

"No apology is necessary," said Alex. "How could you have possibly known who I am?"

"Master Vankin mentioned . . . I mean, I heard that you . . . um, well . . ." the apothecary stammered.

"It seems your reputation has preceded you," Arconn said to Alex in a low voice.

"It's quite all right," Alex said to the shopkeeper. "No harm has been done."

The apothecary swallowed and said, "Let me see, some of these items are a bit expensive. Would you prefer to buy them or trade for them?"

"Trade?"

"I am always looking for supplies for my shop," said the apothecary. "Some items are extremely hard to come by. If you like, I'll give you a list of items that are always in short supply."

"That would be nice," said Alex. "I might have something to trade, Mr.—?"

"Oh, I'm sorry," the apothecary said brightly. "I haven't introduced myself. I'm Treevander Fern."

"Mr. Fern. I do have something you might find of interest." Alex reached for his magic bag again and extracted his dragon's bane plant, which had grown to the size of a small bush.

"Oh! Oh, my," said Mr. Fern, his eyes growing large.

"I don't want to trade the entire plant," Alex said quickly. "However, I could divide it and let you have half."

"You are most kind," Mr. Fern beamed. "Dragon's bane is incredibly hard to come by, after all. I mean, a single seed is worth at least ten gold coins—if you can even find one—and a flower . . . well, I haven't seen a flower in years."

"Sadly, I don't have any seeds or flowers at the moment," said Alex. "However, with proper care, I'm sure you could coax this plant to bloom in time."

"Yes, yes, of course," said Mr. Fern. "Let me get a pot and then we'll discuss prices."

As Mr. Fern rushed off to find a pot, Alex heard Arconn laughing quietly.

"What's so funny?"

"I fear your treasure room is about to grow larger," said Arconn.

"Why?"

"The dragon's bane plant is worth much more than all the items you've selected," said Arconn. "Even a plant this small could make an apothecary rich."

"I see," said Alex. "I knew it was rare, but I didn't think it was that valuable."

Mr. Fern quickly returned, smiling and looking from Alex to the dragon's bane plant.

Alex nodded and carefully divided his plant into two large pieces. Shaking the loose dirt from one of the pieces, Alex handed it to Mr. Fern.

Mr. Fern carefully put his half of the plant into its new pot. Brushing the dirt from his hands, he said, "I suppose a price needs to be agreed upon."

Alex nodded, taking into consideration what Arconn had told him about the plant's worth. After several minutes of discussion, and a few remarks from Arconn, Alex and Mr. Fern shook hands on a price. Alex stored all of his new items in his magic bag, while Mr. Fern hurried to the back to get the money he owed Alex.

"I didn't think I'd make money on this trade," said Alex, slightly embarrassed.

"It is a fair price," Arconn said. "Hopefully, Mr. Fern will have success with this plant, and it will not be so rare in the future."

"That would be nice," Alex agreed. "The plant has wonderful healing powers and is useful in dozens of potions."

"I know a few of them," said Arconn. "Though I will not pretend to be an expert on potion making."

Mr. Fern soon returned, carrying two bags with him. "One hundred gold in each. And as much again if and when the plant blooms."

"You are most generous," said Alex, accepting the two bags.

"Not at all," said Mr. Fern. "A fair price and a wonderful trade. Now, let me see. Yes, here is a list of items that are always in demand at my shop. You can trade them at any apothecary shop in the known lands, but I would be in your debt if you could bring any items you find here to trade."

"Thank you very much," said Alex, taking the list from Mr. Fern. "I will. And when I return to Telous, I would like to see how your new plant is doing."

"Yes, of course. You are always welcome here, Master Taylor."

Alex returned his staff and the gold to his bag and said good-bye to Mr. Fern. He was pleased with the trade and hoped that Mr. Fern's half of the dragon's bane plant would thrive. As they left the shop, Arconn looked over Mr. Fern's list of items.

"He was good enough to suggest trade values," Arconn said, handing the list back to Alex. "Not all apothecaries are so honest."

"You're not thinking of changing professions, are you?" said Alex. "It looks like good money can be made by supplying apothecaries."

Arconn laughed, but did not reply. Alex, of course, knew that Arconn had a great deal of treasure in his magic bag and that money was not a concern for the elf. The two of them walked back to the Golden Swan, talking casually.

As they waited for the rest of the company to return for the evening meal and the official start of the adventure, Alex told Arconn more about his last adventure. He told Arconn about the brownies he had met and how they had helped save the adventure. Arconn laughed at the story and promised not to mention the brownies to anyone.

"So, you've met Sindar," Arconn said when Alex had finished his story.

"Do you know him?" Alex asked.

"No, though I do know *about* him, as he is well-known among all the elves."

"I thought he might be," said Alex. "I could tell that he was old, even for an elf."

"Indeed he is," said Arconn. "Sindar is one of the eldest who still remain in the known lands."

Alex and Arconn's discussion about Sindar was interrupted as the rest of the company appeared. Thrang led everyone back to the dining room they'd used earlier that day. Thrain seemed happier than he had been before, if that were possible, and Alex guessed that he had found an excellent weapon at Mr. Blackburn's. Thrang took his seat at the head of the table and gestured for Arconn to sit at his left and Alex at his right. Once the entire company was seated, Thrang cleared his throat.

"You all know the goal of our adventure," said Thrang. "We have one first-time adventurer with us, so I will ask you all to help him learn as much as he can. Master Taylor is also carrying a lost bag and wishes to return it to the adventurer's heir, who lives in the city of Kazad-Syn. Since we will pass through the city as we travel, I have promised Alex time to return the lost bag."

Thrang paused, letting his words sink in. Returning lost bags was the sworn duty of all adventurers as well as an honor and a burden.

After a moment, Thrang rang a golden bell. Servants

appeared carrying pitchers. They filled mugs for the entire company, then left the pitchers on the table and departed.

"I will ask you all to drink with me," Thrang said, raising his mug. "To the adventure, to the bargain, and for luck."

"The adventure, the bargain, and luck," the rest of the company repeated, and they all drank from their mugs.

"We leave for Thraxon in the morning," said Thrang, setting his mug back on the table. He rang the bell once more, and the servants instantly appeared with their meal, departing as quickly as they had come.

"Arconn told me this is your first time as a leader," Alex said softly to Thrang as they ate. "I'm honored to be going with you."

"You are very kind, my friend," said Thrang. "I never thought I'd be leading an adventure, you know, but King Thorgood insisted."

"I suppose this means you won't be retiring anytime soon," Alex said with a smile.

"Perhaps not," said Thrang. "Though I might follow Skeld and Tayo's example and find myself a wife. It's time I started thinking about an heir."

"Don't tell Halfdan." Alex laughed. "He was very disturbed by the lovestruck way Skeld and Tayo acted when we saw them in Norsland."

Thrang chuckled but didn't reply. Alex turned his attention to his meal and the rest of the company. Nellus asked a few more questions about Alex's last adventure. Kat seemed interested in hearing more about Alex's friendship with Whalen and wanted to know about the acts of wizardry he had done before taking his staff. Barnabus and Thrain were both happy to just listen, though Thrain would often blurt out a question in pure excitement. As they finished their meal and started for the door and their beds, Alex pulled Nellus aside.

"How is Tara?" Alex asked softly.

"Much happier since she met you, my friend," said Nellus, his eyes shining brightly. "I've never seen such a change in a person, and I'm very glad for it."

"As am I," said Alex.

The two of them hurried to catch up to their companions, who had already moved out of the dining room. Alex would be sharing a room with Thrain, which pleased them both.

"Don't let your excitement get the best of you," said Alex as they climbed into their beds. "Try to stay calm, and pay close attention to what you're told."

"That's exactly what the oracle said." Thrain laughed. "It's so exciting! I hope I do well. Grandfather will be so pleased if this adventure is a success."

"I'm sure you'll do fine." Alex turned down the lamp next to his bed. "And I'm sure we'll find some success as well."

"Do you really think so?" Thrain asked, showing no signs of being tired. "I mean, with so many experienced adventurers I suppose we should, but I'm a little nervous. What if the Ring of Searching is lost forever?"

"Sleep," said Alex in a soft tone. "We will find out soon enough if the ring is where Thrang suspects it to be."

"Well, yes, I suppose so," said Thrain, turning down his own lamp. "But what if we don't find *any* treasure at all?"

"The amount of treasure we find has little to do with the

adventure's success," Alex said sternly. Then he softened his tone. "But, don't worry, I'm sure we'll find *some* treasure."

Thrain didn't answer, but Alex knew he was still awake. Alex understood Thrain's excitement and his hopes of doing well. He felt the same way, though he was more concerned about finding the Ring of Searching for Thorgood than he was about finding treasure. Thrang was one of Alex's best friends and he wanted Thrang's first adventure as a leader to be a complete success.

CHAPTER THREE
THRAXON

———◦◦◦◦◦———

Alex woke early the next morning. He moved quietly around the room as he dressed, not wanting to wake Thrain. He slipped into his magic bag to inspect his new greenhouse. He was happy to see that all of the plants seemed to be adjusting to their new home. It took some time to get everything in order, and after he finished, he left the magic bag and shook Thrain awake.

"It's time for breakfast," said Alex.

"Already?" Thrain said sleepily. "I've only just fallen asleep." He climbed out of his bed and dragged himself to the basin. Thrain's excitement seemed to still be asleep, but Alex knew it would return over breakfast. He remembered his own first adventure, after all.

As they prepared to leave the room, Alex reminded Thrain to take his new magic bag with him.

"I can't believe I almost forgot it." Thrain shook his head they walked toward the dining room. "Please don't tell anyone."

"I won't say anything," said Alex.

Thrang and Arconn were already waiting in the dining

room when Alex and Thrain arrived. Kat appeared soon after, followed shortly by Nellus and Barnabus. Thrang looked happy, though a little tense. Alex smiled at Thrang as he took his seat and then glanced at the dark sky outside the window.

"Starting early, then," Alex said.

"Early starts are always best," said Thrang, ringing the bell to summon their breakfast.

"Where will we be starting our adventure?" Nellus questioned as they ate.

"We will be stopping first at Benorg—the city of King Thorgood," said Thrang. "He wishes to meet you all before we begin our search."

"Checking to see what kind of company you've put together?" Arconn asked in a sly tone.

"No," Thrang said quickly, his smile fading slightly. "He just wants to meet you. He is sponsoring this adventure, after all."

"Is Thorgood a good king?" Kat asked, a thoughtful look on her face.

"Of course he is," said Thrang. "He's one of the best kings Benorg and the dwarf realm has ever had."

"I meant no offense," said Kat.

Alex looked at Kat curiously. He knew Kat was a seer, but her question had seemed a bit odd.

"How long will it take us to reach Benorg?" Thrain asked, his voice full of excitement once more.

"Five, maybe six days," answered Thrang absently.

"You have said little about where we will search specifically for Albrek's tomb," said Barnabus, pushing his chair away from the table. "Can you tell us more?"

Thrang looked worried again. "As I've said, there are three possible locations for the tomb of Albrek. These locations are not marked on any map, however, and I have only a general idea of where they are."

"Which is why we have a seer," said Arconn, bowing his head slightly to Kat.

Thrang nodded as well. "King Thorgood already has a team searching the libraries and archives of Benorg for information. I'm hoping we will learn a great deal more about Albrek's journeys when we reach Benorg."

As the meal and the discussion came to an end, the company prepared to leave the Golden Swan. Alex went to the stable with Nellus and Barnabus to collect the horses, while the rest of the company waited in front of the tavern. Soon they were riding south toward the great arch, Thrang and Arconn in the lead, Alex and Kat directly behind.

"You seem troubled," Kat said quietly to Alex.

"Simply curious. I have been wondering why you asked about King Thorgood."

"I have met several kings," answered Kat. "Some are good, most are fair, and a few are evil."

"And you wanted to know what kind of king Thorgood was before we reached his city," Alex said with a nod.

"It is best to know something of your host before arriving at his house."

Alex was glad Kat was a member of the company. A seer could often see things that even a wizard could not, and Alex could tell that Kat was a clever person who thought things through. Her interest in King Thorgood had made Alex think. Whalen had once warned Alex that kings and lords often hid their dark desires from even those closest to them. Alex trusted Thrang, and he knew that Thrang would never go on an adventure for an evil king, but he wasn't sure, however, if Thrang would be able to see the evil if it was well hidden.

"Can you tell us anything more about the libraries of Benorg?" Alex asked Thrang as they rode along.

"I can tell you they are large."

"What language are the records written in?"

"Several languages. Mostly in dwarvish, though some things are written in elvish."

Alex could read elvish easily, as the letters were similar to magic letters. He had studied dwarvish a little after his last adventure, but it was a difficult language to learn, especially if you didn't have someone who spoke it to help you.

They continued toward the great arch, and Alex felt happy to be starting a new adventure. He enjoyed listening to Thrain's excited questions from where he rode between Nellus and Barnabus. He smiled as the two older adventurers tried to answer the young dwarf's questions as fast as he asked them.

The company stopped for their midday meal, and Alex headed to a spring to refill his water bottles. When he returned, Barnabus was busy cooking their midday meal, and Alex noticed that Thrang was watching Barnabus closely. Thrang had been the cook on Alex's first adventure, and watching him hover around the campfire made Alex laugh out loud.

"Miss cooking, do you?" said Alex.

"Old habits die hard," answered Thrang, looking a little sheepish.

"If you'd like to take over, just say so," said Barnabus.

"No, no, not at all," Thrang said quickly. "I've heard about your ability, Barnabus, and I'm happy to let you do the cooking."

"You are most kind. But perhaps you should wait until you taste it before making up your mind."

The entire company laughed, but there was no need to worry. Barnabus was an excellent cook, and Thrang made a point of telling him so.

"Now then," said Thrang as he finished his meal. "I have a few final instructions before we distribute our food shares and arm ourselves. First, we will be following the standard rules for adventures on our journey. If anyone gets lost, we will search for thirteen days, as is customary. After the thirteen days, the lost person or persons will be free to do what seems best to them. Second, our quest is not widely known in Thraxon, so I must remind you all not to speak of it openly. We will be passing through areas with lots of people, and the temptation to talk will be great."

"Especially for those of us who might meet kinsmen," Arconn said, looking at Thrain.

"There is that," agreed Thrang. "Most of our journey will be in lands peopled by dwarfs, but we will also meet many men as we travel, and possibly elves as well."

"Are there many men and elves in Thraxon?" Alex asked.

"More men than elves. The elves of Thraxon are not very friendly, and, if Arconn will forgive me, a bit secretive."

"Reluctant to mingle might be better," said Arconn.

"Reluctant to mingle, then," Thrang repeated. "There is one last thing of importance. Remember that the honor of each member of our company is linked to the honor of us all. It is possible that we will meet people who will question or doubt our honor. I would ask that we all be willing to stand up for each other if such questions arise."

"You are most kind, Master Silversmith, though I fear it will be myself alone who will be questioned," said Kat, her voice a mix of sadness and pride.

"I won't deny that seers are not as well respected as they should be in parts of Thraxon," said Thrang, bowing to Kat. "However, you are part of this company, and I will not have your honor called into question."

The rest of the company agreed, and Kat smiled and thanked everyone for their kindness.

"Now, we will share our food so that we all have plenty in our bags," said Thrang. "Then we will arm and ride into our adventure."

They all cheered at Thrang's words and quickly started swapping packages. Alex accepted several parcels from both Thrang and Barnabus, who seemed to be carrying most of the company's food between them. He still had a fair supply of food in his bag from his first two adventures, however, and he was not surprised to find that none of it had spoiled.

As Thrang and Arconn helped Thrain store packages in his new magic bag, Alex turned to his weapons. He attached his magic sword, Moon Slayer, to his belt, along with his true-silver knife. Taking a deep breath, he retrieved his staff from his bag as well. He had never carried a staff on an adventure before, and he felt a little odd carrying it now.

"A fine-looking staff," Arconn commented. "I have never seen one quite like it."

"It is different than most," said Alex.

"I wish I could have been there when you took the oath," said Thrang, also looking at Alex's staff. "Halfdan told me about it, but still . . ."

"I missed you both on my last adventure," said Alex. "But we are together again for this adventure."

"And I hope we find as much success as we did the last time we rode together," said Thrang.

Alex nodded and then looked around to see how the rest of the company would be armed. Nellus wore a long sword at his side and carried a bow, while Barnabus carried a short sword and a fair-sized ax. Kat was carrying both a finely made scimitar and a bow. Arconn and Thrang were both armed as they had been on Alex's first adventure: Arconn with his longbow and dagger, Thrang with his short sword and ax. Thrain was attaching a short sword to his belt, though he already had a crossbow slung across his back.

"A fierce-looking company," Thrang said with pride.

"Very fierce," said Arconn. "Though I doubt we will meet trouble so close to the arch."

"It's not likely," said Thrang. "But it's always best to be prepared."

Alex agreed, though he wondered if it might actually be a good thing if they did meet something not too dangerous, because then they could see how well they fought together as a group.

"If we are ready, then," said Thrang, "let us ride to Thraxon and hope for success."

"Success!" the rest of the company echoed loudly.

They rode toward the great arch. Alex found that his staff was a little awkward to ride with at first, but he soon got used to it.

As they rode through the arch, Alex immediately noticed how different Thraxon was from the other lands he had visited. The hills instantly changed to towering, jagged mountains. Tall pine trees were scattered on the mountainside, and Alex was amazed that not only had the trees managed to take root but also that the narrow spaces where they grew had not collapsed under the weight of the trees. The well-made road under their feet stretched along the base of the mountains in a southerly direction.

"Are these the Gray Mountains of Thraxon?" Alex asked.

"They are," Thrang answered. "The Gray Mountains are large, however, and there are no dwarf cities between the arch and Benorg."

"What about other things that live in the mountains?" Arconn asked.

"What other things?" Thrang questioned.

"Goblins," Alex answered, knowing exactly what Arconn was thinking.

"There are none that I know of," said Thrang. "There are goblins in Thraxon, but they are mostly in the Blue Mountains, which are far to the south and west."

"Yet goblins move and are seldom seen until they wish to be seen," said Arconn.

"That is true," Thrang agreed. "However, my people are more watchful than most."

Alex hoped Thrang was right. He had battled goblins on his last adventure and was in no rush to face more of the evil creatures.

Riding along the edge of the mountains, Alex studied the landscape and the rugged beauty around him. The mountains formed an uneven wall, broken by wide, green valleys with deep rivers running through them and narrow valleys with smaller streams. Across all the rivers and streams were well-built stone bridges. The water flowed to the west across open grasslands, and Alex wondered if they joined together at some distant point.

They spoke little as Thrang led them forward. Even Thrain seemed happy to simply watch the countryside slip by and not ask questions. As the sun set over the grasslands to their right, Thrang called them to a halt in an open space close to a stream.

"I've used this campsite many times," said Thrang. "There are several adventurers who live in Thraxon, and we all use the same campsites as we travel to and from the arch."

"Well-used campsites are not always the best," Arconn said.

"Do you feel something?" Thrang asked in concern.

"I do not," said Arconn. "I was simply thinking that such a campsite might be a target for bandits."

"If bandits had ever attacked one of these campsites, I would have heard about it," said Thrang, shaking his head.

Once they had taken care of their horses and set up their

camp, Thrang waved for Thrain to join him. Alex watched as Thrang piled up branches for their campfire, and he knew that Thrang wanted to teach the younger dwarf how to magically light and put out a fire. He remembered the first time he had tried this bit of magic, as well as the effect his untrained magic had on the pile of branches.

"Watch your beard," said Alex to Thrang with a smile.

"I don't think that will be a problem," said Thrang, stroking his beard. "I doubt very much that young Thrain will be able to ignite it, as you once did."

"You lit Thrang's beard on fire?" Thrain asked in shock and surprise.

"Not his beard," said Alex. "I overdid the inferno command, and the effect was more than Thrang bargained for."

"My own fault for not explaining things clearly." Thrang laughed. "Though I should have known better, as we knew about your abilities even then."

"You might have known, but I still had doubts," said Alex. "I didn't know Thrain had magical ability."

"Only simple dwarf magic," Thrain said, looking embarrassed.

"Only?" Alex questioned. "Magic is magic; it all has the same root. And if you were to master all the dwarf magic there is, you would know a great deal indeed."

"You're talking more and more like a wizard," said Thrang, shaking his head. "Soon you'll be harder to understand than Arconn."

Alex laughed and took a step back. He watched as Thrang showed Thrain how the *inferno* and *quench* commands worked.

Thrain was impressed, and Alex smiled as Thrang carefully told the young dwarf to concentrate on a single branch, something he had not told Alex the first time Alex had tried the spell.

Thrain stood still for several minutes, concentrating. Finally, he pointed at one branch and spoke the magic word. A thin wisp of smoke rose from the branch but was quickly blown away by the breeze. Thrain looked disappointed, but Thrang was extremely happy.

"Not bad for your first try. It normally takes several tries to summon a flame when you first learn the magic."

"But it was only a little smoke," said Thrain in a dejected tone.

"Perhaps you weren't concentrating hard enough," Alex said.

"Perhaps not," Thrang agreed. "Try once more, and this time try to focus all your thoughts."

Thrain obeyed and closed his eyes. Alex winked at Thrang, who immediately took a step back. After a few moments, Thrain opened his eyes and, pointing at the branch once more, spoke the magic word. This time a flame sprang to life as soon as the word had left his lips.

"Well done," said Thrang, returning Alex's wink when Thrain wasn't looking. "Very impressive. Now try the *quench* command."

Thrain obeyed once more, and, as he spoke the word, the fire sputtered for a moment and died. Thrain, pleased with himself and his newfound ability, quickly relit the fire. Alex smiled at his young friend and commented on how well he had done.

"You shouldn't have helped him," Thrang said to Alex in a low tone.

"I only helped the first time," said Alex. "He needed a little confidence, that's all."

"And the *quench* command?" Thrang asked.

"Again, only a little help. As his confidence grows, he will be able to do the spells on his own."

"Still, you shouldn't have helped him," said Thrang with a smile on his face.

"Why not?" Alex asked. "You helped me the first time."

"I most certainly did not," said Thrang, sounding shocked by the idea.

"Even if you didn't know it, you helped. You believed I could do it, even though I didn't."

"Will we be setting a watch?" Arconn asked, walking toward the fire.

"There is little need so close to the arch," said Thrang. "Though it might be wise to start now, just to be safe."

"If nothing else, we will be prepared for later," Alex said.

Thrang considered the idea for several minutes and then decided it would, indeed, be best to start keeping a watch. Alex, with his normal luck, drew the first watch, which made him happy. He knew from experience that Arconn would sit up with him, and he was looking forward to spending time with his friend.

CHAPTER FOUR

BENORG

———— ◆ ————

O n the fifth day of their journey, the road turned east into the mountains and followed a large and noisy river flowing through a narrow, green valley. The river snaked between huge boulders and had many impressive waterfalls and rapids, some of them so close that they covered the road with a damp mist. The path twisted and turned almost as much as the river did, but always stayed close to the water's edge.

"Did your people build all these bridges?" Alex asked Thrang over the roar of the river.

"Yes, indeed," Thrang shouted over his shoulder. "King Thorgood owns this road and insists that the bridges be maintained. After all, this is the road that leads to his capital. The stone bridges make a good impression on visitors and are useful for trade."

"Do your people trade much with other lands?" Kat questioned.

"More and more," answered Thrang. "King Thorgood has been trying to open trade with all the known lands."

"And having a good deal of success, I would guess," Arconn said.

"Honest trading makes for success," said Thrang.

Alex wondered what was awaiting them in Benorg and beyond. Thraxon was one of the larger known lands, and the map of it in the *Adventurer's Handbook* was better than most of the others. Alex had spent some time studying it, trying to get a feel for the land that he and the company would be traveling through. He knew that Benorg was in the heart of the Gray Mountains, with many roads leading to it, but that most of Thraxon—at least according to his map—was east and south of Benorg.

The day passed with little talk, except when they stopped for their midday meal. Kat asked a few more questions about Thorgood, and Alex knew she was still nervous about meeting the king. He was too. He tried to relax his own mind, but even when he managed a moment of peace, Kat's nervousness pressed in on him.

The sun was well to the west when Thrang at last halted them in the road. The valley opened wide before them, and they could see that the land had been divided into neat, little farms. The road stretched through the farmlands and crossed a wide stone bridge before leading directly to a huge city made of stone.

"My friends, welcome to Benorg!" Thrang turned in his saddle and smiled. "A wonder of the dwarf realms."

"I didn't know that dwarfs built cities so high above the ground," Alex said as they started forward once more.

"Benorg is different than most dwarf cities. The part of the city you can see isn't very old. It is built on top of and around the older city, which is thousands of years old. When we get closer, you will be able to see the difference in the work," said Thrang.

They moved forward to the bridge, where dwarf guards clad in shining true-silver armor stood proudly. The guards must have recognized Thrang, because as the company approached, they lowered their spears as a sign of welcome.

Thrang led them into the heart of the dwarf city, waving now and then to someone he knew. Many of the dwarfs would wave back or toast them as they passed, and it appeared that Thrang was well-known. Horses were allowed in Benorg, at least in the aboveground parts, so they rode along the stone-paved streets, smiling and nodding to the dwarfs as they went.

When they reached what looked like the tallest building in the city, Thrang directed the group to one side where several dwarfs were waiting, ready to take their horses to the royal stables. Alex gave Shahree's reins to a bowing dwarf and whispered words of comfort to her.

"King Thorgood will be waiting," said Thrang, looking nervously at the others. "I believe there will be a feast in our honor."

"And if Thorgood doesn't like the look of us?" Arconn asked.

"He will," said Thrang, scowling at Arconn.

"Elves are not always welcome guests of dwarfs," Arconn said.

"You have nothing to worry about," Thrang answered.

"Thorgood knows a good deal about adventures and about the importance of mixing the company."

"Was King Thorgood an adventurer once?" Thrain questioned.

"No, but he's known a good many adventurers in his time," answered Thrang, still scowling. "He thinks very highly of our profession, and he is a kind and generous host."

"Then lead on," said Arconn, bowing to Thrang. "It would not be polite for us to keep our host waiting."

Thrang did not reply, but his scowl softened. He turned toward the large building and led the company forward, dusting himself off slightly as he went. Arconn caught Alex's eye and gave him a quick wink.

They followed Thrang toward the grand entrance hall, where more armored guards stood at attention. They bowed as Thrang approached and allowed the company to pass without questioning them. Alex looked in wonder at the inside of the building, which was really just an open space surrounded by a high wall and filled with fountains and trees, like a park. In the middle of the open space was a small pavilion, and standing beneath it was King Thorgood.

"Welcome, my friends, welcome," said Thorgood, coming down the steps of his royal pavilion with a smile. "You've made good time, Thrang; I didn't think you would be back so soon."

"I was fortunate to find the members of the company quickly," said Thrang, bowing to the king.

"And what a company," said Thorgood, looking over Thrang's shoulder at the rest of them. "I am glad you come as friends, for it seems Thrang has assembled a fierce group of warriors."

"If you will permit me, Your Majesty," said Thrang, moving to stand beside the king. "Allow me to introduce you to my companions."

"Yes, I suppose introductions are in order," said Thorgood, moving forward with Thrang. "I thought the pavilion would be more comfortable than the throne room. Not so stuffy or formal. There are always fewer of the lords out here, and you know how they can be."

Alex and the others quickly lined up in front of Thrang and the king. Alex could see that Thrain was extremely nervous, which surprised him. Thrain's grandfather was king of the dwarf realm of Vargland, after all, and Alex thought he would be used to meeting royalty and other important people.

Thrang moved down the line, introducing each of them to the king and saying something about their accomplishments as adventurers. Alex listened closely when Thrang introduced Kat, Nellus, and Barnabus because he didn't know as much about them yet. When Thrang introduced Alex, Thorgood stopped him before he could list Alex's accomplishments.

"The young wizard," Thorgood said with a quick glance at Thrang. "The one you and Halfdan have told me so much about."

"The same," answered Thrang, beaming at Alex.

"A great honor," said Thorgood with a bow. "I had hoped Thrang would find a wizard for this adventure, but I did not dare hope that it would be you."

"The honor is mine, great king," said Alex, bowing to

Thorgood. "Master Silversmith was good enough to invite me on this adventure, and I am pleased to be in your fair city."

"Yes, well, we do what we can," said Thorgood with a laugh. "Perhaps you will tell me the truth of Thrang and Halfdan's stories, if time allows."

"It would be a pleasure and an honor, great king, though I am sure Thrang and Halfdan have been most truthful in their tales," answered Alex.

"No doubt they have. Though it is always good to hear the story from a different point of view."

Alex bowed to Thorgood once more as Thrang, looking proud and pleased, continued down the line. Thorgood stopped again when they reached Thrain, asking about his grandfather and Vargland.

Once all the introductions had been made, Thorgood returned to his pavilion, speaking in a low voice to Thrang. Thrang appeared to agree with the king and was smiling as he returned to the company.

"Now that the formalities are complete, let me offer all of you some refreshment," said Thorgood, taking his seat in the pavilion. "Tonight we feast and sing; tomorrow you begin your work."

As he finished speaking, Thorgood clapped his hands. Dozens of dwarfs instantly appeared from various places around the walled-in space. While Alex and his companions looked on in wonder, the dwarfs set up several round tables and covered them with food. A dozens more tables and chairs were set up, and silver lamps were placed at the center of each table.

"An old dwarf custom here in Benorg is to welcome friends with a small gathering so they can mingle without the formality of a traditional feast," Thrang explained. "Thorgood wants us to mingle with his people, so they will have a chance to get to know us."

"An interesting custom," said Nellus. "We do something similar in my homeland, but not on such a large scale."

"Well then, let's mingle," said Barnabus with a smile. He moved away from the others, heading for one of the main tables that was filled with food.

Alex soon discovered that he was something of a legend in Benorg. It seemed that all the dwarfs knew who he was and what he had done on both of his previous adventures. He talked and mingled with the dwarfs, feeling very much at ease among them, relieved that they were so willing to accept him.

As the night grew darker, more lamps were lit and placed around the walls, illuminating the open space. Alex eventually gave in to the pleading of some of the younger dwarfs and conjured several small weir lights. He sent the balls of light dancing around the park, changing their colors as they went. All of the dwarfs laughed and clapped as the weir lights whirled past them, and even King Thorgood watched them with wonder.

As the evening wore on, Alex put out the weir lights one by one until there was only one light left, floating above his own head. As one of the servants came forward to lead Alex and his companions to their rooms, Alex sent the last light dashing through the crowd before shooting it up into the sky where it vanished from sight.

They were led out of the pavilion park to a large guesthouse nearby, which Thorgood declared was theirs for as long as they needed it. The house was impressive, stocked with everything they might need or want. There were bedrooms and baths for everyone, as well as several small sitting rooms and a large common room that could comfortably seat as many as thirty or forty people.

It was late, and Thrang decided that it was time for all of them to be in bed. Thrain was unhappy about the order because he had been having such a good time at the feast. Thrang insisted, however, reminding him that they all had a great deal of work to do in the libraries and archives the next day.

"I'll need your eyes sharp tomorrow, Thrain," Thrang said. "You and I are the only ones who can read all of the dwarvish letters. Arconn may know a few of them, and I don't believe Alex has learned them all yet."

"Not yet," Alex said through a yawn. "Though I have been studying. It was a difficult task—studying alone, without any dwarfs to help me. I will be glad for your help at the archives."

The company said good night and headed to their various rooms. Alex did not feel sleepy so he wrote a short message to Whalen to let him know how things were going. Once the note was sent, he remained seated at the small writing table, taking out one of his books about dwarf runes and writings and beginning to study.

When morning came, Alex was tired from his night's work, but felt his time had been well spent. He had learned all the dwarf runes from his book and could read most of the writing with only a little hesitation. He sat down to breakfast with his friends, looking forward to spending the day in the libraries.

"Thorgood has had his people searching the libraries for us," Thrang announced. "They haven't found anything important yet, but with their help, I think we should find what we need quickly."

"Are you in such a rush to leave Benorg?" Alex questioned.

"No, not at all," answered Thrang. "But our adventure is not in Benorg or in the archives of this city. The sooner we find what we need, the sooner we can continue with the adventure properly."

"And as most of us don't know how to read or speak the dwarvish language, I, for one, will be happy for all the help we can get," Nellus said.

After breakfast, Thrang led them out of the house and toward the mountains that stood behind the city. Alex admired all of the buildings in Benorg, which were quite beautiful and impressive to look at, and wondered how long it had taken the dwarfs to build such a fine city. He listened closely as Thrang pointed out various buildings and explained what each of them was used for.

The libraries were located in several huge underground vaults, containing thousands and thousands of books and even more scrolls and pieces of parchment. Alex suspected it would take him a hundred years or more just to look at everything the libraries contained, and several hundred more to read it all, and he was grateful for the help Thorgood had offered them.

"Thorgood said that these last two chambers hold the documents from the time of Albrek, so anything about him should be there," said Thrang, leading them through the underground maze.

"That narrows the search a bit," said Barnabus with a short laugh.

"It narrows it a great deal," said Thrang, missing the joke. "And with the help Thorgood has sent, it shouldn't take us more than a month or two to find what we need."

"Oh, is that all?" said Nellus sarcastically, elbowing Barnabus in the ribs.

When they reached the second-to-last chamber, they found a dozen or so dwarfs busily sorting various documents. Thrang introduced his company to the chief librarian and then stepped aside to speak with a few other dwarfs.

"I'm not sure what good I'll be, as I don't read dwarf or elf runes," Nellus said.

"I can read some dwarf runes, but no elf at all," Barnabus added.

"Then you can help move things about," Thrang said, looking up from his discussion with one of the other dwarfs.

Alex and the others spread out through the enormous vault, looking for a place to begin. The chief librarian did indeed put Barnabus and Nellus to work moving stacks of documents. Arconn sorted through a large pile of documents written in elvish, and he was pleased to find that some of the books had actually been written by the elves of Thraxon. Thrain and Kat sat on the floor together at the back of the vault, looking through a large leather-bound volume she had found.

Alex found a large table near one wall and started thumbing through the pile of documents that was stacked on it. He could read most of what was written on them, but there were some runes that were completely new to him. He tried not to read everything on every document, instead he skimmed the words he knew, hoping to find a passing reference to Albrek or perhaps even a map. Searching the documents was tiring, but Alex enjoyed it more than the others did. His ability to read dwarf runes improved as the day went on, and he found that he could move quickly through the old pages as long as he remembered to skim them and not read every word.

They stopped their search at noon for a quick meal, which Thorgood had sent down to the vaults for them. After lunch, the chief librarian ordered Barnabus and Nellus out of the vault, saying that they were just getting in the way. Thrain watched them go with a sad look on his face and then returned to the enormous volume one of the librarians had given him. Alex suspected that this was not Thrain's idea of an adventure.

The documents in the vaults seemed endless as Alex and his friends returned day after day to the caverns. Barnabus and Nellus, still banned from the library, had taken to exploring the city, and on their fourth day in Benorg, Thrang sent Thrain along with them.

"I need someone to keep an eye on those two," said Thrang. "I don't want them getting into any trouble."

"Well, if you really need me to," Thrain said, a hopeful look on his face.

"Go on, then," Thrang said gruffly.

"That was kind of you," Alex said as Thrain left the library. He shifted a stack of documents off his table.

"Well, it's his first time out and all," said Thrang. "I really should have had this part of the adventure done before putting the company together."

"What, and deprive us of all of this?" Alex joked.

Thrang laughed with Alex and reached for another stack of papers.

Alex was actually enjoying his time in the vaults. He had found the dwarfs to be both helpful and willing to explain any of the runes he did not yet understand. They were also impressed that a man, especially a wizard, had taken the time to learn so much about their methods of writing.

"Not many men ever learn this lore," the chief librarian said. "It does my heart good to know that a wizard would take the time to learn our ways."

On their tenth day in the vaults, Kat finally found something that was useful. It was a piece of parchment, almost too dirty to read. Placing it carefully under a bright light, Thrang and the chief librarian were able to piece together what it said. Some parts were impossible to make out, but other parts of the page were clearly legible.

"This is part of the tale of Albrek," said Thrang excitedly.

"Does it say where he traveled?" Arconn questioned.

"Just a moment," answered Thrang, looking back at the paper.

"The Isle of Bones," the chief librarian muttered.

"Isle of Bones?" Kat repeated with a worried look on her face.

"In a moment, in a moment," said Thrang, holding up his hand for silence.

Alex looked over Thrang's shoulder at the parchment, reading as much of it as he could, but several of the runes were still unfamiliar to him.

"Ah, yes, of course," said the chief librarian, slapping his head as he looked up. "This indicates that the full story of Albrek is written in the special history of the city. I never even thought of looking there."

"Special history?" Alex asked.

"Oh, it's not secret or anything like that," the librarian said, moving toward the back of the vault. "We just keep a record of special events—things that are outstanding in some way or another."

"And Albrek's search for new mines was outstanding?" Arconn questioned.

"Well, the stories say that he took more than five hundred dwarfs with him," said Thrang as the librarian hurried away.

"A large party to go looking for mines," said Kat.

"Not really," said Thrang. "Mining is a labor-intensive job, after all, and you need to sink a shaft or two before you know if your mine is worth anything."

They waited in a tense silence for the librarian to return. When he did, he carried with him a thick volume bound in black leather. He set it on the table and began thumbing through the pages. He seemed to be looking for a certain page, flipping large groups of pages all at once and making dust fly from the book's cover. In a surprisingly short time, he had found what he wanted, and he and Thrang huddled around the open book. Alex, standing nearby, also began to read the book.

"Interesting," said Thrang. "It seems Albrek planned to travel farther than I thought."

"And?" Arconn asked.

"The story is a bit confusing, but basically it says where Albrek was going, or at least where he planned to go," said Thrang. "According to this, he was going to the Isle of Bones. After that he was going south to the Lost Mountains, and finally to Gal Tock."

"What is Gal Tock?" Alex questioned.

"What is the Isle of Bones?" asked Kat at the same time.

"The Isle of Bones actually has nothing at all to do with bones," answered Thrang. "It's a mountainous island in the Eastern Sea. We call it that because the mountains are rocky and remind us of the bones of the earth."

"And Gal Tock?" Alex asked again.

"Gal Tock is a dwarf name meaning gold rock, or golden rocks," answered the librarian. "The exact location isn't known, but the stories tell of a place where the morning sun shines on the rocks and make them look like gold. All I can tell you is that it is supposed to be far to the south."

"That would make sense, because the Lost Mountains are also well south of here," Thrang added. "It looks like Albrek went northeast to the Isle of Bones first, then south to the Lost Mountains. If he went farther than that, then he must have gone looking for Gal Tock."

"Does the story say if he made it to any of those places?" Arconn questioned.

"It mentions some of his group returning," said Thrang. "They came back while Albrek was still on the Isle of Bones, so we know he made it that far."

"It seems we know where we are going," said Kat, a slightly troubled look on her face.

"Yes, yes, we do," said Thrang happily.

"How soon will we depart?" Alex asked.

"As soon as possible," answered Thrang. "It will take at least a month to get to the Isle of Bones, maybe longer. Summer has already begun, and I'd like to head northeast while the weather is warm."

"Tomorrow, then?" Arconn questioned.

"The day after, I think," said Thrang. "We should make sure we are well stocked with provisions and warm clothes." He turned to the librarian. "It would also be useful to look at some of the older maps of Thraxon to get a better idea of Albrek's journey."

"Does anyone live on the Isle of Bones?" Kat asked.

"Not that I've ever heard of," answered Thrang. "It's a rugged island, and being as far north as it is, a very cold place in the wintertime."

"Hopefully we will be there while it is still summertime," said Alex.

"If all goes well," Arconn added.

"And if things go really well, and we find the Ring of Searching on the Isle of Bones, we could be back here before winter sets in." Thrang laughed. "Though I doubt it will be quite as easy as that."

"It never is," said Alex.

CHAPTER FIVE

EAST BY NORTH

———————◆———————

That night, as the company ate dinner, Thrang presented his plans for their journey. They would travel east from Benorg and follow the main road, which would take them out of the mountains and into the open plains beyond. From there they would travel as directly east as possible, though they would eventually need to turn northeast to reach the Isle of Bones.

"How far away is the Eastern Sea?" Nellus questioned.

"About two hundred miles," answered Thrang. "If we travel straight from here to there. But since we need to go north as well as east, that will add at least fifty miles to our journey."

"Is this Eastern Sea the border of Thraxon?" Barnabus asked.

"Not at all," Thrang said with a laugh. "In high summer we could travel around the sea to the north, though few people have ever done so. And you can easily sail around the bottom of the sea to the south, though you would have to go extremely far south to do so."

"Are there cities along the sea coast?" asked Thrain, his excitement showing yet again.

Thrang nodded. "There are; though I've never visited any of them. The southern coast is well populated—more than the north, but as I've mentioned, northern winters are hard, and not many people want to live in so rugged an area."

"I wonder if there will be anyone at all on the Isle of Bones," Kat said. The troubled look Alex had seen before on her face had returned.

"Why do you say that?" Alex questioned.

"Something about the place," said Kat, not meeting Alex's eyes. "I cannot say why. It is just a feeling."

"Any feeling a seer has is worth paying attention to," Arconn said.

"It may be nothing," said Kat, smiling weakly. "I thought of another place when I first heard the name, so now I have the two linked in my mind. The other place was a terrible place— somewhere I hope never to go again."

"If you feel there is danger on the Isle of Bones, we should know about it," said Nellus, his voice kind but firm.

"No, nothing like that," answered Kat with a wave of her hand. "Please, do not be troubled. A memory from my past has darkened the name for me, that is all."

"Very well then," said Thrang, glancing from Kat to Alex and back. "We will leave the day after tomorrow, and we should easily reach the seacoast long before winter comes."

With Thrang's final words, the group began separating for the night. It was late, and everyone was thinking of bed and their last day in Benorg. Alex stayed in his seat for a minute, watching Kat as she crossed the room toward the stairs leading to her room. He wondered what experience she was remembering that caused her such pain, but he knew better than to ask. Perhaps he would ask later, when the time was right and they were alone.

———————

They woke the next morning to a light rain. Alex didn't know when they would be coming back to Benorg and had wanted to spend the day wandering the streets and seeing at least some of the city. He hoped Thrang would offer to show them around the city, but he said he needed to talk to Thorgood again and finish preparing for their journey.

Arconn offered to accompany Alex into the city after breakfast, despite the rain. Alex jumped at the chance and quickly found a hooded cloak to wear. He considered inviting Thrain to come along and show them what he had discovered during his days of exploration, but Thrain was busy repacking his magic bag. Nellus, Kat, and Barnabus were likewise busy with their own preparations for the long journey ahead of them.

"Just the two of us, then," said Alex to Arconn.

"Two strangers in a strange city," said Arconn. "Though I doubt we will find any trouble among our friendly hosts."

"And don't you two start any trouble either," said Thrang with a grunting laugh. "I don't want any of Thorgood's people turned into farm animals."

"Oh, and here I was hoping to practice my craft," said Alex.

Arconn laughed and followed Alex into the street. The rain

was still light, and the air was warm and full of sweet smells. They wandered the streets of the aboveground city for a time, entering a few of the shops they passed along the way. The dwarfs were all friendly, though many seemed shy of Alex and his staff. Alex asked Arconn about it as they left a shop where Alex had bought several bags of dwarf candy.

"I expect a lot of people are shy of you and your staff," said Arconn. "A wizard with a staff makes a great difference to most people, which is not always a disadvantage."

"I have noticed a difference in the way people look at me," said Alex with a hint of unhappiness in his voice.

"Do not let it bother you," Arconn said. "There have never been many wizards and to see a wizard as young as you are is somewhat unexpected."

"Whalen said that most wizards are at least thirty or forty years old before they take a staff," Alex said.

"That is true," Arconn said. "Or at least, it is for all *true* wizards."

"Do some false wizards take staffs at a young age?" Alex questioned.

"There are some people who carry staffs who are not wizards," said Arconn. "You will find in your travels that some magical people wish to be called wizard, but do not know what the title truly means. It is a matter of pride for some, power for others, and foolishness for all who do not deserve the staff or the title."

"And some people take a staff just to give the appearance of being a wizard," said Alex, considering Arconn's words.

"They do. Though many of them can actually use the staff,

as you could have if you'd taken one on your first adventure," said Arconn. "Not knowing what a true wizard is does not mean the staff will not work."

"That is true. However, it won't work as well as it might if someone took the time to become a true wizard."

"I would not know about that," said Arconn. "I have known a few wizards and have always chosen not to associate with pretenders."

"Is it easy to spot the pretenders?"

"There are ways to know, but it is not always easy."

"Can you explain the ways?" Alex asked, wondering if he would be able to detect a false or pretend wizard.

"You would know," said Arconn in a definite tone. "Power knows power, and like knows like. You would see the pretender and know that they were not what they pretended to be. And if they had any magical ability at all, they would know you for what you are as well."

"Perhaps, perhaps not," said Alex softly. "Though I hope I never run into a pretender."

"You might not," said Arconn. He directed Alex toward the entrance to the underground part of Benorg. "Few pretenders would want to be caught by a true wizard. I believe there are some harsh penalties for pretenders."

"There are," said Alex, remembering what Whalen had taught him. "The punishments are usually left up to the wizard who finds the pretender."

"Posing as a wizard is a dangerous game to play," Arconn agreed.

Alex was a little surprised that Arconn knew so much about

wizards and their rules, but then he remembered that Arconn was several hundred years old—perhaps even a thousand years old—and the elf knew a great many things.

The two of them spent the rest of the day exploring as much of the city as they could, returning to their home in time for their evening meal with the rest of the company. The others were already seated around the table, and Thrang was glaring at Thrain. While Alex and Arconn had been exploring, Thrain had taken everything out of his magic bag looking for a log-book he wanted to use as they traveled. Thrang had stumbled over some of Thrain's gear as he was rushing around the house and had hurt his ankle. Nellus and Barnabus had been quick to intervene, helping Thrain store his gear and explaining more clearly how to use his magic bag.

"That ankle isn't going to keep you out of the saddle, is it?" Nellus asked Thrang as they ate.

"It will take more than a bad ankle and Thrain's foolishness to keep me from this quest," said Thrang in a grumpy tone.

Thrain went red and slouched in his chair, his boundless enthusiasm dampened by Thrang's dark mood.

"It's your own fault, you know," Alex said to Thrang.

"My own fault!" Thrang said hotly. "How could it possibly be my fault?"

"If you'd explained the magic bag properly, Thrain could have found his logbook without taking everything out of his bag," said Alex in a matter-of-fact tone.

"I explained everything," said Thrang loudly. After a pause, he admitted, "Though I may not have been as clear on some things as I should have been."

"That's as close to an apology as you're likely to get," Arconn said to Thrain.

"It was *my* fault," said Thrain, sounding and looking sorry. "I should have asked for help and not scattered things about like I did."

"Oh, no serious harm was done," said Thrang, his voice softening. "Just ask for help the next time you don't understand something."

"I will," said Thrain. "I promise."

"Now that that is settled, do we have anything else to discuss?" Barnabus questioned. "I'm bone tired and would like to go to bed. I imagine we'll be leaving before the sun comes up."

"We will," said Thrang, his voice returning to normal. "We should all get a good night's rest. We have a long road ahead of us, and who knows when we will have such a fine place to stay again."

"Kat might," said Alex with a grin.

"I'm a seer, not an oracle," said Kat.

"Then I suppose we'll have to trust to luck," said Nellus.

"And a good night's sleep is always a lucky thing," Thrang added, draining his mug and setting it on the table with a thump.

Alex went to his room and stretched out on the bed. His excitement about the adventure was beginning to grow inside him once more. The dust-covered papers and books in the library had been interesting, and he was glad his ability to read the dwarf runes had improved, but for him, being on the road was the best part of any adventure.

The next morning they were all up early. Thrang was eager

to get underway, and the night's sleep, what little there had been of it, seemed to have healed his sore ankle. After a large breakfast, Thrang led the group to the stables, where their horses had been groomed and saddled and were waiting for them. Several dwarfs were moving around the stables, ready to help the company with any last-minute details.

Before the sun had fully risen, the company had left the city of Benorg behind them. Alex thought it odd that Thorgood had not come to see them off, but he kept his concerns to himself. They rode east through the mountains, enjoying the warm sun and talking about past adventures. Barnabus told them a story about one of his own adventures, but Alex only half-listened as his mind was already racing ahead of them to the Isle of Bones.

The Isle of Bones was a strange name. Of course, dwarf names did not always translate well into the common language. Alex thought a better translation would have been "the place where the earth's bones can be seen," but that was a bit much. He wondered how the translation he read from the runes had changed into the Isle of Bones. Thinking about the name made him think about Kat, and he wondered again why she seemed so nervous about traveling to a place called the Isle of Bones.

They camped early that night. Alex helped Nellus and Arconn look after the horses while Barnabus prepared their evening meal. Watching from a distance, Alex saw Thrang help Thrain practice starting and extinguishing the campfire before starting it for good. Alex wondered how many adventures Thrang had been on and how many first-time adventurers he had helped train.

"I've lost count," said Thrang, when Alex asked him. "A fair few, I'd say, but I've never sat down and counted them out on my fingers."

"More than all your fingers and toes put together, I expect," Arconn said with a laugh.

"Quiet," said Barnabus, joining in the fun. "He'll lose count and then we'll all have to take off our boots for him to add it up."

Thrang laughed along with the rest of them and they finished their meal in high spirits.

After the others had gone to bed, Alex and Arconn remained beside the fire. After some time, when Alex felt certain that the others were asleep, he asked Arconn if he knew anything about Kat's worries or about her dark feelings when she'd heard the name of the Isle of Bones.

"Perhaps it is best that you asked me about this," said Arconn after a moment of thought. "There are places I have heard of and seen that would trouble a seer more than most adventurers, so I feel I can guess what is troubling Kat."

"What sort of places have you heard of?"

"Most of them are desolate places," answered Arconn. "The Valley of Bones. The Tower of Bones. The River of Bones."

Alex nodded in understanding. "Places where a great many people died. Places where no one remained to bury the dead."

"Or did not wish the dead to be buried," said Arconn. "Yes, there are places like that. Most of those places are evil in one way or another, and all of them are very sad. I would not question Kat too closely about this if I were you. Such memories are best left in the past and forgotten, if possible."

"Then I'm glad I asked you about it first," said Alex. "I wouldn't want to trouble Kat or cause her to remember such dark places."

"You are kind," said Arconn. "You have some connection to Kat already, though I cannot see what it is."

"To be honest, I can't see what it is either," said Alex with a slight laugh. "I feel as if I've known her for years, and at the same time, I don't think I know her at all."

"That is strange," said Arconn and then remained silent.

———

The next morning the company was up early once again, each of them sipping a bit of Thrang's dwarf cure for soreness as they stretched and walked off their discomfort. Alex reminded himself to make some of this secret potion himself so he would always have it on hand if he needed it.

By the end of their third day's ride, they came to the edge of the mountains, and the road they had been following turned sharply to the south. Since their journey required them to travel east, they left the road and halted for the night at the edge of an open plain that spread out before them. Alex looked out over the country they would be traveling across, admiring the peaceful scene of rolling hills covered with tall grass. Several hills appeared to be rocky toward their tops, and Alex wondered if the rocks might be ruins of some earlier time.

"No, they are just rocks," Thrang answered when Alex questioned him. "No one has ever lived on these hills, at least as far as I know."

"I'm surprised," said Barnabus. "It looks like a nice place to live."

"Men do live in the plain, but farther to the east," said Thrang. "I think they like a little room between themselves and the dwarf realm."

"Is there trouble between men and dwarfs in Thraxon?" Alex asked.

"No, but a little distance helps keep the peace." Thrang laughed. "Don't want neighbors to live too close or overstay their welcome."

"Wise words," said Kat. "Though your people seemed happy to have us in their city."

"But we were not there long," Arconn said. "And we are on a quest for their king."

"The nature of our quest is not known in Benorg," said Thrang, stroking his beard by the firelight. "People know that we are doing something for Thorgood, but exactly what we are doing is something only Thorgood and I know. Though I suspect Thorgood may tell a few of the dwarf lords about our quest before we return."

"Do his ministers not know, then?" Nellus questioned.

"Well, yes," Thrang admitted. "They had to agree to the terms of our contract, after all. I daresay they will keep quiet, though. They won't want anyone to know how generous Thorgood has been to us. It might make people think Thorgood has lost his bargaining edge."

"Is it not the sign of a great king to be generous?" Barnabus asked.

"Men see it that way, as do elves," said Arconn. "Dwarfs

are not stingy, but they are more careful with their wealth. To be overgenerous might be seen as a sign of weakness in the king."

"Thorgood is not weak," said Thrang, staring into the fire. "He knows our quest will be a hard one. Possibly dangerous. He is willing to pay a fair price for what he has asked us to do."

"Dangerous?" said Kat. "You've said nothing about known dangers."

"Simply the normal dangers that accompany any adventure," said Thrang, his eyes still fixed on the flames. "Nothing out of the ordinary."

"Still, the king must suspect something," Kat went on.

"Albrek did not return from his travels," said Thrang, speaking more to himself than to Kat. "The only members of his company to return came from the Isle of Bones, and they went back there after a short visit to Benorg. Where Albrek went and what he did after that is unknown. Something must have happened to him to keep him from returning or sending word, but who can say what."

"The book in the library seemed to say more than simply where Albrek was going," Alex said, thinking back over what he had read.

"Yes," said Thrang, shaking himself from his thoughts. "The tale said that fifty of Albrek's people returned to Benorg, bringing a fair amount of wealth with them. Those fifty reported to the king and then returned to the Isle of Bones with two hundred others dwarfs."

"So Albrek had seven hundred dwarfs with him," said Nellus.

"The dwarfs said that Albrek had planned to leave between one hundred and two hundred dwarfs on the island to work the mines he had found there," Thrang said. "Once the fifty had returned to him and everything was in order, he was going to lead the rest of the group to the Lost Mountains and continue searching there."

"And no one ever returned from the Isle of Bones again, or from the Lost Mountains?" Kat questioned.

"Nothing more was ever heard from them," said Thrang, sinking once more into his own thoughts. "However, it's not unusual for new settlements to remain isolated for long periods of time. If the dwarfs on the island chose their own king, the new leader would not want the king of Benorg making a claim on his new realm."

"Is that likely?" Barnabus asked.

"If Albrek was still there, no," answered Thrang. "But if Albrek had already gone south, who can say?"

"Well, we won't know what happened until we get there," said Arconn, stretching out on his blankets.

"And we won't get there if we don't get some sleep," added Thrang.

Alex's companions rolled themselves in blankets and went to sleep, but Alex sat by the fire, keeping watch and thinking about Thrang's words. Closing his eyes, he pictured the writing in the old leather book from the library. The runes had sounded hopeful, even happy. There was nothing in the story—or at least in the part of the story he had seen—that would make him think there had been any problems at all. There was a chance, however, if the dwarfs had found some wealthy mines, that some of Albrek's followers might have become greedy.

All of the dwarfs Alex knew were both kind and generous, but he had to admit that he didn't know that many dwarfs—even though this was his third adventure. He suspected that some dwarfs, just like some men, could be corrupted by wealth and dreams of power. If that had happened on the Isle of Bones, there was no telling what they might find when they reached it. A new dwarf realm might be waiting for them, or the ruins of a dream gone badly wrong.

That night, after he had finished his watch, Alex dreamed about the Isle of Bones. He could see the beginnings of a beautiful dwarf city made of stone. The city faced south, and the sun warmed its stone houses all day long. In his dream, Alex wandered the newly made streets and entered the huge stone caverns in the mountains close to the city. It was a wonderful place, but nobody was there. The caves and mines of the city were empty, and he could see no sign that anyone had lived there for hundreds of years.

When Alex woke the next morning, his dream was already fading. He lost the dream completely as he rolled out of his blankets and found that it was starting to rain. Barnabus was at the fire, cooking their breakfast and looking unhappily at the cloudy sky.

"Unusual," Thrang said as they ate. "It doesn't often rain this time of year, but when it does, it doesn't last."

"Perhaps our wizard friend can push this little storm away," Kat joked.

"A clear day here might mean a flood somewhere else," said Alex. "And a little rain never hurt anyone."

As the day went on, however, Alex began to doubt the wisdom in his own words. The rain grew steadily worse as they traveled and showed no sign of quitting. By midday, they were all soaked to the skin, and Alex had to start their cooking fire because neither Thrain nor Thrang could coax anything more than smoke from their pile of wet branches.

"A little rain never hurt anyone," Arconn joked. Of the entire group, he seemed the least bothered by the rain.

"Oh, shut up," said Alex.

They ate quickly and resumed their journey, moving slowly across the muddy grasslands.

Thrain muttered something about the weather, and Nellus and Barnabus teased him about adventures not being all sunny days and dragon hoards.

When they stopped for the night, the rain finally started to let up. They set up their tents and took care of the horses. Everyone changed into dry clothes and felt their spirits lift once more. Barnabus cooked their evening meal, and while they ate, Thrang told a story about one of his early adventures where he had experienced some remarkably bad weather.

"Rained for thirty days and nights, did it?" Nellus joked.

"I'll bet crossing the road was more like fording a river," Barnabus added.

"Laugh if you will," said Thrang, brushing aside their jokes. "I'll tell you this, though, it took me six weeks to get all my gear dry after that adventure, and that's a fact."

"You should have taken your gear out of your bag," said Kat with a smile.

"Or at least dumped out the water," Alex added.

"Maybe I should have added a swimming pool to my bag and saved myself the trouble," said Thrang with a laugh of his own.

It was a merry night, and they were all happy to see the moon rising over the open grassland. Alex spent his watch looking at the sky and not really thinking about anything. The clouds were drifting to the west and south, and before his watch was over, there were more stars than clouds in the sky. As he went to his tent, he took one more look at the sky. The clouds seemed to be shifting again, and he feared they might have more rain the next day.

Chapter Six

THE LOST FIDDLER

Alex's premonition that more rain was coming proved correct, as a light mist was falling when he woke. The clouds were not as dark as they had been the day before, so he hoped that the rain would not last. Thrang looked at the sky and grumbled to himself about it being strange weather for that time of year.

"Perhaps we will have rain for thirty days and nights," Barnabus joked as he cooked their breakfast over the fire.

"Oh, I hope not," said Thrain, glancing at the clouds, worried.

"It will clear off," said Thrang, as he rubbed his chin and looked at the sky. "Storms don't last long this time of year, and a few days of rain won't ruin our adventure."

"I imagine we'll experience worse things than rain before this adventure is over," Alex said, stamping his boots. "And if rain is the worst thing we meet, then I say thirty days of it would not be so bad."

As they broke camp and were preparing to leave, the sun broke through the clouds, flooding the land with golden light.

Their spirits rose along with the sun, and they talked happily as they continued eastward.

The land they rode across was still completely uninhabited. Alex remembered Thrang's words about how men lived farther east, but he still thought it odd that there weren't at least a few farms or a path in the open land. He kept looking at the ground from time to time, but if there had been any tracks, the rain had washed them away.

"Do you sense something?" Kat questioned after the third time Alex looked around.

"No," answered Alex. "I just thought there might be some tracks about. It seems a fair land to be so empty."

"It is not empty," said Kat. "There are many birds and beasts living in this land."

"But no people," said Alex. "Not that people always make a land better, but it seems a little odd."

"It wouldn't seem odd if you saw a winter here," said Thrang. "We may not be that far north, but winters in this open land are hard. It would be difficult to farm here during the cold months."

"How many months of the year are cold?" Alex questioned, remembering that the Thraxon calendar had fifteen months instead of twelve.

"Normally only six," said Thrang. "Of course, there are two months of spring and two of fall when the weather is unpredictable."

"Five months of summer, then," said Arconn.

"Yes, in a normal year we can expect five months of fair and warm weather," said Thrang. "Though some years it is less and some more. Luckily, it is still early summer. We passed the last days of spring on our way to Benorg."

"That means we will have at least four months to reach the Isle of Bones and search it before the weather starts to change," said Kat.

"Yes, that sounds about right," agreed Thrang. "Though it shouldn't take us more than a month to reach the island."

Alex wondered how long it would take to search the Isle of Bones once they got there. He assumed it must be a fairly large island or it wouldn't be worth trying to mine there. He worried that it might take a long time just to find any sign of Albrek's party.

As the days passed and they continued riding just north of due east, they discussed the size of the island and several other things, but there were no real answers to many of their questions.

One of the most important questions, however, was how they would get to the island once they had reached the Eastern Sea. Luckily, Thrang had an answer for that one.

"There are cities and villages along the coast," he said. "We can hire a boat to take us there and bring us back when our search is done."

"How did Albrek get to the island?" Alex questioned.

"I don't know," said Thrang in a thoughtful tone. "The records didn't say anything about him taking boats of his own, so I have to assume that he hired boats to carry him and his people to the island just as we will."

"Perhaps the dwarfs built boats when they reached the sea," Arconn offered.

"Perhaps," said Thrang, considering the idea. "Though I don't know of any dwarf who's ever built a boat big enough for that. We're land folk and not much for riding water and waves."

"I'll remember that when we make our own crossing," Alex teased.

One evening, as they were looking for a campsite, the unmistakable smell of smoke filled the air. Arconn rode up a small hill to the south of the company in order to take a look around. Alex wondered where the smoke was coming from and if there might be trouble close at hand.

Arconn soon returned with a smile on his face. "A town. A mile or so ahead of us."

"How large a town?" questioned Thrang.

"Perhaps thirty houses," answered Arconn. "If we turn south here, we will come to the main road."

"I don't remember there being a town so near the mountains," Thrang said. "Though it has been a long time since I or any of my people have come this way."

"Did it look like there was a tavern in the town?" Nellus questioned.

"I believe there was," Arconn answered.

"It would be good to sleep indoors if we can," Thrang said. "Let's stop at this town and see if the tavern will put us up."

"An excellent idea," said Barnabus.

"And remember," said Thrang, turning in his saddle to

look at them all, "our honors are bound together. Small towns are not always friendly to outsiders, so try not to cause any unwanted trouble."

They all agreed and followed Thrang as he and Arconn led them to the main road. The town was not impressive to look at as they rode into it. A handful of small wooden houses were clustered together along a single dirt road. Alex noticed a few fields that looked well cared for, but nothing that could be called a proper farm.

"The Lost Fiddler," read Nellus, nodding to the sign outside the tavern.

"He must have been lost to find himself here," said Barnabus.

Thrang dismounted and entered the tavern, returning with a thin, balding man and a red-faced boy.

"Seven of you?" the thin man said, a look of surprise on his face. "Not many travelers in these parts."

"Can you put us up for the night?" Thrang questioned.

"Yes, we have room," said the thin man. "If you don't mind doubling up."

"That will be fine," said Thrang. "Though we will require one single room for one of our company."

The man nodded. "Three doubles and a single. That won't be a problem. Ned here will take care of your horses."

Ned seemed more cheerful than the tavern owner and bowed politely to them. Alex whispered softly to Shahree and then followed Thrang and Arconn into the tavern. The smell of cooking meat and smoke met him as he entered the building, and he realized how hungry he was.

"If you'd like something to eat or drink, Rose can get you what you need," said the thin man, pointing toward the bar area. "I'll see to your rooms."

With these final words, the man hurried off, and Alex and his friends walked into the bar. A few locals were sitting at tables around the room, and a group of three rough-looking men was standing together at one end of the bar. Another man stood alone at the far end of the bar, and something about him caught Alex's attention.

Rose, a middle-aged woman with dark brown hair, welcomed them and asked what she could get for them. They all ordered drinks and whatever she had to eat, not wanting to make things difficult for her.

"I can fix most anything," said Rose, smiling at the group. "How about some steaks and eggs and perhaps a few potatoes?"

"That would be nice," said Thrang.

Rose nodded and hurried off to get their drinks. Alex and his friends sat down at two small wooden tables, speaking softly to each other while they waited. Alex's attention returned to the man standing alone at the bar. He sensed something about the stranger, but he couldn't make up his mind exactly what it was. He didn't think there was any danger, but still, there was something vaguely magical about the man.

Rose returned with their drinks and a basket with fresh bread, butter, and jam. Alex helped himself to the bread and let his eyes wander around the room. The locals glanced at them from time to time, as did the three men standing together at the bar. Only the man standing alone seemed to pay no attention at all to the company, which Alex thought was a bit odd.

"Walsh, the landlord, says the town's only been here for about thirty years," Thrang said.

"It looks a hundred years old," said Arconn. "The weather has been hard on the wood—and the people."

Thrang nodded. "They would have done better to build from stone."

Alex was only half-listening to his friends. Kat had gotten up from the other table and was approaching the solitary man at the bar. He wondered what Kat was doing, and without thinking about it, he nervously shifted his staff in his left hand, ready to use it if necessary.

"Alex," said Thrang, a bit louder than normal.

"Sorry, what?" Alex looked away from Kat and back to Thrang.

"I was just asking if you thought the weather would hold," Thrang said, looking unhappy about having to repeat himself.

"It should," answered Alex absently. "The weather should be good for the next few months."

"Away, witch!" the man at the bar shouted in a commanding tone.

All eyes turned to the bar. Kat backed away from the man, turning and hurrying to the back of the bar. She sat at a separate table, obviously shaken.

Alex looked quickly at his friends. They all looked as stunned as he felt, but none of them made any kind of movement. He felt a wild and reckless surge of anger rising up in him, and he gripped his staff in his fist.

"Alex, no," said Thrang, his voice low and urgent.

"What?" Alex had started to rise to his feet, but Thrang's voice stopped him.

"Don't," said Arconn.

"What are you saying?" Alex asked in surprise. "Did we not agree to uphold each other's honor?"

"This is different," Thrang whispered.

"How?" Alex asked, confused.

"He's not just a man," said Arconn, nodding toward the man at the bar. "He's a paladin."

"A what?" Alex asked, angry that his friends were trying to hold him back.

"A paladin," Thrang repeated. "A holy or sacred warrior."

"And that means we should let this insult pass?" Alex said hotly.

"They have powers of their own," said Arconn, putting his hand on Alex's shoulder and guiding him back into his seat. "Some say they are the equal of wizards—if not greater."

"I doubt that is true," said Alex, the reckless feeling getting the better of him.

"Perhaps it is not true, but this is not the time to find out," said Thrang, his voice full of fear.

"The little one wishes to defend the witch," one of the three men at the bar said loudly.

"Listen to the dwarf and the elf, boy," the second man added. "They know better than to meddle in things that do not concern them."

"But the little one carries a staff," said the third man with a laugh. "Perhaps he thinks himself a wizard, free to meddle when and where he chooses."

It happened too quickly for Thrang or Arconn to say or do anything. In a flash, Alex was on his feet, his staff blazing like the sun and filling the room with light. The three men at the bar were picked up and thrown across the room, pinned to the wall by Alex's magic. The locals screamed and ran for the door, and Alex ignored them. He moved closer to the men he magically held against the wall, the reckless feeling burning inside of him and threatening to overtake him completely.

"Enough," the man at the far end of the bar said loudly. "Release them, wizard, and face me."

Alex did not release the three men, but he turned toward the man who had called Kat a witch. The man looked directly into Alex's eyes with a slight grin on his face, as if he had heard everything Thrang and Arconn had said and was not at all amused by it. Alex moved to meet him, shifting his staff from his left hand to his right, ready to confront the paladin and whatever powers he might have.

The room seemed to vanish around him, and all Alex could see was the stranger by the bar. He held the paladin's gaze and felt the contest of power and will begin. Alex immediately knew he was the stronger of the two. Time seemed to stand still. For Alex, there was nothing but the stranger in front of him and the recklessness inside of him.

You must bow to me, said a voice in Alex's mind. *You must bow and acknowledge that I am greater.*

No, Alex answered in his own mind, directing his thoughts back at the stranger. *You will bow to me and apologize for your rash words.*

They stood, locked in combat that no one else could see,

for what seemed like a long time, Alex resisting the words of the stranger and forcing his own will and words back at him.

The end came as quickly as it had begun. There was a flash in Alex's mind, and he knew that he had overcome the stranger. He blinked once to clear his eyes and the wild, reckless feeling slipped away from him. He stood in the middle of the room, though he didn't remember moving there.

"Forgive me," said the stranger. "Forgive my pride and arrogance."

Alex looked down and saw the stranger kneeling in front of him. He glanced at his friends, their faces frozen in fear and amazement. The three men he'd held against the wall had fallen to the floor, pale and gasping for breath.

"What is your name?" Alex questioned the kneeling man.

"I am known by many names," the stranger answered, his head bowed almost to the floor. "In this land, I am called Bane."

"Why did you attack as you did?"

"I felt your power when you entered," the paladin answered. "I heard your conversation with the dwarf and the elf. For a moment, I thought they would convince you to let my harsh words pass. I was already angry with myself for speaking too quickly to the seer, and I wanted you to confront me. Then my friends spoke out of turn, and you attacked them instead. I could not let them suffer for what I had done."

"Why did you not just apologize to my friend?" Alex asked, his tone softening.

"My pride would not allow that. It was also my pride that forced me to test myself against you. I thought myself more powerful, but I was wrong. Forgive me, master wizard, I have been a fool."

"Will you take back your hasty words and apologize to my friend?" questioned Alex.

"Gladly," said Bane, looking up for the first time. "I know you could force me to apologize, and I appreciate the opportunity to ask the seer for her forgiveness."

"Then I will forgive you as well," said Alex, putting his hand out and helping the man back to his feet. "I am Alexander Taylor, but my friends call me Alex."

"Then I hope to be among your friends, young wizard," said Bane, smiling weakly.

Alex nodded. "There is only one thing left for you to do before we can be friends." Alex glanced to the far corner of the room where Kat sat, looking as shocked as the rest of the company.

"As you wish," said Bane, bowing and walking quickly toward Kat.

Alex watched for a moment and then turned back to his friends at the table. Thrang and Arconn still looked dumbstruck, as did Nellus and Barnabus. Thrain looked pale and terrified, like he wanted to run and hide. Alex sat down at the table, and that seemed to break the spell that was holding his friends motionless.

"I . . . I don't know what to say," Thrang stuttered, looking at Alex. "I've never seen or heard of anything . . ."

"An impressive feat," Arconn said, his voice a little shaky. "I have never heard of a paladin bowing to a wizard."

"How did you . . . ?" Nellus stammered, unable to finish his question.

"It was a test of will, but it is over now," Alex answered. "And I was only doing what Thrang asked us all to do."

"Yes, but . . . a paladin," Thrang managed to say.

At that moment, Kat and Bane walked up to the table.

"My thanks, Master Taylor," said Kat, bowing to Alex. "I am in your debt."

"As am I," Bane added, also bowing.

Alex glanced at the three men who were struggling to get off the floor. "Perhaps your friends need some assistance," he said to Bane. The paladin hurried over to them and said something that Alex could not hear, and then returned to the table.

"If it's all right," said Bane slowly. "They would like to ask your forgiveness as well."

"Perhaps I should ask for theirs," said Alex. "I don't make a habit of throwing people around magically, and I'm afraid I've hurt them more than their words hurt me."

"No, master wizard," said the first man, kneeling down with his two friends. "We spoke as fools, and you were right to punish us."

"Forgive us for our rash words," said the second man in a pleading tone.

"We did not think, and we are sorry that we offended you," the third man added quickly.

"Then rise as friends," answered Alex.

The three men stood up and bowed to Alex and the rest of the company. Bane nodded to his friends, and they quickly made their way out of the tavern.

"And all is well between us, then?" Alex questioned, looking from Kat to Bane.

"All is well," answered Kat. "And I ask that you not place all of the blame on Master Bane. I offered help where it was neither needed nor wanted."

"And I spoke too quickly, without thought," Bane added. "In the future I will not be so hasty."

"Good," said Alex. "Now, I think we should eat. Bane, you are welcome to join us."

Bane glanced at Thrang. "The leader of the adventure should be the one to invite guests," he said politely.

"My apologies, Master Silversmith," said Alex. "I seem to have forgotten my place."

"What's that?" said Thrang, looking between Alex and Bane. "Oh, yes, we would be honored if you would join us."

"The honor is mine," said Bane, bowing to Thrang. "I would count it a great blessing to share a meal with your company."

Thrang offered Bane a chair, and Alex suggested they push the two tables together into one long table. Bane and Thrang sat at opposite ends of the table, and Alex sat next to Bane. He wanted to talk to the paladin and find out more about him.

"Changed the seating, then, have you?" Rose remarked as she returned with a large platter. "And added a new friend as well. The two of you have scared away my regular customers, you know," she said to Alex and Bane.

"I am sorry," Bane said. "The fault is mine, and I will gladly compensate you for the loss of business."

"Oh, that's not needed," said Rose with a laugh. "Those

old grumps needed a bit of shaking up. They sit here every night and drink one mug apiece, and they never leave a tip. After tonight, I expect they'll be drinking a bit more for the next few days."

"If it's not too much trouble, there will be eight for dinner," said Thrang. "And please, put the mugs on our bill."

"No trouble at all," said Rose, putting the large platter of potatoes on the table. "I'll be just a minute with the rest of it, and then I'll leave you be."

Rose moved surprisingly fast, and soon everyone in the company had filled their plates with hot food. Alex noticed that Bane made sure everyone had enough of everything before helping himself, and he smiled approvingly. He had never met a paladin before, and he didn't remember reading anything about them in any of his studies.

"Have you traveled far?" Bane asked, looking at Thrang.

"Not yet," said Thrang, cutting into his steak. "Our adventure is just beginning, and we have a long road to travel before its end."

"May I ask which direction that road lies?" Bane asked. "Of course, if you'd rather not say, I understand."

"We go east," said Thrang simply.

"I have just come from the east," said Bane. "I had heard stories of trouble there, though I had none myself."

"What kind of trouble?" Thrang questioned.

"Rumors of bandits or maybe trolls," Bane answered. "I saw few tracks in my travels, so I can't say which, if any, of the rumors are true."

"Trolls have more wealth than bandits," Alex pointed out.

"And are often more dangerous," Arconn added.

"And both are best avoided," said Nellus, his voice troubled.

"Well, we won't go looking for them," said Alex. "I was just thinking if we had to face one or the other."

"I doubt that either would be much trouble for Master Taylor," Bane said.

"You are too kind," said Alex. "And please, call me Alex."

Their meal went on with a great deal of talk, but not much laughter. Bane knew a great deal about the land to the east, and they all listened closely as he told them about the difficulties he had run into and rumors he had heard.

"There are more dangers in Thraxon then there once were," Bane concluded, pushing his chair back from the table.

"Not enough adventurers," said Thrang, nodding his head. "If more adventures were going on here, many of the troubles you've heard of would be removed."

"Perhaps," Bane allowed. "Though the people of the land have some responsibility as well. They should not wait for adventurers to come and solve their problems for them."

"True," said Thrang, stroking his beard. "And the different peoples of Thraxon have not worked together for many years. I will mention it to King Thorgood when we return to Benorg."

"Do you know the king well?" Bane questioned.

"Better than most," said Thrang. "I have been one of his ministers. And this is his adventure, in a manner of speaking."

"Then perhaps I could impose on you," said Bane, leaning forward intently. "I am on my way to Benorg, and I need to search its history. Perhaps you could send a message to the king, asking for his assistance in my quest."

"We know nothing of you or your quest," said Thrang carefully. "I would need to know something about you and what you are looking for before I could ask the king to help you."

"Yes, of course," said Bane. "I will be happy to tell you anything I can."

"But not everything," said Alex, looking at Bane.

"You see much," said Bane with a nod. "Yes, there are some things that I cannot tell, not even to a wizard like yourself."

"Then tell us your story if you will," said Thrang. "If there are parts you must leave out, we will understand and not ask questions."

Chapter Seven

The Paladin's Tale

Alex and his companions leaned back in their chairs, waiting expectantly. For several minutes Bane said nothing. His head was bowed slightly, as though he was trying to remember something from the distant past. If Alex hadn't known better, he would have thought that Bane had fallen asleep.

Bane lifted his head, and Alex was surprised to realize that Bane was actually a great deal older than he appeared to be. The paladin looked worn and tired, and his face had turned a slight gray color.

"I was born in Goval," said Bane slowly, "before it was divided into two lands. I had an easy childhood, or at least as easy as any childhood can be. Nothing of great importance happened to me as a child, and I mention it only so you will know that I was once a normal man."

Bane paused, a troubled look crossing his face, but it was quickly gone, and he continued his story.

"When I was sixteen years old, the wars in Goval began. At the time, I didn't know who started the wars, or why. To me, war looked like a great adventure, an opportunity to win fortune and fame. With such thoughts in my mind, I left my happy home and joined one of the many armies that marched across the land.

"I was a boy pretending to be a man. I knew nothing of war and less of life. Sadly, I learned too much about both, for I had a gift. The art of war came naturally to me, too naturally, in fact. I should have stayed at home, but that thought did not occur to me until it was much too late to go back. By the time I was seventeen, I had killed twenty men in single combat, and many more than that in the massed attacks between the armies.

"War is bloody, dirty work, but I took to it willingly, and my fame began to grow among the soldiers of our army. I was respected as a warrior, though I was still a boy. The fame went to my head, and I became proud and arrogant, two things I struggle with even today."

Bane took a long drink from his mug. Alex could understand Bane's feelings and desires, as he had sometimes felt a similar thirst for battle when wielding his sword, Moon Slayer.

"As my reputation grew," Bane continued, "so did my responsibility. When I was eighteen, I commanded a squad of men. By the time I was twenty, I commanded a company. In four short years, the army had become my life. I had almost forgotten the home and family that I'd once had.

"When I was twenty-one years old, our army joined with another, and we received a new lord to rule us in our deadly game. He was a wise man, cunning on the battlefield and careful with the lives of his men. He had heard about me and ordered me to stand before him. At the time, I thought it was the greatest moment of my life.

"He began to train me to be more than just the mindless leader of a company. He taught me tactics and strategies. He showed me how to win men's loyalty and get the most out of them. Those were the good lessons he taught me—but there were other lessons as well."

A look of pain crossed Bane's face. He stared at the table in front of him, lost in thought. When he spoke again, his voice was tight, and he had some difficulty with the words.

"I learned to be cold and cruel," he said. "In war, the ruthless often have the advantage. Under the training of my new master, I learned to put aside my own feelings, to do what needed to be done—no matter what. It was a hard lesson for me to learn because, up until that time, I had always thought that mercy and honor had a place on the battlefield.

"I did things that I will never speak of, things that should not have been done. My master praised me and my actions, but deep in my own heart, I knew I had done wrong. I hid my doubts and buried my feelings deep. If I did evil, it was only to bring about a greater good, or so I told myself at the time. If the innocent had to pay the price for our victory, well, that was not my concern because only our final victory mattered. The innocent would be taken care of once my master was king of all the land.

"It was during this time that I began to understand what evil really is. My master seemed to change as time passed as well, becoming more desperate to win battles and less careful with his army. We were coming to the end, but I could not see it. All that mattered to me was that we fight. Victory could still be ours, if only we could keep going.

"The end of that time in my life is a bloody story, and I will not retell it now. Simply know that the end did come, and when it did, I was at my master's side, though even then I did not realize what was truly happening. I was blinded by the hate he had poured into me."

Bane paused, taking a few deep breaths and running his hands through his hair.

"The end came," he repeated grimly. "We were caught by our enemies. I tried to help my master escape, tried to run to the hills and start again. We would rebuild our army, even if it meant traveling to another land. But our attempt was in vain. We were cornered. Not by soldiers, but by wizards.

"Four wizards—true wizards like Master Taylor here—who did not seek power for themselves, but justice for the people of Goval. I was bound by their spells and made to watch what they did to my master. At first I thought they would torture him and make him pay for the dark deeds that he had done and that others had done in his name. Torture was not what the wizards were about, and that was something I had not expected.

"They spoke a magic spell together, and a shadow of darkness tore away from my master's body. I did not understand what I was seeing. I knew little of magic and even less about the dark creatures that exist in the known lands. The shadow spoke to the four wizards, but I did not hear what it said. Before the wizards could capture or destroy the shadow, my old master rushed at them, distracting them from their final task.

"The old man was destroyed, but the shadow that had been inside of him escaped. I thought the wizards would destroy me as well, but they did not. With a few kind words, they removed the darkness and shadows from my mind so I could see the truth, so I could understand the evil that had been done. I could finally understand what I had done in the name of victory, and, for the first time in years, I could feel with the emotions of a man.

"It was an act of kindness, but still the guilt for my evil deeds overcame me. For a long time I wished for death, but that was not to be. The wizards helped me overcome my guilt and found ways to heal the wounds I had inflicted on the land and people of Goval. I traveled for many years in the company of one or another of these wizards, until finally the four of them came together once more."

Bane closed his eyes and leaned back in his chair. He shook his head as if trying to wake himself from a dream.

"These four great men asked me to take on a final quest," said Bane, half-smiling as he spoke. "They explained to me what the shadow I had seen was, though words fail to express its true nature and horror. I will simply say that it was a shadow of evil that could posses a person and use that person for its own ends. I have heard it called by many names in many lands, but the result is always the same: war and pain.

"I accepted the quest, thinking it would be a way to repay some of the evils I had done. I did not know then that my quest would last so long, but even now, I feel the punishment is light compared to my crimes."

Bane stopped as a sudden cough racked his body violently. It was several minutes before he caught his breath again, but no one said anything or even moved.

"So, my new masters gave me power," said Bane, rubbing his chin. "They passed some of their own power to me and sent me into the known lands as a paladin. Now I hunt the shadow that possesses men, and my quest will not end until I find it and destroy it, or it destroys me."

There was a long silence as Bane finished speaking, and the only noise came from the fire burning in the hearth.

Alex considered Bane's story, remembering something his own teacher, Whalen Vankin, had told him.

"I see now why my friends were so concerned when I wanted to confront you," Alex said at last. "I did not recognize you for what you are, and I did not understand what they meant when they called you a paladin."

"A name for common people to use," said Bane.

"Yet I know another name, a name that I will not speak in this company," said Alex. "If I had known that that was what you are, I would not have confronted you as I did."

"And yet you proved the stronger," said Bane, a look of wonder on his face.

"How long have you been on this quest?" Arconn asked quietly.

"A long time," Bane answered. "Sometimes it feels like forever, and I think the quest will have no end. But I cannot give it up."

"Your story rings true," said Thrang after a moment. "I will gladly ask King Thorgood to assist you in your quest."

"You are most kind," said Bane, inclining his head to Thrang.

"I think I may also be able to assist you," said Alex.

"Perhaps more than the libraries of Benorg, unless I miss my guess."

"You know of the creature? The shadow of which I spoke?" Bane questioned, a hint of excitement in his voice.

"I believe I do," said Alex. "If it is the same creature, and I feel sure that it is, I have confronted it twice."

"Twice?" Bane repeated in amazement.

"It tried to tempt me," said Alex. "It wanted me to join with it. It made me promises of power, wealth, and fame."

"Promises it could not keep, unless it used the power in you to bring such things to pass," said Bane. "Will you tell me where these meetings took place?"

"The first was in Vargland," said Alex, glancing at his friends. "The shadow was controlling several wraiths there. I was not yet a trained wizard and did not understand what I was facing. It nearly destroyed me, and I was saved only because my friends called me back from the wall."

"More than one called you back?" Bane questioned in surprise.

"I called him back partway," said Arconn, a pained look on his face. "I did not have the power to call him back completely."

"Perhaps not," said Alex. "But you had the presence of mind to take me to one who could call me back—or, as you once said, demand that I return."

"A close thing, even for her," said Arconn.

"Yes, it was," agreed Alex.

"So you escaped it once when you were not trained, and then you met it again?" Bane asked.

"By chance, it traveled with an adventurer who was part of the company I had joined," Alex explained. "I was still being trained and had not yet taken my staff so I did not see or feel the shadow until it was almost too late."

"The adventurer—were you able to save him?" Bane questioned in a worried tone.

"I was not," said Alex sadly. "He was lost, and the shadow escaped. That was in the far north of Norsland, not long ago."

"Twice you have met the shadow and twice you have overcome it. I think the shadow will avoid meeting you a third time," said Bane with a nod.

"Perhaps," Alex agreed. "I think I could hold it now, but I do not know how to destroy it."

"I have little doubt that you could destroy it if you needed to," said Bane in a confident tone. "You overcame me easily, and I was sent to be this shadow's bane."

"Yes, but your powers are not fully yours to use," said Alex. "I think your powers would have been greater if I had been evil. If I had accepted the shadow's offer, I would be less than I am. You would have prevailed."

"I wonder," said Bane softly. "I am glad that such a test will never come."

"As am I," said Alex.

"Now that you have some idea where the shadow has been, will you still go to Benorg?" Kat asked Bane.

"Yes," said Bane. "I would still like to search the records of the city to see if there is any mention of the shadow. I doubt that the records will name it as such, but I will know just the same."

"I doubt that the shadow remained in Norsland anyway," Alex said. "It was going to look for a new servant, or perhaps I should say victim. Though it may wish to return to Norsland, once that victim is found."

"Why do you say that?" Bane questioned.

"It thinks there is something waiting for it there," answered Alex.

Bane looked at Alex, confused. Alex smiled and told the story of the last time he'd met the shadow. As he spoke, he could feel his friends' eyes on him. He hadn't told them the entire story of this part of his last adventure, and he was a little embarrassed to be telling it now.

"It will be disappointed when it returns," Bane said with satisfaction. "Though I am sorry that the adventurer could not be saved."

"He made his own choice," said Alex. "I feel sorry for him, but he had to pay the price for the choices that he made."

"As do we all," said Bane with a bleak smile.

"What happened to the four wizards who sent you on this quest?" Thrain asked shyly.

"That is not important," Alex interrupted. "What is important is that Bane is still on his quest. I, for one, will help in any way I can."

"You have already helped a great deal," said Bane. "More than anyone else I have met in my journeys."

"But—the wizards?" Thrain persisted.

"We should go to bed," Alex suggested. "Tomorrow we must start on the road again, and I know that Bane has a long journey ahead of him as well."

"Yes, of course," said Thrang, catching the quick look Alex gave him. "To bed, and the road in the morning."

Alex and Bane remained seated as the others got up from the table and left for their rooms.

"Aren't you coming, Alex?" Thrain questioned.

"I'll be along shortly," said Alex.

Alex watched as Thrang pulled Thrain aside, whispering something in his ear. He felt a little sad for his young friend, but he knew there was nothing he could do about it just now.

"You were kind to deflect his question," Bane said once he and Alex were alone.

"I knew the answer would trouble you," said Alex. "I will explain it to him later, if he still wishes to know."

"I suppose you wish to know the parts of my story I did not tell," Bane said.

"I will not pry," said Alex. "Much of what was missing I could see without your speaking it. Anything that I could not see is not important for me to know."

"Thank you," said Bane. "You have been both kind and helpful."

"What will you do now?" Alex questioned. "I know your trip to Benorg will be a short one."

"After hearing your story, I will admit I thought of going to Norsland," Bane answered. "I could wait for the shadow to return and hope to take it by surprise."

"Yet you have doubts about that plan," Alex stated.

Bane nodded. "Time means little to the shadow, and . . ."

"And?"

"I feel that something else is happening. Something is

wrong in the known lands, something that I cannot clearly see."

"What do you mean?" Alex questioned.

"The shadow slips away, and, at times, it seems to vanish completely. It is as if someone or something is helping it to escape me," Bane answered. "I feel as if some great conspiracy is taking place, yet I can find no proof or trail to follow."

"A conspiracy to hide this shadow?"

"Not just the shadow. I have seen things in many lands—things that should not be. Yet it seems that people don't notice the danger. Or perhaps they don't care as they once did."

"What is this conspiracy? What is it they want? Power? Wealth?"

"I don't know," said Bane. "Sometimes I feel that I should know, but the answer remains just out of sight. I do know that things are changing, and not for the better. Kingdoms are weakening, and old friendships are being forgotten. Perhaps that is what the conspiracy wants, but I don't know why."

"If that is true, it must be a large conspiracy," said Alex. "And a large group is easily discovered."

"Not if they were patient," said Bane. "Not if they worked slowly over hundreds or even thousands of years. You know how long ago the wars in Goval started, Alex. You know how long I have been on this quest."

"Long enough that you would notice things like a careful and patient conspiracy."

"Yes," said Bane. "I would ask you to do something for me."

"What can I do?"

"Talk to the wizards that you know, pass on my thoughts to them," said Bane. "Alert them to what might be happening and ask them to act, if they can."

"I'll do what I can," said Alex.

Bane nodded and sat silently for several minutes, looking into the fire across the room.

"I think it would be best if I am gone before your company wakes in the morning," he said at last.

"Must you always travel alone?" Alex questioned quietly.

"People's lives are too short, and I am too old. I am a paladin and must always be on the move. I do not have time for ties to family or friends."

"Very well," said Alex, feeling sorry for Bane. "I wish you good hunting in your quest."

"Thank you," said Bane.

"If ever I meet this shadow again, I will let you know," Alex promised. "And if you ever need my assistance, please, feel free to call on me."

Bane nodded, but Alex knew that the paladin was unlikely to ever ask for assistance. The ancient warrior had searched the known lands for many long years, and Alex knew that in all that time, he was the first to offer him any kind of help.

Alex stood up from the table and shook hands with Bane. He did not speak, but simply turned and left the paladin sitting alone at the table.

CHAPTER EIGHT

ROAD TO DANGER

———◆———

The next morning Alex was up before any of his companions. He wrote a letter to Whalen, explaining Bane's thoughts about a conspiracy, and then went down to the bar and took a seat at one of the tables. He knew Thrang and the others would be along soon so he ordered breakfast for the entire company. While he waited, he wondered how far Bane had already traveled toward Benorg.

"You're up early," Thrang said as he entered the room.

"Or you're up late," said Alex.

"I'm surprised you slept at all," Thrang said. "I thought you and your new friend would be up all night talking. I suspect there were things you needed to talk about that were best discussed in private."

Alex nodded. "And other things that were best not to speak of in front of the company."

"Like Thrain's question? Did you have to ask Bane or did you already know the answer?"

"Once I knew what Bane was, I knew the answer to Thrain's question. Though what should concern us now are the rumors that Bane heard in his travels. I know I said trolls

109

have more wealth than bandits, but I'm not in a hurry to meet either."

"Nor am I," said Thrang. "Bane said he saw nothing as he traveled, so perhaps we will not be troubled either."

"Bane traveled alone," Alex said. "There are seven of us. We will be easier to spot than he was."

"He traveled alone?" Thrang questioned. "Then who were the three men with him?"

"Some things should not be asked," Alex answered softly.

Their discussion was interrupted as the rest of the company entered the room just as Rose arrived to serve breakfast. Alex noticed that Thrain looked dejected and not his normal happy self. Alex knew that it had taken a lot of courage for Thrain to ask Bane about the four wizards and suspected he was unhappy at not hearing the answer. But when Thrain seemed reluctant to look Alex in the face, Alex sensed that there was more to the problem.

"I see Master Bane has gone," said Arconn, taking his seat.

"He had far to travel," said Alex.

"But he never answered my question," said Thrain quietly, his eyes fixed on the table in front of him.

"I will answer your question," Alex said gently. "But when we are on the road once more, not here."

"We should discuss the road ahead," Arconn said.

"Alex and I were doing just that before you arrived," said Thrang. "We will need to be careful and choose our campsites well."

"But Bane said he saw nothing," said Nellus.

"But he did hear rumors," said Barnabus.

"The trouble with rumors is you never know what to believe," Kat said. "There might be bandits or trolls along our path, or there might be nothing at all."

"Or there might be something even worse," Arconn added.

"It's no use trying to guess what we might or might not meet. We'll be careful as we go, and our road goes east," said Thrang.

The sun was coming up as they left the tavern, and Alex was pleased to see that Ned had taken good care of their horses. As Thrang settled the bill, Alex handed Ned a couple of silver coins and thanked him for looking after the animals. Ned seemed stunned by the generous gift and thanked Alex several times before they rode away.

"That was probably more than he makes in a month," Kat commented, riding beside Alex.

"Then he is underpaid," said Alex with a laugh.

Soon the small town was far behind them, but Thrang decided they should continue to follow the road simply because it was going in the right direction. Alex wondered about the wisdom of that decision, but he kept his thoughts to himself.

After they had ridden for some time, Thrain drew up alongside Alex. "If I was wrong to ask about Bane, I'm sorry," he said quietly.

"You were not wrong to ask," said Alex. "There is no secret that needs to be kept."

"Well then, can you tell me the answer?" Thrain asked.

"Bane is a paladin," Alex began. "But wizards use a different word, which is why I didn't understand when Thrang and

Arconn tried to warn me last night. The wizard word has much more meaning, of course, but paladin will do."

"Yes, we know he is a paladin," said Thrang. "But what happened to the four wizards who gave Bane his quest?"

"It is not a simple question to answer, even for me," said Alex. "To create a paladin requires a great deal of magical power. It's not as if the wizards could simply say, 'You're a paladin. Go on this quest.' There is much more to it than that. To give Bane the power he would need, they had to let go of some of their own. The four wizards poured their own power into Bane. Once that was done, they were no longer wizards, but they were not simply men either."

"You mean they gave up their magical powers so Bane could go on his quest?" Thrain asked in a puzzled voice.

"Yes," answered Alex.

"So Bane has the power of all four wizards in him?" Kat questioned after a long pause.

"Yes," Alex said again.

"Yet you proved stronger in your test of will," said Arconn, looking over his shoulder at Alex. "He bowed to you, not you to him."

"That is true," said Alex. "However, Bane could not use all of his power against me. His full power can only be used against the shadow he chases or against those who serve that evil."

"Still, you were stronger than the four," Kat said.

"I am not evil, and I do not have the same restrictions that Bane has," said Alex. "I said as much last night while telling him about my meetings with the shadow."

"It was impressive to see," Barnabus said from behind Alex.

"What was?" Alex asked, not sure what Barnabus meant.

"The contest of power," Barnabus answered. "It was impressive to see."

"What exactly did you see?" Alex questioned.

"You don't know?" Barnabus asked in reply.

"I was a bit busy at the time," said Alex with a slight smile.

"You passed through the table like a ghost," said Barnabus. "That alone was startling."

"And when you and Bane locked eyes, it was as if all light and sound had been drained from the world," Arconn added.

"All we could see was the two of you, standing there surrounded by a shining white light while the rest of the world was in darkness," said Thrain, his voice shaking slightly.

"It seemed to me that nothing else in all the known lands mattered but the outcome of your contest," said Nellus. "Though I don't think any harm would have come if Bane had prevailed."

"Perhaps no harm, but less good," said Kat, looking away from Alex and toward the east.

"I . . . I didn't realize," said Alex, shaking his head. "For me, you all just melted away until only Bane existed."

"When Bane knelt, it was like the world snapped back into being," said Thrang, rubbing his nose on the back of his sleeve.

"I will have to be more careful in the future," said Alex. "I did not realize the effects of such a test on those not involved."

For a while they rode in silence. Alex now understood the stunned looks on his friends' faces and the reason Thrain was reluctant to look him in the eye. They had seen a contest of two great powers—powers that they did not really understand. Alex knew it was fortunate that his contest with Bane had been nothing more serious than a test. If it had been real battle—a battle that his own reckless feelings had almost started—then things might have turned nasty.

When they stopped for their midday meal, Arconn surveyed their surroundings. "This road seems little used, but the grass and weeds have not grown over it."

"Perhaps grass and weeds grow more slowly here. Or perhaps the rain from last week has washed away any tracks," Nellus suggested.

"Perhaps," said Arconn, looking east along the road. "There is a strange feel to this road, but I cannot make out what it is."

"Should we perhaps leave the road and travel across open ground?" Alex questioned, voicing the thoughts he'd had earlier in the day.

"The road goes in our chosen direction," said Thrang, stroking his beard in thought. "To leave it would slow our progress."

"And to stay on it might lead us to danger," Barnabus said.

"We don't know there is any danger," said Kat. "If there is, it will find us as easily in the open as along the road."

"We will stay on the road for now," said Thrang, his voice final. "If there is danger, then we will meet it when it comes. If there is no danger, we will move quicker on the road."

They all agreed, though Arconn's comment about a strange feel to the road stuck in Alex's mind. He, too, felt there was something strange about the road, but he also understood Thrang's point about wanting to travel as quickly as possible.

When they camped for the night, Alex felt more watchful than he normally did. There was nothing definite to trouble his thoughts, but something in the back of his mind continued to nag at him. He kept his worries to himself and listened while the others talked around the campfire. When the others went to their tents, Alex stood and looked into the darkness. There was danger ahead; he was certain of it.

"May I speak with you?" Kat asked.

Alex turned to look at her, unsurprised by her presence. He had half-expected her to remain at the fire when the others went to bed. "Of course," he said.

"I . . . I wanted to thank you for what you did," said Kat, her voice halting as she spoke. "At the tavern."

"I did only what I said I would do," said Alex.

"Yes, but to face a paladin . . . that was a risk."

"I did not know what a paladin was. If I had known, I may have been more hesitant to face him."

"You would not have hesitated," said Kat, sounding sure of her words. "To hesitate is not in your nature."

"You know me so well already." Alex laughed.

"I am a seer, and I often know things about people without knowing them for long."

"Can you see the possibilities, like an oracle?" Alex questioned.

Kat shook her head. "There are different kinds of seers. Some see as oracles do, only not so clearly. That is not my gift."

"What is your gift?" Alex asked.

"I have a gift for finding," said Kat. "It is my strongest gift, though not my only one."

"You also have a gift for knowing the intentions of others," said Alex. "If Bane had been evil, you would not have approached him as you did."

Kat smiled and nodded. "A useful gift, though at times it is unwelcome."

"Bane has many demons to fight. He was not angry with you, but with himself."

"I do not blame him," said Kat. "But I do thank you for your actions."

Alex nodded and smiled at Kat. She was different than he thought she would be, and yet at the same time, almost exactly what he thought she would be. It was difficult to explain, and he did not try.

Kat returned his smile and then headed to her tent.

Alex watched her go, then turned to look into the darkness again. He knew there was nothing there, but for a long time he stood watching just the same.

The following day passed with no sign of danger or other travelers. Alex began watching the road more closely, looking for anything—a footprint, a track, even a bit of garbage—that would show that other people had used it. There was nothing to be seen, however, and his thoughts remained troubled.

After three days of following the road, Alex had given up on looking for any signs, and he turned his thoughts to other things. At first he spent his time practicing some methods that relaxed his mind but allowed his body to function as normal. He found this very restful, though it removed his need to sleep at night. After a few nights of not sleeping, he decided to practice some sensory exercises instead. They were supposed to help him know when someone was coming or if danger or enemies were close. He found these exercises much more difficult to do than relaxing his mind, and he guessed that having so many people around made it more difficult than it would be if he were alone.

On their seventh day of following the road, Thrang stopped them next to a stream, the first they had found since leaving the mountains.

"We have traveled far already, and a little extra rest will do us good," Thrang said. "We will camp here."

"I would guess we are getting close to the Eastern Sea," said Nellus, looking across the grasslands. "I think we've traveled at least a hundred and fifty miles from the mountains."

"Closer to two hundred," said Arconn, jumping lightly from his saddle.

"As you are so light on your feet, perhaps you can hunt us up some fresh meat," Barnabus said to Arconn.

"I have seen little to hunt, but I will try," Arconn answered.

"May I come along?" Thrain asked, his enthusiasm for the adventure having returned over the past several days.

"Don't go too far," Thrang warned. "And keep both eyes open for trouble."

"We'll do that." Arconn laughed. "And perhaps, if we have a spare moment, we might look for game."

Thrang grunted as Arconn and Thrain walked away from camp.

Alex knew that Thrang was worried about Thrain. It was true that this was Thrain's first adventure and the young dwarf didn't know a great deal about the dangers that came with adventures, but as long as he was with Arconn, he should be all right. Alex walked forward and stood by his dwarf friend, who was still looking north at where Thrain and Arconn had disappeared.

"He'll be fine," Alex said. "Arconn is with him, after all."

"Yes, I suppose he will," said Thrang. "And I suppose I'd better get a fire going, since Thrain has managed to sneak off before doing it."

Alex laughed and helped Thrang gather wood for their campfire, an easy task because there were more trees along the stream than there had been along the road. They soon had a large pile of wood, and Thrang ignited a small fire and began heating water for tea.

Alex left the campsite and climbed a small hill to the northeast, wanting to get a good look at the countryside. Kat asked if she could walk with him, and he happily agreed.

The hill was small and it took them only a few minutes to climb to the top. Alex leaned on his staff and looked around, taking in the change in landscape to the east and the distant mountains to the west. He glanced at Kat and saw that she was gazing north with a look of expectation on her face.

"What is it?" Alex questioned, his voice lowered so as not to startle Kat.

"Something strange," answered Kat in a slow and dreamy voice. "Evil intentions, but I cannot name the source."

"Are we in danger?"

"I do not think so," Kat whispered. "Not now, not yet."

The dreamy look suddenly left Kat's face, and she blinked and rubbed her eyes. She gave Alex a questioning look, and he explained what had just happened.

"A trance?" Kat questioned.

"Not exactly," said Alex. "I think you were seeing or at least feeling something that was there. I couldn't tell if you were looking at something in the future or at something that is some distance away from us."

"But that's never happened before," said Kat, a note of worry in her voice.

"If it had, would you know?"

"No, I suppose not."

"You will need to learn how to remember such things," said Alex. "Perhaps I can help you with that. For now, I think we should mention this to the others."

"No," Kat said quickly. "Not yet. Not until we know if my words hold any meaning."

"By the time we know, it might be too late for your words to do any good."

"If we remain watchful and careful, we should be fine."

"As you wish," Alex agreed. He thought Kat's prediction or premonition was a good thing. The more he thought about it, the more he felt that they were not in any immediate danger, so he was willing to do as Kat requested and not mention what had happened to any of the others.

The two of them walked back to the camp in silence, but they had not been back for long when Thrain came rushing back to the camp alone. He looked worried and afraid, and it took several minutes for him to catch his breath before he could speak.

"A huge snake," Thrain managed to say at last. "Arconn told me to come back and let you know. He said it was a nag-something and that he was going to follow it."

"A nagas?" Alex questioned.

"Yes, that's what he said," Thrain answered, still breathing hard and looking terrified.

"What's a nagas?" Thrang asked.

"As Thrain said, a giant snake," answered Alex, looking north. "They have a human-looking head, and they can speak to people if they choose to."

"Are they dangerous?" Kat questioned, looking slightly panicked.

"They can be if they are startled or angered," said Alex. "They are also known to protect treasure, or hoard treasure if they have not been given one to protect."

"And Arconn is following this thing?" Thrang asked, looking back to Thrain.

"He said he would return shortly," Thrain answered. "He didn't seem to think there was any real danger."

"There may not be," said Alex. "But some nagas are evil, and they have been known to attack unsuspecting travelers."

"That would explain why Arconn sent Thrain back to warn us," Nellus said.

"Yes, but not why he chose to follow the serpent in the first place," said Alex.

"I'm sure he had a good reason," said Thrang. "Arconn would not do anything foolish."

"Should we look for him?" Barnabus questioned, glancing between Alex and Thrang.

"He didn't say anything about needing us to come after him, did he?" Thrang asked.

"No," said Thrain. "He said he would return shortly and told me to hurry back."

"Then we will wait," said Thrang, his hand going to his beard as he thought. "If Arconn does not return soon, then we will go and look for him."

"I would suggest that I go and look," said Alex, taking his eyes off the northern horizon to look at Thrang. "If all of us happened upon the nagas, it would feel threatened and might attack."

"Very well," Thrang agreed. "I know from experience that you can take care of yourself in any situation."

The others settled back around the fire, but Alex stayed where he was. His eyes returned to the horizon, and he tried to use his powers to sense what was ahead of them on the road. The concern and high emotions of his friends at the fire made this difficult for him, but slowly he managed to expand his thoughts to the north. He was surprised to feel Arconn's mood, and more surprised that the elf was not overly concerned with the creature he was following.

Alex stretched his thoughts further, his hands gripping his staff with the effort. He could sense the nagas moving unconcerned between the trees and through the tall grass, apparently unaware that Arconn was following it.

After several minutes Alex let his mind relax, shaking the blood back into his hands. He was not worried about Arconn, but a small part of him was worried that the nagas might still prove to be dangerous.

With his heightened senses, he could hear his friends talking around the fire.

"How long should we wait?" Barnabus questioned.

"What exactly did Arconn say?" Thrang asked Thrain.

"That he would return shortly," Thrain answered, still pale from the shock of seeing the giant snake.

"It will be dark soon," Nellus pointed out.

"Arconn can see in the dark," Kat commented.

"But we cannot," said Thrang, sounding worried and irritated.

They all stopped talking and sat staring into the fire. Alex continued to study the northern horizon, his senses on alert. Kat joined him by his side.

"Could this be what I spoke of?" Kat questioned, her voice low so the others could not hear.

"Perhaps," answered Alex.

"Then its intentions are evil, and it is waiting for a better time to attack us," Kat said softly.

"Yes," Alex agreed. "I was thinking of the rumors Bane heard. A nagas would make travelers vanish, just as bandits or trolls would."

"So you think the rumors had something to do with this nagas creature?"

"I do," said Alex.

Just then Arconn appeared, hurrying toward the camp with a grim but satisfied look on his face.

"Thrain explained, then?" Arconn asked as soon as he could make himself heard over the questions of the others.

"He did," said Thrang. "And a foolish thing it was for you to go off following a giant snake."

"I had my reasons," said Arconn calmly.

"And what might they have been?" Thrang questioned, a note of anger in his voice.

"I wanted to see where the creature made its home," answered Arconn. "I thought the nagas might be the source of the rumors Bane had heard."

"I was thinking the same thing," Alex added.

"And did you find the pit where this serpent sleeps?" Thrang asked.

"Yes, and my suspicions were verified," said Arconn. "Bones and debris littered the ground in front of the serpent's cave. I fear it has been waylaying travelers for some time now."

"And would waylay us, too, if it had a chance," said Thrang.

"It may have already seen us," said Kat.

"What's that? How? When?" Thrang asked.

Kat explained what had happened on the hill and that she now felt certain that the evil intentions she had felt came from the nagas, and that it was only waiting for a convenient time to attack them.

"What should we do?" Barnabus asked.

"Attack it first," Nellus suggested.

"It is growing dark, and the nagas would have great advantage in the dark," said Arconn.

"Yet we cannot remain here," said Thrang thoughtfully. "If the nagas has seen us here, we should move. Then at least it will not find us where it expects us to be."

"There is some wisdom in that, though where to move to is a problem," said Alex. "The nagas can move swiftly, and it will try to follow us wherever we go. If it does not find us here, it will be on guard, making it harder for us to attack it."

"What, then?" Thrang questioned, looking at Alex.

"Perhaps we can draw it in," Alex suggested. "It knows we are here, but it does not know that *we* know it is here."

"How difficult are these things to kill?" Thrang asked, fingering his ax.

"They are powerful creatures, and some have stings in their tails," said Arconn.

"Their teeth are long and sharp, and they can raise as much as half their body off the ground," Alex added.

"Dangerous at both ends, then," Thrang said. "Still, we must do something before this creature attempts to attack us."

"It is a difficult problem," said Alex, thinking it through. "I would suggest not being in the tents where we are separated and vulnerable to attack, but if we are all in the open, then the nagas will see us and might wait for another time to attack."

"There are also the horses to consider," said Arconn. "If it cannot get at us, it may go for the horses."

"Well, we must do something," Thrang repeated, looking worried and desperate. "And we must do something *now.*"

CHAPTER NINE
THE NAGAS

———————◆———————

Alex sat alone beside the fire, watching as the flames began to fail. All of his senses were alert, and his mind searched the ground around their camp for any sign of the nagas. The others were crowded into two of their four tents, waiting for any sound that would indicate the nagas was attacking. It was a desperate plan, but they couldn't think of anything else to do.

As a precaution, Alex had put a hiding spell on their horses, so at least the nagas would not be able to find them easily. It was not a difficult spell, but there were seven horses, and it had required more time than Alex would have liked. Still, the horses should be safe, and once the nagas appeared, his friends would be close at hand.

The nagas was both cunning and intelligent. No simple tricks would deceive the giant serpent, and they didn't have time to plan anything too difficult. So Alex sat alone as bait, watching the fire and waiting for the nagas to arrive. He worried that his ability to feel the nagas was limited, and he hoped that he would have time to act before the nagas could attack him.

Suddenly the hair on the back of Alex's neck stood up. The nagas had arrived. Alex could feel its eyes looking at him from the darkness, searching the camp. Alex remained still, as if dozing by the fire during his watch. He needed the nagas to come closer before he tried anything or else it might escape into the darkness.

Concentrating, he could feel the snake moving, circling the camp, and looking for the best place to attack.

Alex stayed still, focusing his mind on the nagas. He knew exactly where it was, and he was impressed and a little surprised by the snake's patience. The nagas was considering every possibility before it attacked, as if it half-expected some trick. For a moment Alex wondered if the creature had seen Arconn following it earlier, but he didn't think that was the case. This was a careful creature by nature, but it was also ruthless in its desire to destroy.

The movement was quiet and quick, and almost before Alex realized what was happening, the nagas was closing in on him. He spun around, lifting his staff as he turned. Without waiting to get a clear view of his enemy, he cast a freezing spell and called out for his friends to join him.

The freezing spell caught the tail of the nagas, immobilizing the last third of the giant snake. Unfortunately, its front two-thirds was still very mobile, and the spell had infuriated the nagas. It had expected easy prey, but now it had to face six warriors and a wizard.

The nagas lunged toward Alex, and he dove left to avoid being caught in its massive jaws.

Alex rolled quickly to his feet, his hand frozen halfway

to his sword. For a moment he stood, undecided about what to do. He could cast another spell using his staff, or he could draw his magic sword and attempt to fight the nagas physically.

As he debated what to do next, he heard the sound of Arconn's bow and Thrain's crossbow. Arconn's arrow hit the nagas squarely in the body, but it broke on the thick scales of the serpent. Thrain's bolt, however, sank deep into the nagas's body just behind its head.

The nagas screamed in pain and rage. Rising up, it turned away from Alex, angling toward Thrain. Thrain was too busy reloading his crossbow instead of paying attention to the nagas and was unaware of the danger.

Alex launched himself toward his friend, knocking Thrain away just as the nagas's head struck the ground where Thrain had been standing. Alex rolled away from his friend, turning to see what the serpent would do next. Raising his staff, he prepared to cast another spell, but the nagas was too quick for him. Its massive head shot forward, missing Alex but striking his staff instead. The staff shuddered in Alex's grasp, and he was thrown backward, slightly dazed.

By the time Alex was back on his feet, the nagas was closing in on him. Nellus and Barnabus were staggering to their feet, having dodged the attack. Arconn and Kat were firing arrows, trying to find some soft spot on the monster where their arrows would do some good. There was a loud twang and the nagas rose up once more, screaming for a second time. Thrain had managed to fire a second bolt, this one striking the nagas in the eye.

Alex didn't wait to cast a spell; instead he drew his sword

and ran forward. The reckless feeling he had experienced when he faced Bane returned once more, but now it was directed toward this snake that dared to attack him. The nagas's head was ten feet in the air, so Alex swung his sword at the massive body in front of him and felt his blow slice through the scaled armor of his enemy, cutting the body almost in half.

"Quickly!" Alex heard Thrang shout from behind him.

The head of the nagas dropped toward the ground, unable to lift its broken body.

Thrang charged with his ax, striking the head of the serpent as it tried desperately to crawl away. The nagas jerked wildly, and Thrang was thrown back. Alex ran to the head as well, lifting his sword for a final blow. The nagas wriggled madly on the ground, trying to twist its body over its head for protection, but its frozen tail made that impossible. Alex brought his sword down with all the strength he had.

For a moment the nagas continued to move, but Alex knew that it was already dead. The reckless feeling was slipping away from him, but he realized how close it had come to controlling him completely.

Barnabus and Nellus put their weapons away and helped Thrang to his feet, commenting on his bold attack. Alex smiled at Thrain, who looked pale and afraid but determined to stand his ground.

"More dangerous than a dragon," Thrang said, retrieving his ax from the severed head of the nagas.

"Not as bad as that," said Arconn.

"It moved faster than I thought it would," said Alex.

"Lucky you were able to partially freeze it," Thrang said, wiping his ax on the grass.

"You . . . you saved me," said Thrain, walking up to Alex. "It would have killed me if you hadn't knocked me out of the way."

"You would have done the same for me," said Alex. He looked around at his companions. "It appears that we are all unhurt."

"Yes, it does," said Nellus, standing close to the fire.

"I don't suppose any of us wants to spend the rest of the night so close to that thing," Kat said, a look of disgust on her face as she pointed at the dead nagas.

"We will have to move camp," said Thrang. "Even dead, this creature is unpleasant to be near."

They went to work at once, taking down tents and packing their things. Alex removed his hiding spell from their horses as Thrang asked Thrain to put out the fire. Arconn suggested they move closer to the nagas's cave and search it once the sun had come up.

"That would be best," agreed Thrang. "I have no desire to be searching caves in the dark. Who knows what other creatures we might find."

"I doubt there are many creatures that would share a cave with a nagas," said Alex.

They followed the stream north for about a mile before setting up a new camp. The night was warm and clear, and since they didn't plan on staying there long, they didn't bother setting up their tents again. None of them felt tired after their fight with the nagas, so they spent the last hours of darkness sitting around the fire and talking.

"A masterful final blow," Barnabus said to Alex. "You were quick in the attack."

"A useful trait for the person who is the bait." Kat laughed.

"I was almost too slow," said Alex. "The nagas moved much faster than I thought it would."

"But not fast enough." Thrang laughed. "Though it was a close call for some of us. Young Thrain here was so busy thinking of attack, the creature almost had him. You should pay more attention to your enemy," Thrang said to Thrain.

"In the heat of battle, it is easy to forget the danger," Alex said, glancing at Thrain, who looked a little embarrassed.

"True enough," Arconn added. "I have often seen warriors take terrible wounds simply because they were trying to attack and forgot their defense."

"All that you say is true," said Thrang, his voice softer. "And Thrain did draw first blood. That's not bad for a first-time adventurer—not bad at all."

The last few hours before sunrise passed quickly, and their talk dwindled to silence as the new day arrived. As the company ate breakfast, Alex noticed that Thrain still seemed a little shy of him. He wondered if the contest of power with Bane, and the fact that Alex had saved Thrain's life, had made Thrain unsure of their relationship.

Alex remembered the wild, reckless feelings that had almost overcome him while fighting the nagas and facing off against Bane. It was something he had never felt before, not even when he was fighting goblins with his magic sword. He considered asking Whalen about it, but he knew Whalen would tell him to control his emotions. The trouble was, the feeling wasn't really an emotion. It was a sense of power, greater power than he had ever experienced before, and a recklessness that came from knowing he could not be defeated. It was strange, and it scared him more than he liked to admit.

After breakfast, Arconn led them through the trees to a wide clearing full of wreckage. Broken wagons, carts, and bones were scattered over the ground. To one side of the clearing, a large cave opened into a small hillside, its dark opening looking like a patch of midnight that morning had forgotten to wipe away.

"Why would so many people bring carts and wagons here?" Nellus questioned.

"The nagas tricked them," said Alex. "It must have made promises to these travelers to lure them close to its den."

"Then why did it not do the same with us?" Kat questioned.

"Travelers are easier prey than adventurers are," Arconn answered.

"Yes," agreed Thrang, looking around the clearing. "Arconn, Alex, and I will enter the cave. The rest of you, search the wagons and carts."

"For what?" Thrain asked.

"Treasure, of course. The nagas could not easily move items from carts and wagons," Thrang said. "It would be best for us to make a complete search."

The others did as Thrang asked, dismounting from their horses and beginning their work. Alex and Arconn rode forward with Thrang to the cave opening and tied their horses to a broken wagon wheel just outside the dark entrance.

"We'll need torches," said Thrang.

Alex smiled, and with a wave of his hand, conjured up several weir lights and sent them into the cave.

"Yet another good reason to bring a wizard along," said Thrang with a grin.

"I find them easier than torches, and faster," said Alex.

"Halfdan said you used them to great effect on your last adventure together," Thrang said.

"They have many uses," said Alex. "Right now they will make our search quicker. I don't want to spend any more time in this cave than we have to."

"Nor do I," said Arconn.

Thrang nodded his agreement and led the way into the cave. The weir lights moved ahead of them, lighting the cave better than a dozen torches. Fortunately, the cave did not extend deep into the hill. It took only a minute or two for the three of them to find the main chamber, and when they did, they stopped in surprise.

"You said these creatures hoarded treasure, but I did not expect this," Thrang said to Alex.

The floor of the chamber was covered with wealth. Gold and silver coins were scattered everywhere, making it appear as if the cave floor was solid metal. The weir lights reflected brightly off the treasure.

"It will take at least two days to get all of this out in the open," Thrang declared.

"Yet well worth the labor," Arconn said.

"Yes, but I do not wish to remain in this dark place for two days or more," said Alex.

"So you would leave all of this behind?" Thrang asked, stunned.

"That is not what I said," Alex answered. "If you will allow me, I can quickly move all of this into my bag, and then we can find a better place to do the sorting and dividing."

"Not going to try and put one thing in your bag at a time, then." Arconn laughed.

"You two have taught me well," said Alex with a bow, remembering the trouble he'd had the first time he'd used a magic bag. "Now, if you wouldn't mind standing back—I wouldn't want to accidentally add the two of you to my bag."

Thrang and Arconn both laughed and stepped behind Alex. Alex lifted his bag and concentrated on the room in front of him. He had done something similar before, so he knew it would work now. He spoke softly so Thrang and Arconn would not hear the secret password to his magic bag, and in one shimmering moment, the chamber was emptied.

"I've never seen that done before," Thrang said, an astonished look on his face. "Piles of bags or stacks of wealth, yes, but never an entire room in one instant."

"Useful, if you are in a rush," said Arconn.

Thrang insisted on checking every corner of the empty cavern, so Alex sent the weir lights dancing around the room as Thrang searched. He even made a couple of them circle Thrang's head. Arconn stifled a laugh when Thrang stood up too quickly and the weir lights bounced off his head, spinning wildly around the chamber.

"Well, it seems you've done your work well," said Thrang at last, swatting at one of the weir lights that had returned to circle his head. "Let's get out of this hole and see what the others have found."

They left the empty cave, and Alex put out the weir lights as they returned to the bright morning sunshine. The others were having more difficulty with their search than Alex, Thrang, and Arconn had had. Many of the wagons and carts had been tipped over, making it difficult to see what was under them. Alex noticed that his friends had stacked a fair-sized pile of bags and boxes already, and he wondered how much wealth the nagas had managed to hoard.

"Any treasure in the cave?" Barnabus questioned.

"A fair amount," answered Thrang. "Master Taylor has put it in his bag for now, thinking it would be best to sort and divide later."

"There is wisdom in that," Nellus said, lifting a broken cart to see what was under it. "The bones of the dead are all around this place."

"The sooner we are away from here, the better," said Thrang. "What have you found so far?"

It turned out the others had searched about one-third of the clearing. Alex, Thrang, and Arconn joined in the search and were soon sweaty and dirty with the work. Alex was surprised by the amount of treasure they found in the broken wagons and carts, and he wondered who would be traveling with so much wealth in this open and empty country. He had little time to ponder because Thrang soon called him away from the cart he was searching.

"Magic books," said Thrang, holding up a large, leather-bound volume. "A strange find, and something you should have a look at."

Alex took the book from Thrang, looking at it for several minutes before noticing the pile of nine or ten other books that Thrang had recovered from a broken-down wagon.

"With your permission, I would like to add these to my bag," said Alex slowly, looking at Thrang.

"They are yours, of course," said Thrang. "None of us has any use for magic books, and they should not be left about for just anyone to find."

Alex bowed to Thrang and began looking at the books more closely. After several minutes, he put the books inside his bag and began walking around the clearing in a wide circle.

"What are you doing?" Thrang questioned, dragging a heavy chest out from under one of the wagons.

"Looking for something," Alex replied.

As the others finished their search, Alex continued to wander back and forth, across and around the clearing.

"Well, that's done," said Thrang, loudly enough for Alex to hear him. "Now if Alex will add all of this to what we've already taken from the cave, we can find a better place to do our sorting."

"In a moment," said Alex, finally spotting what he was looking for and hurrying toward it.

He moved carefully into the trees on one side of the clearing, and when he returned, he was carrying two staffs.

"The nagas was even more dangerous than I thought," Thrang said in a whisper.

"We were lucky to defeat it," Nellus added.

"But a wizard?" Barnabus questioned.

"Perhaps," said Alex. "It is a wizard's staff, but the person carrying it may not have been a true wizard."

"How did you know it was there?" Kat asked.

"The books," said Alex. "They are too advanced for most, and I thought it unlikely that just anyone would be carrying them."

"But a wizard would stand a fair chance against the nagas," said Barnabus.

"A true wizard would," said Alex. "We do not know who carried this staff, so we cannot say that he was a wizard."

"Alex is correct," said Arconn. "There are some who carry a staff and pretend to be wizards. This staff might have been carried by one of those."

"Yes, but a staff," Thrain said breathlessly.

"A staff is a tool and a symbol of a wizard, not the power of the wizard," Alex explained, looking at Thrain. "The power is in the wizard, not in his staff."

"What will you do with this second staff?" Thrang questioned.

"I will take it with me," said Alex, "and send a message to Whalen and the counsel of wizards. They might be able to tell us who the staff belonged to. If they can't, then I will have to assume the person who carried this staff was a pretender."

"Very well then," said Thrang, looking at the staff with interest. "We should move on, so if you will add this pile to what we've taken from the cave . . ."

"As you wish," said Alex, reaching for his magic bag.

They moved back to the road and continued to head east.

At midday Thrang began looking for a spot to camp. He wanted to sort the treasure they had taken from the nagas, and he wanted a good place to do it. After a half an hour of searching, he found a spot that suited him, and they set up camp once more. Barnabus began cooking a meal for them, and Alex marked out an area to gather their treasure for sorting.

"Will it fit there?" Thrang questioned as Alex scratched a circle in the dirt with his staff.

"It might be a little tight," Alex said with a laugh.

"Leave room for us to sort," Thrang said. "Don't pile it so high that we're in danger of being buried if a pile tips over."

Alex laughed again and finished scratching his circle. When they had all finished eating, Thrang gathered the company near the circle and asked Alex to produce the treasure. Alex bowed and spoke softly into his bag. In a rush of sparkling light, the treasure of the nagas appeared in the circle he had drawn. The late afternoon sun reflected brightly from the enormous pile.

"You're sure you did not add some of your own treasure?" Arconn teased, smiling at Alex.

"Of course not." Alex laughed.

"It looks like our work is cut out for us," Kat said. "It will take two, maybe three days, to sort all of this."

"Then let's begin," said Thrang happily.

"And you were worried we wouldn't find any treasure," Alex said to Thrain.

Thrain blushed slightly but didn't reply.

Thrang set them to work sorting the treasure into piles. He was pleased as the various piles grew larger and larger, while the pile in the center seemed to remain the same size. As the sun was setting, he asked Alex to conjure the weir lights so they could continue their work.

Alex laughed and suggested that a meal and a good night's sleep might be a better idea.

"Yes, of course," said Thrang, glancing at the treasure. "I suppose this is safe enough here."

"Unless something worse than the nagas comes looking for it," Arconn said.

"Oh, don't say that," said Thrain, glancing over his shoulder into the gathering darkness.

That night was a happy one around the campfire. Nellus and Barnabus joked that Thrang had prevented them from attacking the nagas when he jumped in front of them. Thrang replied that he had to jump in front of them because he was afraid they would bungle the job. Alex commented on how well Thrain had done, and Arconn and Kat were both quick to agree. Thrain blushed at the praise, pleased by the attention.

It took them two full days to sort and divide everything they had found in the cave and the clearing. Thrang insisted that all the odd numbers go to Alex since he was the one who actually killed the nagas. Alex wasn't happy about it, but he accepted Thrang's decision, simply because he knew it would do no good to argue.

On the morning of the third day after their battle with the nagas, they resumed their journey. The weather was warm and dry, and they all knew they would soon reach the Eastern Sea. What would happen once they reached the sea, however, was something that none of them could tell.

CHAPTER TEN

DUNNSTAL

———◆———

See there," said Thrang, pointing to the east. "The Eastern Sea."

Alex and his friends paused at the top of a small hill in the road. As they looked to the east, they could see the unmistakable glimmer of sunlight on water in the distance.

"There is a small city at the edge of the water," Arconn said, shading his eyes with his hand. "I see several sails on the water as well."

"That would be Dunnstal," said Thrang. "Not the largest of cities, but we should be able to find a ship there to take us to the Isle of Bones."

"Do the people of Dunnstal often travel to the island?" Kat questioned.

"I do not know," answered Thrang. "If any of Albrek's people are still on the Isle of Bones, I would guess that ships from Dunnstal make the trip often."

"And if none of Albrek's people remain?" Arconn asked.

"Then we may have some difficulties," Thrang answered, looking slightly worried. "Though I imagine we can find someone to take us, if the price is right."

"Take us? What about bringing us back?" Alex asked.

Thrang didn't reply, but simply prodded his horse forward. Alex and the others followed, their eyes on the sea and the distant city in front of them. The city of Dunnstal was more a large town than a city, but it looked inviting enough, sitting on the shore of the Eastern Sea.

"Thraxon must be a peaceful land," Alex said.

"Why do you say that?" Thrang questioned.

"The city has no wall," said Alex.

"Some of the people around the Eastern Sea don't build walls to protect their cities," Thrang said. "Or, at least, the smaller cities like Dunnstal don't. If trouble comes, they simply get in their boats and sail away."

"What about their homes and riches?" Kat asked.

"Their wealth is the sea and their homes are their boats," Thrang answered. "At least, that's what the old dwarf songs say."

"Yet they have houses on land," Arconn pointed out.

"Well, old dwarf songs don't always give the whole story," said Thrang.

As they approached the city, they found that, even without a wall, Dunnstal was well guarded. Watchtowers stood at several points along the road and in the fields around the city. Each of the towers contained a bell, and as they passed by, each bell would ring once.

When Alex and his friends were about half a mile away from the city, the meaning of the bells became clear. A large company of well-armed men on horses rode out to meet them, and Thrang stopped in the road, waiting for the men to approach.

"Greetings, travelers," said a rugged-looking man riding up to Thrang and looking at him closely. "Not many people come from the west, so we must ask your business before we allow you to enter our city."

"We mean no trouble to your fair city," said Thrang. "We are hoping to find passage here to the Isle of Bones."

"There is little hope of that," said the man as his horse moved back and forth in front of Thrang. "Few of our people hire out their boats, and fewer still would sail to that island."

"And why is that?" Thrang questioned.

"For what reason do you seek the Isle of Bones?" the man countered.

"We are looking for lost dwarfs," said Thrang. "Many of my people came this way long ago, and I have come with my friends in search of them, or at least to find out what happened to them."

"There are some old stories about dwarfs," said the man thoughtfully. "Perhaps they are true, perhaps not."

Alex noticed the man's eyes moving quickly over all of them, deciding if they were a danger to the city or not.

"You are a strange company," the man said, "but we will allow you to enter the city."

"You are most kind," said Thrang. "Perhaps we will find what we seek here, or at least we may hear some of the stories you have spoken of."

"You are more likely to hear stories than to find passage to the Isle of Bones." The man gestured. "Come. We will find you a place to stay."

The man rode back to his companions, and Thrang and the rest of them followed at a distance.

As they entered the city, the armed men quickly disappeared down side streets. The commander of the group led Alex and his friends to a large, two-storied tavern with lots of chimneys poking out of the roof at odd angles. A large, round-faced man in an apron was standing in the doorway, watching as they approached.

"The Sea Mist is the only tavern large enough for your entire company," the commander said, nodding toward the tavern. He bowed to Thrang. "May the wind blow true for you," he said formally before riding off deeper into the city.

Thrang dismounted and took a couple of steps toward the door of the tavern, when the man in the apron spoke.

"Passed old Top Mast's test, then, did you? Most do, though he doesn't get to test people as often as he'd like."

"Yes, well," Thrang began, surprised by the man's sudden words.

"I'm Ishly Prow, owner and keeper of the Sea Mist," the man said. "You can call me Ishly, if you like."

"I see, Ishly," said Thrang, trying to regain his train of thought.

"You'll be wanting rooms, and stables for the horses, I expect. I'll get one of the lads to take care of the horses for you, and then we can discuss rooms and rates and all that," said Ishly, turning away from Thrang and yelling back into the building.

A pair of young men who looked like they might be Ishly's sons appeared in the doorway.

"Very good, then," Ishly went on. "Both of you, take care of these horses, and I'll skin you alive if they don't receive the best of care."

The boys nodded and hurried forward to take the horses from Alex and his friends, leading them around the corner and toward the back of the tavern. It appeared that they knew what they were doing, and Alex decided that he didn't have to worry about Shahree, or the boys being skinned alive.

"Now then, if you'll follow me, we can see about your rooms," said Ishly, smiling and waving his hand toward the door.

"We may be here some time," said Thrang, looking flustered by Mr. Prow's quick way of speaking. "You see, we are looking to hire a boat to—"

"Well, this is a good place to hire a boat, seeing as we're so close to the sea," Ishly interrupted. "Of course, I don't know why you'd hire a boat if you weren't near the sea, but to each his own."

"Of course," said Thrang, and tried again. "You see, we wish to sail to the Isle of Bones, and—"

"Not many sailors here in Dunnstal are keen on hiring out their boats. I suppose old Top Mast told you that," Ishly went on, either not hearing or not caring what Thrang said.

"Well, yes, he did," Thrang said, "however, we would be willing to pay, and—"

"Don't mind doubling up, do you?" Ishly questioned, still

not listening. "I have a nice single room for the lady, and if the rest of you don't mind doubling up, it will make things easier."

"That will be fine," said Thrang with a resigned sigh.

"I'll just show you to your rooms," Ishly continued. "Let you freshen up a bit, and then we'll talk about dinner. We can make whatever you'd like, but fish is our specialty."

Alex was amused by the exchange between Thrang and Ishly, and he could see from the looks on his friends' faces that they were too. Only Thrang seemed unhappy about how things were going, but just as he was about to attempt another question, Ishly offered up some useful information.

"Speaking of dinner—most of the captains stop in for a drink now and again," Ishly remarked. "They normally start turning up about suppertime. Your best bet of finding a boat would be to talk with some of them—not that I'm saying they'll hire out, of course."

"Is their business so good that they can turn down paying customers?" Thrang questioned.

"'Course, there are a few who might be interested," Ishly went on as if he hadn't heard Thrang. "Might cost you a bit. I doubt they'd take less than nine or ten gold coins a day."

"Payment is not a problem," said Thrang. "However, we do not know anyone here, so if you could—"

"And here are your rooms," Ishly interrupted. "Feel free to join the common room whenever you are ready."

"Yes, but—" Thrang tried again.

"I'll leave you to it, then," said Ishly. "And if I happen to see any of the captains, I'll be happy to let them know you're looking for a boat. I can't say I hold out much hope, but you never know."

"Thank you," said Thrang as Ishly hurried away.

"You tried valiantly, my friend." Arconn laughed.

"I don't think he heard a word I said," Thrang grumbled.

"At least he knows we're looking to hire a boat," said Kat hopefully.

"And he did say some of the captains might be interested, though the price seemed a bit high," Barnabus added.

"Getting a boat to take us to the island seems a small problem. It's getting one that will bring us back that worries me," said Nellus.

Alex agreed with Nellus. Since it sounded like only a few sailors might be willing to go to the Isle of Bones, Alex thought that meant they were unlikely to find any of Albrek's people there.

Thrang suggested that they all wash up quickly and then meet back in the common room.

Alex was sharing a room with Arconn, and it only took them a few minutes to wash up and change their clothes. The two of them entered the common room a short time later and sat at a table to wait for the others.

"Ishly seems to talk fast and listen little," Alex commented, looking around the common room. He kept his voice low so only Arconn could hear him.

"I think he hears quite a bit more than he lets on," said Arconn. "After all, he did say the ship captains would be here later and that there might be a few who would take the job."

"Who might be *interested* in the job," Alex corrected. "I

have my doubts. I would like to know what stories are being told about the Isle of Bones."

"No doubt they are bad," Arconn allowed. "The man that Ishly called Top Mast looked grim when Thrang mentioned the island."

"I noticed," said Alex. "It has made me doubt that any of Albrek's people are still on the island."

"Where would they go if not back to Benorg?" Arconn questioned.

"South with Albrek, perhaps," Alex answered. "Or perhaps they didn't go anywhere at all."

"A dark thought for such a sunny day," said Arconn.

"Dark or not, it is a possibility that Albrek's people died on the island," Alex insisted.

"I hope your guess is wrong, but we will not know until we reach the island," said Arconn.

Thrang entered the room, followed closely by the rest of the company. He looked around the sparsely filled common room as he joined Alex and Arconn at their table.

"Too early for much business," Thrang said. "Though I don't doubt things will pick up as the day grows old."

"You think we should wait?" Alex asked.

"What else can we do?" questioned Thrang, a puzzled look on his face.

"We could go down to the docks," said Alex. "There are a few ships there. Perhaps we can find one to take us to the Isle of Bones."

"Perhaps," said Thrang, stroking his beard as he thought. "However, if all seven of us go, we may have a hard time getting anyone to speak with us. We are strangers, after all, and most men are not overfond of strangers."

"Then only one or two of us should go," Arconn said.

"It might speed things up," said Thrang, considering the idea carefully. "Still, I'm not sure it's a good idea."

"No harm will be done," said Alex. "And I want to know what stories the men of Dunnstal are telling about the island."

"As do I," Thrang said thoughtfully. "I suppose you'd best go and see what you can learn. Take Barnabus with you. If the people here have reason to fear the Isle of Bones, they may blame the dwarfs for that fear."

"Very well," said Alex, bowing slightly. "We will find out what we can and return before the evening meal."

"Be careful," Thrang said as Alex and Barnabus headed for the door. "Sailors can be a rough crowd, and they tend to be a bit superstitious."

Alex and Barnabus left the tavern and made their way toward the waterfront.

"I would expect more trade to be going on," Barnabus said as they approached the docks. "If the sailors of Dunnstal are so busy, there should be a great deal more happening at the warehouses."

"It does seem odd," Alex agreed, noting how few people were moving about the city. "Perhaps this is a slow time of year for them. Or maybe most of the ships are away at other cities."

"Perhaps, but it still seems strange," said Barnabus.

They reached the docks, but only a few people were walking around. Alex noticed that two small ships were tied up to one of the docks, but nothing appeared to be happening on either of them. He saw several men sitting near the back of one of the warehouses, talking to each other and playing cards.

"Perhaps they can tell us something," Alex suggested, nodding toward the men.

"I was thinking the old fisherman might be a better bet." Barnabus pointed in the opposite direction to where an old man sat in the afternoon sun, mending his nets. "He could probably tell us what stories there are about the Isle of Bones and give us some idea as to who we might hire to take us there."

"You think he will know more than the others?" Alex questioned.

"I think that he will be more willing to talk to strangers since he is alone," Barnabus answered.

Alex considered Barnabus's words. It was likely that one man alone would be more willing to talk to them than a group of men who seemed only interested in their card game. He nodded his agreement, and the two of them walked toward the old fisherman.

"Good day, master," said Barnabus in a jovial tone.

"Not so good when you've got nets to mend," said the old man, glancing up at Alex and Barnabus before returning his attention to his nets. "You're new here, and landlubbers as well."

"Your eyes are keen," said Alex. "We are looking for a ship to aid us in our travels."

"Lots of ships in these waters," said the old man.

"That is true, but we are looking for a ship that might take us and several of our friends to the Isle of Bones," said Alex.

"Argh!" said the old man, looking up at them once again.

"Not likely to find anyone to take you there. They're all too superstitious for that."

"Can you tell us why they would be too superstitious to travel to the Isle of Bones?" Alex asked.

"'Cause that island is haunted, of course," the old man answered, returning to his nets. "Haunted, or cursed, or something."

"If nobody goes there, how do you know it's haunted?" Barnabus asked politely.

"A fair question," said the old man, pausing in his work. "The answer is a long one, however, and I have nets to mend."

"Perhaps we could help you with your task if you could take the time to explain," said Alex, taking a step nearer to the nets.

"Help me?" the old man asked, and then laughed out loud. "You two have never mended nets. I don't know how you could help me."

"I could put a spell on your nets so they would never need mending again," Alex offered.

"Oh?" said the old man, looking hard at the staff in Alex's hand. "I suppose you're a wizard, then."

"I am," said Alex, bowing slightly.

"I don't know much about wizards, but you look awfully young to be one," commented the old man.

"I assure you that I am a wizard, though I am young," said Alex in a serious tone.

"Maybe you are, maybe you aren't," said the old man. "Not my place to argue the point, and it would be rude to say that you don't know what you're talking about."

"And dangerous." Barnabus glanced quickly at Alex to make sure the old man's words hadn't angered him.

"Yes, I suppose that's true," the old man agreed.

"So, then," said Alex. "Do we have a bargain?"

"I'm not sure," said the old man thoughtfully. After a moment, he shrugged. "I suppose there's no harm in telling you what I know, which is little enough."

"If you wouldn't mind," said Alex.

"Well, to begin with, not many people from around here have ever gone to the Isle of Bones," the old man began. "Not much reason to go so far north when the fishing is fine here. There are only a few towns along the coast north of here, so not much trade goes that way either."

"That makes sense," said Alex.

"'Course, now and then somebody gets it in their head that fishing might be better up north. Not many fishermen up there so there should be plenty of fish—or so you'd think," the old man went on. "I was up north once—years ago. Went with an uncle of mine who had that idea about better fishing. Anyway, we spent a week, ten days, sailing all around that island. Didn't catch many fish, but that wasn't the worst of it. All the time we were there, it felt like someone was watching us."

"Did you land on the island?" Barnabus questioned.

"We thought about it," said the old man, shifting his position slightly. "Heard the old stories about dwarf mines on the island and piles of treasure for the taking. Don't know if any of that's true, but we talked about taking a look."

"But you never did," said Alex.

"No, we never did," said the old man. "That feeling that

someone, or maybe something, was watching us got worse when we sailed closer to the island. It was like someone was keeping an eye on us for some reason. None of us were keen on staying close to that island, let alone going ashore."

"So you think the island is haunted?" Barnabus asked.

"There's something going on there, that's for sure," said the old man, lowering his voice. "I figure there must be something living on that island because we didn't catch any fish. You'd expect good water like that to have loads of fish, but if there were fish, we couldn't find them."

"Did you see anyone or anything on the island? Or was it just a feeling of being watched?" Alex questioned.

"Didn't see nothing. Not a sign. No boats or ships. Nothing," the old man answered, his thoughts trailing off. "Course there was a harbor, we saw that clear enough."

"And now the men of Dunnstal avoid the island, believing it is haunted," said Alex in a thoughtful tone, watching the old man.

"For the most part," said the old man. "Now and then someone still talks about going to the island, but not many ever do more than talk. In fact, old Bill Clinker was talking about going up north just last fall. Doubt he'll ever do it; he'd had plenty to drink along with his talk, if you know what I mean."

"Yes, of course," Barnabus said with a smile.

"Well, that's that," said the old man, returning his attention to his nets.

"You've certainly given us something to think about," said

Alex. "I don't suppose you know of anyone, besides Master Clinker, who has thought of going north?"

"Oh, I suppose most of them have," the old man answered with a slight laugh. "We all heard the stories when we're young. Old dwarf mines left abandoned, piles of gold and jewels lying about for anyone to pick up. But there's a difference between thinking about it and actually doing it."

"I suppose we could buy a boat and sail there ourselves," said Alex, looking out at the water.

"If you know how to sail, you might," said the old man, chuckling. "But if you don't, it would be a fool's journey."

"Perhaps," agreed Alex. "Now, I will repay your kindness and put a spell on your nets so they won't need mending in the future."

"Oh, no." The old man laughed. "Wizard or not, nets need mending. It's best to leave them as they are so an old man like me has something to do."

"Then how can we repay your kindness?" Alex questioned.

"Well," said the old man, looking straight into Alex's eyes, "if you ever get to that island and find out what is there, you could come back and tell me."

"That I will do," said Alex, bowing to the old man.

CHAPTER ELEVEN
ACROSS THE OPEN SEA

———————◆———————

Alex and Barnabus decided not to ask anyone else about the Isle of Bones. The old fisherman had made it clear that most, if not all, of the men of Dunnstal believed the island was haunted, or worse.

"It seems their old stories confirm that dwarfs were on the island at one time," Barnabus observed as he and Alex walked back to the tavern.

"Yes, but it also sounds like they haven't been there for a long time," said Alex. "I would guess they have been gone almost as long as Albrek has."

"Perhaps Albrek's tomb is on the island, and we will find the Ring of Searching soon," said Barnabus hopefully.

"Perhaps," agreed Alex, though he had his doubts.

The fact that the people of Dunnstal knew that there were dwarf mines on the Isle of Bones made sense. If Albrek had sent a great deal of treasure back to Benorg it would have been noticed. Of course, the wealth might not have passed through Dunnstal, but even then, stories would have spread along the coast, and everyone would have heard them by now.

What didn't make as much sense was that the people didn't

seem to know anything about when or if the dwarfs left the island. The old fisherman's story hadn't said anything about the fate of the dwarfs, only that they were no longer there. What that meant, Alex didn't know.

"Haunted," Thrang said, after listening to what Alex and Barnabus had learned. "That's going to be troublesome, to say the least." Thrang sighed. "I agree that it doesn't sound like there are any dwarfs left on the island. However, we still need to go and see for ourselves."

"It will be difficult for us to go to the island if everyone here is afraid to sail there," Arconn said. "Perhaps we should travel to a city farther south, where stories of a haunted isle are not told."

"That would take time," said Thrang. "We would have to travel some distance. Besides, I'm sure the stories are told all along the coast."

"Perhaps along all the coasts of the sea," Kat said. "Such stories are common in seaports, and most sailors believe them."

"Then what can we do?" Nellus asked.

"We could buy a boat and sail it ourselves," Thrain suggested with a doubtful tone in his voice.

"And if we had wings we could fly there," Thrang snapped, his mood having taken a dark turn the more they discussed their situation.

"Thrain's suggestion might be the only one that will work," said Alex, cross with Thrang for taking his bad mood out on Thrain. "I'd considered the same thing myself."

"I hate to have come this far and not make it to the island, that's all," said Thrang, softening his tone.

"Perhaps we can still talk someone into taking us," Barnabus said. "The old fisherman said that the younger captains sometimes talk about going north. He mentioned a Bill Clinker by name. He said Bill had talked just last year about going to the island."

"But he also said Bill had been drinking at the time," Alex pointed out.

"If we could just find someone who *wanted* to go," said Thrang thoughtfully. "Perhaps you could magically encourage their desire, Alex?"

"No," said Alex after he considered Thrang's idea. "I will only agree to that option if there is no other way for us to reach the island."

"We should talk to the captains when they come in. We still might be able to find someone," Arconn said.

"And if we said that they didn't have to wait for us at the island, but drop us off and return at a prearranged time to pick us up again, they might agree," Alex added.

"If, if, if," said Thrang, taking a deep breath and blowing it out loudly. "I suppose we have to try something, though, and sitting here talking about it won't help."

"Perhaps we can arrange a meeting with Clinker," said Arconn. "Perhaps we could appeal to his pride, or encourage his natural desire. Without using magic, of course."

"Yes, that might work," said Thrang. "At least until we were at sea, but then what? If we get halfway to the island and he loses his nerve, we'll be right back here, or worse."

"The only thing we can do is try," said Alex. "Unless we

take the time to learn to sail, which I'm sure will take longer than finding someone to take us."

"Very well," said Thrang, sounding both depressed and desperate. "I'll talk with Ishly and have him arrange a meeting with this Clinker fellow."

Thrang's talk with Ishly seemed to go better than expected, or at least Ishly seemed to pay more attention to what Thrang was saying. Ishly nodded and said he would see what he could do, and then asked a series of questions about what Thrang and his company would like for dinner. Thrang wasn't convinced that Ishly had heard a word he'd said, but Alex thought the innkeeper had probably heard more than Thrang meant to say.

As Alex and his friends were eating their evening meal in the common room, Ishly appeared at Thrang's elbow and whispered something in his ear. Thrang nodded and thanked Ishly. Once Ishly had left, Thrang addressed the rest of the company in a lowered voice.

"Ishly says that Master Clinker will meet with myself and two other members of our company," said Thrang happily. "Apparently he's asked that Alex be one of the two, but Ishly doesn't know why."

"Obviously because he's a wizard," Arconn said.

"Yes, perhaps," said Thrang, slightly distracted. "Ishly has resevered a small room for us to meet in. I think Arconn should be the third member of our company to meet with this Bill Clinker."

"When is the meeting?" Alex asked, setting his mug on the table.

"Now," said Thrang. "Master Clinker is already waiting."

The others wished them luck as Thrang, Arconn, and Alex left the common room and headed to a back room.

When they entered the room where Bill Clinker was supposed to be waiting, the lamps were burning low. Thrang hesitated at the doorway. Alex wondered if perhaps Thrang had led them to the wrong room, but then someone spoke.

"Come in, please," said a voice.

Thrang moved forward, followed closely by Arconn and Alex. As Alex shut the door behind them, the person who had spoken turned up the lamp. Alex was stunned to recognize the man sitting by the table. It was the same man who had granted them entrance to the city, the same man Ishly had referred to as Top Mast. The man seemed amused by their surprise, but he didn't laugh.

"Forgive my secrecy," he said. "There are some here in Dunnstal who would be upset if they knew we were speaking together."

"And why is that?" Thrang questioned, moving to a chair next to the table.

"The Isle of Bones has a legend all its own," the man answered. "Most say that it is haunted, some say worse. Those that fear the worst would not like the idea of my taking you to the island."

"I take it that you are Bill Clinker," Thrang said, clearing his throat.

"I am."

"And Ishly has told you what we are looking for?"

"He has."

"Are you willing to take us to the Isle of Bones?"

"Perhaps," came the slow reply. "I have not made up my mind, but I am willing to discuss the possibility."

"May I ask you something?" Alex asked.

"Of course."

"You say that your name is Bill Clinker, but Ishly referred to you as 'Top Mast.' Can you tell us why you are known by two names?"

"Ishly has a long memory," answered Bill with a smile. "When I was younger, I always wanted to stand lookout on my father's ship. The lookout's position is on the topmast of the ship, so Ishly started calling me that as a joke."

"The top of the mast is a daring place to be," Arconn said.

"Yes," said Bill. "But youth is a time of pride and the belief that nothing can hurt you."

"Are you more cautious now?" Alex questioned.

"A little, though not as much or as often as I should be," Bill answered.

"There are seven of us who wish to go to the Isle of Bones," Thrang said, retuning to the point of their meeting. "We will require some time on the island, after which we will require passage back to Dunnstal."

"When we first met, you said you were looking for lost dwarfs on the Isle of Bones," Bill said carefully. "Is there more to your journey I should know about?"

"Our business there is our own," said Thrang, not offering any more details.

"A dwarf, an elf, and a wizard," said Bill thoughtfully. "I

think some of the old tales are true. I think you are seeking the treasure that the dwarf lords left behind."

"We are seeking a single item," said Alex, holding up his hand to keep Thrang quiet. "The item is small and unimpressive, but it is of considerable worth to the person who sent us looking for it."

"And if you happen to find treasure along the way . . . well, that's considered part of your payment," said Bill with a knowing smile.

"That is the customary agreement for adventurers," answered Thrang, his voice tight.

"No offense meant," said Bill. "I know something of adventurers after all. What you seek and what you find is none of my affair. My only concern is what it will cost me to take you to the Isle of Bones, and what profit I can make from such a journey."

"Cost?" Arconn asked.

"My time and labor is a cost," said Bill. "The trip will cost me both at least, and probably more. I've mentioned that some here in Dunnstal would not want me talking to you. What they will think of me could cost me my reputation as well."

"You know your business and your people," said Thrang in a thoughtful tone. "We need to make this journey, and can pay you a fair price for your time and troubles."

"A fair price," Bill repeated.

"For you *and* your crew," Alex said. "We understand how few people are willing to sail to the island and how hard it might be to find a full crew."

"That is correct," said Bill.

"What price will you consider fair?" Thrang questioned.

"I will think on it," Bill answered, rubbing his chin. "Meet me here tomorrow night, after your evening meal. I will give you my answer then."

"I would prefer an answer now," Thrang began, but Alex cut him off.

Thrang glanced at Alex and then back to Bill, looking a little put out by the delay.

"Very well," said Thrang after a brief pause. "We will meet you here tomorrow night."

"I will wait until you leave," said Bill, turning the lamp on the table back down.

Thrang nodded and led Alex and Arconn out of the room. Outside the common room, Thrang stopped and turned to Alex.

"Why did you not let me press him for an answer now?" Thrang questioned.

"He is unsure, and pressure to answer quickly might cause him to say no," said Alex. "There are several things he needs to think through besides the price. The members of his crew will have to agree to this voyage as well."

"He is the captain; the crew should go where he says," said Thrang in a firm tone.

"It's not as simple as that," said Arconn. "We know the people here believe the island is haunted and that they would prefer that no one travel there. Perhaps they fear some evil will be brought back from there."

"Yes, of course," said Thrang. "I suppose there are stories of such things happening, and the people here would naturally be careful. They have a pleasant life, after all, and anything that might endanger that life would make them nervous."

"Exactly," said Alex. "So we will wait and see what Master Clinker decides."

Thrang was still unhappy about waiting, but he agreed that Alex and Arconn were probably right. The next day passed slowly for them all, and Thrang spent most of it pacing back and forth in the common room. Alex and the others spent their time telling stories of previous adventures, all of which Thrain listened to with great interest. When it was finally time for their evening meal, Thrang was too anxious for an answer to eat. He picked at his food, continually glancing toward the doorway.

"We will know soon enough," Alex pointed out. "You might as well eat something. Starving yourself won't help."

"I know," said Thrang, setting his fork on the table. "They say that dwarfs are patient, but waiting has always been a burden to me."

As soon as Alex and Arconn finished eating, Thrang insisted they wait in the small meeting room. Alex thought he was being a bit silly, but he didn't say anything. He didn't think Bill Clinker would show up for some time yet. The captain would want to be careful to time his arrival so as to remain unnoticed.

Alex was surprised, then, to find Bill already in the small room waiting for them. He looked tired and pale, as if he had not slept much since the day before. Alex could tell from the look in his eyes and the cool, determined expression on his face that Bill had made his decision.

"If you agree to my terms, we can leave in the morning." Bill spoke slowly, as if he had spent the day practicing the words.

"Let me hear what your terms are," said Thrang, moving to a chair.

"First, neither I nor any of my men will set foot on the island," said Bill. "We will provide you with a rowboat so you may leave the ship and travel to and from the island, but we will not go with you."

"That is agreeable," said Thrang. "What else?"

"For myself I will ask ten gold pieces for each day we are away from Dunnstal," Bill continued. "That includes the days we wait at anchor for you to return from the island."

"Very well," Thrang agreed.

"I estimate that it will take three days to sail to the island and three to return," Bill explained. "It may take longer if storms come up, but that is a chance you will have to take."

"Yes, of course," said Thrang. "How long are you willing to wait for us at the island?"

"We will not wait at the island," said Bill. "We will sail a short distance away and anchor. We will return to Dunnstal after two weeks and one day—with or without you."

"Very well," Thrang agreed grudgingly. "What else?"

"For each of my men, I will ask one gold coin for each day we are away. Those are my terms. Do you accept?"

"How many men do you have?" Arconn questioned.

"There will be twelve, besides myself," Bill answered.

"That comes to four hundred and sixty-two gold coins, if everything goes well," Arconn said, looking at Thrang.

"Those are my terms," Bill repeated.

"Very well, we accept," said Thrang.

"Payment in advance," Bill added quickly.

"Half when we reach the island, and the other half when you pick us up," said Thrang.

"Half now, and the second half when we return to Dunnstal," Bill countered.

"Done," said Thrang, holding out his hand for Bill to shake, sealing their bargain.

Thrang took out his magic bag and counted out the gold. He handed Bill the two hundred and thirty-one gold coins, counting them slowly so Bill knew exactly what he was getting. With the payment made, Bill shook hands with all of them and gave them directions to his ship.

"Be there an hour before sunrise," he said. "With favorable winds, we can be well on our way by the time the sun is up."

"We'll be there," said Thrang.

Bill left the room without another word.

"Well, we have a ship," said Thrang after a moment.

"The price was higher than I thought," Arconn said.

"A small matter if we find what we are looking for on the island," said Thrang.

"We don't know how large the island is. It may take more than fourteen days to search it," Alex pointed out.

"Kat's gift for finding things should speed up our search," said Thrang. "And we know that Albrek's city was on the southern end of the island. We will start there."

"And if there *is* something there? Something worse than ghosts?" Alex asked.

"That's why we've got you with us," said Thrang with a grunting laugh.

Alex managed a weak smile. His thoughts returned to the wild, reckless feeling he had felt when facing danger on this adventure. A touch of fear entered his mind as he thought about what it might mean, but he didn't say anything to his friends.

That night Alex dreamed about the Isle of Bones, but it was not a normal dream. He was flying over the sea, desperate to reach the island for some reason he could not name. He knew that all his questions would be answered if only he could reach the island. But whenever he flew near the island, it vanished in front of him. When he finally woke, he felt exhausted, but sleep was the last thing he wanted. Instead, he lay awake on his bed, forcing his mind to relax and wondering what his dream might mean.

When morning came, Thrang's spirits were high and his happy mood rubbed off on them all. They ate a large breakfast at the tavern, and when they had finished, Thrang made arrangements with Ishly for their horses to remain stabled at the Sea Mist. Ishly agreed and said he would only charge them if and when they returned from their voyage. If they did not return, he would take the horses as payment.

The eastern sky was beginning to change from black to dark blue when Alex and his friends boarded Bill Clinker's ship, the *Seeker.* Alex thought the name was a good omen. The *Seeker* was not a large ship, but it was still larger than a regular fishing boat. Instead of cabins on board, there were only a couple of small rooms below deck that Alex and the others would have to share.

"Could be worse," Thrang said. "At least we'll be out of the rain and the night air."

"I thought it did not rain this time of year," Barnabus joked.

"It's not likely to, but at sea—who knows? If it does rain, at least we will stay dry," said Thrang.

Alex went back up on deck to watch the crew cast off. The work looked hard, but Bill's crew seemed to know what they were doing. Soon the sails were out, and they were moving slowly away from Dunnstal. Alex watched the city grow small behind them, wondering what they would find on the Isle of Bones once they got there.

The wind grew stronger as the sun came up, and Alex moved to the bow of the ship to see where they were going. He found that the rolling waves under the ship helped relax his mind. Unfortunately, when he returned to his room, he saw that this was not the case for most of his friends. Arconn seemed all right, but everyone else had become seasick almost as soon as they had set sail. Thrain was the worst off, but none of the others looked very healthy.

Alex reached for his magic bag to see if he had something that might help. He made a potion to help calm their seasickness, but unfortunately, it did not remove the sickness completely. Even worse, the potion tasted so bad that Alex's friends thought they would rather be sick.

"Not all potions can be sweet as honey," Alex told them.

"A drop of honey would help that mixture of yours," Nellus said.

"I suppose it would," Alex agreed. "However, honey would make it completely useless, so there's no point in using it."

The three days at sea were a great deal of fun for Alex, even though his friends remained sick and in their rooms below deck. Alex made a point of checking on his friends several times a day, and he always offered to make more of the seasickness potion, but no one ever took him up on his offer.

Alex made friends with Bill's crew and helped them do the work of sailing the ship. He learned a great deal in those three short days, and he won the respect of the men and their captain. Arconn also helped with sailing the ship, and he proved very good at running up and down the rope ladders to set sails and tie lines.

On the afternoon of their third day at sea, the Isle of Bones appeared on the horizon. Thrang managed to come up on deck. He stood, looking silently for a long time at the island where they hoped to find some sign of Albrek. Finally he turned away, and with Arconn's help, returned to his room.

"Your friends do not take to the sea so well," Bill said to Alex as they watched Thrang and Arconn descend below deck.

"They are used to dry ground under their feet," said Alex.

"Yet you take to the sea and the work of sailing as if born to it," Bill observed.

"I've never sailed before, but I find that it feels natural," said Alex.

"Tell your friends that we will put you ashore in the

morning," said Bill, returning to his work. "We will anchor south of the island tonight—well away from the shore."

"There may be a harbor on the southern end of the island," said Alex, remembering the old fisherman's story. "It would be helpful if we could find it and start our search from there."

"We shall see," said Bill as he walked away.

Alex stood on the deck for a while longer, looking north to the Isle of Bones. He had a strange feeling about the island, as though something inside him was calling him toward the island. Or perhaps not calling him *toward* the island, but calling to him *from* the island. He thought about this for several minutes trying to decide which it was, but the feeling was gone.

Turning away, Alex headed below deck. He knew the news that they would be going ashore in the morning would please his friends—especailly Thrang. Alex knew that Thrang was hoping to find dwarfs on the island, and while Alex thought that was unlikely, part of him hoped Thrang was right.

"One more night on this rolling monster," said Barnabus, looking pale and a little green in the lamplight.

"You should come up on deck and get some fresh air," said Alex, looking around at his friends.

"The movement is too noticeable on deck," Thrain complained. "At least here I can only feel it; I don't have to see it as well."

"You'll have a hard time getting into the rowboat tomorrow," Arconn said with a laugh.

"That trip will be a short one, with the promise of dry land at the end," Nellus said.

"And the promise of another sea voyage at the end of two weeks," Alex pointed out.

"Don't mention that now," said Kat sourly. "I'm not sure I'll ever feel right again."

"Have none of your adventures included sailing?" Alex questioned.

"Not until now," Barnabus replied.

"And not again if I can help it," Kat added.

Alex smiled and once again offered to make his seasickness potion. They all thanked him but refused, so he left them and returned to the open air of the deck. Arconn followed and the two of them stood together watching the sun sink in the west. Tomorrow they would reach the Isle of Bones and face whatever was waiting for them there.

Chapter Twelve

The Isle of Bones

———————◦❀◦———————

Morning came early so far north, and Alex and Arconn were already on deck helping prepare for their departure from the ship. Bill had guided the ship close to the southern coast of the island during the early morning hours, looking for the harbor Alex had mentioned.

"Your friends are slow to emerge," Bill said.

"They still haven't found their sea legs or tamed their stomachs," Alex said.

"They are lucky the weather was so fair," said Bill with a smile. "If the weather had been rough or if we'd run into a storm, then they would know what sickness really is."

"Harbor—three points off the starboard bow," a sailor called from the topmast.

Bill's eyes went to the point the sailor had called out. Soon even Alex could see what the lookout had spotted. A large stone pier appeared along the edge of the island, reaching out into the water. Bill corrected their course slightly and made for the far end of the pier. Bill expertly guided the ship into the harbor, and the crew quickly rolled up the sails as the ship grew still on the calm waters.

"It seems that someone has sailed here at one time," said Bill, studying the pier. "It would take a great amount of work to build this harbor, and I don't imagine it was done quickly."

"It probably took several years," said Alex. "The dwarfs were supposed to have been here for some time."

"You will find no living dwarfs here," said Bill, a note of sadness in his voice. "If there were dwarfs on this island, we would know about it."

"That may be," Alex answered. "But Thrang still has hope."

Alex moved forward to help the sailors lower the large rowboat that would take him and his friends to the shore. As they eased the boat into the water, Thrang appeared on deck with the rest of the company. They all looked happier than they had in days, and Alex knew they were looking forward to being on solid ground again.

It didn't take long for Alex and the others to climb over the side of the ship and into the rowboat. Alex thanked Bill and the sailors for all their help before waving good-bye. They all wished him and the others luck in their quest.

"We will return to this spot in two weeks' time," Bill called. "We will wait for one day and then leave. Do not forget your days, or you may remain here for the rest of them."

"We'll be waiting," Thrang called back, gripping the side of the rowboat tightly.

As Alex and his friends rowed away, the sailors on the *Seeker* quickly let out their sails. By the time the rowboat had reached the island, Bill had maneuvered the *Seeker* out of the harbor and was sailing away.

Alex felt strangely alone as he looked across the sandy beach, trying to get a feel for the island and some idea of where the dwarfs might have mined. He could see several tall, rocky hills nearby, but little else. Dark green pine trees seemed to be growing everywhere on the island except on the beach, which was wide near the harbor.

"It's good to be on dry land," Thrang said as they dragged the rowboat high up on the beach to prevent the tides from pulling it away. "No more rolling about on the water."

"Please," said Kat. "No talk of rolling about."

Thrang was eager to start searching, but only Alex and Arconn felt well enough to do much exploring; the others were still weak from seasickness and hunger. Even Thrang, for all his desire, had to walk slowly and rest often.

"We should be able to find some sign nearby," Arconn said, his tone hopeful. "If the dwarfs built the harbor, they would have build something else close by as well."

"Perhaps Arconn and I should look around a bit," Alex added. "The rest of you should take things slowly until you've recovered from our voyage."

"Yes, that might be best," agreed Thrang. "If you find anything or run into trouble, call out. We'll come along as quickly as we can."

Alex and Arconn left the others and started off across the sand. The beach was wider than Alex had thought, and much steeper than it looked. It was difficult to walk in the dry, loose sand, and both he and Arconn had to stop to catch their breath once they reached the edge of the trees.

"I would guess," Arconn began, pausing to breath deeply. "I would guess we will find a path into the trees somewhere close."

"By now, the trees would have grown over any paths," said Alex. "If Albrek's people made a road of stone, we might be able to find that."

"Stone roads are slow work," Arconn pointed out. "Though if they built the pier for the harbor, perhaps they built a road as well."

"I would think they'd need a stone road all the way to the sea," said Alex. "It would be hard work carrying supplies across the open sand, and I would guess they had a lot of supplies and other things to carry."

"Which way, then?" Arconn questioned, looking at the trees in front of them.

"Left?" Alex guessed. "There were some hills that way. Perhaps that's where the dwarfs began their mining."

Arconn agreed, and the two of them walked along the edge of the trees. Alex thought about the dwarfs coming to the island looking for mines and hoping to become rich. According to the story from the archives of Benorg, some of those hopes had come true. But, then, why weren't there any dwarfs here now? It seemed unlikely that the dwarfs, having found mines here, would suddenly decide to leave.

"Here is something," said Arconn, bringing Alex back from his thoughts.

Arconn hurried forward and bent down to pick up

something from the ground. Alex followed him, wondering what his friend had found. When Arconn stood up, he held something shiny in his hand. He looked at it for a moment and then held it out to Alex. Alex lifted the egg-shaped sapphire from Arconn's hand, holding it up to catch the sunlight.

"No dwarf would let that drop by accident," Arconn said, his eyes fixed on Alex and not the gem.

"A sign?" Alex asked.

"A strange place for a sign."

Alex looked at the empty beach around them before turning his attention to the trees. He noticed that some of the taller trees were scarred on the side facing the beach, and looked as if they had been burned at one time. He moved forward to take a closer look at the burned trees, Arconn walking beside him.

"Strange," Alex commented.

"Very strange," Arconn agreed. "Some of these burn marks look like letters or runes, but it is impossible to tell for sure."

"Let's continue," said Alex, returning the gem to Arconn. "Maybe we can find an answer to this riddle."

Arconn placed the gem in his pocket as they continued walking along the edge of the beach, their eyes scanning the ground in front of them. If the egg-sized sapphire had indeed been meant as a sign, then there might be others. After walking several hundred yards, they both stopped at the same time. They were standing close to the trees, and without noticing it, they had walked into a grove hidden from the beach. Trees grew almost all the way around them, and to their right, between the pine trees, was an unmistakable stone path.

"Odd that this path should be hidden from view," Arconn said.

"Maybe the dwarfs didn't want just anybody finding the path to their homes," Alex suggested.

"Or perhaps the trees have grown since the dwarfs left."

They were both silent for a moment.

"I feel uneasy," said Arconn.

"So do I," said Alex. He knew there was no reason for him to be nervous, yet the feeling was there all the same. "I don't know why, but something about this island doesn't feel right."

"Should we call the others?"

"Let's look along the path a bit first," said Alex, stepping forward.

Alex and Arconn walked along the stone path through the trees. They hadn't gone very far when they spotted a fair-sized bag lying on the path. Alex bent down and picked up the bag, which seemed unusually full. He looked at Arconn, and then back to the bag in his hands. Slowly he untied the knots that held the bag shut and was amazed by what the bag contained.

"Nobody would drop these," Alex said, holding the bag open so Arconn could see the hundreds of small gems inside. "A single sapphire, maybe—but this?"

"The puzzle is a hard one," said Arconn, gazing along the path. "I feel uncertain about this place. I feel like we are being watched, but I know there is no one near."

"I feel it too," Alex agreed. "Let's go a little farther, just to see if the trees start to thin. Then we'll go back and get the others. Maybe Kat can help solve this puzzle for us."

Arconn nodded his agreement. Alex walked slowly beside

his friend, pondering his own feelings. He had felt strangely alone as he watched the *Seeker* sail away but not at all uneasy. Now he felt both alone and uneasy, and he didn't like it.

There was something wrong here on the Isle of Bones, and Alex wasn't sure he wanted to know what it was. In the back of his mind, however, was a longing he didn't understand, a strange desire to be here and to find the answers to questions he couldn't remember. It was confusing, and he struggled with his thoughts, trying to keep things clear in his mind.

They walked for about a half a mile, picking up three more bags all containing riches of some kind as they went. With each bag they picked up, Alex's uneasiness grew, and he began to wish they had never come here. Finally, the trees around them started to thin out, and they reached the edge of a small valley. They could see several stone houses in the distance, though they looked like they'd been empty for a long time. Alex reminded himself that Albrek had been there nearly two thousand years before.

"Let's return to the others," said Arconn, a sad note in his voice. "Thrang will want to know what we've found, and I would feel better if we were all together."

Alex agreed that it would be best to continue the search as a group, and he hurried back along the path with Arconn. When they reached the beach, Alex's feelings of unease were almost gone.

"I feel much calmer here," Alex said as the two of them walked back toward the rowboat and their friends.

"Yes," said Arconn. "It is as if a great worry has been lifted from my mind. It reminds me of something from the distant past, but I can't remember what."

"What do you think it means?" Alex questioned.

"I wish I knew," was Arconn's only reply.

The others were all interested in what Alex and Arconn had found. Thrang seemed troubled when they showed him the bags of treasure they had found along the path. He looked at the four bags, scowling at the items and stroking his beard in thought.

"Not things you'd drop carelessly," Thrang said at last.

"Or throw away without good reason," Nellus added.

"We were thinking the same thing," said Arconn.

"And the village looked deserted?" Thrang questioned, his scowl remaining.

"From what we could see, yes," answered Arconn, glancing at Alex.

"It's more than what we found," said Alex, leaning against his staff and gazing back toward the woods. "The feelings of unease, our troubled thoughts, even the feeling of being watched—they all seemed so strong when we were near the village."

"And now they are gone," Arconn added.

Alex turned to Kat. "Do you feel anything strange? A presence, perhaps?"

"There is something," Kat began and paused. "There is something here that does not wish to be found."

"Something?" Thrang asked. "What do you mean?"

"It is confusing," said Kat, rubbing her head. "I can't seem to focus on what it is. Whenever my thoughts get near, it moves away."

"How long have you known that something was here?" Alex asked.

"Not long," said Kat. "After you left to look for a path, I started to worry. But the feeling didn't seem to be my own. My thoughts wandered for a time, and I felt confused, even lost."

"I don't like this at all," Thrang said, looking around at each of the members of the company. "But there's nothing we can do about it, so we'll just have to carry on."

"Carefully," Arconn added.

"Yes, carefully," Thrang repeated.

It was still early in the day so Thrang decided they should follow the path through the woods back to the deserted village. If their feelings of unease increased, they would return to the beach and make camp for the night. If the feelings were not there or not very strong, they would explore the village.

Alex was not excited about returning to the village, but he knew Thrang was right. All that they could do was carry on. They set out for the stone path that Alex and Arconn had found, but Alex lagged a little behind the rest of the company, trying to sort out his feelings. His uneasiness reminded him of something, but he couldn't remember what it was.

As they walked back through the trees, Alex concentrated on his feelings and thoughts. He wanted to know exactly when the uneasy feeling started or when his thoughts became confused. This time, however, there was no uneasy feeling. In fact, there was nothing at all. The sun was bright and warm, and the walk along the path was pleasant. Alex began to wonder why he'd felt uneasy before; there seemed to be nothing to trouble his thoughts now. But the fact that he didn't have the same feelings now bothered him.

"Is this as far as you came?" Thrang asked when they reached the edge of the trees and looked down at the dwarf village.

"We thought it best to continue as a group," answered Arconn. "Though now that we are all here, I don't feel troubled at all."

"Neither do I," Alex added, walking up from behind. "It's as if our earlier feelings did not exist."

"Kat," Thrang began, looking hopefully toward her. "Do you still sense something?"

"Nothing," said Kat, closing her eyes. "There is nothing here, or at least, nothing that I can sense."

"Then we'll continue to the village," said Thrang, sounding relieved. "Perhaps we can find some clues there that will tell us what happened to Albrek's people."

"Clearly none of them remain here," Barnabus said. "The village is deserted."

"But where could they have gone?" Thrain questioned, looking from face to face for an answer.

"They could have gone anywhere," said Thrang, trying to sound hopeful. "Thraxon is a large land, after all, and just because they didn't return to Benorg doesn't mean they didn't go someplace else."

"It's been a long time, and they've sent no word to their old home," Nellus said, his eyes fixed on the village.

"That doesn't prove anything," said Thrang, starting to

walk toward the village. "We won't find out anything if we don't go and look."

Alex followed Thrang as soon as he moved forward, but the others hesitated for a second. Thrang pretended not to notice, but Alex saw the troubled look on his friend's face. Alex understood the company's concerns because he had many of the same concerns himself, but he also understood Thrang's determination. They had to find out what had happened here, and the only way to do that was to search the village for clues.

The walk from the trees to the village was a short one, but every ten or twelve yards along the path there was another bag—sometimes more than one—containing some kind of treasure. The scattered treasure was troubling because none of them could think of a reason for why it was there. Thrang muttered to himself as they walked. Alex stopped looking for the bags in order to focus his attention on his own feelings, but they remained neutral and he had no reason to think they would change.

"It doesn't make sense," said Thrang, stopping to pick up yet another bag. "Dwarfs don't throw their treasure away."

"What if they were pursued?" Barnabus asked. "If something was chasing them, they might have thrown these things away to lighten their load."

"That is a possibility," Thrang allowed. "But I don't know what would have scared a village full of dwarfs into throwing their wealth away."

"I don't suppose there are many things that would pursue a village full of dwarfs," Nellus added. "Dwarfs, as a rule, do not scare easily. If they were running, something terrible must have made them run."

"Perhaps they had run out of food and were forced to leave the island," suggested Arconn. "I don't suppose they could grow much here."

"No, not this far north," said Thrang, continuing along the path. "If they were short on supplies and winter was coming, they might abandon their treasure. Of course, they'd try to come back later to claim it."

"I don't think they'd throw it along the path," Kat commented. "They would have hidden it somewhere—somewhere they believed was safe."

Alex listened to all the ideas but didn't comment. He thought the idea of dwarfs being pursued was the most likely explanation, but he couldn't think of anything that would chase the dwarfs away and leave their treasure lying on the ground. Even dwarfs fleeing from a host of goblins would have been an ordered escape, and besides, goblins wouldn't have left treasure behind. It was a mystery he couldn't solve, and that troubled him more than anything else that had happened that day.

When they reached the outskirts of the village, they paused, looking at the long rows of empty houses.

"Let's split up and search the houses," said Thrang. "Alex, you go with Kat and Barnabus. Search the house on the left. The rest of us will search this one on the right. If anyone runs into trouble, call out."

Alex nodded and moved toward the house on the left with Kat and Barnabus. It was obvious the run-down house had been abandoned for a very long time. They had some trouble opening the house's heavy wooden door because the hinges had almost rusted shut.

"I'm surprised the door is still so solid when the hinges have rusted it closed," Barnabus said.

"The wood has a binding spell on it," said Alex, looking at the door. "Dwarfs are known for the binding spells they can put on wood to make it almost as hard as stone."

"You'd think they'd rustproof the hinges as well," said Kat with a slight smile.

Kat's smile made Alex smile as well, and he felt better than he had all day. He let his mind relax as they began looking around the ancient house, but he wasn't sure what they were looking for. He knew, and he was certain Thrang also knew, that the dwarfs would not have left their records in one of these houses. They would have built an underground chamber, or at least a special stone building to keep their records safe.

"Not much here," said Barnabus after several minutes of wandering around the house. "Nothing of value, and the furniture has all but turned to dust."

"Wait. There is something," Kat said, staring at a blank wall.

"A hidden room?" said Alex, walking toward the wall. "I suppose the owner of the house would need someplace to keep his treasure."

"It is well hidden," said Kat. "I can't see it, but I know it is there."

Alex looked at the wall for several seconds and then reached out to tap it with his staff. For a moment nothing happened, and then the outline of a door appeared on the wall.

"Lucky we brought a wizard along." Barnabus laughed.

"Lucky we have a seer to find hidden doors," said Alex.

"Finding the door is not difficult, but getting it open might be," said Kat.

It took Alex three tries to open the door. Behind the door was a small room filled with piles of treasure that looked as if they had been searched through in a hurry. To Alex, it looked like the owner of the room had been in a terrible rush to find something, and then left quickly without straightening up. Barnabus and Kat both seemed happy with the discovery, even if Alex was troubled. Absentmindedly he picked up a golden necklace. *Why?* That was the only thing he could think of. *Why would the dwarfs leave all of this behind?*

"We should get the others," said Barnabus after several minutes.

"Yes," Alex agreed, returning the necklace to a nearby shelf. "Thrang will want to know what we've found."

"I sense you are troubled by this," Kat murmured.

"I can't find a reason for it," Alex answered, turning to go. "No one leaves their wealth and their home for no reason."

The others followed Alex out of the house. Nellus and Arconn were waiting for them in the street, but they were alone.

"Where are Thrang and Thrain?" Kat asked, looking up and down the street.

"They believe they've found a hidden room," said Arconn. "They're trying to find a way to open the door."

"They'll have a hard time with it," said Alex. "We found one as well, and it was guarded better than I expected."

"I would guess that all the houses have hidden rooms," Arconn said thoughtfully.

"And I would guess that Thrang will want us to open them all," said Alex.

Alex found Thrang and Thrain inside a house, standing next to a blank wall and looking unhappy. Thrang knew only a few opening spells, but he had tried them all. Alex explained about the hidden room they had found in the other house and smiled when Thrang insisted on trying one more ancient dwarf spell. Thrang stood still for a moment, deep in thought. He took a step back and spoke the words, but nothing happened.

"I suppose you'll have to do it, then," said Thrang, looking at Alex hopefully.

Alex bowed slightly and touched the wall with his staff. Once again the outline of a door appeared, and this time Alex was able to open it on his first try. Thrang and Thrain both hurried into the small treasure room as Alex watched from the doorway.

"Did the room in the other house hold this much treasure?" Thrang questioned.

"About," said Alex with a shrug.

"I suppose we've added to our wealth, then," Thrang said with a laugh.

"That is true, but the real question remains," said Alex, turning away from the room.

"What question is that?" Thrang called after him.

"Why?" said Alex, walking out of the house.

Chapter Thirteen
Salinor

———✦———

"W hy what?" Thrang questioned, following Alex out of the house and into the road.

"Why has all this been left?" said Alex. "Why are there no dwarfs here? Why do we feel troubled and then not troubled? There is something wrong here, and I want to know what it is."

"Yes," said Thrang, nodding his head. "I agree that none of this makes any kind of sense. I suppose we should look for the colony's records and leave the treasure hunting for later."

"That would seem the wisest course," said Arconn.

"Yes, well," Thrang said, looking down the stone-paved street, "I suppose we'll have to move farther into town. It's customary for the archives to be built near the center of the settlement, unless the dwarfs built most of the city underground."

"It looks like most of this city is aboveground," Nellus said.

"Kat, if you sense anything—anything at all—please say so at once," Alex said to the seer.

"Whatever I sensed before has either left or hidden itself very well," said Kat, sounding both relieved and unhappy at the same time.

Alex could not explain it, not even to himself, but he knew there was something on the island, and even if Kat could not sense it, it was still there. Whatever it was, Alex couldn't do anything about it, not unless it wished to reveal itself to him, so he settled on the next best thing—finding the records of the city and whatever answers they might hold.

"Come on, then," said Thrang, starting off down the road that led to the center of the deserted town.

Alex and the others followed, looking from side to side as they went. They didn't bother picking up the small bags anymore; there would be time for treasure hunting after they'd found out what had happened to the dwarfs.

Fortunately the village was fairly small, with only about sixty stone houses. Each of the houses had an area of open land around it, which seemed odd for a dwarf colony, or at least it did to Alex.

"They must have expected the colony to grow," Thrang said in a thoughtful tone. "As a rule, dwarf houses are closer together and often share walls."

"The treasure we've found so far would indicate that this was a promising place," Nellus said. "If the dwarfs here had found so much wealth, others would surely have come to join them."

"Yes," said Thrang. "But it appears that no one ever did."

The discussion ended as Thrang spotted what he was looking for. A large stone building made of white marble stood alone in the center of the town square. Polished bronze doors still gleamed brightly in the afternoon sun.

"Locked," Thrang said, pushing on one of the doors. "I suppose we should have expected that."

"The bronze has not tarnished," said Barnabus in surprise, rubbing one of the doors with his hand.

"A little dwarf magic," said Thrang, a note of pride in his voice. "The dwarfs of this village took great care in building their storehouse."

"This looks too grand to be a storehouse," Nellus said.

"A common name for such buildings," said Thrang, pushing on the door again. "The dwarfs would have used this building to store supplies as well as their records. There is also a chance that they stored community treasure here as well."

"I suppose we should find a way to open the doors," said Alex.

"If you would, master wizard," said Thrang, bowing to Alex.

Alex stepped forward and put one hand on the bronze doors. He could feel the dwarf magic vibrating through his fingers and palm as if the door had a life of its own. This was deeper magic than the hidden rooms in the dwarf houses, deeper and much more powerful. For several minutes he stood motionless, letting his mind explore the spell that held the doors shut. Slowly he stepped back, then lifted his staff and knocked on the bronze door twice. For a moment nothing happened, then the shining bronze seemed to dim. The others looked in wonder as what had once been solid and locked bronze doors melted away, vanishing completely.

"Amazing," said Thrain, a stunned look on his face.

"An interesting spell," Alex commented. "Whoever put it here knew what they were doing."

"Well then," said Thrang, looking at the dark open space in front of him. "I suppose we should have a look inside."

Alex could see how nervous Thrang and the others were, but he knew there was no danger. He stepped forward into the darkness, and, seeing no source of light inside the building, conjured up several weir lights. Thrang hurried in behind him, and then smiled as the weir lights moved along the dark passage showing them which way to go.

"Strange there are no windows," Thrang said, walking at Alex's side.

"The dwarfs might have been afraid of being robbed," said Alex. "The door was impressive—though I wouldn't think that the colony's records would require so much protection."

Thrang didn't comment as they continued to walk into the darkness. A short distance into the building, they came to a broad staircase that led steeply into the ground.

"It seems the building is only a marker," said Thrang, walking down a few steps. "Perhaps the dwarfs here had a great deal more than archives to protect."

The stairs went down for a long way before opening into a vast hall. Alex magically lit the torches and lamps along the walls, and then turned to look at Kat.

"Any idea where the archives might be?" asked Alex.

"Lower down," said Kat after a moment's thought.

"That sounds right," said Thrang as he started off into the hall. "This would be a feasting hall. Kitchens and stores would be on the left, and perhaps some private rooms there on the right. There should be another staircase at the far end of the hall that will lead us to a second level. That is where the archives should be."

"There is a third level as well," said Kat thoughtfully.

"Oh," said Thrang, looking back in surprise. "The only reason for a third level would be to store treasure. We'll have a look there after we find the archives."

"And after a meal," Barnabus said.

"It has been a long day already," Arconn added, smiling at Thrang.

"Yes, of course," said Thrang as if he'd only just remembered that none of them had eaten since that morning. "Barnabus, Nellus, Thrain, perhaps you would be so good as to return to the surface and set up our camp. The rest of us will go to the archives and see if there are any records of what happened. We will not explore the third level until tomorrow."

Barnabus and Nellus nodded and started back to the stairs. Thrain took a step then turned back as if to argue about leaving.

"You can see it all tomorrow, Thrain," said Thrang in a kind but stern voice.

Thrain nodded and reluctantly followed Barnabus and Nellus back up the stairway. Thrang smiled as he watched the young dwarf go, and then turned back toward the hall and started across it.

Alex held back a laugh as he caught Arconn's eye. He knew how excited Thrain was to explore this abandoned dwarf building, but he also knew that Thrang was right to send him back for the time being. There might still be dangers here, and Thrain was not yet ready to face the unknown.

They found a second set of stairs at the end of the hall, and once again they went down them. The weir lights Alex had conjured had been hovering above his head, and now they rushed down into the darkness to light the way.

At the bottom of the staircase was a solid-looking iron door. Alex stepped around Thrang, who was pushing on the door, and placed his hand on the cold metal. The dwarf magic was stronger here than it had been in the bronze door. After a few moments of thought, Alex spoke a few words in the dwarvish language, and the door slowly creaked open on its own.

"Impressive," Arconn said.

"Yes," agreed Alex. "The dwarfs who lived here must have had at least one wizard with them."

"There have been few dwarf wizards," Thrang said thoughtfully. "I know of one who lived in Thraxon at about the same time as Albrek. His name was Languinn, but there aren't many stories about him."

"It seems we've found the hall of records," said Kat, looking around the room that was filled with books. "I would say the door at the far end of the hall leads to the lowest level of all."

"Yes," said Thrang, looking in the direction of the door. "First things first, however. Let's see what the records have to say about the colony and if there is anything about why the dwarfs left."

Left, or were destroyed, Alex thought but didn't say.

Alex lit the lamps and then joined the others in looking through the records. There were far fewer records here than there had been in the archives of Benorg, and it didn't take them long to find what they were looking for.

"Here now," said Thrang, looking down at a large leather-bound book that was sitting on a stone table. "This is a listing of what the colony had mined. It seems they found some rich mines here, including at least one mine of true silver."

"The amount produced drops after the third year of mining," Alex said, looking over the information. "For the first three years, the numbers increase, and then they drop off by quite a bit."

"That would make sense," said Thrang, running his finger down the page. "If Albrek took most of his people south, there would be far fewer dwarfs here to do the mining."

"So it would seem that Albrek left the Isle of Bones after three years, and went . . . where?" Arconn frowned.

"To the Lost Mountains, no doubt," said Thrang. "We know that was his plan from the start, but it would be nice to find something written to confirm that fact."

"It will take some time to go through all these records," Alex said. "Kat, do you have any impression about where we should start?"

Kat was silent for a minute, her eyes closed. Slowly she moved to one side of the room and put her hand on a huge volume.

"This one," said Kat, blinking several times as if to focus her eyes.

Arconn and Thrang lifted the book onto one of the stone

tables. Alex had never seen a book so large, and he wondered why the dwarfs would make something that no single dwarf could move alone. His thoughts about that were soon forgotten as Thrang began reading from the book.

"Yes, this is the complete history of the colony," said Thrang, turning the pages. "We should learn what happened here when we see where the history stops."

Thrang paged quickly through the book, looking for the place where the writing stopped. It took only a few minutes, but those minutes seemed to last for hours as Alex and the others waited.

"Ah, here we are," said Thrang, turning back a few pages from the end of the writing.

For several minutes Thrang read in silence, Alex and Arconn skimming the words over his shoulder. Kat stood back, looking around the room and waiting to hear what had happened.

"It sounds like things were going fine, and then all at once every dwarf on the island started feeling uneasy and tense," Thrang summarized, taking his hands off the page so Alex and Arconn could finish reading.

"That sounds similar to the way Alex and I felt earlier today," Arconn said.

"Too similar," Alex added. "Something on the island was affecting the dwarfs."

"But what could it be?" Thrang asked. "The record gives no clue at all, and the writing stops without explaining anything about what happened. Kat is unable to sense anything on the island, so what could the trouble have been?"

"I don't know," said Alex, pacing back and forth. "Yet there is something here. Something that doesn't want to be found."

"Whatever it is, it seems to be leaving us alone," said Thrang, closing the book with some effort. He sighed in frustration. "We're not here to find out what happened to the colony, we're here to find the tomb of Albrek."

"So you think we should continue our quest and not worry about what happened here?" Alex asked.

"We should worry about it, but not let it get in the way of our quest," Thrang answered. "We have two weeks on the island, so we should make good use of them. Tomorrow we will explore the third level and gather all the treasure we can find in the time we have. As long as these troubled feelings don't return, I don't know what else we can do."

"And if they do return?" Arconn questioned.

"Then we'll do what we have to do to protect ourselves and complete our adventure," said Thrang.

"Very well," said Alex, refocusing his thoughts. "We should all pay attention to our feelings, though. Hopefully we won't have any problems before the *Seeker* returns."

They all agreed, and Thrang led them up the stairs toward the deserted dwarf village. As they went, Alex tried to relax his mind, but something was poking at his thoughts. The troubled feelings he'd had earlier in the day still reminded him of something, but even now he couldn't think of what it was.

When they climbed out of the dwarf ruins, they found that Barnabus had their dinner nearly ready. Nellus and Thrain were watching the empty space where the bronze door had been and seemed relieved when Alex and the others emerged.

"What happened?" Nellus questioned.

"I'll explain as we eat," said Thrang, moving toward the campfire. "We've learned some things, but not everything."

Barnabus served the food, and Thrang slowly recounted what he had read from the giant book.

Alex had a hard time paying attention to the story or his food; he was still trying to remember what it was he had forgotten and what his strange feelings reminded him of. He knew the answer would come to him eventually, but for now, his thoughts were cluttered and confused.

As the others prepared to sleep, Alex remained by the fire. They all agreed it would be a good idea to keep watch, and Alex had drawn the first shift. Arconn also remained by the fire, but remained still and quiet. Alex listened to the breathing of his friends as he watched the fire burn down, still trying to relax his mind.

"You seem troubled," Arconn said at last.

"The feelings we had earlier today remind me of something, but I can't remember what," said Alex, shifting his position slightly.

"Yes, I feel the same way, though I don't know why. Perhaps an answer will come to you in your sleep. Often our minds find answers when we stop looking for them."

"Yes," Alex agreed. "I suppose I should try to sleep."

Arconn said nothing more, and Alex slowly moved away from the fire and lay down on his blanket. Closing his eyes, he forced himself to relax, and before he knew it, he was asleep.

How strange, Alex thought in his dream.

He felt awake, even though he knew he wasn't. He was

sitting on a beach, possibly the beach they had landed on that morning. The wind blew his hair, and the smell of the sea reminded him of the sailors he'd met on the *Seeker*. For several minutes he remained seated, and then he slowly rose and looked toward the land. It looked exactly as he remembered it from earlier in the day, with one large exception.

Sitting directly behind him was an enormous dragon.

"So, you are what Kat could feel. The presence that moved away when she got too close," said Alex.

"I thought it best that we meet in your dreams," said the dragon, its voice softer and friendlier than Alex had expected. "I hope you will forgive my intrusion, but meeting face-to-face would have been difficult."

"I am surprised to see you here," said Alex, watching the dragon for any sudden movement and trying not to look into its eyes.

"And I am surprised that you are so young," said the dragon.

Alex was not afraid, though he thought perhaps he should be. This dragon was much larger than Slathbog had been, and even if this was only a dream, he knew the dragon still had a great deal of power.

"I require your assistance, young wizard," the dragon said. "I can offer several things in return for your services."

"Why do you require my help?" Alex questioned.

"Because you are what you are," the dragon answered. "You are a wizard of great power, and I need that power to accomplish my goals."

"Why would I agree to help a dragon?" Alex asked. "I've

met one of your kind before, and I doubt your goals will be something honorable."

"Yes," said the dragon, its voice sounding thoughtful. "You met Slathbog and destroyed him, as was right. And because of your encounter with Slathbog, you mistrust me, which shows wisdom on your part. However, I am not like Slathbog; I do not hoard wealth nor seek out the lesser races to destroy them."

Alex considered the dragon's words for several minutes before he replied. It seemed to be true that this dragon did not care about the dwarf treasure scattered across the island. Still, dragons were dragons, and Alex knew he had to be careful.

"What is it you wish of me?" he asked.

"A spell," the dragon answered. "A spell to hide this island from all who seek it."

"Why do you wish that?" Alex questioned, surprised by the dragon's request.

"So the past will not be repeated," said the dragon, sounding strangely sad.

"It was you, then," said Alex as he considered how dangerous a dragon might be in a dream. "You destroyed the dwarfs that lived here."

"Sadly, yes," said the dragon. "I did not mean for it to happen, and while most of the blame is mine, the dwarfs still share some of it."

"Will you tell me what happened?" Alex asked.

"Long ago I chose this place to hide," the dragon began. "I had grown tired of my long travels and wanted only to sleep and to dream. This island was a good place, far from the lesser races and secluded by the sea. For hundreds of years I slept here, and then the dwarfs came."

Alex remained quiet.

"At first I was not aware of them," the dragon continued. "The dwarfs dug their mines and found their treasures, and I remained asleep. Then they opened new mines and looked for more treasures. That is how dwarfs are, so I cannot blame them for that. The mining was noisy, and it slowly woke me from my long sleep. They had a wizard with them, and he was the first to realize I was here."

"So you destroyed the dwarfs before they could attack you," said Alex.

"No, nothing like that," answered the dragon. "The dwarfs attacked me while I was not yet fully awake. Their wizard, a dwarf named Languinn, had great power. He believed that he could drive me away or even destroy me. When I woke fully, it was to his attack. Startled by his magic, I thought only of defending myself. But my anger began to burn inside of me, and being a dragon, my rage got the better of me. I swept down on my attackers and destroyed most of them before I was able to shake off my madness."

"You destroyed most of them, but not all?" Alex questioned.

"No, not all. Languinn and some of the other dwarfs hid themselves in the underground archives. I tried to apologize, to make things right, but Languinn would not speak to me, even in dreams."

"So he and his people are still down there?" Alex asked, stunned by the idea.

The dragon shook his head. "They died off, until only Languinn was left. Even then, alone in the dark, he would not speak with me, though I tried many times."

"So we will find their remains on the third level when we go there tomorrow," Alex said, wondering how much of the dragon's story was true.

"Yes," answered the dragon. "Perhaps that will convince you I speak the truth, though there is an easier way, if you dare."

"You would have me look into your eyes," Alex said, feeling a strange desire to look, despite knowing the danger.

"We are in a dream so our powers are not what they might be," the dragon said. "And I will give you something to protect you, if you will trust me."

"What can you give me for protection?" Alex asked. He wanted to trust the dragon, yet he knew that trusting any dragon could be fatal.

"I will give you my true name," the dragon answered.

Alex considered the offer. He knew that dragons often had many names, but they each had only one true name, a name that gave them their power and made them what they were. He also knew that having that true name would give him power over the dragon, power to control and command the dragon to do whatever he wanted it to do.

"How will I know the name you give me will be your true name?" Alex asked.

"You will know," said the dragon with what might have been a smile on its face. "I am Salinor, oldest remaining of my race. I am the lord of dragons, the most ancient, the guardian of the past."

"Salinor," Alex repeated, feeling the incredible power of the name even in his dream. "Yes, I will trust you. I will look into your eyes."

Even before he looked, Alex knew that Salinor had told him the truth. As their eyes met, Alex could feel Salinor's power, and he could see some of the details of the dragon's long life. Salinor was far more powerful than Slathbog had been, and Alex knew that he could not defeat this dragon, not in the same way he had defeated Slathbog and not in any other way he could think of. Then, to his surprise, Alex realized that Salinor could not defeat him either. They were equals, an even match.

"There is more to you than I thought," Salinor said, sounding pleased and perhaps a little proud. "It is good that we have met this way. If we had been forced to battle, I think we both would have lost in the end."

"I am glad we have not met as enemies, then," said Alex, letting his mind move closer to Salinor's.

The mixing of thoughts was amazing, and for a moment Alex considered breaking away and forcing himself to wake up. At times Alex had felt that his own mind was cluttered and full, but that feeling was nothing compared to what he felt now. And he sensed something else as well—the same wild, reckless feeling he had felt twice before on his journey.

"Open the third level for your friends, then come and talk with me," said Salinor, blinking and breaking the link between the two of them. "There are things we need to speak of, things you will need to know."

"I will come," said Alex.

"Until then," said Salinor, turning to leave the beach of Alex's dreams. "I will see you soon, young dragon lord."

"Dragon lord," said Alex, waking up with a start.

"What's that?" Thrang asked, turning away from the cooking fire to look at Alex.

"Oh, nothing," said Alex, looking around to see if anyone else had overheard him.

"Well, come and get your breakfast," said Thrang. "We have a long day ahead of us."

Alex got up, still thinking about his dream. He knew that it had been real, though he had never actually spoken to anyone in a dream meeting before.

"We'll go down to the third level this morning," Thrang said as they finished breakfast. "It should be worth our time to look around and perhaps find a bit of treasure."

"I have something to do after I open the door to the third level," said Alex.

"Oh? What is that?" Thrang questioned, a puzzled look on his face.

"I have to go and talk to someone," answered Alex.

"Who are you going to talk to?" Thrain asked, looking even more puzzled than Thrang did.

"A friend," Alex answered with half a smile.

"That's no kind of answer," said Thrang, standing up and running his hand down his beard.

"A dragon, then," said Alex, and almost laughed at the

shocked looks on his friends' faces. "That's where the uneasy feelings are coming from and what Kat could feel but not get close to. There is a dragon on the island, and I'm going to talk with him."

"How do you know about the dragon?" Nellus asked, looking worried and pale.

"Because I spoke with him last night in my dreams," said Alex. "I don't have time to explain everything, but I can tell you there is no reason to worry. I'll open the door to the third level where you should find the remains of some dwarfs and the dwarf wizard, Languinn. Once that is done, I will be leaving for a few days."

"You're going to talk with a dragon?" Thrang repeated, looking confused.

"The risk is great," said Kat, looking from Alex to Thrang and back again.

"No, it's not," said Alex. "Enough talk. Let's go and open the door to the third level. Or perhaps I should show Thrain how to open the hidden doors in the houses first."

"You seem determined to go," Arconn said.

"I am. And I'm sure there is no danger," said Alex.

Thrang and the others looked as if they wanted to argue, but Alex wouldn't hear any of it. He turned and walked into the stone building behind their camp, and the rest of them had no choice but to follow.

The door to the third level was better protected than either of the previous two. It appeared that Languinn had spent most of his time casting spells on the third door to protect himself and his comrades from the dragon. Just as Alex thought he had removed all of Languinn's spells, however, he started sneezing uncontrollably.

"I didn't expect that," Alex said, shaking off the effects of Languinn's spell. "A strange spell to put on a door."

"Not so strange." Thrang laughed. "Dwarfs often use such spells if they're afraid of someone sneaking up on them. The sneezing would alert them to an enemy's presence."

"Yes, I see," said Alex, wiping his nose.

Returning to the door, he removed the sneezing spell and quickly checked for anything else he might have missed. Confident that he'd removed all of the magic from the door, he told his friends to move to the sides of the short hallway. He carefully pushed the door open with his staff and a volley of arrows came flying out of the darkness, clattering against the stairs behind them.

"You should be careful as you search the third level," Alex said, checking his staff for arrows.

"How did you know about the trap?" Arconn questioned, looking at the open door in concern.

"I thought Languinn might do something like this," said Alex. "He was afraid, and he couldn't be sure that his magic would be enough to protect him from a dragon."

"The same dragon that had trapped him," said Thrang, looking Alex in the eye. "The same dragon you want to talk to. The same dragon that killed my people on this island."

"I told you I would explain later," said Alex, his voice stern and slightly cold as it echoed into the darkness of the third level. "Languinn acted foolishly. He was only trapped here because he would not listen to reason."

"But . . . a dragon?" said Barnabus softly.

"Enough," said Alex, trying to stay calm. "I know what I'm doing."

"We are concerned for your safety as much as our own," said Arconn soothingly. "We aren't questioning your ability or belief."

"Forgive me," said Alex, taking a deep breath. "I know you don't understand and would like an explanation, but there isn't time. Believe me when I say that I will be safe and that the dragon will not bother you. Languinn's traps might be another story, though, so be careful."

"Very well," said Thrang, though he still looked unhappy. "We'll all go up while you teach Thrain to open the hidden doors. We'll need to make torches anyway, before we can search the third level since we won't have your weir lights."

With Thrang's words they all moved back up the stairs. Alex felt bad that he couldn't tell his friends everything he knew, but he wanted to hurry to his meeting with Salinor and telling his friends about his dream would only lead to dozens of questions that he didn't have time to answer, even if he knew all the answers.

Thrain quickly learned how to open the hidden doors once Alex had explained how it was done and taught him the correct magical words to use. Thrang also paid attention, and, with some effort, he was able to open the hidden doors as well. With that task completed, Alex walked into the street and turned to look at his friends.

"I don't know how long I'll be gone, but I promise to re-turn before the *Seeker* gets here to take us back to Dunnstal," said Alex. "I suggest you spend your time gathering everything of value here, including the archives. Once we leave this island, no one will ever be able to return."

"Why not?" Thrang asked.

"I'll tell you this much and then I have to go," said Alex, leaning on his staff. "When we leave here, I will be casting a spell that will make the island impossible to find. The dragon has asked me for this favor. He regrets what happened to the dwarfs here, and he doesn't want anything like that to happen again. I agree with him, and as he was here first, the island is rightfully his."

"How do you know all of this?" Arconn questioned.

"The dragon told me," said Alex, turning away. "I'll answer the rest of your questions when I return."

Alex walked quickly through the empty dwarf village and into the woods without looking back, making his way toward the low rocky hills. He knew where he would find Salinor, and he hoped that the dragon was as friendly in real life as he had been in the dream. Of course, knowing the dragon's true name gave Alex an advantage. He still wondered why Salinor had done that; usually dragons closely guarded their true names. Still, Alex knew that Salinor had told him the truth and there was little chance the dragon would change his mind now.

Salinor's cave was extremely well hidden, and it took Alex more time to find it than he thought it would. Salinor had cast several spells over the entrance of his cave in order to remain hidden from anyone or anything that might come to the island, and the dragon's magic was impressive. It was only because Salinor had told him where to look that Alex was able to find the cave at all.

Alex spent the next eleven days and nights with Salinor, learning from the ancient creature and telling his own story to the dragon. Time seemed to melt away, and Alex didn't remember sleeping or eating at all; he wasn't even a little bit tired or hungry. When it was finally time for him to go, Alex was reluctant to leave the dragon behind. There was so much that Salinor knew, and so many more questions that Alex wanted to ask. Salinor also seemed sad that Alex was leaving, but he promised to visit Alex in his dreams from time to time.

"You are now a dragon lord," said Salinor as Alex was preparing to leave. "If ever you need me, you need only call my name."

"You have been very kind, my friend," said Alex. "I hope I will never need to disturb your rest."

"There are a few more things," said Salinor, turning his giant head toward the back of the cave. "There are books that you should take with you."

"Books?" questioned Alex. He'd never thought of dragons as reading or writing books.

"Ancient writings," said Salinor. "Mysteries and knowledge that have long been lost. You may need what they hold."

Alex went to the back of the cave and found a small gap in the wall. Moving through the gap, he entered a second cavern full of old-looking books. The number of books in the cave surprised him, and he wondered how they might have gotten there. Salinor could never have slipped through the gap, not even when he was a very young dragon. Alex picked up one of the books and glanced through its pages. The writing was different from the magic letters he had learned, but yet also strangely familiar. Without taking time to look at all the books, Alex held up his magic bag and moved them to his own library.

"The books are not written in letters that I understand," Alex said when he returned to the main cave.

"They are not so much read as experienced," said Salinor. "When you read these books, it will not be like reading, it will be as if you are there."

"I don't understand," said Alex.

"In time you will," answered Salinor in a confident tone. "And now one last thing before you go."

"Yes?" said Alex, looking up at Salinor's ancient face.

"Your family," said Salinor. "You need to find your family to find yourself."

"I have no family," said Alex, turning away.

"We all have families," said Salinor with a booming dragon laugh. "Your parents had families before they were your parents. Seek them out. They will need you, and you, I think, will need them as well.

"I will tell you this as a final gift in parting," Salinor went on. "There was a time—a time long forgotten by most—when dragons and men were of one race. Not all men, but the great and noble men, the men who later became kings and rulers in the known lands, had the blood of the dragon in their veins. I was there, so I know what I say is true. I also know something about you that you have not yet guessed."

"What is that?" Alex questioned nervously.

"You are of my own bloodline," Salinor answered. "Both

of your parents had dragon blood in their veins, and it flows very strongly in you as well, my child. In fact, I think that you alone among wizards could take the dragon form without fear of losing yourself."

"The dragon form is warned against by all wizards," said Alex.

"That is because most wizards would lose themselves in the form of a dragon. They would feel what it is to be a dragon and forget that they were ever men."

"And you think I should take this form?" Alex asked.

"Not until you are ready," said Salinor. "You will find great power in the dragon form, greater than you have now, greater than any I have ever had. Yet even with this power, I think you will be able to return to your human form at will. Unless I am much mistaken, you have two true forms—man *and* dragon."

Alex wanted to ask more questions but Salinor lowered his head to the cave floor and closed his eyes. Alex bowed to the great dragon, and then left him in his hidden cave. It was a long walk back to the dwarf village, and as he went Alex considered everything Salinor had told him and the promises he had made to the dragon.

The first promise was a small thing, really, and one that Alex had decided to do before ever meeting Salinor face-to-face: cast a spell on the Isle of Bones to hide it from any who might come looking for it. The other two promises Alex had made were more complicated, and he needed time to consider exactly what they meant.

Salinor's words about his family filled his mind as well, and Alex wondered why he had never thought to ask about his parents' families before. The idea that he might have living grandparents, aunts and uncles, even cousins, was something new; he wondered how he could find them.

There was one other promise that had come as something of a surprise to Alex, hardly something he'd expected the dragon to think about.

"Always go to your friends in their times of need," said Salinor in a serious tone. "If a friend calls for your help, go as quickly as you can."

Of course he would, wouldn't he? If any of his friends were in trouble, of course he would go to them. That's what friends did. It seemed natural, the kind of thing he would do without thinking. So why had Salinor made him promise to do it?

As he approached the deserted village, Alex reflected on Salinor's parting words. Salinor thought that Alex could take the dragon form and still return to his own form again. That was something no wizard had ever done, at least as far as Alex knew. Most wizards would not even try to take the shape of a dragon. Every wizard Alex had read about who had tried had either flown away as a dragon or gone completely mad and died. As he walked along, lost in his thoughts, Alex thought he could hear Salinor's voice echoing inside his own mind.

"Through your friends and your family you will find your true self," the dragon's voice said softly. "Go to them when they need you."

What did that mean? Alex knew who and what he was, didn't he? Well, no, he didn't. He was still learning about *what* he was, and he had no real idea about *who* he was. Iownan, the Oracle of the White Tower, had told him on his first adventure that he was a mix of races. He'd always thought of himself as human, but that wasn't exactly true. Somewhere in his family's history there were other races—elves, dwarfs, and apparently even dragons, according to Salinor. Could that be part of the reason Salinor had told him to look for his family? Was there something in his future that the dragon could see? The questions were enough to drive him crazy, so he tried to push them to the back of his mind. There would be time to think about them later, right now he had to get back to his friends and prepare to leave the Isle of Bones behind.

CHAPTER FOURTEEN

THE ROAD TO KAZAD-SYN

A lex soon left the woods and entered the empty dwarf village. It was a depressing sight now that he knew how sorry Salinor was that the dwarfs had been destroyed. Alex could see that his friends had been busy while he was away, because when he entered the town square piles of treasure glimmered all around him. Some of the piles were stacked almost as high as he was tall, and it was like moving through a giant maze to find the company's campsite. It was almost midday, and Alex quickened his pace, hoping to reach his friends before they started their meal.

"Well, look who's back," said Nellus, looking up with a smile as Alex approached the camp. "Been hiding and getting out of the *real* work."

"Something like that," said Alex, returning the smile. "Though eleven days and nights with a dragon is no easy task."

"I think I'd rather sort treasure than spend any time with a dragon," Barnabus said as he stacked wood on the campfire.

"I would say both have been profitable," answered Alex. "Where are the others?"

"They'll be along soon," said Nellus. "Thrang's had us all working down on the third level for days."

"The colony was rich, then," said Alex.

"They were doing well, that much is clear. Took us nearly a week to collect what you see here, and that's just what came out of the houses." Barnabus shook his head. "I'm not sure we'll be able to get Thrang to leave."

"The *Seeker* returns tomorrow and we must leave on it," said Alex.

"Thrang will argue the point," said Nellus, taking a seat beside the campfire. "Dwarfs aren't keen on leaving treasure behind."

"Perhaps I can help with that," said Alex, sitting down by Nellus.

"I hope so," Barnabus said. "Thrang's been moody since you left."

"Moody is hardly the word for it," said Nellus, looking troubled. "Thrang's temper has gotten steadily worse, and so has young Thrain's."

"What do you mean?" Alex asked.

"The look in their eyes," said Nellus, trying to explain. "It's a wild, hunted kind of look. I've seen it in men who have spent too much time in the wild, or adventurers who have been on one too many adventures."

"It is true," Barnabus added. "They are both consumed, I think. The treasure, the loss of their people who lived here—and then you heading off to talk with the dragon. It's changed Thrang and Thrain. They won't listen to reason anymore."

"They will have to listen," said Alex. "We must leave tomorrow or remain on this island forever."

"Thrang's been mumbling something about revenge," Nellus added. "He's convinced himself that your dragon friend is to blame for what happened here. Even Arconn can't talk to him about it."

"Well, he'll have to give up any ideas of revenge," said Alex, feeling more than a little worried. "Even if Thrang were to call all the dwarfs of Thraxon to his aid, I doubt he would do more than inconvenience this dragon."

"What's that about revenge?" said Thrang's voice.

Alex looked up and saw Thrang and Thrain coming around the piles of treasure.

"I said revenge is a dangerous game, and is often more dangerous to those looking for it than to anyone else," said Alex.

"I see you've come back, then," said Thrang, his voice colder than normal. "I suppose you've heard what this dragon has to say about my people. I suppose he told you that their destruction wasn't his fault at all."

"No, actually that's not what he said," said Alex. "As soon as the others are here, I'll tell you exactly what he said, if you care to hear it."

For a moment Thrang didn't speak or move, but simply stood with a look of mixed rage and fear on his face. Alex could see that Thrang had been worried about him, but he could also see that he had made up his mind about Salinor, and about all dragons for that matter.

"Alex," said Arconn happily as he walked into camp. "I thought we might have to come looking for you."

"I said I would be back before the *Seeker* returned," said Alex. "And it looks like you've all been busy while I was away."

"We won't be leaving on the *Seeker* tomorrow," said Thrang, his voice tight. "There is far too much treasure to collect still, and I won't leave the island until we have it all."

"I've never known you to be greedy, Thrang," said Alex, his tone calm and even.

"Greed has nothing to do with it," Thrang snapped. "The treasures of this island were gathered by my people. It is my duty, and yours as a signed member of this adventure, to collect it all before we leave."

Kat moved up beside Arconn, a troubled look on her face. Alex could tell that all of them were worried about Thrang's mood. And Thrain looked almost as serious as Thrang did.

"Very well," said Alex after a moment. "Forgive me if I have offended you. Collecting the treasure will not be a problem. We will still be able to leave tomorrow."

"I don't see how," Thrang answered, ignoring Alex's apology. "We've been sorting treasure for nearly two weeks, and we're not even half done yet."

"The sorting can wait for another time," said Alex, trying not to become angry with Thrang. "As before, I can quickly place all of the treasure in my bag. That is, if you trust me to hold it for you."

"Trust?" Thrang repeated, looking away from Alex. "Once the question of trust would never have come up between us. But now . . ."

"Now that I've spoken to a dragon, you're not sure if you can trust me," Alex finished for him. "You've made up your mind that the dragon is to blame for everything that happened here, and you long for revenge."

"Revenge is not enough," shouted Thrang, his face growing red with anger. "How can a single dragon pay for the hundreds of lives it has taken? No, I want the dragon destroyed, so it will never harm another creature."

"You don't know what you're saying," said Alex, his own temper starting to rise.

"You've been enchanted by this dragon," Thrang went on. "You can't see what really happened here, and you won't admit that the dragon is to blame. A fine wizard you've become." Thrang spat on the ground.

"Silence!" Alex commanded in a tone both deeper and stronger than his normal voice would be. The ground beneath them shook, and a dark cloud moved in front of the sun. "You will listen to what I have to say, and then you can decide if I am enchanted."

Alex looked around at his friends, who were shocked and scared by his sudden command and display of power. He had never spoken so strongly before, and Thrang looked petrified with fear, as if something terrible was about to happen to him.

"Now," said Alex, regaining control of his emotions. "The dragon that you blame has told me the whole story of what happened here. If you'll sit down and listen, I will tell it to you."

Thrang inched forward and slowly sat down, his wide eyes never leaving Alex's face.

Thrain stood as if he had turned to stone, and he didn't move until Alex pointed to a chair and told him to sit down.

Slowly, Alex told them what he had learned since they'd arrived on the island. Everyone remained silent as he spoke, though Arconn would often nod his head in understanding. As Alex told the story, he worked some special magic that would help Thrang accept what he was saying. He hoped that Thrang could let go of his anger and hate long enough to see the truth.

When Alex finished the story, he could see that they all had questions for him, but they held back, waiting for Thrang to speak first.

"So, Languinn attacked the dragon while it was still asleep," said Thrang, his voice almost a whisper.

"Yes," said Alex. "A good idea, but only if you're sure you can destroy the dragon before it wakes up."

"Yes," Thrang repeated. "And a foolish move if you cannot defeat the dragon."

"How could you know?" Thrain questioned. "I mean, how could you know how powerful the dragon was until it woke up?"

"It would not really be possible," said Alex. "And the dragon on this island is not evil. He was here, hidden from the world, trying to stay out of harm's way."

"But you could destroy it," Thrain went on, a hopeful tone in his voice. "I mean, you defeated Slathbog, so you could defeat this dragon as well, couldn't you?"

"No, I could not," answered Alex. "I could control him because I know his true name, but if it came to open battle . . ." Alex trailed off and took a deep breath. "I think if it came to open battle, we would destroy each other, and probably this entire island as well."

"You know the dragon's name?" Arconn questioned, a look of surprise on his face.

"Yes," said Alex.

"Then you . . . you are a dragon lord," said Arconn, his surprise changing to wonder.

"A dragon lord?" Thrang repeated, looking at Alex, his expression changing from confusion to understanding. "Yes, of course. How stupid of me. Forgive me, Alex, I have been a fool."

"There is no need for forgiveness," said Alex. "Your feelings are understandable. But know that the dragon regrets what happened here."

"Yes, I see that now," said Thrang, looking away for a moment to dry his eyes. "We will leave on the *Seeker* when it arrives. We will take as much treasure as we can, but whatever we cannot gather will be left behind without regrets."

The tension was broken now that Thrang had agreed to leave, and Alex's friends all looked relieved. Barnabus quickly started preparing their meal, and Thrang walked slowly away from the campfire. Alex followed Thrang, wanting to reassure his friend that there were no hard feelings. He caught up with Thrang outside the dwarf archives.

Thrang led Alex down to the third level. Alex was amazed by the amount of treasure in the cavern. His friends had been busy sorting, but they hadn't even started to store treasure in their bags.

"With your permission," said Alex, bowing slightly to Thrang.

"Do what you can," said Thrang, his voice weak. "Time has run out, and what remains here will remain forever."

Alex wanted to comfort Thrang, but he didn't know what more he could say or how he could say it. Thrang's confidence had been shaken when Alex had commanded him to listen, but it had been broken when he saw the truth. It had been for the best, Alex was sure of that, but Thrang had lost face in his own eyes. Alex could see that Thrang doubted his own ability to lead the company, and that could be a problem.

With a few magic words and a command whispered into the top of his magic bag, Alex emptied the giant chamber of its treasure. The hoard glimmered for a moment in the torchlight, and then sped into Alex's magic bag with a sound like a cracking whip.

When they returned to the surface, Alex saw that the rest of his friends had managed to store the treasure they'd gathered from the village in their own bags. Thrang said nothing, but simply returned to his seat by the fire and silently waited to leave the island.

———————

The next morning they returned to the beach. Everyone seemed to be in a dark mood, and Alex knew there were doubts about Thrang's ability to lead them on the rest of their adventure. If Thrang did not regain his confidence, it seemed likely that the adventure would end and they would divide the treasure and part ways. This was not acceptable to Alex, and he tried to think of a way to help Thrang get back his old confidence.

About an hour after they arrived on the beach, the *Seeker* sailed into the harbor. Alex and his companions pushed their rowboat back to the water's edge, climbed inside, and quickly made their way back to the ship. Bill Clinker and his crew greeted them happily, though they could tell something was wrong with the company. Bill, being quick to grasp what the problem was, asked Thrang for permission to get underway. Thrang didn't speak but simply nodded, and Bill gave the orders for the crew to set sail.

"A moment, please," said Alex, looking at each of his companions in turn. "I promised to cast a spell on this island, and I think you all should bear witness."

They all agreed, though only Arconn seemed happy about it. As the *Seeker* made its way out of the harbor, Alex and his friends gathered on the raised stern of the ship. Alex waited until they were a few miles away from the island, and then turned and looked at Thrang.

"With your permission," said Alex, bowing to Thrang.

"Yes," said Thrang, slowly returning the bow. "Yes, of course."

Alex stepped away from the others and raised his staff. Salinor had explained the spell to him, and he remembered the dragon's voice as he quietly spoke the words. As he worked the magic, the sun seemed to dim as if a cloud had moved in front of it. A strange mist began to grow out of the sea, circling the island. Alex focused all of his thoughts on his task. He could feel Salinor's magic joining his own as he wove the spell, and he knew that the island would be hidden forever.

Soon the island was hidden by a great cloud that sat on the surface of the water. Slowly Alex finished his work, binding the magic forever as he lowered his staff. He felt drained of strength, but oddly happy as he looked toward the island. The cloud remained where it was for a minute or two, and then blew away in the sea breeze. There was nothing but open water where the Isle of Bones had been.

"Impressive," Arconn said, looking surprised. "I thought the cloud would remain to hide the island."

"That would be a marker," said Alex in a tired voice. "This way is better, as it leaves no trace."

"You've done well," said Thrang, smiling weakly. "And I suppose it's for the best."

Alex smiled and bowed once more to Thrang. The others all seemed impressed by Alex's work, but they also wanted to get below deck. They still didn't like sailing, and the ship was already starting to roll on the waves of the open sea. They made their way below, leaving only Alex and Arconn standing on the stern of the ship, watching the spot where the Isle of Bones had been.

As night fell, Arconn went down to check on the rest of the company. Alex remained on deck, looking across the open water. He wanted to talk to Thrang, but he didn't want to do it in front of the rest of the company. He hoped that Thrang would shake off his doubts on his own, and he tried again to think of something he could say that would help. Then, to his surprise, Alex saw that Thrang was making his way across the deck toward him.

"Do you have any of that seasickness potion left?" Thrang asked, holding tightly to the railing of the ship.

"Of course," said Alex with a smile. "Decided it might not taste as bad as you remember?"

"I can't bear to remain below deck," said Thrang, looking as troubled as Alex had ever seen him. "They all have doubts now—even Arconn."

"I don't," said Alex. "And I'm not sure the others do either. I think perhaps you see your own doubt reflected in their faces."

"Perhaps," said Thrang. "But I have no idea what to do now."

"We carry on, of course," said Alex, handing a small bottle to Thrang. "You'll want to sip that a little at a time."

Thrang took a swallow of Alex's potion.

"I'm a fool," Thrang said. "I let my own foolish beliefs take over and cloud my judgment. I forgot what we were really after."

"You made a mistake; all of us do," said Alex. "The only thing you can do now is learn from it and try not to make the same mistake again."

"You are very kind, Alex. You've tried to help me save face, but—"

"But nothing," Alex interrupted. "You are the leader of this adventure, and you are the one who says where we go and when. You made a mistake. So what? Everyone makes mistakes."

"You didn't," Thrang pointed out.

"I didn't this time," said Alex. "I've made mistakes before, and I'll make them again. I just hope I don't make the same mistakes over and over again. And when I do make a mistake, I hope that I'm the only one who has to pay for it."

"You've changed a great deal since we first met," said Thrang with a short laugh. "You seem so much older now. I suppose that's your wizard training coming out."

"I suppose it is," said Alex. "I've never really thought about it, but I guess being a wizard has changed me quite a bit."

"Yes, but you're still the same friendly, trusting boy I met that day in Clutter's shop," said Thrang.

"And you're still the confident and wise dwarf I met that day as well. You've had your confidence shaken a little, but you are still the same."

"Perhaps," Thrang allowed. "And perhaps I'm a bit wiser than I was, thanks to you."

"What are friends for?" said Alex.

Thrang finished off the seasickness potion, and then remained on deck with Alex. They talked about their first adventure together, remembering a time that seemed so long ago, but wasn't really long ago at all.

"I suppose we should ride south and west when we get back to Dunnstal," Thrang said at last. "We'll stop at Kazad-Syn before starting for the Lost Mountains."

"That sounds like a good plan," said Alex.

"We might even be able to get some information about the Lost Mountains in Kazad-Syn," Thrang went on. "I have family in the city, and it would be good to see them."

"It is always good to see family," said Alex, remembering Salinor's comments.

"And you'll be able to return the lost bag to its heir."

"Yes, I need to do that, don't I?"

The stood in silence for a moment, and then Thrang patted Alex's shoulder. "Well then, I guess I'll try to get some sleep. I only hope the weather stays calm; I don't think I could take any more rolling than we're doing now."

Alex watched Thrang stagger across the deck, working his way back to the rest of the company. He was happy that Thrang had decided to continue with the adventure, and he hoped that his other friends would be happy about it too.

The days remained clear and calm as they sailed back to Dunnstal, which was a good thing for Alex's companions. When they arrived, Alex and Arconn helped the others off the ship while Thrang paid Bill Clinker and his crew. Alex noticed how hard Thrang was trying not to look sick, and he was quick to help his friend off the ship once payment had been made.

"I hope I never sail again," Thrang said, leaning on Alex. "Even your potion did little to calm the sickness."

"Yes, well, I was reading up on that," said Alex with a slight laugh. "It seems the potion works best if you stay in the fresh air, above deck."

"Oh, that's nice to know," said Arconn, laughing as he took Thrang's other arm.

Thrang did not find Alex's information as amusing as Arconn did, but he still managed a weak smile.

It was late afternoon, and Thrang and the others wanted nothing more than to return to the Sea Mist and find a bed to lie down on and recover from their voyage. As it turned out, Ishly had expected them, and he had rooms ready for all of them. Alex and Arconn remained in the common room for a short time after the others had gone to bed, and then wandered out into the streets of Dunnstal.

"Thrang's mood has improved since we left the island," Arconn commented, looking at Alex.

"We had a talk," said Alex. "He knows he made a mistake, but he's learned from it. Now I think he's prepared to move on."

"I am glad to hear that," said Arconn. "For a time I thought he would give up."

"I think he wanted to, but that would have been unacceptable," said Alex.

"Unacceptable to you or to him?"

"Both of us, I think," said Alex. "And I think you would agree with that as well."

"I would," said Arconn.

There wasn't much to see in Dunnstal, but Alex liked the sea air and the soft breeze blowing in his face. He and Arconn went down to the docks and found the old fisherman who had told Alex the story about the Isle of Bones. The old man seemed pleased to hear Alex's story about the lost dwarf mines, though Alex left out the fact that a dragon lived on the island. Once again Alex offered to put a spell on the fisherman's nets, and once again the old man laughed and said no. At sundown, Alex and Arconn left him on the docks and returned to the tavern. Only Thrain and Barnabus had managed to make their way

222

down from their rooms for dinner, and Alex thought it best to let the others sleep.

The next morning all of Alex's friends looked much happier and healthier than they had the day before. The long sleep in soft beds had done wonders for them, and they all ate their breakfast without wasting time to talk. As they were finishing their meal, Thrang stood up, looking around the table at each member of the company.

"I've decided that we will ride south to Kazad-Syn," said Thrang. "We should be able to get some information about the Lost Mountains there, and Alex has the bag of a lost adventurer that needs returning. The heir lives in Kazad-Syn, so we should be there for a few days at least."

"What do we know about the Lost Mountains?" Arconn asked quickly.

"Well, we know they are not actually lost," said Thrang with a soft laugh. "They are called the Lost Mountains because it is easy to get lost in them. I've never been there, but I've been told that there are hundreds of narrow canyons winding through the mountains."

"Is anything dangerous supposed to live there?" Nellus asked.

"I don't know of anything, but I'm sure we'll find out more when we reach Kazad-Syn," answered Thrang. "I believe some of the dwarfs who live there have been to the Lost Mountains, and their knowledge might be useful to us. After all, we don't want to search all of the mountains looking for signs of Albrek."

There was general agreement with Thrang's comment, and

they all got up together, ready to ride south. Alex and the others made their way to the stables, while Thrang stayed behind to find Ishly and pay for the company's stay. Alex could see that Thrang's renewed confidence had impressed the others, and they all looked a great deal happier than they had when they left the Isle of Bones.

"How far is it from here to Kazad-Syn?" Thrain asked as he worked to saddle his horse.

"Ten days—maybe two weeks' ride," said Alex, remembering the map of Thraxon he'd studied in Benorg. "Of course, the roads could be difficult, so it may take longer than that."

"At least we'll be riding," said Kat with a laugh. "I've never been as sick as I was on that boat."

"Nor have I," Barnabus added. "It'll be good to be on horseback again."

"I rather enjoyed the voyage," Arconn said with a laugh.

"As did I," Alex agreed, rubbing Shahree's neck as he spoke. "Though it is good to be back to a normal mode of travel."

The others laughed as they made their way out of the stable. Arconn led Thrang's horse along with his own, and they found Thrang waiting for them at the front of the inn.

"Ishly suggests that we follow the coast road south," said Thrang, climbing into his saddle. "He says there is a good road from Darvish to Kazad-Syn, and Darvish is only four or five days south of here."

"Are you sure you want to stay so close to the sea?" Alex asked with a smile.

"As long as we're not in it," said Thrang with a grunting laugh.

They quickly fell into line behind Thrang and rode out of Dunnstal. Alex looked back once before the city was lost to view, wondering what stories his friends from the *Seeker* would be telling at the inns tonight.

———

The coast road was a good one, and it was still early on the fifth day away from Dunnstal when they reached Darvish. Darvish was a much larger city than Dunnstal, with high stone walls around it. The gatekeepers were friendly enough, however, and let them pass after only a few questions. Thrang decided they would spend the rest of the day in Darvish and ride on toward Kazad-Syn the next morning.

"A few weeks out of the saddle and I'm not fit for a long journey," Thrang complained.

The rest of the company agreed. They were eager to explore the city of Darvish, but Thrang insisted they find an inn before anyone went exploring. They were surprised to learn that there were few rooms available in the city.

"A busy time of year," one innkeeper told them. "The calm sea doesn't last all year, after all, and many merchants don't like shipping their goods when the weather is bad."

Eventually they found an inn that had three rooms available, and Thrang was quick to take them all. Thrang and Thrain would share one room, as would Nellus and Barnabus. Arconn and Alex would share the third room with Kat, though their room was actually a small suite, with two bedrooms attached to a fair-sized sitting room. Alex was concerned that each of the bedrooms had only a single bed, but Arconn wasn't troubled.

"I do not need to rest like you," Arconn reminded Alex. "I will be quite comfortable in front of the fire. Though I've noticed that lately you can go for days without sleep as well."

"Only when I need to," said Alex. "And I don't think there is much need today."

With the sleeping arrangements taken care of, they all set off for a look at the city. Alex was surprised by the number of dwarfs in the city, but Thrang explained that Darvish did a great deal of trade with Kazad-Syn as well as with several other dwarf cities.

"My brother owns some property here," Thrang said as they walked along a crowded street. "He's done a lot of trading, and he's paid for ships to trade at most of the larger ports on the sea."

"He must be prosperous, then," said Nellus as they entered the city's main square. It was filled with hundreds of little tables covered with all kinds of goods and items for sale. "It seems there is a little of everything here."

"Darvish is one of the largest ports on the Eastern Sea," said Thrang. "Thorson says they are a hard people to deal with, but always fair."

"Thorson would be your brother, then," said Arconn, looking at Thrang.

"Yes," Thrang answered. "He's quite a bit younger than I am, but he's done very well for himself."

Alex could tell from Thrang's words and the look on his face that he was proud of his younger brother. It was strange to hear Thrang talk about his brother, as Alex had never really discussed family with any of his friends. For a moment Alex thought about his own family, the family that Salinor had told him to look for. Would Mr. Roberts know something about his family? And if not Mr. Roberts, then who?

"I'm going to look for some new boots," said Barnabus, breaking Alex's train of thought.

"You should take someone with you at least," said Thrang.

"You don't think there is any danger here, do you?" Thrain asked.

"No, but we should stay alert all the same," said Thrang.

They agreed, so Nellus and Kat went off with Barnabus to look for boots. Thrang insisted that Thrain stay with him, which left Alex and Arconn free to wander the city together.

They worked their way through the open market in the square, looking at several items and even buying a few. The people of Darvish didn't seem at all surprised to see a man and an elf together, though a few of them did take a second look at Alex when they noticed his staff. It was a pleasant morning, and at midday Alex and Arconn bought some food from one of the market stalls and went looking for a place to sit and eat.

"A fair city," said Arconn as they walked along. "I wish we had more time to spend here."

"I expect Thrang wants to see his brother," said Alex, spotting a patch of green that looked like a public park and pointing it out to Arconn. "How much do you know about Thrang's family?"

"I know he has several brothers," Arconn answered as he and Alex sat on a bench in the shadow of a tall tower. "Families are not often discussed between adventurers, though I don't know why."

"Not something that comes up as part of the adventure," said Alex.

"No, I suppose not," said Arconn.

"Do you know anything about ancient books?" Alex questioned, changing the subject because he didn't want to consider how little he knew about his own family.

"How ancient?"

"I would guess that they are older than the elvish writing, maybe older than the magic writing as well," Alex answered.

Arconn thought for a moment. "Why do you ask about such books?"

"I have some," said Alex. "The dragon on the Isle of Bones gave them to me. I've only looked at one of them, and only for a few seconds, but I could see it wasn't written in either the magic letters or the elvish language."

"Why would a dragon have books?" Arconn questioned, as much to himself as to Alex.

"I don't know," said Alex, wishing Salinor had explained things a bit more. "He told me to take them and that they had a great deal of lost knowledge in them."

"I would say almost anything in them would be considered lost knowledge," said Arconn, looking up at the sky. "I've heard stories of such books, but nothing more."

"And what do the stories say?"

"These ancient books are rare," Arconn began slowly, as if trying to remember. "The oldest of them would date from the time just after the creation of the known lands, before the different races spread out from their own lands."

"So they tell about how the lands were created and who did what? Where each race came from and things like that?" Alex asked.

"Perhaps," said Arconn. "Who can say for sure? What I've heard is mostly rumor and legend. I don't think the oldest elf alive could say what was true about such books."

"And what do the rumors and legends say?" Alex pressed, noticing that Arconn hadn't really answered his question.

"They say such books can be dangerous," said Arconn. "Some of the legends say that the books give power to the reader. Depending on who the reader is, such books could either be very dangerous or possibly very profitable."

"Or both," said Alex, considering Arconn's words.

"If the books the dragon gave you are from the ancient times, you should be careful when exploring them," Arconn advised. "Perhaps you should ask Whalen about them."

"Yes, I suppose I should," said Alex thoughtfully.

"Masters," said an old-looking man, interrupting Alex and Arconn's conversation.

"May we help you?" Alex asked.

"I would like to ask why you are here," the old man answered.

"We are traveling through your city on our way to Kazad-Syn," said Arconn.

"Oh, no, I mean *here,* in the shadow of the empty tower," said the old man with a smile.

"Should we not be here?" Alex asked.

"There is no law against it," said the man in a reassuring tone. "It is just that few people ever sit so close to the tower, as they know its dangers."

"Dangers?" Arconn questioned.

"This is the Empty Tower of the Oracle," the man explained. "I am Kathnar, the keeper of the grounds. I, and my people, are known as the Servants of the Empty Tower."

"And how long have you served?" Alex asked.

"My family has cared for the grounds of the tower for more than a thousand years," Kathnar answered proudly. "We have kept watch, waiting for the oracle to come."

"A long time to wait," commented Arconn.

"Yes, but we will wait as long as we must," said Kathnar in a sad tone.

"Who is this oracle that will come?" Alex asked as he looked up at the tower.

"The dragon will bring her," Kathnar answered reverently. "At least, one of the legends says that. It is difficult to know which legends are true, as so many have been told."

"May we enter the tower?" Arconn asked.

"Oh, no," Kathnar answered quickly. "It is most dangerous. The tower is sealed by magic."

"Take us to the entrance," said Alex. "I would like to see what magic holds the gates of this tower."

"As you wish," said Kathnar with a bow. "The gate is not far. I will show you."

Alex and Arconn followed Kathnar through some trees and along a stone path. The tower had a high wall around it, and as they came around one corner of the wall, Alex saw Nellus,

Barnabus, and Kat standing in front of the gates. Barnabus and Nellus both looked worried, but Kat seemed perfectly calm as she walked toward the gate.

"Kat, no!" Arconn called, racing forward.

"You should not stop her," yelled Kathnar, hurrying along behind Arconn. "She has a right to try."

Stepping between Kat and the gate, Alex stuck the ground with his staff. The rolling sound of thunder filled the air, and Kat's eyes turned from the tower to Alex in surprise.

"This is not for you," said Alex, his voice full of power. "You have other tasks to do."

"Yes," Kat said in a dreamy voice. "I have promises to keep."

"But the time is so short," Kathnar shouted. "If the oracle does not arrive soon, the tower will be lost forever."

"What do you mean?" Alex demanded, turning to look at Kathnar.

"Legend says that the tower will remain empty for only so long," said Kathnar, looking from Alex to Kat and back again. "If the oracle does not arrive before that time is up, the tower will vanish like the mist."

"How much time is left before the tower vanishes?" Alex questioned.

"It is hard to say," said Kathnar, his anger fading into help-lessness. "The exact count was lost years ago." He shrugged. "A year, maybe less. Forgive my anger, I . . . It's just that I feel that the time is almost over, and I don't want the tower to fade."

"There is no need for forgiveness," said Alex, glancing at

Kat. "My friend is a seer. The power of the tower called to her as I'm sure it has called to others."

"Yes, there have been others who have tried," said Kathnar. "They have all failed to enter the tower, but that doesn't mean your friend shouldn't try."

"Those who failed, what happened to them?" Arconn questioned.

"They lost themselves," Kathnar answered slowly. "They had no sense of who they were or even where they were. Some went mad. Others wandered away from the city. Still others simply refused to eat and, well . . ."

"Yes, I understand," said Alex. "The tower is seeking a new oracle. The power of this place is trying to find someone who can control it, and it will call to anyone who might fill its need."

"That sounds more than a little evil," Arconn said, glancing at the tower.

"No, not evil," said Alex. "It is a test of magic and will. The magic of the tower does not destroy those who try to enter; it is their failure to enter and their inability to accept that failure that destroys them. I don't think Kat is ready for this test—at least not yet—and I won't let her go blindly forward. When she understands what has happened and what might happen to her, then perhaps she will wish to make an attempt to enter."

"As you wish, master wizard," said Kathnar, bowing to Alex. "I hope that she will not wait too long before making the attempt."

"And I hope that the oracle appears before the tower fades," Alex answered.

Kathnar bowed to Alex and walked away.

Kat was still looking at Alex, her eyes blank and distant, and it was only when he softly spoke her name that the trance was lifted.

"I don't know why I came here," said Kat after the others told her what had happened. "It was like a dream, but the more I try to remember it, the more it slips away from me."

"Don't be troubled by it," said Alex. "We have an adventure to finish first. If you decide that you want to try to enter the tower once you understand what your attempt might mean, well, then I will come with you and help in any way I can."

Kat nodded her acceptance of Alex's words without speaking, and they all returned to the city without looking back at the tower. Alex worried that Kat might slip away from them and return to the tower, but she didn't. Kat did seem to be thinking about the tower, and she said very little to anyone for the rest of the day.

"Kazad-Syn is a wonderful city," Thrang said at dinner. "A week or ten days and you will see it shining like a jewel in the sun."

"I've never heard you speak so fondly of any city," Arconn said, looking at Thrang.

"It is the city my family comes from, my home," said Thrang with a smile. "My brother Thorson still lives there, though the rest of my brothers have moved away. Still, I have cousins and other family there, so our visit should be a happy one."

"Then let us drink to Kazad-Syn, and hope to reach it quickly," said Nellus, raising his mug.

The others followed Nellus's example, which made Thrang happy.

"One final drink and then off to bed," said Thrang as they finished their meal. "We'll make an early start in the morning, and if we're lucky, we'll reach Kazad-Syn in less than ten days."

They all drank and headed to their rooms. Thrang motioned for Alex and Arconn to wait as the others departed. When they were alone, he spoke in a lowered voice.

"Do you think she will try to return to the tower?"

"I don't think so," Alex said softly. "I've blocked the magic that called to her, at least for now."

"And when you remove the block?" Arconn questioned.

"Then the magic of the tower will call to her again," said Alex. "If she wants to try to enter the tower then, well . . . In any event, I won't let her do anything without really understanding what the attempt might do to her."

"It's good that we'll be leaving tomorrow," said Thrang in a thoughtful tone. "Arconn, keep an eye on her tonight, just in case she tries to slip away."

Arconn nodded and the three of them hurried after their friends. Alex felt certain that Kat would want to return and try to enter the tower after their adventure was finished, even once she knew what might happen to her. He was also troubled because he knew he could do almost nothing to help her if she tried and failed.

CHAPTER FIFTEEN

THE THIRD BAG

———◆———

Thrang's prediction of when they would reach Kazad-Syn was correct. Just before midday on the ninth day out from Darvish, the company stopped at the top of a hill. Spread out before them was the dwarf city of Kazad-Syn, shining like a jewel, just as Thrang had said.

"It's beautiful," said Thrain with breathless excitement. "I've never seen anything like it."

"Do all dwarf roads lead up hills before reaching cities?" asked Nellus. "It seems the roads are designed to give us the most impressive view of the city possible."

"I don't know if the roads were designed that way." Thrang laughed. "But it is a splendid view."

Alex agreed that the city was beautiful, and to his surprise, it was also very green. The city was built close to the mountains, and a long wall stretched out from the mountainside to enclose part of the city in a half circle. The wall was a pale and milky green color; it looked more like a giant hedge than a wall of stone. They could see many large buildings inside the wall, most of them made of the same jade-colored stone as the wall. There were also many trees growing in and around the city, which only added to the effect of the green stone.

"Kazad-Syn is known for its jade-colored marble," Thrang said as they started forward once more. "Stone from this area has been shipped to most of the known lands."

"It is impressive," Arconn said. "I never thought a dwarf city could look so vibrant and alive."

"Wait until you see the underground parts of the city," said Thrang with a smile.

When they reached the city gate, the guards greeted Thrang as an old friend and let the company pass without hesitation. It didn't take long for news of the company's arrival to spread through the city, and they were soon being followed by dozens of young dwarfs who were all calling Thrang's name.

"I have a bit of a reputation here," said Thrang with a grin. He reached into his pocket and took out a handful of silver coins, which he tossed over his shoulder to the youngsters following them. "I always toss a few coins to them, and I always have good luck," he explained.

"A custom?" Arconn questioned, looking back as the young dwarfs rushed in to gather up the coins.

"It is for my family," said Thrang. "My great-grandfather started the practice, and now, whenever anyone from my family returns here, we carry it on as a tradition."

Thrang looked like he was going to say more, but at that moment, a crowd of happy dwarfs shouted greetings to him from the street. Thrang called back, waving to them, and Alex could see that Thrang was glad to be home once more.

They followed the main road through the city, but as

they went, the crowd around them grew, and soon they could hardly move at all. Alex wondered if Thrang always had this kind of reception when he came to the city, but decided it might not be a good question to ask. Instead, he rode slowly behind Thrang, smiling at the dwarfs who were so happy to see Thrang and his company.

It took some time, but they were finally able to move away from the crowds and turn off the main road onto one of the many side streets leading toward the mountains. After a short time, Thrang stopped in front of a fine-looking house built right up against the mountainside. There was a high wall around the house, and the gate was closed. Thrang climbed off his horse and banged loudly on the solid wooden gate.

"Cousin Thrang!" the young dwarf who opened the gate exclaimed in surprise. "We didn't know you were coming. I would have had the gate open for you."

"I didn't have time to send word," said Thrang, smiling at his young cousin and motioning for the others to follow him through the gate.

"Thorson will be happy to see you," the dwarf went on, apparently unaware of the rest of the company. "He was saying just the other day that he should write and invite you to come and stay for awhile."

"I hope there's room for my friends as well," said Thrang, turning to gesture at the others.

"Always room for your friends," the dwarf answered, also turning to look. At the sight of the group of adventurers, his eyes grew wide and his mouth dropped open. Alex thought that the dwarf might have lost the ability to speak.

"I didn't know you were on an adventure," the dwarf managed to say after several seconds. "Forgive me, cousin, I shouldn't keep you and your friends waiting here in the courtyard."

"No harm done," Thrang said with a laugh. "And as you are here, you might as well meet everyone. Everyone, this is my cousin Dain. Dain wants to follow in my footsteps and become an adventurer, but he's not yet come of age."

Dain bowed to the company, blushing slightly as he rose. Thrang introduced each member of the company in turn, saving Alex for last.

"Alexander Taylor?" Dain repeated. "The wizard who defeated Slathbog?"

"The very same," said Thrang, smiling and winking at Alex. "And he's done a great deal more than that as well."

"A great honor, sir," said Dain, bowing to Alex.

"The honor is mine," said Alex, returning the bow and Thrang's wink.

"I'll take your horses to the stables for you," Dain said to Thrang.

"And who will tell Thorson we've arrived?" Thrang questioned.

"Well, I . . ." Dain began, then trailed off.

"Go on, then." Thrang laughed. "Take the horses for us, and I'll let my brother know we are here."

Dain took the reins of their horses and started off across the courtyard.

Thrang motioned for the company to follow him in the opposite direction. Alex could see that the house was large on the outside, and he guessed that a great deal more of it was either underground or inside the mountain, which was close to the back of the house.

Thrang seemed to know exactly where his brother would be at this time of day. He led them through a small part of the house and out into a large, walled-off garden. Several dwarfs were sitting at a stone table near a fountain, talking loudly.

"I don't care if he is of age. He'll have to wait until arrangements can be made for his trip to an oracle," said a dwarf who looked a great deal like Thrang.

"He doesn't want to wait, cousin," a second dwarf said. "He says he's of age and will do as he likes."

"Then he can go by himself and without my help," the first dwarf answered. "Tell him to be here this evening and I'll tell him so myself."

"Who wants to go to an oracle?" Thrang asked loudly.

"What's that?" said the first dwarf, turning to see who had spoken. "Thrang, you old rascal, when did you get here?"

"Just now," said Thrang, moving forward and embracing his brother. "Dain met us at the gate and has taken our horses to the stables. We haven't come at a bad time, have we, Thorson?"

"Ah, a company," said Thorson in delight. "You should have sent word; I'd have had a feast prepared."

"The feast can wait," said Thrang with a laugh. "Do you have room for the seven of us to stay? We'll be in the city for a week or two."

"You know I have room," said Thorson. "And if you're staying for at least a week, there will be time for several feasts."

"You are most kind," said Thrang. "Let me introduce my friends to you."

Thrang introduced the company to his brother and to the other dwarfs in the garden, once again saving Alex for last. Thorson was happy to meet them all, and the dwarfs all smiled and bowed as they were introduced. Alex tried to remember all of their names, but Thrang's relatives looked so much alike it was hard to keep the names and faces straight.

Thorson gestured to the table by the fountain. "Please, make yourselves at home. I'll have the midday meal brought out here as well as have rooms prepared for all of you." Thorson quickly turned to one of his cousins and rattled off some instructions. Alex thought the cousin's name was Bulbur, but he wasn't completely sure.

"Now then," said Thrang, walking over to the table. "Who is it that wants to run off and see an oracle?"

"Your nephew, Fivra," Thorson answered, shaking his head. "Just came of age last month, and already he wants to run off and find an oracle."

"That's natural enough," Thrang said, taking a seat. The rest of the company joined him around the table.

"So it would seem, but he doesn't want to go and see just any oracle. He wants to go to Vargland and see the Oracle of the White Tower," said Thorson, joining Thrang at the table. "Halfdan's trading company will be going that way, and he's already agreed to take several young dwarfs with him."

"For a price," said Thrang, nodding.

"One hundred gold coins each," Thorson said. "I told

Fivra if he would save half the money, I'd give him the other half, but I don't think he has two coins to rub together."

"But he still wants to go, and he still wants you to pay for it," said Thrang, nodding once more.

"He says he'll go if I pay or not," said Thorson in a slightly worried tone. "Has his mind made up, and you know how stubborn he is."

"Even if he gets to Vargland, there's no promise the oracle will talk to him," said Thrang, glancing quickly at Alex.

"No, there's not," said Thorson. "But I refuse to pay the entire price, and now he's off sulking about it somewhere."

"He always was a bit of a sulker," Thrang said.

"And he's never been any good with money," Thorson added. "He's got it in his mind that he'll be an adventurer, like you and Halfdan. Seems to think adventures are an easy way to get rich quick."

"I've told him a hundred times that being an adventurer is hard work," said Thrang, shaking his head. "Even if he goes to Vargland, and even if the oracle speaks to him, odds are he won't be chosen as an adventurer."

"I know," said Thorson, shaking his head as well. "I've tried to explain it to him, but he won't listen. Now, with you and your friends here, I know he'll be more determined than ever to go."

"Perhaps we could talk to him," offered Arconn. "We could tell him how hard adventures can be."

"A kind gesture," said Thrang, smiling at Arconn. "It might not hurt, but I hate to bring you all into family matters."

"It is the least we can do," said Nellus.

"But he mustn't think we put you up to it," Thorson warned. "If the subject comes up naturally, fine, but don't bring it up."

They all agreed, and Thorson thanked each of them individually. Just then, the midday meal arrived, and they were soon eating and talking about other things.

"So, an adventure in Thraxon," Thorson said, glancing at Thrang. "Can you tell me anything about it?"

"You know I can't," said Thrang with half a smile. "But there is something you can help us with."

"Anything, anything at all," said Thorson.

"My friend, Alex, is carrying a lost bag. We need to find the heir and arrange for the bag's return."

"Do you know the heir's name?" Thorson asked Alex.

"Haymar Glynn," said Alex, pushing his plate away and leaning back in his chair. "The bag maker in Telous gave me the name."

"Haymar Glynn," Thorson repeated. "Yes, I think I know him. Nice fellow. I'll send word this afternoon that you wish to speak with him."

"Excellent," said Thrang. "With any luck, we can take care of this task and be on our way. Oh, yes, I should ask one other thing."

"Just the one?" said Thorson with a laugh.

"We need information about the Lost Mountains," said Thrang. "Anything will be helpful, but we don't want every dwarf in the city knowing that we're going there."

"Yes, of course," said Thorson, looking more serious. "I'll

see what I can find out. Make it sound like business of my own, if that's all right."

"That would be wonderful," said Thrang.

Later that afternoon, Alex was sitting in the garden talking with Kat and Arconn when Thrang and Thorson came looking for him.

"We've run into a bit of a problem," said Thrang, a troubled look on his face. "It seems there is some dispute about the bag you want to return to Haymar Glynn."

"What kind of dispute?" Alex questioned.

"Haymar's half brother, Halbrek, is disputing Haymar's claim as heir," said Thorson. "He claims that their father was going to change his will and name him heir to his bag, but he died before he had the chance."

"The bag maker gave me Haymar's name," said Alex. "As far as I know, Haymar is the heir and should receive the bag. If his half-brother wants to make a claim, he'll have to do it some other way."

"It's not as simple as that," said Thrang as he took a seat. "Halbrek has made a public claim, and now the claim has to be settled before you can return the bag. It's a very old dwarf law, and I don't think anyone has tried to enforce it for several hundred years."

"Who decides the dispute?" Alex asked, looking from Thrang to Thorson.

"Well, there are two ways," Thrang began. "The king can hear both sides of the story and then make a ruling, but that might take months, or even years."

"And there's no way to know if the king will choose the

true heir or not," Thorson added. "There is always a chance he might make a mistake."

"Or that he or one of the officials hearing the claims will accept a bribe," said Thrang in a troubled voice.

"And the second way?" Alex questioned, afraid that he already knew the answer.

"As a wizard, and the bag holder, *you* can decide who the true heir is," said Thorson, smiling weakly.

"How would I do that?" Alex asked.

"The ceremony to return the bag would be much the same as you've done before," said Thrang quickly. "However, in this case, both Haymar and Halbrek would come forward to claim the bag. The simplest way would be to have them both tell you the passwords to the bag, and if they're different, the one with the correct passwords would be the true heir."

"And if they both know the correct passwords?" Alex questioned, feeling that he'd rather have the king resolve the dispute.

"Then you'll have to come up with your own test," Thorson answered.

"Oh," said Alex, looking down at the ground. "What kind of test could I use?"

Thrang shrugged. "This law is very old, and there have been only a few cases like this in our history. Perhaps there is some magical way to find out who the owner of the bag wanted to be his heir."

"There might be," said Alex, not looking up. "Or I could use magic to force both Haymar and Halbrek to tell the truth.

But, of course, if they both believe what they're saying is the truth, that magic is useless."

"It will be a difficult task, that is for sure," Thorson agreed. "However, both Haymar and Halbrek have asked to speak with you. Perhaps you can find the truth some other way."

"Did they both want to talk to me at the same time?" Alex asked.

"No, they each requested to speak to you alone," said Thorson. "No doubt they each want to press their own case with you, hoping that you will decide in their favor."

"When do they want to see me?" Alex asked, feeling a weight settle in his stomach.

"Haymar said he will come whenever you ask him to," said Thorson. "Halbrek insisted on seeing you only after you have spoken to Haymar."

"Very well," Alex agreed reluctantly. "Ask Haymar to come tonight, and Halbrek can come tomorrow morning. I will listen to what they both have to say and see if I can find a solution to their dispute."

"It will be as you request," said Thorson with a bow.

"There must be some way to find out who's telling the truth," said Thrang after Thorson had gone.

"They both must believe what they're saying is true or else they wouldn't have invoked the ancient dwarf law," Kat pointed out.

"That's true," Thrang agreed. "But even if they both believe in their claims, they are taking a huge risk. The one you decide against will lose a great deal of honor."

"Yet Haymar's claim is already the stronger," said Alex thoughtfully. "His name was given as the heir."

"What appears to be true is not always true," Arconn said in a thoughtful tone.

Alex nodded but didn't say anything more. He wasn't happy about the turn of events. He thought that returning the lost bag would be a simple task and a happy event. Now he feared that returning the lost bag might tear a family apart. He wondered if perhaps he should refuse both Haymar and Halbrek, at least until they agreed on who the true heir should be.

Alex had little time to think about what he should do, because Thorson arranged for Haymar to arrive less than an hour later. Alex remained in the garden alone, waiting for Haymar and thinking over his options.

As the sun was going down, Haymar Glynn walked into the garden. He looked nervous. Alex was sitting by the fountain, watching as the dwarf approached.

"Master Taylor?" Haymar questioned, a look of surprise on his face.

"Yes," said Alex, trying to look wise.

"I'm sorry. I . . . I thought you would be older," said Haymar, bowing. "Of course, I've heard the stories, but still . . ."

"I seem young to be a wizard," Alex finished for him.

"I mean no offense," said Haymar, bowing once again. "It is not my place to judge wizards or their ways."

"But it seems that it is my place to judge you and your half-brother," said Alex.

"I am sorry for that," said Haymar. "I've tried to talk to Halbrek, but he won't listen to me. I've offered him an equal share of anything the bag holds, but he won't accept. He insists that he is the rightful heir of the bag and that the honor of receiving it should be his."

"And you are not willing to give up that honor," said Alex, looking closely at Haymar.

"I would give up everything in the bag, but not the honor of being the heir," said Haymar.

"Is this honor more important to you than your family?"

"Halbrek is my half-brother, but we've never been close. I am my father's first son by his first wife, heir to his fortune and titles. Halbrek is my father's first son by his second wife, and he is unwilling to accept that he can never be the true heir."

"A difficult problem," Alex commented.

"It has been, yes. I've tried to be understanding, but Halbrek doesn't want understanding; he wants to be heir."

"So you don't believe your father ever said anything about making Halbrek his heir?"

"My father was old when he went on his last adventure," said Haymar. "Old and tired and he shouldn't have gone, but he did. He told me he was going to give any treasure he found on his last adventure to Halbrek. It was his way of making up for the fact that Halbrek could never be his heir, I think."

Alex thought about Haymar's words for several minutes before speaking again. Everything Haymar said made sense to Alex, but then it should. Haymar had probably known about his father's death for some time, and he would have made up a convincing story to explain Halbrek's claim.

"You have answered all of my questions without really answering them," Alex said, watching Haymar's every move.

"Yes, I suppose I have," said Haymar. "I have tried to explain things that may not have needed explaining. I will say this: My family is more important to me than any honor or riches, but giving up the honor of receiving my father's bag would, I think, do more to harm my family than not giving it up. I do not believe my father ever told Halbrek that he would be the heir of the bag, but I do believe that *Halbrek* believes that such a promise was made."

"Why do you think giving up your claim on the bag would harm your family?" Alex asked, surprised by Haymar's words.

"If Halbrek is given the honor of receiving the lost bag, he will use that status to make other claims," said Haymar in a sad tone. "I fear Halbrek would try to take everything my father left to me and my brothers, and that I cannot allow."

"Very well," said Alex, looking Haymar in the eye. "I have heard your side of things. Tomorrow I will hear what Halbrek has to say. Once I've heard both sides, I will try to make a fair decision."

"You are most kind," said Haymar, bowing to Alex.

"One more thing," said Alex as Haymar turned to leave. "Is there any chance that Halbrek knows the passwords to the bag?"

"There is always a chance," said Haymar. "As I told you, my father was getting old. He may have told Halbrek the passwords, but I don't believe he did."

"And I suppose you'd rather not tell me the passwords until I'm ready to return the bag," said Alex with a smile.

"I would trust you with the passwords if you asked me for them," said Haymar sincerely. "Are you asking me to give them to you now?"

"I am not," said Alex, bowing slightly. "I will talk with Halbrek and then let you both know what my decision is in a day or two."

"As you wish," said Haymar, bowing once more before he left.

Alex remained alone in the garden for some time, considering what Haymar had told him. He thought Haymar was telling the truth, but there was no way he could be completely sure. He wondered if he should have asked Kat to join him when he talked to Haymar, but he knew that wouldn't have been right. Kat was not a wizard, and she could not make this decision for him, even if she wanted to.

"Did your meeting with Haymar go well?" Thrang asked when Alex finally returned to the main house.

"As well as possible. I'm not at all sure that I should be the one to settle this question. No matter what I decide, either Haymar or Halbrek will be unhappy, and they may continue to contest who the true heir is."

"No, they wouldn't do that," said Thrang, his expression serious. "They have both accepted you as the judge in this matter, so they will both have to live with your decision. The law is very clear on that point. They will not be able to complain about the decision or contest it at all."

"Making the correct decision will be hard," said Alex with a sigh.

"You'll do what's right," said Thrang confidently. "I'm sure you'll be able to decide who the true heir is."

Alex smiled at Thrang and nodded.

The next morning Alex was back in the garden, waiting for Halbrek to arrive. He wondered what Halbrek would have to say, and why he had insisted on coming after Haymar. Alex thought that if he were in the same situation, he would want to talk to the person deciding things first. Halbrek arrived slightly late and was led into the garden by Thrang's cousin Dain.

"Master Halbrek Glynn, Master Alexander Taylor," said Dain, bowing to Alex and Halbrek.

"A great pleasure," Halbrek said, stepping forward and extending his hand.

Alex shook Halbrek's hand but said nothing, waiting for Halbrek to begin after Dain left.

"I suppose Haymar has told you all about me," said Halbrek, stepping back. "I can always count on him to tell people how terrible I've been to him."

"The topic did not come up," said Alex.

"I suppose there is a first time for everything," said Halbrek, looking surprised. "He probably thought it would be a mistake to tell his stories to you. After all, you're a wizard and can see through such falsehoods easily."

"At times I can," said Alex, watching Halbrek.

"Yes, of course," Halbrek said, not meeting Alex's eyes. "So, to the matter at hand."

"As you wish," said Alex, motioning for Halbrek to take a seat.

"I'm sure Haymar told you how he's the oldest son of our

father's first wife," said Halbrek. "How only the oldest son can be the true heir and all of that nonsense."

"We did go over that," said Alex, taking the seat opposite Halbrek. "Though I know adventurers can name anyone they wish as the heir to their bag."

"Yes, that's true," said Halbrek with a smile. "Haymar doesn't believe that, of course, but as you say, adventurers can name anyone they want to. My father named *me* his heir, and so I must insist that the bag be returned to me."

"But your father did not name you as his heir," corrected Alex. "The bag maker in Telous listed Haymar's name. Your father might have told you he was going to change this, but he never did."

"He may not have had time," said Halbrek quickly. "He told me before he left on his last adventure that I would be his heir once he returned home."

"Though he never returned home, did he?" Alex said thoughtfully.

Alex's thoughts turned to Hathnord, the owner of the bag and the father of both Haymar and Halbrek. Haymar had said little about his father, though he had shown concern regarding his father's health and age. Halbrek didn't seem concerned about his father at all, only about the magic bag and his own claim as Hathnord's heir. Alex thought it was an important point, and one that made him favor Haymar's claim even more.

"No, he did not, and it appears that he never bothered to change the named heir of the bag with the bag maker,"

Halbrek went on, not noticing the tone in Alex's voice. "Still, my claim is just, and I'm willing to pay for my rights."

"Pay?" Alex questioned.

"Of course," said Halbrek. "What's in the bag is nothing compared to the honor of being named the heir. I'm sure Haymar made you a generous offer to return the bag to him, but whatever he's offering you, I'll give you more."

"The subject of reward for the bag's return is part of the returning ceremony," said Alex flatly. "Haymar and I did not discuss it at all."

"No, of course not," said Halbrek, a twisted smile on his face. "And I'm sure that we won't discuss it either. Though I might suggest something along the lines of one-half of all the bag contains."

"As I said, such things should not be discussed now," said Alex.

The more Halbrek talked, the more Alex disliked him. And after this conversation, he was sure that Haymar was the true heir.

"Yes, of course," said Halbrek with a wink.

"I suppose you know the passwords to your father's bag?" Alex asked, getting to his feet. He tried not to let his feelings of anger show.

"I'm sure I will when the time comes," answered Halbrek, winking at Alex again. "As long as Haymar goes first, I'm sure there won't be any trouble with passwords."

"I'm sure there won't," said Alex coldly.

"Well then, if we understand each other, I'll be on my way," said Halbrek happily.

"I understand you perfectly," said Alex, fighting to control the rage building up inside of him.

Halbrek stood and held out his hand again for Alex to shake, but Alex turned away, walking toward the fountain.

"I will send word about the ceremony," said Alex over his shoulder, not wanting to look at Halbrek. He was afraid his feelings would make him do something terrible to the lying dwarf.

"Yes, of course," said Halbrek, and he quickly departed.

Alex stared into the fountain for several minutes trying to control his emotions. Halbrek had no claim at all; he only wanted to steal Haymar's honor and whatever treasure he could. Worse than that, he thought he could bribe Alex into helping him, and that was a dishonor Alex would never allow. For a moment Alex considered changing Halbrek into something terrible as punishment for his attempted bribe, but then decided that exposing Halbrek for what he was would be a more suitable punishment.

"So, you've spoken to both of them now. What do you think?" Thrang asked when Alex returned to the house for the midday meal.

"I know who the true heir is," said Alex without explaining. "How soon can the ceremony be arranged? I'd like to announce my decision and return the bag at the same time."

"I'll have to talk to Haymar and Halbrek to see how soon they can be ready," said Thorson. "Though I doubt the two of them will agree to the decision of who the true heir is and the ceremony of the bag's return at the same time."

"Tell them that is the only way the bag will be returned,"

said Alex with a smile. "They should both be there for the decision as well as to witness the bag's return to the true heir."

"It will be as you wish," said Thorson with an understanding smile.

As it worked out, it took two days to prepare for the ceremony. Haymar and Halbrek argued about how many people should attend the ceremony and who those people should be. Then they argued about where the ceremony should take place and even what time of day it should begin. In the end, Thorson made most of the arrangements and decided most of the questions about who should be there. The only two things Alex insisted on were that some of the guests in attendance not be related to either Haymar or Halbrek, and that all of his companions be included as guests. He also suggested that Thrang's nephew, Fivra, should be there.

"It might enlighten him a little," said Alex. "After all, a lost bag means a lost adventurer, something I'm sure Fivra has not considered in his thinking."

"Ah, yes," said Thrang with a nod. "A cunning plan to show him the hard facts about adventures without saying anything. Very good, Alex, very good."

As they waited for the ceremony to begin, all of Alex's companions seemed to be getting nervous. They were interested to know what decision he had made, but Alex wouldn't tell them. He thought it best not to say anything until the day of the ceremony, mostly because he wanted to see how Haymar and Halbrek would act between now and then.

"Halbrek seems confident," Thorson observed as Alex and his friends made their way into the feasting hall on the day of the ceremony. "There are some rumors in the city that he will be named the true heir."

"Rumors that Halbrek started, no doubt," said Thrang, looking unhappy.

"Loose talk seldom holds truth," Arconn said, taking a seat next to Alex.

"You *have* discovered who the true heir is, haven't you?" Thrain questioned in a worried tone.

"Yes, I have," said Alex with a slight smile.

Once all the guests had arrived, Thorson stood up to address the crowd. Since Thorson had made most of the arrangements, he had been chosen to supervise both the decision about who the true heir was and the ceremony of returning the lost bag.

After several minutes of greetings and a quick explanation of the events for those dwarfs who didn't already know what was going on, Thorson introduced Thrang and his company, and then he called both Haymar and Halbrek forward.

"Master Taylor, if you will," said Thorson, bowing to Alex.

"I've been asked to judge who the true heir of Hathnord is," Alex began, standing between Haymar and Halbrek. "It was not a simple task, but I know who the true heir is, and who I will be returning the lost bag of Hathnord to."

Alex paused for a moment to look at both Haymar and Halbrek. Haymar looked a little nervous but stood firmly in his place. Halbrek looked pleased with himself and was bouncing up and down on the balls of his feet.

"The true heir of Hathnord is Haymar Glynn," said Alex

in a loud, clear voice. "His claim on the bag is recognized, and I offer to return his father's lost bag to him."

"No!" cried Halbrek, his smile gone and his face growing red with anger. "We had an agreement. You were supposed to name me the rightful heir."

"*You* had an agreement," Alex corrected. "I agreed to nothing. You admitted to me that you did not know the passwords to your father's bag. Worse, you tried to bribe me into naming you as Hathnord's heir."

"I never said I didn't know the passwords," said Halbrek angrily. "And I would never think of offering a bribe for something that is rightfully mine."

"I was asked to decide who this bag belongs to, and I have," said Alex firmly. "If you know the passwords as you claim you do, tell me now."

"I . . . well . . . we agreed that . . ." Halbrek stuttered.

"You are a fool, Halbrek Glynn," said Alex coldly. "You have tried to cheat your brother out of his rights and honors, and worse, you have tried to bribe a wizard. Admit what you have done, or spend the rest of your life trying to hide it."

"There's nothing to admit," Halbrek shouted. "You've made a mistake, but I suppose there is nothing I can do about that. Serves me right for putting my faith in such a young wizard, but what's done is done."

"Halbrek, please, tell the truth," said Haymar, a look of concern on his face.

"You should talk about truth," Halbrek spat back. "It's obvious to me that you're the one who's done the bribing around here. You've cheated me out of my inheritance, just as you've tried to cheat me out of everything else."

"You cheat yourself," said Alex calmly. "You will take back what you've said about bribes, or I might take offense."

"Take what offense you like," Halbrek sneered. "You've taken my honor this day, so offending you is of little concern to me."

"Forgive him, Master Taylor," Haymar pleaded. "He doesn't know what he's saying."

"Because of the day and because Haymar asks it, I will take no action against Halbrek for his insults," said Alex, fixing Halbrek with a glare. "However, if you ever even suggest that I would accept a bribe again, I will track you down and claim my revenge on you. And I promise you, Halbrek Glynn, that my revenge will be far worse than the loss of honor you've suffered this day."

Halbrek paled. He seemed to be frozen in place. Once Alex had finished speaking, Halbrek tried to say something, but no words came out of his mouth. His face twisted with rage and fear.

"Go now," Alex commanded. "You have no place among these honorable people."

Halbrek turned and rushed out of the room. Alex and Haymar watched him go, as did everyone else in the hall. The guests looked stunned and surprised, and everything was quiet until Thorson spoke once more.

"Well, let the ceremony of returning the lost bag begin," said Thorson nervously.

With Thorson's words, the tension was broken and the

dwarfs in the hall began to whisper. Thorson moved to where Alex and Haymar were still standing, and, speaking over the whispers, he started the ceremony.

Haymar managed a weak smile and offered Alex one-half of all that the bag contained. Alex thought Haymar was being overly generous and in the end accepted only one-third of the treasure in Hathnord's bag. He would have asked for less, but he knew only too well that asking for too little would be an insult to Haymar.

With the bag returned to the rightful heir, the feast began and the noise in the room increased. Alex returned to his seat next to his friends. Thrang was upset about Halbrek's outburst and his insults to Alex, and he insisted that Halbrek be punished in some way.

"I think he will be punished enough," said Alex. "Everyone here knows what he has done, and the news will spread through Kazad-Syn quickly."

"Still, he has insulted you," said Thrang. "Something more than public shame is called for."

"He will make his own punishment," said Alex. "Everyone in the city will know what he's done, though I think he will continue to deny it. Yet, the more he denies the truth, the easier it will be for others to see what he truly is."

Thrang didn't respond but it was clear that he thought some other punishment should be given to Halbrek. The feast, however, was very good, and soon the conversation turned from punishment to more pleasant topics.

It took several days for Alex's payment to be arranged; Hathnord had been on many adventures and had collected a huge amount of treasure. Alex didn't mind waiting because Kazad-Syn was a wonderful city to be in, and he spent his days meeting people and wandering the streets. Thorson took great pleasure in introducing Alex and his companions to all of his friends, and every night there was another feast to attend. It seemed that after the return of the lost adventurer's bag most of the city knew who Alex was, and all of them greeted him wherever he went.

After a few days, Thrang began talking about leaving Kazad-Syn to continue their quest, but Alex reminded him that they still needed a place to sort and divide the treasure they had collected on the Isle of Bones. Thrang asked Thorson if he had a place large enough to put the treasure.

"We won't be in the city long enough to sort and divide it all," Thrang told Thorson. "Still, it would be good to make a start."

"You can use the lower chambers," said Thorson. "They have been empty for some time. And, if you like, you can leave the treasure here, and I'll have some of our cousins do the sorting for you."

"That would save time," said Thrang. "If the rest of the company agrees, we'll leave the treasure here to be sorted and divided."

That night at dinner Thrang asked the rest of the company what they thought about his plan, and they were all in favor of leaving the treasure with Thorson. Thrang was pleased by their willingness to trust his family with so much treasure, and he accepted Thorson's offer at once. Thorson thanked them all for their trust, rising from his seat and bowing several times to the company.

"Well, with that settled, I have some other news for you," said Thorson, his smile changing to a serious look as he returned to his chair. "I've learned a few things about the Lost Mountains, though I'm not too happy about what I've found."

"Trouble?" Thrang questioned quickly.

"Possibly," said Thorson. "You should know that there are a few dwarf villages in the mountains, mostly on the western edges. There might even be a few cities, but I can't confirm that. The dwarfs who live in the Lost Mountains seem to be prosperous, though they try to hide that fact as much as possible."

"Don't want thousands of dwarfs rushing in on them, most likely," said Thrang.

"True, that would explain their secrecy," Thorson allowed. "Still, there are rumors of trouble. Nothing solid, of course— just rumors."

"What kind of trouble?" Arconn asked, leaning back in his chair.

"Rumors about an ancient evil reborn," said Thorson as he nervously looked around at his guests. "An evil that is killing people, and the dwarfs in the villages seem unable to stop it."

"An ancient evil?" Alex prompted, seeing Thorson's hesitation.

"The stories say there are packs of wolflike creatures in the area," said Thorson, glancing quickly at Thrang. "Vicious creatures that show no fear."

"Wolflike creatures," Thrang repeated, stroking his beard. "Are you saying what I think you're saying?"

"The rumors—and mind you, these are just rumors— sound like . . . Well, they sound like the hellerash," said Thorson, his eyes dropping to his plate.

Alex quickly glanced around the table at his friends, but it was obvious that none of them had the slightest idea what a hellerash was either. Whatever they were, both Thorson and Thrang were afraid of them.

"It can't be," said Thrang, a stunned expression on his face. "There hasn't been a hellerash seen in almost a thousand years."

"Well, they are only rumors," said Thorson hopefully. "I've had a hard time getting any information about the Lost Mountains, and it's possible this rumor was started by the dwarfs of the area to keep others away."

"Yes, that must be what it is," said Thrang, looking only slightly happier.

"What in the world is a hellerash?" Nellus asked, voicing the question they all wanted answered.

"The hellerash were vicious creatures, like giant wolves," said Thrang slowly. "They killed just for the sake of killing, and they almost always traveled in packs."

"The dwarfs used to hunt them down and kill them," Thorson added. "They were dangerous and clever creatures, so never fewer than thirty dwarfs would go in a hunting party."

"But the last hellerash was killed almost a thousand years ago," said Thrang, more to himself than the others.

"Then perhaps this is just a rumor," said Barnabus.

"It must be," said Thrang, shaking off the fearful look that had been on his face. "These rumors must be false, but we will stay alert along the road, just in case."

"A wise plan, considering what happened the last time we heard rumors of trouble," Arconn said.

CHAPTER SIXTEEN

THE HELLERASH

———◆———

The days before Alex and his friends left the city were spent depositing the treasure from the Isle of Bones in the lower chambers of Thorson's home and sorting as much of it as they could. Thorson was amazed by the amount of treasure they had, and he worried that the lower chambers would not be large enough to hold it all.

"Well, brother, I can see you're far richer than you've let any of us know," said Thorson, smiling at Thrang.

"I've had a great deal of luck," said Thrang. "Been on some good adventures with good people, and Master Taylor here has added a great deal to my wealth."

"Never hurts to have a wizard along on an adventure." Thorson laughed. "That's what our grandfather always said, and I can see he was right."

"It may not hurt to have a wizard, but it's better to go with good people," said Alex. "I'd remind Thrang on our first adventure together that I was not a wizard, and yet we managed to collect a fair amount of treasure on that trip."

"Perhaps not a wizard in name," said Thrang with a sly

smile. "Still, you're correct in saying that it's better to go with good people."

With their treasure safely stored, Thrang was ready for the company to move on. Thorson seemed a little worried about the time of year, reminding Thrang that winter was coming.

"We should have a month or so of fair weather before winter arrives," said Thrang thoughtfully. "Plus we'll be moving south, so winter won't catch up to us too quickly."

"And with luck, you'll reach a village in the Lost Mountains before snow comes," Thorson added. "Still, I wouldn't mind having you all spend the winter here."

"But you might mind before spring came again." Thrang laughed. "No, we'll move on in the morning, and return quickly after we find success."

That night's feast was a grand one, even compared to all the feasts they'd already been to. Alex suspected Thorson had been preparing it for several days, and the preparation showed. Most of Thrang's family was there, along with several other important dwarfs from the city. All of them wished the company good luck and a quick return to Kazad-Syn, once they'd completed their quest. The party went late, and would have gone on all night if Thrang had not put an end to it.

"We've a long road ahead of us still, and if we sit here much longer we won't be away before midday," Thrang said. "I'll thank you all for my companions and myself, and wish you each a pleasant good night."

It still took some time for Alex and his companions to make their way back to their rooms. Alex was sad to be leaving Kazad-Syn, but at the same time, he was happy to be moving on. They still had a long way to go on their adventure, and unless he was mistaken, there would be time for dinner parties when they returned from their journey.

Alex was preparing to climb into his bed when a small popping noise and a loud ding announced the arrival of a geeb. He was only slightly surprised to find that the geeb had a message from Whalen; he'd been expecting and hoping for one for quite some time.

> *Dear Alex,*
>
> *I apologize for the delay in getting back to you, but I've been busy with several other matters. I would point out that you haven't been sending nearly as many messages as you should, but as I haven't been sending any at all, let's start over and this time I promise to keep up with you.*
>
> *Looking back over your messages, I see you've met Bane. He's an interesting fellow with an even more interesting story. I'm happy to hear that the two of you have become friends; I'd hate to have to clean up the mess if the two of you were enemies. I'd like to talk about Bane and his suspicions of a conspiracy in the known lands the next time we meet.*
>
> *Nice work with the Nagas. I've run into a few of them in my travels and I know how quickly they can move and how deadly they are. It's lucky you have some good people around you.*
>
> *Now, on to more important things. The dragon on the Isle of Bones is of great interest, both to myself, and*

the council. It is a pity that you had to hide the island from everyone, though I suppose the dragon asked for that, and I can't say that I blame him. And you're a dragon lord now, which is something very special. There hasn't been a true dragon lord for at least two thousand years, and even I don't know all the details of the title. The council is hoping you will come to our next meeting. The date and location aren't set yet because we don't know when everyone will be available to attend.

Keep me posted on what's happening, and I'll try harder to write to you on a regular basis. I'm sorry to say I don't know why you are having reckless feelings. Perhaps it is your age. As long as you are able to control the urge to be reckless, I wouldn't worry. I'll remind you again, though, as I've done so often in the past, don't let your anger get the best of you. Never act out of rage alone as something really terrible might happen. Enough said.

Yours in fellowship,

Whalen

P.S. If you want to know more about your family, I would suggest you talk to Mr. Clutter. He should have the records on your father, and he might know something of your mother as well.

Alex read the letter twice then smiled and put it in his bag. It seemed like it had been a long time since he'd heard from Whalen. He knew he hadn't been sending as many messages as he should have, and he promised himself that he would make time to send at least one message every two or three weeks from now on.

Alex was surprised by the council of wizards' invitation for him to attend their next meeting. The only wizard Alex knew was Whalen, and while he did want to meet others, he was a little nervous about meeting the entire council at one time. He was still young, and even though he'd already done some impressive things, he wasn't sure the other wizards would take him seriously. After all, they were all much older than he was and had a great deal more experience.

In the end, Alex decided not to worry about meeting the council of wizards. He would have time to worry if and when the meeting came. He moved on to Whalen's comments about his reckless feelings. Alex knew where those feelings were coming from now, even if he wasn't completely comfortable with the answer. He would have to tell Whalen what Salinor had said, but maybe he would wait until he could talk about it with Whalen face-to-face. With that final thought, Alex dropped into his comfortable bed and quickly fell asleep.

The next morning was gray and windy, and it looked almost certain to rain before the day was over. Thrang's mood darkened with the change in weather, but he remained determined to get back on the road.

"A gloomy day to part on," Thorson said as he stood beside Thrang. "I wish you all a safe journey, and promise a great welcome when you return."

"You've been most generous to us," said Thrang, bowing to his brother. "We will not forget your kindness."

"Oh, stop it," said Thorson. "I know very well that your

adventurer's code demands that you say such things, but it means little here. You are family, and you and your friends will always be welcome."

"You are most kind, my brother," said Thrang. "I hope we will return soon to take advantage of your kindness."

Thorson laughed, then he and Thrang embraced. Alex and the others bowed and thanked Thorson as they moved toward their horses. Thorson waved off their thanks, though he looked pleased just the same. They all mounted their horses—except for Thrain.

"Thrain, are you coming with us?" Thrang questioned loudly.

"Yes, I'm coming," said Thrain, hurrying to climb onto his own horse.

"Where did you run off to?" Thrang questioned, a knowing smile on his face.

"I wanted to say good-bye to Dain," said Thrain in an apologetic tone. "I didn't get a chance to last night, and I thought it would be rude not to."

"And Fivra?" Thrang questioned.

"Well, yes, Fivra was there as well," said Thrain, his face turning bright red.

"Plotting with my own family, I see," said Thrang with a laugh. "So has Fivra agreed to wait for your return before going to Vargland?"

"Oh, well," Thrain stammered, clearly surprised that Thrang had guessed the truth. "Yes, he said he would wait until I could go with him."

"That may be a long time," Thorson said. "After all, you have this adventure to finish before you can go anywhere."

"Yes, well, I did say I'd try to come back," said Thrain. "Or I thought maybe Fivra could come to Benorg, once our adventure is done."

"At least Thrain was able to talk Fivra into waiting," Arconn pointed out. "I don't think any of us could have done that."

"I suppose that's true," said Thrang with a laugh. "But I think I would keep a closer eye on our young friend just the same."

"Until you return, my friends," said Thorson. "And perhaps Fivra will indeed be able to go to Benorg when you return."

"Farewell, my brother," Thrang said. "Keep an eye on the youngsters—they seem to be plotting together."

Thorson laughed and waved to them all as Thrang led the company through the gates, away from Thorson's house and into the city.

It appeared, however, that the people of the city were unwilling to let them leave without wishing them good luck once again. The streets of Kazad-Syn were crowded, and all along the way dwarfs were cheering them on and wishing them a safe journey.

"You are well thought of by the people of this city," Arconn said as he rode beside Thrang. "They honor you greatly by this display."

"Their wishes are for all of us," said Thrang, smiling and waving to some friends as he spoke.

"Yet I doubt we would receive such a send-off if you were not our leader," said Kat.

Soon they left the cheering crowds behind, and the city became a small green spot on the road behind them. Thrang's good spirits did not falter, however, even when a soft rain began falling after their midday meal.

"Winter moves south quickly," said Barnabus. "I am glad we are going south and not north."

"This rain is hardly winter," Thrang said with a laugh. "Though I confess I also am glad to be moving south. Winter is hard in the north, and travel is almost impossible."

"How long will it take us to reach the Lost Mountains?" Alex questioned.

"Two, maybe three weeks," said Thrang. "They are south and a little east of us, but the people Thorson spoke to in Kazad-Syn said the road is good. If we stay on the main road we shouldn't have any trouble."

"That's what we thought when we left Benorg," said Nellus with a grin.

"And there is the rumor of the hellerash," Thrain added.

"That's just a rumor," said Thrang, looking a little uneasy. "I doubt we will see anything."

"Some creatures grow strong when rumors remain rumors," said Kat, her voice so low that only Alex heard her.

As they made camp for the night, the rain stopped and the clouds slowly broke apart and drifted away. Alex glanced up at the thousands of stars in the sky, letting his mind wander freely. It was a pleasant evening, yet something in Alex's mind made him nervous. He glanced around the campsite, wondering if something was watching them, but he could see nothing.

"You felt something," Kat said, moving up beside him; it was not a question.

"A nervous feeling, nothing more," said Alex.

"I felt it too," said Kat, a look of concentration on her face. "There is nothing there now, only the empty land."

"Perhaps that is why I'm nervous," said Alex, laughing softly.

"Too many dangers," said Kat.

"What do you mean?"

"You've faced too many dangers for one so young. Now you feel nervous when there are no dangers to face."

"Perhaps," Alex agreed. "Though I'm not in any rush to look for danger."

"Danger seems to find you," Kat answered with a smile. "I find that strange, but I am at a loss to explain it."

"Don't be troubled by it," said Alex, turning back to the campfire.

Kat remained at the edge of the camp for a few minutes and then returned to the campfire as well.

The days passed and the weather seemed to change with each new day. Some days were warm and dry, others wet, and still others windy. Alex and his friends were not troubled by the weather, but they were starting to feel strangely nervous as they moved south. Nellus and Barnabus both tried to lighten the mood with jokes and songs, but were not always successful. Alex felt watchful, and he noticed that both Kat and Arconn would often stand and stare into the darkness around their camp at night.

On the eighth day away from Kazad-Syn, they camped beside a small stream, eating in silence as rain poured down on them. The campfire popped and sizzled in the rain, but because Alex had conjured it up with magic, it would not go out.

"Winter is moving south fast," Thrang said, looking at the dark sky. "But we should still reach shelter in the Lost Mountains before the weather gets too bad."

They finished their meals and hurried off to their dry tents. Alex let the conjured fire burn, though he had some misgivings about such a bright light on such a dark night. Arconn remained at the fire during Alex's watch, and Alex had the feeling that the elf was listening for something, something that he could not hear over the noise of the falling rain.

The next morning, the rain had stopped, but the uneasy feelings had grown stronger. They were darker than the uneasy feelings they had experienced on the Isle of Bones. As they were eating their breakfast, Arconn wandered down to the stream, and then quickly returned with a troubled look on his face.

"What is it?" Kat questioned, setting aside her plate.

Alex jumped to his feet, looking around the campsite as if expecting a sudden attack.

"Just tracks in the mud," said Arconn, trying to sound calm.

"Tracks?" Thrang questioned. "What kind of tracks?"

"They are difficult to read," said Arconn. "I have never

seen anything like them before, though they look something like wolf tracks."

"Wolf tracks?" Thrang questioned. "There aren't any wolves this far south in Thraxon."

"Show me the tracks," said Nellus as he got to his feet. "I've tracked many creatures in the past, and may be able to make some sense of them."

Arconn led Nellus and the rest of the company back to the stream and pointed out the large tracks. They were all on the far bank, though none of them had come within five feet of the water.

"They do look a little like a wolf's tracks, but they are too large," Nellus said.

"That's what I thought," said Arconn, looking quickly at Thrang and then back to the tracks.

"Hellerash," Thrang whispered. "Those are hellerash tracks."

"What?" Barnabus asked, turning to look at Thrang.

"I thought the hellerash were vicious," said Thrain softly. "If they're as vicious as the stories say—and I heard a lot of stories in Kazad-Syn—then why didn't it cross the stream and attack our camp?"

"Who can say?" answered Thrang, looking a little pale. "Perhaps this is the boundary to their territory, or perhaps they were afraid of the light from Alex's conjured fire."

"Or perhaps it was a single hellerash, and it has gone to get others," Kat said darkly.

"Perhaps," Thrang allowed. "Whatever the reason, we

should all remain extra alert from now on. We should also have a double watch at night, just in case."

"A wise precaution," said Arconn. "And I think we should keep the horses closer to our tents as well."

"Yes, that is a good idea," Thrang agreed quickly, leading the company back toward the camp.

The journey that day was slow, and everyone kept glancing around them as they traveled, looking for any sign of movement. They saw nothing that day, and by the time they made camp for the night, Alex's troubled feelings were beginning to subside. Thrang, however, seemed more nervous than ever, and he asked Alex to conjure up a fire that would burn brightly all night.

When they started off again the next morning, most of their fears had slipped away. They had heard nothing during the night, and there were no signs of tracks anywhere near their camp. Arconn and Alex had both walked a wide circle around the camp just to make sure. Thrang seemed relieved, but he still made sure that Arconn and Kat had their bows ready and that Thrain had his crossbow loaded.

"Better safe than sorry," said Thrang with a weak smile as they started off.

Alex thought it unlikely that they would see anything along the road, but he kept his staff ready. They continued riding south, and the afternoon sun and the warm, damp air made Alex feel slightly sleepy. He was jolted awake by the sound of Arconn's and Kat's bowstrings snapping at the same moment, followed quickly by the high-pitched spring of Thrain's crossbow. Neither of those sounds shook him as much as the terrible cry that followed. It was an almost-human cry of agony and despair, a cry that forced his eyes toward the creature that made it.

Thirty yards to the right of the road, a huge, black, wolf-like creature crouched with arrows sticking out of its shiny black hide. Alex could see the bones of the creature's ribcage. It bit madly at the shaft of Arconn's arrow. Kat's arrow had hit the creature higher in the neck, but it couldn't get its head around to bite at that one. Then it turned and ran, darting between some large rocks, the shaft of Arconn's arrow snapping off as it ran.

The hellerash was fast, vanishing from view before Arconn could fit a second arrow to his bow.

"That shot should have killed it," Arconn said, turning his horse toward the hellerash's trail. "If not mine, then Kat's for sure."

"I'm sure my bolt hit it as well," said Thrain, following quickly.

"I saw no wound from the bolt," said Thrang gruffly.

"It seemed pained, but uninjured from the arrows," Nellus added.

Arconn dismounted and bent to pick up the broken shaft of his arrow. Thrain moved about the rocks, looking for the bolt he had let fly. As Arconn walked back toward the group he looked troubled, almost afraid.

"No blood," Arconn said, holding the broken arrow out for Thrang. "There is no blood on the shaft."

"Well, it broke away from the wound," said Thrang, glancing at the arrow.

"There is no blood on the rocks or grass either," Arconn added.

"And there's no blood on my bolt," Thrain said, coming up beside Arconn and holding out the bolt he'd recovered.

"You may have missed it completely," said Thrang in a dismissive tone.

"I didn't miss," Thrain insisted defiantly.

"Thrain is correct," Arconn broke in. "I saw the bolt pass through what should have been the creature's stomach. I would not have expected it to pass clear through, but it seems to have done so."

"What are you saying?" Thrang questioned, his pale face growing hard.

"Isn't it clear?" said Kat, causing all of them to jump.

"No, it's not clear at all," said Thrang, looking as if he didn't want to hear anything Kat had to say.

"That creature was not a true hellerash," Kat said flatly. "It has no blood and no life in it."

"Impossible," said Thrang weakly.

"But that can mean only one thing," said Arconn, glancing at his arrow and then turning to look at Alex.

"Necromancer," said Alex, a chill running down his back as he said the word.

"No, it can't . . ." Thrang began and trailed off.

"It is the only explanation," said Alex. "It is the only thing that could call a long-dead hellerash back to life, or at least to a half-life."

Alex felt his friends staring at him, but their confused

and frightened looks did not trouble him as much as the next words he had to say.

"I must face him," said Alex, looking down at his saddle.

"No, it is too dangerous," Kat broke in.

"We will find another path to the south," Thrang said quickly.

"You do not understand," said Alex, holding up his hand. "As a true wizard, I must seek out this evil and try to destroy it."

"I forbid it," said Thrang forcefully. "You are part of this company, and I am the leader. You will not seek out this danger that has nothing to do with our quest."

"I know you speak from friendship, Thrang, but I have no choice," said Alex. "My vow as a wizard is more binding than our agreement, and if I must, I will break the adventurers' bargain and go on alone."

"Not alone," said Arconn quickly.

"Thank you, my friend, but you cannot break the bargain without losing honor," said Alex. "I would not allow you to leave the company in any event, as they will need you more than ever, once I leave."

"Arconn is right," said Thrang forcefully. "If you must seek out this evil, then you will not do it alone. Even if our adventure fails completely, I will not leave you to face this evil by yourself."

"Then we continue south," said Alex, grateful for Thrang's words.

"We continue south," Thrang repeated. "And may evil fear our approach."

The rest of the company cheered Thrang's words, and Alex couldn't help but feel grateful to his friends. He was worried, however, because he knew, perhaps better than any of them, the danger that a necromancer presented. He also knew that, in the end, he would have to face the necromancer alone. That meeting would be incredibly dangerous, not just for him, but for all of Thraxon as well.

They continued south along the road, moving as quickly as they could and looking for a safe place to make their camp. As the sun dropped in the west, Thrang called them to a halt and moved them a short distance off the main road. A series of large boulders formed a horseshoe shape, the center of which provided the perfect campsite.

"A good spot," Nellus observed. "The creatures can come at us from only one direction."

"They might jump down from the rocks behind us," said Thrain in a worried tone.

"And they might bar our path from leaving," Thrang added nervously. "Still, it seems the best place we'll find today, so we might as well make camp."

There was little talk and no joking or stories around the campfire that night. They were all tense, and even the slightest sound from outside their camp was enough to draw all of their eyes. When Thrang and the others went to their tents, leaving Alex and Arconn on watch, Alex took his writing things out of his magic bag. He needed to let Whalen know about this latest development.

"You are sending word to Master Vankin?" Arconn said.

"Yes," said Alex, looking up at his friend.

"He knows a great deal, and may be able to advise you on dealing with this evil," said Arconn, his eyes fixed on the campfire. "Though I confess, I am concerned about you meeting a necromancer."

"So am I, but there is nothing that can be done about it," Alex answered, folding the letter he'd been working on. "I am here, so I must face this test."

"And if you fail?" Arconn questioned, a pained look on his face.

"I will not allow myself to be used by this evil," Alex said forcefully, guessing at Arconn's greatest fear. "I will summon the dragon to destroy me before I become the puppet of a necromancer."

"I hope it will not come to that," Arconn replied softly, glancing at Alex.

"So do I," said Alex with a weak smile. "So do I."

There was no sign of the hellerash that night, and they saw no tracks or signs of the creature for the next few days. Alex could tell that the others were beginning to hope they had left the hellerash behind them. Thrang even voiced the hope that there was no necromancer and that the company could continue on their quest without any trouble.

Alex, however, knew there was a necromancer. Ever since he'd seen the hellerash, he had felt the presence of evil. Worse, Alex knew knew the necromancer was aware of him as well.

"We should reach the Lost Mountains in a day or two," Thrang said as they were breaking camp one morning. "Then perhaps we can get some news of Albrek and his people."

"I doubt it will be that easy," Kat commented in a low tone.

"Oh, the dwarfs of the Lost Mountains should be friendly enough," Thrang went on, trying to avoid the point Kat was trying to make.

The others did not comment, because they were all thinking of the hellerash, even though none of them would say so.

"You sense the presence of the necromancer," Alex said quietly to Kat as they started off.

"Yes," said Kat, looking pale and tired. "I fear that I will be overcome if you fail."

"Then I must not fail," said Alex, forcing a smile.

The morning was sunny and warm, but by midday dark clouds rolled across the sky and the smell of rain filled the air. Thrang urged them forward, hoping to find a dwarf city or village for them to spend the night in. As darkness began to grow around them, Alex noticed movement out of the corner of his eye. For a moment he wasn't sure he'd seen anything at all, but he knew that he had.

"Yes," Arconn said, noticing Alex's look. "I see them too."

"What's that?" Thrang questioned, taking his attention off the road ahead.

"Several of the hellerash," said Arconn. "They have been circling us for the last hour."

"As long as they keep their distance," Nellus said, looking over his shoulder.

"They won't attack until it's dark," said Kat. "They will want as much cover as possible before coming at us."

"Then we should hurry," said Thrang in a worried tone.

"We may arrive at a village soon, and any dwarfs we find will be sure to help us against these creatures."

Alex had his doubts. If they had been close to a dwarf city or village, the hellerash would not be circling them now. Even as he considered their chances against the evil creatures, he saw that the hellerash were getting closer to them.

"There," said Arconn, pointing to a large hill to the left of the road. "If we can reach the top, we can make our defense there."

"Yes," Thrang agreed quickly. "It will be better than meeting them in the open. Quickly now—to the hilltop."

Thrang spurred his horse forward and the others followed him. At first the horses seemed reluctant to run toward the hill, but when a sudden piercing howl rose from behind them, the horses all shuddered and dashed forward. Alex knew that the howl had been a signal, a call to the attack, and he could feel Shahree trembling beneath him.

"Easy, girl," Alex said softly to his horse. "We have faced greater dangers before."

Shahree seemed to calm down, but only slightly as she raced forward. Alex could sense her desperation to reach the safety of the hilltop before the hellerash could attack.

The landscape became a blur and the company was spreading out. Kat's horse was not as swift as the others, and she was falling behind, and fast. Alex slowed Shahree, unwilling to leave Kat, but the others rushed on. It looked as if they had completely lost control of their horses and were struggling just to hold on.

It happened suddenly, but to Alex it seemed that everything

was moving in slow motion. A scream and a horse's terrified whinny came from behind him, and without thinking, he reined in Shahree, turning her back the way he had come.

Shahree stamped her hooves impatiently, but he held her on the spot for a moment, and then spurred her forward, back across the ground they had just crossed.

Kat struggled to get to her feet; her horse lay on the ground ten feet behind her. Alex saw the black shapes of several hellerash tearing at the fallen horse, and a flame of rage began to burn deep inside him.

As quickly as Shahree could run, he charged forward, whispering magical words as he went. The end of his staff flared in the darkness, and a sudden ball of flame shot toward the dark shadows in front of him. A hellerash burst into flame, and several others jumped away. He wanted to press his attack on the evil creatures, but Kat was on foot, dazed from her fall, and it was up to him to save her.

"Leave me," Kat yelled as Alex rode up to her. "There is no time, and your horse cannot carry us both."

"Come," Alex commanded, putting out his free hand and catching Kat's arm. With a single movement, he swung her up behind him, and then let loose the reins, giving Shahree the freedom she demanded. "Run now, my friend! Run like the wind."

Shahree leaped forward. Back into the darkness she raced, back toward the hill that stood so close and yet so far away. Alex could feel Kat clutching at him, trying desperately to hold on. He could feel Shahree struggling for more speed, but the added weight on her back was slowing her down. Desperate to give them more time, Alex raised his staff over his head, its burning light driving back the darkness, and, he hoped, the hellerash as well.

As they reached the bottom of the hill, Shahree stumbled and Alex felt himself lifting off the saddle. Kat tried to grab hold of him, but it was no good. Together Alex and Kat flew helplessly through the air, and as Alex's staff went spinning out of his hand, its light went out.

Fighting to get to his feet and drag Kat up with him, Alex blurted out the summoning spell to call his staff back to his hand. He had barely managed to relight his staff when his eyes met the evil, yellow-green eyes of the advancing hellerash. His voice seemed to leave him, and all he could do was stare. The hellerash was moving fast, charging down on him before he could do anything to defend himself. For a moment Alex thought his life was over, but then a silver-gray shadow blocked the hellerash from his view.

"No!" Alex screamed, realizing what had happened.

There was the sickening sound of tearing flesh, followed by the sound of Shahree's body falling to the ground. The evil eyes of the hellerash returned. The light from Alex's staff showed the bloody jaws of the hellerash opened wide as if it were laughing at him. Anger and sorrow rushed through Alex, blinding him to reason and thought. The hellerash in front of him let loose its chilling howl, calling its companions to the feast, and in that moment Alex's rage overcame everything else.

The hellerash standing next to Shahree burst into flame, dissolving almost instantly into ash. Alex brought his staff down forcefully, striking the ground and finishing the magic words at the same moment. For a few seconds, the darkness vanished as a wall of bright, blue-white flame grew up around Alex. The burning wall stood motionless for less than a second, and then rushed outward in all directions.

Kat cried out in fear, but Alex took no notice. As darkness reclaimed the night, Alex sank down to the ground, tears pouring down his face as he reached out to touch the neck of his lost friend.

After some time, Alex became aware of the sounds around him. He could hear Kat whimpering behind him, and he could hear the rest of the company moving carefully down the hill toward them. He didn't want to explain what he'd done or why; he just wanted to be left alone.

"Alex," Arconn's concerned voice said softly. "Alex, are you all right?"

"I'm fine," answered Alex, not turning to look at his friend. "Take care of Kat and make camp. There is no danger now. I'll be along in a little while."

Arconn did not reply, but Alex could hear him helping Kat to her feet and moving away. He was grateful to Arconn for leaving him alone and not insisting on answers or reasons. But sorrow filled his mind and he had no place for other thoughts.

Alex didn't know how long he sat there with Shahree's dead body. The spell he had used had taken a great deal of power out of him, and when he finally tried to get to his feet, his legs wobbled beneath him. Leaning on his staff, Alex looked down at Shahree. He wiped his face on his sleeve and slowly forced himself to cast another spell.

The silver-gray horse faded into the ground like mist, and a large silver-gray stone rose out of the earth where she had been. Three words written in golden letters appeared on the monument. Resting on his staff for another moment, Alex managed a weak smile, then turned away.

Alex found the others easily, though he was not sure he wanted to answer questions even now. His sorrow had lessened, but the death of his horse was still clear in his mind, and the fact that she had willingly sacrificed herself to save him made her death harder to bear.

Thrang and the others said nothing as Alex sat down beside the fire. He could feel them looking at him nervously. He was sure Kat had told them what had happened and what she had seen, but that would not explain everything. Alex had done something out of pure anger, and now he wondered if he had been right to do it.

"Something to eat?" said Barnabus, holding out a bowl of stew for Alex.

Alex accepted the bowl, but he did not eat. For several minutes he just looked at the stew, and then he spoke. "I destroyed them. All of them. Forever."

"The wall of flame?" Arconn asked.

"Yes," said Alex. "It has moved across all of Thraxon and destroyed every hellerash that ever has been."

"All of Thraxon?" Thrang questioned nervously.

"Yes," said Alex, setting his bowl down and putting his head in his hands. "Nowhere, in all of this land, does even a bone of a hellerash remain."

"A powerful spell," Kat said softly.

"Perhaps too powerful," said Alex.

"How so?" Thrang asked. "Surely you don't feel sorry for destroying those evil creatures."

"No, I don't feel sorry for that," said Alex, looking up. "But now I fear the necromancer will try to hide. He may no longer wish to face me. If that is the case, it may take me years to track him down."

"Will you . . ." Thrang began but did not finish.

"I will finish this quest regardless of what the necromancer chooses to do," said Alex, answering Thrang's unasked question. "If he remains, I will face him. If he flees, I will pursue him. But after this adventure is over."

The others remained silent and Alex picked up his bowl. He didn't feel hungry, but he forced himself to eat anyway. He knew that he would need his strength, and he knew that he had to write to Whalen immediately.

CHAPTER SEVENTEEN

THE CURSED CITY

———✦———

No one slept that night. When dawn finally came, they quietly collected their gear and prepared to resume their journey.

"Where are your horses?" Alex questioned, noticing for the first time that none of his companions' horses were anywhere near the campsite.

"They broke away when we were trying to get up the hill," Thrang answered. "Arconn's carried him to the hilltop, but the rest ran."

"And even mine ran when the hellerash closed in on us," Arconn added.

"How close did they get to you?" Alex asked.

"Too close," said Nellus with a soft laugh.

"We were standing back-to-back on the hilltop," said Thrang. "The hellerash were closing in slowly, looking for a weak spot, I guess."

"I'm sure they were about to charge us when the wall of flame appeared," said Barnabus. "If your spell had been a few seconds later, I doubt we would have survived."

"I shouldn't have left the group," said Alex bitterly.

"No harm was done," said Thrang. "And you saved Kat from those foul creatures."

Alex could tell that Thrang and the others wanted to hear about how he had rescued Kat and destroyed the hellerash. He suspected Kat had told them what had happened while he had remained with his fallen friend, but he knew they still had questions. He was grateful that none of them asked about it, and the conversation trailed off quickly.

They moved down the hill toward the spot where Shahree had fallen, and a fresh wave of sorrow filled Alex. He noticed Kat glance at him as if she wanted to say something, but she quickly turned away.

"A fine monument," said Thrang when they reached the spot Alex had hoped to avoid. "And never a truer statement has been carved."

"'A True Friend,'" Arconn read from the stone. "Yes, I would say that is fitting."

Kat made a strangled, sobbing sound and hid her face. Alex thought for a moment that he'd seen tears in her eyes, but he couldn't be sure. Turning away from the monument, he wished the hollow feeling inside him would go away. The pale morning light shined on the open land in front of them, but in several places Alex could see where the stones and grasses had been scorched black.

"It appears that there were quite a few of them," Arconn said, moving up beside Alex. "More than I would have guessed."

"And now there are none," said Alex, starting off across the open ground without looking back.

Arconn's comment had not angered him, but Alex wasn't ready to think about what had happened. He wanted to forget about it for a time, and move ahead with the business at hand. But he knew that he would not forget, and perhaps that made it harder for him to turn away from the monument and leave his fallen friend behind.

His companions hurried after him, not saying anything more about the monument he'd created or the spell he'd cast. They fell into line behind Thrang and Arconn. Alex noticed that Kat kept her head turned away from him. At first he didn't know why, but then he realized that she blamed herself for Shahree's death. She felt that Shahree's death was her fault, and she feared that he would blame her for the loss of his friend.

Alex's own sorrow melted away like ice, and he suddenly found himself concerned about Kat's worries. Shahree's death had not been Kat's fault, and Alex could not blame her even if he'd wanted to. She had told him to leave her behind. She had warned him that her weight would be too much for Shahree to carry.

For one long, terrible moment, the images of Shahree's death rose once more before his eyes. If Alex had been a little quicker or if he hadn't frozen when the hellerash had charged him, then Shahree would not have had to sacrifice herself to save him.

But Alex knew that he was not to blame either. The only person to blame was the necromancer who had called the hellerash back from the dead. It was the necromancer who had killed his friend, and it was the necromancer who would pay for that death.

Alex wanted to say something to Kat, something to ease her troubled thoughts, but her sorrow seemed almost as deep as his own, and nothing he could think to say sounded right in his mind.

"I don't blame you," Alex finally said softly.

"I know," answered Kat, looking at him for the first time since the night before. "But I blame myself."

"Don't," said Alex forcefully. "There is only one person responsible for what has happened, and he will answer for it, to me."

"A dangerous attitude," said Kat in a lowered voice.

"No, not really," said Alex, forcing a weak smile. "I do not wish to take his place or steal his power. I will simply call him to account for what he's done, as I must."

"And if he is the stronger?" Kat questioned. "Necromancers are said to have a great deal of magical power."

"Then he will go on," said Alex with a sigh. "Though I think my dragon friend might put an end to him, if I were forced to summon him."

"You are set in your course, then," Kat said flatly. "You will summon the dragon to destroy you before you let yourself be used by the necromancer."

"Better to die once in flame than live forever in the half-life of the necromancer," said Alex. The words were not his own, and he was a little shaken by what he heard himself say.

Kat gave him a puzzled look for several seconds before she turned away.

As the day wore on, they began to look for any sign of a dwarf city or possibly even a party of dwarfs on the road.

The road, however, remained empty, and for all they could tell there were no cities anywhere nearby.

"Can you sense anything, Kat?" Thrang asked as the afternoon was wearing away. "Anything at all?"

"Sadness," Kat answered slowly. "There is great sorrow near, but I cannot see why."

"Perhaps because of the hellerash," Arconn suggested, gazing across the land in front of them. "I'm sure any dwarfs in this area would have suffered from those creatures."

"Yes, that would make sense," said Thrang, looking at Kat, his expression clearly hoping for more information.

"To the east of the road," said Kat, a pained look on her face. "East and south of us, at the base of the mountain—there is a city."

"Are you certain?" Nellus questioned, looking from Kat to the southeast and back. "I see no sign that would indicate a city."

"And you wouldn't," said Thrang. "The dwarfs of the Lost Mountains are careful to hide themselves. We could walk right past a city and never see it if the dwarfs living there didn't want us to."

"I doubt that," said Alex.

"Well, perhaps not right past," Thrang admitted.

"In Vargland, many of the smaller cities are hard to find, even if you know what to look for," said Thrain.

"The same is true here," Thrang added. "But we have several things in our favor. We have a seer who can lead us, a wizard who can sense things others cannot, and I know the ways that dwarfs hide their cities here in Thraxon."

"Then we should be able to find this city quickly," said Barnabus. "And I hope they have horses for sale, because—"

Barnabus stopped quickly. For a moment they were all silent, and then Barnabus cleared his throat.

"Forgive me, Alex. I did not think."

"You have done no harm," said Alex, trying hard to smile. "And I really don't want to walk all the way across Thraxon."

As darkness gathered around them, the road began to bend toward the mountains, but when it became clear that they would not reach the city that night, Thrang reluctantly ordered them to make camp. The memory of the hellerash attack was still sharp in all of their minds, and only Alex was certain that there was nothing to fear.

As Barnabus prepared their meal, Alex found a comfortable spot and sat down. He knew he should write to Whalen—he needed his friend's advice—but he didn't really feel like writing down everything that had happened. Just then, Barnabus called them all to eat, and Alex was grateful that he could postpone writing a difficult letter, at least for a little while longer.

"We should reach the mountains tomorrow," Arconn said as they ate.

"And what then?" Nellus asked.

"What do you mean?" said Thrang, looking around at them all. "We go on with the adventure, of course."

"Yes, of course," said Nellus quickly, glancing at Alex.

"You are thinking perhaps I will leave the company to chase the necromancer," said Alex, looking at his food. "I have already said that if the necromancer should flee, I will complete this adventure."

"And if he does not flee?" Arconn questioned.

"Then I will face him sooner rather than later," said Alex.

"I think," Thrang began, not looking at Alex, "well, I think we are all a little worried about what might happen . . ."

"If the evil is stronger," Alex finished for him.

"It is a possibility," Thrang said softly.

"Yes, it is," agreed Alex. "I have told Kat and Arconn, and now I will tell you all, I will not be a tool of the necromancer. If he has the power to overcome me, I will be less than I am now. If it comes to that, I will use the last of my will and power to summon the dragon to destroy me. I will not become a slave to evil."

"Let us hope it does not come to that," said Thrang, trying for a hopeful tone.

Alex knew his friends were more concerned about him and his ability to face evil than they were concerned about the rest of the adventure, and he was grateful for their care. Of course, they all knew about the time he'd faced the dragon Slathbog, but necromancers were not dragons, and Alex knew better than any of his friends that their power was something to fear.

As the others rolled themselves into their blankets, Alex remained by the fire with Arconn in companionable silence. Arconn seemed to be deep in his own thoughts, so Alex took out his writing things.

For a long time the page remained blank because he could not find the words to explain things to Whalen. He reviewed the events again and again in his mind, finally forcing himself to put it all on paper.

In the end, the letter was long, but Alex had somehow

managed to express all of his doubts and fears, as well as his sorrow. It seemed that pouring his sadness into the letter had removed some of the weight from his mind and heart. He was glad that he had forced himself to write everything he had been feeling.

He summoned a geeb to take his message to Whalen and put away his writing things. To his surprise, the entire night had almost slipped away.

"You should get some rest," Arconn said as the geeb vanished with a small pop.

"I have no need of sleep," said Alex. "The others will need it more than I. Let them enjoy what rest they can."

Arconn nodded, returning his attention to the darkness around their camp.

When the eastern sky showed signs of the coming morning, Arconn woke the others.

"You should have woken us in turn for the watch," said Thrang as he walked toward the campfire. "Though I suppose you know what you're doing."

"Why would you suppose that?" Alex asked with a half smile. He was surprised to realize that he felt much better than he had the day before.

Thrang answered with a grunting laugh as he brushed frost off a log and sat down for breakfast.

They marched all that morning, and as midday approached, Thrang suddenly shouted in excitement and rushed toward a pile of fallen stones. The rest of them hurried to follow, uncertain about the reason for Thrang's shout.

"A boundary marker," said Thrang, kneeling beside the

fallen stones. "It has been pushed over, and some of the inscription has been chiseled away."

"And the part that remains? What does it say?" Nellus asked as he looked at the surrounding countryside.

"The city of Neplee lies ahead," said Thrang, tilting his head to one side as he read the fallen marker. "The instructions for reaching the city and requesting entry have been removed, but not too long ago, I would guess."

"Who would destroy the marker?" Thrain asked, a worried look on his face.

"Hard to say," said Thrang as he got back to his feet. "Enemies of the dwarfs, perhaps."

"Or the dwarfs themselves," said Kat.

"Why would dwarfs destroy their own marker?" Thrang questioned, a hint of worry in his voice.

"Perhaps they do not wish to be visited," Alex said. "It is possible this is a warning to outsiders."

"I have heard of such things," said Arconn. "Dwarf cities in distress or some other kind of trouble will sometimes destroy their boundary markers."

"I would think any dwarf city in trouble would send for help," Thrang said. "There are many dwarfs in Thraxon, and it would be a simple matter for another city to send assistance."

"Then this may be a call for help," said Alex. "Though I think we can all guess the reason for Neplee's troubles."

"You don't think the necromancer is in the city, do you?" Thrang asked nervously.

"No, he would not remain in a city of the living," said

Alex. "Though he may be forcing the people of the city to do his bidding."

"Perhaps we should avoid this city and move on," Barnabus suggested.

"They are in need and are unable to send for help," Kat said in a pained voice.

They all looked at Kat, who was standing a short distance behind them. She seemed to be looking at something that no one else could see, and her face had gone pale.

"Do not dwell on it," said Alex, realizing that Kat was feeling the pain and troubles of the entire dwarf city. "Turn your mind from the darkness ahead of us, or it may overcome you."

"It is difficult to close it out," said Kat, turning to face Alex.

For a moment Alex didn't realize what he was seeing, but when he did, he was quick to act.

"Depart from her," Alex commanded, moving his hand in front of Kat's eyes. "Leave her, and do not return."

"What is this?" Thrang questioned, looking from Alex to Kat and back again.

Kat was still for a moment, staring at Alex without speaking. Suddenly she dropped to the ground as if someone had struck her from behind. The others rushed forward to see what was wrong.

"She will recover," said Alex, watching as Nellus and Barnabus helped Kat to her feet. "Darkness clouded her mind for a moment, and our enemy seized his chance to get a good look at us all."

"The necromancer used her?" Thrang questioned, his voice shaking slightly.

"Yes, but he will not be able to do so again," said Alex. "I have blocked the darkness from her mind so he cannot return."

"And the rest of us?" Arconn asked.

"Kat is the only one he could use from a distance," said Alex. "He would have to make eye contact with the rest of us to gain power over us."

"I . . . What happened?" Kat questioned, her voice weak and confused.

"A moment of darkness," said Alex. "It will not return."

"I don't remember," said Kat.

"I have blocked it from your mind. When you are ready, and when the danger has passed, I will remove the blinders," Alex explained.

"We should move on," Arconn said after a short silence.

"Yes, yes, we should," agreed Thrang, and he started marching down the road once more.

Alex felt certain they would find the city of Neplee before dark, but he didn't know what kind of welcome they would find when they arrived. He didn't have to wait long before the answer to that question appeared. A few hours later, the air rang with a sudden whistle and the soft thud of an arrow striking the ground. Thrang stopped in his tracks.

"Not as friendly as I'd hoped for," Thrang said in a soft voice.

"Who are you, and why do you come here?" a voice called.

"Thrang Silversmith and company," answered Thrang as

he looked around for the source of the voice. "We are adventurers, and have come here by chance."

"Go back the way you came, Master Silversmith," the voice called out. "There is nothing here for you but sorrow and woe. This place is cursed. You must leave before the curse falls upon your party as well."

"I will end the curse," Alex called out as he stepped forward to stand at Thrang's side. "I will end the suffering of Neplee."

"Others have tried before and failed," the voice said, though it was not quite as commanding as it had been.

"I must try, even if you will not willingly assist me in the attempt," said Alex.

There was a long pause, as if the person who had called out to them was considering Alex's words.

"What are you doing?" Thrang questioned Alex in a whisper.

"What I must," answered Alex. "We can't go back and we need help to go on. I must face this evil sooner or later. What other path is open to us?"

"Advance and be recognized," the voice commanded, interrupting Thrang's next question.

Alex and his friends moved forward.

When they approached a small grove of trees, the voice called out, "Hold."

Alex and the others stopped and waited. For several minutes nothing happened, and then an old-looking dwarf stepped out of the trees and moved toward them.

"So, young man," said the old dwarf, looking at Alex. "You say you will end the evil and remove the curse from this city."

"I will if I can," answered Alex.

"A wise answer." The old dwarf laughed grimly, and then turned to Thrang. "We welcome you, Master Silversmith, and your company. We will do what we can for you, and aid you however possible. Lord Turlock will wish to meet with you when we enter the city, and question you further about your adventure."

"We will be pleased to meet Lord Turlock and answer any questions we can," said Thrang with a bow.

The old dwarf did not return Thrang's bow, but simply looked at them all for a moment, and then motioned for them to follow as he started back toward the trees.

Neplee, as it turned out, was extremely well hidden, and Alex saw Thrang stare in surprise and wonder at the great stone doors carved into the mountainside.

"They were made with ancient magic," the old dwarf said. "In a time before darkness came to Neplee."

"Such art has long been lost," said Thrang. "If it has been found again, word should have been sent to King Thorgood."

"Yes, it should have," the old dwarf agreed but said nothing more.

Alex and his companions entered a vast hall, its ceiling supported by dozens of stone pillars that looked like giant gray trees. The hall was empty except for a single chair placed near a large fireplace at the far end of the hall. A troubled-looking dwarf sat in the chair, staring into the low-burning fire. As the company approached, he looked up and quickly stood to greet them.

"Master Silversmith, I am Lord Turlock. I know of you,

though we have never met," said the dwarf, bowing to Thrang. "I ask that you forgive our less than generous welcome, but as I'm sure you've seen, these are not happy times in Neplee."

"We have seen some of your troubles," said Thrang, returning the bow. "But tell us, Lord Turlock, what has happened here? Why have you not sent word to Kazad-Syn, or even Benorg? I'm sure King Thorgood would have sent all the aid he could."

"Yes, I'm sure he would have," said Turlock. "But his help would have done us no good, and more of our people would be under the curse that holds us here. But I am forgetting my manners, please, Master Silversmith, introduce your company to me."

Thrang quickly introduced the company to Turlock. Turlock bowed to each of them in turn and then called for chairs to be brought for them all. Once his guests were seated, Turlock returned to his own chair, his eyes returning to the fire as if he were alone and deep in thought.

"I am sorry you have been caught up in this," said Turlock after a long silence. "I am sorry that we did not see this trouble coming long ago and put an end to it when we had the chance."

"You speak of the necromancer," said Alex.

"Yes," said Turlock, his eyes fixing on Alex's. "We should have guessed, but at the time there was no way to know. He did so much good for the city, we never thought he could become so evil."

"You knew him? Before?" Alex questioned.

"I knew him when he was Nethrom," Turlock answered

in a weak voice, his eyes returning to the fire. "He was gifted in learning, and he had some magical abilities. It was he who learned the ancient magic that hides our city gate. The libraries of Neplee are large, and some of the books in it are very old."

"And this Nethrom learned his magic from those books?" Thrang asked in a puzzled tone. "Magical books are uncommon in dwarf libraries, and few dwarfs have ever been able to read what is written in them."

"He learned some things in the library here," answered Turlock, sounding tired. "Including the existence of a hidden cave in the high mountains beyond the city. The cave was supposed to be guarded by ghosts, or magic, or maybe both. Nethrom became obsessed with the story of the cave, and he spent years looking for it. We became used to seeing him go into the mountains for weeks at a time. He always returned in a dark and unhappy mood."

"But he eventually found the cave," Alex coaxed, trying to understand what Nethrom had gone through in his years of searching.

"Yes, he must have," said Turlock. "It was summer when he went into the mountains, as he always did. When he came back, he was full of happiness. We knew he had found the cave, but we never guessed what was inside of it, and Nethrom never said."

"At first, Nethrom put his powers to good use," said Kat suddenly, and Turlock's head jerked up to look at her. "He learned much about healing and the old dwarf magic, and he used this knowledge to help his people and protect the city of Neplee."

"Yes," Turlock whispered.

"Then, without warning, he changed," Kat went on. "He no longer helped his people, but demanded payment for his services. If the sick could not pay his price, he would do nothing to help them. It was as if Nethrom was no longer the same dwarf he had once been."

"All that you say is true," said Turlock, a questioning look on his face as he glanced from Kat to Alex.

"My friend is a seer," said Alex. "She has felt Nethrom's presence, or rather, the presence of what Nethrom has become."

"A wizard, a seer, and a party of adventurers? Perhaps I should feel hope, but I do not," said Turlock, shaking his head. "I would advise you to leave this place as soon as possible. We will provide you with horses, but I doubt they will last long against the hellerash."

"There are no more hellerash," said Thrang. "Alex has freed you of that curse already."

"You've driven them off?" Turlock questioned in surprise.

"I've destroyed them," answered Alex, turning his own gaze to the fire.

"Perhaps there is hope after all, but I would still advise you to leave," Turlock said, his eyes fixed on Alex.

"The weather is turning, and we may have to winter here," said Thrang in a worried tone. "We need to search the mountains for traces of Albrek and his people."

"Albrek?" Turlock asked as if remembering something.

"Our quest is not to destroy the hellerash, or to fight the

necromancer who called them back from the dead," Thrang explained.

"No, of course not," said Turlock, smiling in a tired sort of way. "I fear you will find little record of Albrek or his company in these mountains. Legend says that he did stop here during his wanderings, but Neplee was already being built. Not wanting to cause conflict, Albrek moved on."

"Then our quest lies farther south," said Thrang, glancing at Alex. "If the weather allows, we will move on as soon as possible."

"I will order that horses be provided for you," said Turlock.

"How long?" Alex questioned.

"How long?" Turlock repeated, his eyes moving to Alex. "How long what?"

"How long since Nethrom changed?"

"With the coming of the new moon, it will be three years and three moons," answered Turlock.

Standing suddenly, Turlock raised his hand. Several dwarfs who had been waiting nearby hurried forward, bowing to Turlock and waiting for his command.

"Find rooms for our guests," Turlock ordered. "Make them comfortable and provide them with refreshment. When they are settled, search the city for whatever horses you can find."

"Yes, lord," the dwarfs answered, bowing.

"Perhaps tomorrow we can speak again," Turlock said, returning to his chair. "And if the weather holds, you can be on your way."

"You have our thanks," said Thrang, bowing to Turlock.

Alex and his friends bowed as well and then followed the dwarfs out of the hall. The dwarfs led them quickly and quietly

through the city to a series of rooms that had already been prepared. Unlike every other dwarf city Alex had been in, Neplee
was dark and quiet. They saw no other dwarfs as they went
along, and many of the passageways had no lights in them at
all. It was depressing, and Alex began to wonder how many of
the city's people had already been destroyed by Nethrom.

"What is wrong with this city?" Thrain questioned as soon
as their guides left them to rest in a large room where there
were several chairs and a fireplace. "In my grandfather's kingdom, no dwarf city is so dark or so quiet, and guests are always
welcomed with feasts and excitement."

"This is not your grandfather's kingdom," said Thrang,
dropping into a chair.

"This city is like a tomb," Nellus said, taking a chair close
to Thrang's.

"They have lived for more than three years in fear," said
Alex, his eyes fixed on the fire. "They have forgotten what happiness is. Now they simply live day to day, while death sits on
their doorstep."

"You still wish to stay and face the necromancer?" Thrang
questioned.

"I will go with the company," said Alex without looking at
Thrang.

"Then you think me wrong to lead us away from here if
the weather holds," Thrang pressed.

"No, I do not think you are wrong," answered Alex. "Our
quest is to find the tomb of Albrek and the Ring of Searching.
Staying here is dangerous. We are honor bound to finish our
adventure, so I will do whatever you think best."

Thrang was about to reply when Arconn broke in.

"Do you think the necromancer will come looking for you?"

"I don't know," said Alex. "I have no idea how Nethrom, or whatever he is now, will react to my being here."

"You don't really think he would attack you openly, do you?" Barnabus asked.

"I have no idea. I've never faced a necromancer before, and I don't know how powerful Nethrom has become. I think, if he feels that he is strong enough, he will challenge me," said Alex. "For now, I'm going to bed."

With that, Alex turned and left the large room, heading for one of the several smaller rooms connected to it. Alex chose a room at random and closed the door behind him. He didn't know what to think or do, and he didn't know what answers to give to his friends. The necromancer was already aware of him, that much was certain. What the necromancer would do now that they had entered Neplee, Alex didn't dare guess.

In the middle of these dark thoughts, Alex heard a sudden popping sound and a loud ding. A geeb appeared on his bed, and for a moment he was too stunned to do anything but stare. When he realized that the geeb could only have come from Whalen, he hurried forward to retrieve the message. Tossing the geeb a small diamond, Alex opened the envelope and began to read.

Whalen's letter did little to make Alex feel any better. For the most part it told him not to feel bad about destroying the hellerash because they were already dead anyway. Whalen had little to say about fighting the necromancer, except to give Alex a lot of advice about gathering his power and preparing himself to face the darkness.

Unhappy with the message, Alex tossed it aside and climbed into his bed. Whatever hope he had felt when the geeb first arrived was gone, and he lay awake in the darkness for a long time before drifting off to sleep.

When Alex finally did fall asleep, his dreams were as confused and troubled as his waking thoughts were. They jumped from place to place as if he was searching for something, but he didn't know what. Twice he woke with a start, looking around wildly as if expecting someone or something to be in the room, waiting for him. The second time it happened, he'd even conjured weir lights, sending them around the room to make sure he was alone.

Lying back on the bed, Alex put out the weir lights and tried to focus on what he was looking for in his dreams. Slowly his mind relaxed, and he felt as if he was lifting off the bed and flying away.

Alex's thoughts moved out of Neplee and turned north. He felt like a bird, flying back along the path that he and his friends had traveled. Kazad-Syn looked small and inviting as he flew past it, and for a moment he wanted to stop, but he felt an urgent need to go on. When his mind reached the shores of the Eastern Sea, Alex knew where his thoughts were taking him. He moved across the wind-tossed sea into the darkness that hid the dragon.

"Your thoughts are troubled, young one." Salinor's deep, steady voice echoed inside Alex's head.

"Yes, I have much to worry about," said Alex.

"The necromancer," Salinor stated.

"You knew about him?"

"Yes, but I did not know you would face him," answered Salinor.

"I'm not sure I will. Thrang wishes to move on as soon as possible, so I may not face him for some time yet," Alex explained.

"Sooner would be better," said Salinor.

"I'm . . . I'm not sure I can face the necromancer," said Alex, expressing the fear that had been nagging at his mind.

"Doubt can be deadly. Would you run from this challenge?"

"I would rather face it and free the people of Neplee, but I don't know how, and I'm not sure that I can defeat this evil."

"Caution is one of your more human traits," said Salinor with a soft laugh. "It may be useful, I would not know."

"I want to ask something of you," said Alex before he could stop himself.

"Ask something, of me?"

"If I cannot defeat the necromancer, if he gains control over me, I want you to come and destroy me. Don't let me be used by this evil," said Alex in a pleading tone.

"Yes, I will come," Salinor agreed slowly. "Though I think there are few things you could not overcome, even though you are still young."

"Thank you," said Alex, bowing to the dragon in his thoughts.

"You should return now," said Salinor, a strange smile curling his gigantic mouth. "Guard your thoughts from the prying of the dark one, and look deeper into what your friend Vankin said in his message to you. If I feel the darkness overcoming you, I will come as you have asked."

Alex bowed once more, and before he could dream himself back across the dwarf realm to Neplee, he woke with a start. Jumping out of bed, Alex retrieved Whalen's letter and reread every line of it carefully, pausing on one line that he didn't remember reading at all.

"There's at least a foot of snow on the ground, and there will be another before we've eaten breakfast." Thrang turned as Alex entered the common room. "If I didn't know better, I'd ask if you'd conjured up this storm," he said.

"Not me," said Alex, smiling at Thrang. "And Nethrom didn't conjure it either," he added quickly.

"Well, we won't be moving anytime soon," Thrang grumbled. "So I suppose we'll have to wait and see what happens."

"You know what's going to happen," said Alex. "I will go into the mountains and face the necromancer."

"Madness," said Thrang, dropping into a chair by the fire. "I'll never understand wizards, not if I live to be a thousand years old."

"It is not madness," said Alex. "It is simply what has to be done."

"Very well. I'll ask no more questions," Thrang said as he got to his feet again. "Besides, there's no time anyway. Turlock has asked us to join him for breakfast, and we'd better be on our way," he said as a guide appeared to lead them back to Turlock.

Once more the city was dark and quiet, though there were a few dwarfs moving about this morning. Most of them moved quickly away as Alex and the others approached, but a few stayed and silently watched them pass.

"Our people are not used to strangers," their guide said. "It has been so long since anyone has come to the city."

"Do they fear us?" Thrang asked as they walked.

"In a way they do," the guide answered. "The evil one in the mountains has sent his servants among us before. Now, we have trouble trusting anyone, even those we hold most dear."

The look on Thrang's face told Alex all he needed to know. Thrang's mind had been made up, and even if the weather permitted them to leave, he would insist that Alex try to free the city of Neplee from the curse of the necromancer.

Turlock greeted the company as they entered a small feasting hall. A large, round table had been set up, and breakfast was already waiting for them. Alex thought Turlock looked tired, as if he hadn't slept in days, so he waited until they were almost done with their meal before asking his question.

"A metal worker?" Turlock asked in response. "We have many metal workers in Neplee, though there is little for any of them to do these days."

"Who is the best metal worker in the city?" Alex asked.

"That would be Volo Silverforge—"

"Volo Silverforge lives here?" Thrang interrupted. "His work is well-known and much prized, even in Benorg."

"Where can I find Master Silverforge?" Alex asked.

"I can have someone take you to him," Turlock answered. "Though I doubt he will be willing to help you. He has taken an oath, and refuses to make anything that might please or aid Nethrom. He has done no work in the past three years."

"I would like to come along," Thrang said, glancing quickly at Alex. "If I may."

"I think I should go alone at first," Alex said to Thrang. "It will be less imposing, and I may be able to convince Volo to aid me."

Thrang reluctantly agreed, though Alex could see that he wasn't happy about it. As soon as they were done eating, Turlock had one of his servants lead Alex through the city to Volo's workshop. Alex asked the dwarf to leave, and then he stood for several minutes looking at the door and wondering what kind of dwarf Volo Silverforge would be.

Alex knocked loudly on the workshop door with his staff, but there was no answer. Alex wondered if Volo might not be in his workshop, but then he heard movement behind the door. He knocked again. He could clearly hear the sound of shuffling feet behind the door, but the door remained closed. Smiling to himself, Alex raised his staff and knocked a third time.

"Volo Silverforge, if you do not answer your door after I've knocked three times, I will blast it off its hinges and turn you into a dormouse," Alex said loudly.

Slowly the door creaked open, and an ancient-looking dwarf stuck his head out from inside the workshop.

"No need to get angry," Volo grumbled, looking closely at Alex. "I'm closed for business, so you can take your threats and your knocking someplace else."

"You prefer to leave the city to Nethrom, then," said Alex as Volo moved to close the door.

"I prefer to be left alone," said Volo sharply, opening the door a little wider.

"So your peace is more important to you than your friends and neighbors are," said Alex, leaning on his staff.

"We are all in the same boat here," said Volo, opening the shop door all the way. "There is no escape from the curse, and no point in searching for false hope."

"If that's how you feel, I must have come to the wrong place," said Alex. "I thought Volo Silverforge would be the dwarf who could aid me in riding Neplee of its curse, but it appears I was wrong. You should go back to gathering dust like your forge; I will find someone else to assist me."

"No need to be rude," said Volo, taking a step out of his shop to get a better look at Alex. "I've never had a wizard knock on my shop door before, so the least I can do is offer you tea."

"Then you are willing to discuss a job I need done?"

"I don't know about that," Volo answered, turning back toward his shop. "Come inside and have some tea. I'll listen to what you have to say before I tell you that you're mad."

Alex smiled and followed Volo into the shop, closing the door behind him. Volo shuffled his way across the room and placed a large copper kettle on top of his forge, pumping the bellows a few times. Alex took the chair that Volo offered him, sitting silently while Volo made their tea.

Chapter Eighteen

Necromancer

Y ou've been working with Volo for weeks. Are you going to tell us what you're up to, or are you going to leave us sitting in the dark?"

Thrang was in a bad mood, and for a moment Alex considered telling him what he had planned. Fortunately, Nellus spoke before he had to answer.

"Sitting in the dark is right. If I don't feel some wind on my face soon, I think I'll die."

"The snow is five feet deep around the city gates. The guards have to shovel it away every night and morning just to open and close the doors," Barnabus said.

"There is little snow once you move away from the mountains," Arconn said.

"That's fine for an elf who can move easily on top of the snow," said Thrang, disgruntled. "The rest of us cannot move so easily. And what were you doing so far from the gates anyway?"

"Looking," Arconn answered. "Feeling what is there."

"Elves," said Thrang, shaking his head and poking at the fire. "You're almost as bad as Alex. If you don't want to say what you're doing, fine, but don't tell us how nice it is to be out in the fresh air."

"You asked," said Arconn with a smile.

"How deep is the snow as you move toward the mountains?" Alex questioned.

"Five or six feet in most places, deeper where it has drifted," Arconn answered after some thought.

"You had a package with you when you came in last night," Thrain said, suddenly turning to Alex.

"Yes," said Alex.

"Then you're going to face him soon," said Arconn, stating what everyone else in the room was thinking.

"I was thinking of going today, if the weather is bad," said Alex, trying to sound hopeful.

"If the weather is bad?" Thrang questioned.

"Bad weather will make it harder for Nethrom to see me coming. I'll need every advantage I can get."

"And how will we get up the mountains in six feet of snow and bad weather?" Kat asked.

"You won't," Alex answered.

"If you think you're going alone, you've got another thing coming," said Thrang in a defiant tone. "I forbid you to go by yourself."

"That is something you have no say in," said Alex. "But I thank you for the thought."

"I will come," said Arconn. "The snow is not a problem for me, and I can help you defeat this evil."

"No," said Alex, his tone almost a command. "This is something I must do alone. I know that you would all go with me, even if I did not ask, but I must go quickly and alone. That is the only hope I have to defeat the necromancer."

Arconn refused to accept Alex's decision, and none of the others were happy about being left behind either. They all knew they could not go into the mountains in bad weather, not with so much snow already on the ground, but Arconn was inflexible in his decision to go along.

"At least, if you fail, I can bring word to the others," Arconn argued.

"If I fail, you will see the dragon," said Alex, reaching for the long cloak Turlock had given him. "There will be fire on the mountains, and you will know the curse is broken."

Alex walked quickly to the door, wanting to get on with his plan. The others followed him out of the common room, continuing to argue against his decision.

"If we all went, Nethrom wouldn't know who to attack first," said Nellus, but unconvincingly.

"And one of us might be able to attack him. Or at least distract him long enough for you to break his power," Barnabus added.

"No," Alex repeated. "I must go alone, and I must go now."

"How will you manage in the snow?" Thrain questioned.

"I will be as the snow," said Alex. "I will move like the wind and arrive at the necromancer's cave without being seen."

"It is too dangerous," Thrang argued. "Couldn't you ask your dragon friend to take care of this, or at least go with you?"

"Dragons care little for the troubles of other races, even the good dragons like my friend," said Alex. "He has promised not to let me be used by the necromancer, and that is as much of a promise as I will ask of him."

The others were silent as they moved through the city, but Alex knew they were all trying to think of ways to make him change his mind. When they reached the city gates, he was surprised to find Turlock waiting for him.

"Volo said you might be going today," Turlock said, bowing to Alex. "I thought I would wish you luck, as I have little more than that to offer."

"It is enough that you have come, Lord Turlock," said Alex with a bow.

"Is there anything I can do for you before you go?" Turlock's eyes were full of sorrow.

"Watch after my friends while I'm away," Alex answered. "One way or another, the curse will be removed from Neplee before I return."

"Then I will thank you now, and thank you again when you return."

Alex smiled and walked to the gate. The guards bowed to him before swinging open the giant stone doors, and then stood back to let him pass. An icy wind rushed into the city, snowflakes swirling with it.

Taking a deep breath of the cold, clean air, Alex turned to look at his friends. "I will return as soon as I can. If I am not back before spring, don't look for me."

"Don't say such things," said Thrang gruffly.

Without another word, Alex turned and stepped into the snow, vanishing from sight in an instant. It was a spell he had been practicing since the first snows began to fall, and he knew

it was his best chance to reach the necromancer's cave unde-
tected. Whalen had warned him about wasting his strength
trying to reach the necromancer, and moving up the mountain
without fighting whatever monsters the necromancer could
send against him seemed like a good idea.

Becoming a gust of wind was not terribly difficult, but
it was dangerous. When Alex had first worked the spell, he'd
had difficulty returning to his own form. The wind was so free
that all of his worries slipped away. It was only when Volo had
started yelling at him for almost blowing out his forge that
Alex had returned to his own natural shape.

Not wanting to lose himself in the shape of wind, Alex
focused his attention on the land around him and began working his way into the mountains. He had only a general idea of
where Nethrom's cave would be, and he was worried it would
take a long time for him to find it. He didn't want to remain
a gust of wind for too long, but he also didn't want to become vulnerable on the mountainside in his own shape; and he
didn't want to start fighting until he had to.

By midmorning he was well into the mountains, and he
let his mind search the land around him, looking for any wild
creature that might help him find the necromancer. The land
was empty, and Alex wondered if it was the winter weather or
the necromancer that had driven away the wild creatures. He
continued searching as he moved higher and deeper into the
mountains.

It was late afternoon before Alex saw something moving in
the snow below him, and he drifted closer to get a better look.
He stopped himself from touching the creature's mind when

he realized it was one of Nethrom's undead creations. A giant bear, making its way down the mountainside in winter was out of place, and Alex was glad he had taken the form of wind and could remain hidden. Alex followed the bear's tracks deeper into the mountains.

When the last gray light of day was fading, Alex stopped in a large grove of trees. He checked to make sure that none of Nethrom's creatures were nearby, then he changed back into himself. After a quick meal, he studied the trees around him. Slowly he let his mind slip into the thoughts of the trees, and with a simple command, he changed forms once more, this time becoming a giant pine in the middle of the grove.

It was in the shape of the tree that Alex discovered where to look for the cave of the necromancer. The tree's thoughts were slower than his own, slower than any living animal. The trees were very much alive, however, and they knew things about the undead land around Nethrom's cave.

When the sun touched the mountainside once more, Alex changed back into the wind. The new day was bright, and the clouds that had covered the mountains for weeks had blown away in the night. It was easy for Alex to see where he was going, and with the knowledge he had gained from the trees, he quickly found the entrance to the cave.

For a moment Alex thought about entering the cave as the wind, but then he thought Nethrom might notice the breeze and possibly capture him before he could change back into his natural form. Instead, he stopped a short distance from the cave's mouth and returned to his own form on the wind-blown path. He looked around at the crushed and packed snow around him and suspected that Nethrom had recently sent a great many creatures out of the cave.

Moving toward the entrance of the cave, Alex paused. A large treelike creature was rooted in the center of the path in front of him. At first, Alex did not realize what it was. He had only noticed the strange creature because there was no snow or ice on it. As he approached, two great serpent heads swung around to watch him, their red eyes shining brightly in the cold morning air. Without waiting for the creature to attack, Alex sent a ball of fire toward it, but it bounced off, hissing loudly as the fireball sank into a nearby snowdrift. He thought about freezing the creature, but since it didn't seem bothered by the winter wind, he didn't think a freezing spell would have any effect. Moving forward carefully, he drew his sword. If magic could not harm this creature, perhaps the edge of his sword could.

One of the serpent heads struck down at Alex as he approached, its reach much greater than he'd expected. Alex spun away, dodging the first head and watching the second. The second head was only a few seconds behind the first, but Alex was ready for it when it came. Sidestepping the attack, Alex brought his sword down directly on the creature's neck. The head went bouncing across the snow and burst into flame at the side of the path.

Stepping back so the remaining head could not reach him, Alex was shocked to see two new heads growing from the flailing stump. He was facing three heads instead of two, and it seemed he would face more if he continued to attack.

"Hydra," said Alex under his breath. He remembered the

story of Hercules, an ancient Greek warrior who had defeated a hydra by cutting off its heads and burning the necks before new heads could grow. Unfortunately, Alex didn't see how he'd have time to burn one neck before one of the other heads attacked him. It seemed impossible, and he wondered how Hercules had managed it.

Alex moved away from the hydra, wondering what he should do. It was only a matter of time before Nethrom or one of his other creatures became aware of him. Now that he was so close to the cave, he had to move quickly, but the hydra was something he had not expected. Alex leaned against his staff and looked around the snowy path, hoping to see some clue of how to defeat the hydra. Icicles hung from the rocks on one side of the path, and Alex jumped when he saw his own reflection in them. He looked around to make sure it was only his own reflection and not some other creature moving behind him. Then the idea hit him, and he smiled at the simplicity of it.

Moving forward once more, he stopped just beyond the hydra's reach. He gripped his sword firmly in his right hand and turned the end of his staff into a blue-white flame. Closing his eyes as he worked the magic, he concentrated on what he needed to do. When he opened his eyes again, he laughed as six copies of himself looked back at him.

The hydra could see the seven different versions of Alex, and its heads began to move back and forth, trying to watch all the images at the same time. The hydra didn't know which of the figures to attack, and the closer the figures got to it the faster it moved its heads.

The hydra stuck at one of the images to Alex's left, but the serpent's head bit nothing but snow and ice. Alex shifted his images, moving them around the hydra slowly and sometimes toward it. The hydra struck a second time on the far side of the path, and Alex knew he would have to wait to launch his own attack.

Five times the hydra attacked Alex's false images and five times it found nothing. On its sixth attack, Alex struck his own blow, slicing off one of the heads with his sword and holding his burning staff against the bleeding neck before two new heads could replace it. The hydra recoiled from his staff, but the work was already done. Now there were only two heads for Alex to watch, and only two heads to watch the seven images of himself.

Alex continued moving his illusions around the hydra. One head almost managed to bite Alex as he was preparing to attack the other head, but he managed to slip away. The hydra seemed to realize that it had found something real to bite this time, and the second head swung around quickly to attack. Alex distracted the first head by having three of his images rush forward at the same time. He cut the second head from its neck and once more pressed his burning staff to the wound.

The final head spun around wildly, trying to defend its body from the seven attackers surrounding it. Alex almost felt sorry for the hydra, but he knew he had to finish the task. He sent five of his images rushing one side of the hydra, forcing its last head to turn and face them. As it turned, Alex rolled forward, swinging his sword with all his strength, and cut the hydra's body off as close to the ground as he could. The long neck and head of the hydra burst into flames as it fell, and

Alex applied his burning staff to the stump that was left in the ground.

The mouth of the cave was open, but the darkness inside it was forbidding.

Taking a moment to catch his breath, Alex waved his hand and his six duplicates faded into mist. He wished he was not alone, but he knew that the danger was too great for any of his friends to face. Taking another deep breath of the cold morning air, Alex stepped into the dark cave and paused, allowing his eyes to grow accustomed to the twilight world he had entered.

The cave was not completely dark, and once Alex was away from the bright entrance, he was a little surprised by how light the cave actually was. Only one path led into the mountain and Alex stepped carefully; if Nethrom was already aware of Alex's approach, and if he had managed to gather too many undead creatures to defend himself, it might be impossible to reach the necromancer at all.

Alex moved slowly, listening for anything else that might be in the cave with him. All he could hear was the sound of dripping water somewhere ahead of him. He continued on, growing more nervous as he went. The cave seemed empty and quiet, and Alex felt even more worried.

After several minutes, the path began sloping downward, deeper into the mountain, before the cave suddenly opened into a large chamber. Alex paused at the entrance, letting his eyes search the darkness for the enemy he knew had to be there. There was nothing to see, though, only stone and more darkness.

Stepping into the cavern, Alex heard a piercingly high squeak, and he raised his sword in time to block a huge bat flying down from the ceiling to attack him. The bat hit the edge of the sword with such force that it cut itself in two, the halves falling to the floor. Alex looked up at the ceiling and saw to his horror that there were hundreds of the bats hanging upside down and looking at him.

He stepped away from the cavern entrance, hoping the bats would not follow him, and he noticed something even more terrible. The bat that had cut itself in half on his sword was growing slowly into two complete bats, their wings flopping along the ground. Without thinking, Alex sent a jet of flame toward the two half-grown bats, but they only seemed to grow faster in the heat.

The light of his flame seemed to stir the rest of the bats, and he could hear the creatures beginning to fly about the chamber in front of him, blocking his path. He considered for a moment sending more false images of himself into the cavern, but given the number of bats he would have to fight, Alex realized it would be pointless.

Another bat shot into the tunnel toward him. He struck it with his staff, whispering a freezing spell as he did so. To his surprise, the bat shattered into a dozen shining gems. Alex bent down and picked up several gems, and he saw that they were real rubies, diamonds, and emeralds. He did not have time to think about why the bat had shattered into gems because a second bat flew into the cave toward him. Once more Alex shattered it with his staff, and once more the shattered pieces of the bat turned into gems.

Thinking quickly, Alex changed back into his wind form, moving forward into the chamber. The bats seemed to be aware of him, but their sonar couldn't detect him hidden in the breeze. They flew around the cavern in a frenzy, clustering in circles in front of the passage that would lead Alex deeper into the mountain and barring his path.

Moving to the center of the chamber, Alex thought of the bright cold morning on the mountainside. He whispered the freezing spell softly, afraid to be heard, and as the bat's movements stilled around him, he spoke another command like thunder. His voice rolled through the cavern, shattering bats and showering him with gems.

Alex knew the thunderclap command would surely alert Nethrom to his presence, but it was the only way he could think of to shatter all the bats at one time. Alex didn't take time to examine the cavern, now covered in jewels, but hurried forward, hoping that he was ready to face the necromancer and whatever other creatures he still had waiting.

The cave went on and on, and Alex began to worry. He didn't have any idea how long it would take him to reach Nethrom, and the deeper into the cave he went, the more nervous he became. Suddenly, he stopped short, catching himself against the cave wall as bits of rock flew out from his feet into empty darkness.

He had stopped at the threshold of what appeared to be another chamber, but this one seemed to have no floor. A dim light shone upward from deep below, but even with the extra light, Alex could not see the far side of the chamber. He put his sword back in its scabbard and leaned against his staff. He was breathing hard from his journey into the mountain, and he had to force himself to relax and breathe slowly and think.

As the sound of his beating heart slowed in his ears, Alex heard a new sound, the sound of digging far below him. Carefully he moved toward the edge of the cavern and looked down into the dim light. Far below him, he could see movement, like hundreds of ants digging in the earth. He watched the shapes moving about until he realized what they were. Hundreds of long-dead dwarfs were digging at the roots of the mountain as if that were the only thing they had ever done. Nethrom was using his own dead people to mine for him, and somehow that was more evil than anything Alex had expected. A feeling of rage began to grow inside of Alex.

Alex looked around for some way down to the miners. He did not know what he would do if he reached them, or what they might do to him, but he wanted more than anything to give the dead dwarfs the rest they deserved. The path he had been following turned sharply to his left as it came out of the cave mouth, moving down the face of the cliff. The path was narrow but well made, and Alex hurried down it.

He tried to calm himself as he descended the cliff wall, but his outrage burned inside him like a flame that would not go out. Alex wondered at how evil Nethrom had become, and at how he could have changed so much from the dwarf who had once helped the people of Neplee. That the same dwarf had enslaved the dead of his own people was too much for Alex to understand.

When he reached the bottom of the cliff, Alex turned to face the miners, wanting to speak to them and tell them that he would return them to their rest. He was surprised to find that the miners had all stopped working and were moving toward him like moths to a flame. He gripped his staff, wondering if the undead dwarfs would try to stop him from reaching Nethrom and if he would have to destroy them to end their torment.

"Hail, great one," one of the dwarfs called out to Alex. "We have heard the clap of doom, and we know our time here is short."

"You know?" Alex questioned.

"Your coming was foretold long ago."

"Foretold by who?" Alex asked.

"It is not for us to say," the dwarf answered. "It is enough for us to know you have come, and that our deliverance is near."

"Quickly, then," said Alex, not wanting to give Nethrom any more time to prepare for him than he had to. "Where do I find the necromancer? Which path leads to him?"

"Do not fear, he does not know of your coming," said the dwarf with what might have been a smile. "We are bound to dig for him, but we are not bound to do more."

"How could he not know I am here? You heard the thunderclap—" Alex started doubtfully.

"We blocked the sound from passing," the dwarf answered. "The evil will not know you have come until you show yourself to him."

"Then I am grateful for your help," said Alex. "I will give you back your rest, but I must act quickly."

"There is one more guardian you must face before you will

find the dark one," said the dwarf. "A golem made of stone. It is bound to guard the entrance to the dark one's prison."

"Prison?" Alex questioned.

"Nethrom is not the evil," answered the dwarf. "He is only a foolish dwarf who did not know what he had found until it was too late. He is controlled by a greater darkness. He has nearly escaped in the past, but the evil needs Nethrom's form to have power in this world. The evil fears what will happen if Nethrom ever escapes."

"I understand," said Alex, considering the dwarf's words. "Is there anything I can do for you—apart from destroying this evil?"

"If you will," the dwarf said slowly. "In life, I was named Set, lord and defender of the dwarf realm of Thraxon. My heir, Thorgood, now rules Thraxon, but he rules without my crown. My crown was broken when I died in this place, binding the evil to these caves, but I have the pieces still. Will you take my broken crown to my heir? Give it to him so that all will know he is the true king."

"You would trust me with your crown?" Alex asked.

"You were foretold," Set replied. "Take my crown to Thorgood, but you must ask what promise he has made for its return before you show it to him."

"I will do as you ask," said Alex, bowing.

"You honor me," said Set as he returned the bow. "You will find the crown waiting for you in the first chamber as you leave. Remember to ask Thorgood about his promise. Farewell, and may fortune smile on you always."

The rest of the dwarfs parted to make a path for Alex to

follow, murmuring words of thanks to him as he passed. Alex looked at their faces as he went, allowing himself to feel their sorrows and their hopes.

At the far side of the cavern, Alex found yet another cave opening. This time, though, there were torches in the cave, and the brightness of them dazzled Alex's eyes. He rubbed his eyes as he stepped forward, trying to remain as quiet as he could. The dwarfs in the great cavern may have blocked the sound of his spell from reaching Nethrom, but Alex feared Nethrom would be searching for him just the same.

As the cave walls extended back into yet another chamber, Alex saw the stone golem standing in the center of the cavern, facing the cave mouth. It began moving as soon as Alex stepped into the chamber. The golem was a slow-moving creature, and it looked as if it took great effort to move its huge stone legs.

Alex thought he could easily avoid the golem and find the path to Nethrom, but even as slow as it was, the golem was relentless. Alex went to the far end of the chamber as he looked for the path, and the golem followed. When Alex moved to another part of the chamber, the golem moved with him. It seemed the stone creature's only task was to attack anyone who entered the chamber.

The golem almost caught him once, but Alex was able to slip under its outstretched arms before it could grab him. The golem was quickly becoming a nuisance, preventing Alex from finding the path that led to Nethrom, a path obviously hidden somewhere in the chamber. With the golem continually following him wherever he moved, however, Alex had no time to look closely at the walls and find the hidden path.

"Fine," Alex said as he tried to think of some way to destroy, or at least disable, the golem.

For the first time, Alex looked closely at the stone creature that was following him. Its face—or at least the features where a face should be—was roughly carved. The golem's body was massive and appeared to be made from a single, solid stone. There were no cracks or marks on the stone body, and the rock seemed to bend whenever the golem moved its arms or legs.

Alex worked his magic quickly, encasing the monster in ice. He thought freezing the creature in place would be the simplest solution, allowing him to move past it and on to the necromancer. For a second, he thought his plan had worked, but the golem was much stronger than he'd anticipated. As the golem continued to try to move toward him, the massive block of ice started to crack, and in less than a minute it had shattered and the golem was free.

The shattering ice gave Alex another idea. He sent a bolt of frost from his staff into the golem's body. The monster slowed, its movements becoming even stiffer than before, but it still didn't stop. Knowing that the stone body was now much colder than any ice, Alex charged forward and struck the golem with his staff, hoping to shatter the stone the way he had shattered the bats. A few bits of rock broke away where the staff hit, and the golem seemed to vibrate, but that was all.

Cold would not work, and fire was out of the question in the confined, underground battlefield. Alex tried to think of something else, something that wouldn't alert the necromancer to his presence. He considered changing the golem into something else, but that was too dangerous. The monster was made of stone and magic, and not knowing how the magic worked meant that any change Alex might try could turn the golem into something even more deadly.

The answer came to him in a flash, and Alex almost smiled at the idea. Long ago, when the company had first entered Thraxon, he had seen trees clinging to the steep sides of the mountains, their roots digging into the solid stone. He sent his magic searching, and it didn't take long for him to find what he needed. The land around the necromancer's cave was a wasteland, but there were still roots of living things hidden underground. It only took seconds before the far wall of the cave began to crack and fall apart like clay, and the noise and motion distracted the golem.

For a moment, the golem just stood there, as if frozen to the spot. Living roots wriggled out of the stone wall, slithered across the floor, and wrapped around the golem's feet. The monster tried to move away, but the vinelike roots were too fast. Larger, stronger roots were already wrapping themselves around the golem's body. As Alex watched, the creature of magic and stone was dragged toward to the crumbling wall and slowly pulled into the darkness beyond.

It was time to face the necromancer. Alex moved to the far end of the chamber, and now that he had time to look, he easily found the door hidden in the stone wall. The door was barred from the outside, and Alex felt sure that meant that Set had been right. Nethrom was still fighting the darkness, still fighting the evil he'd unknowingly set free.

Removing the iron bar from across the door, Alex put his hand on the handle and stopped. He stood motionless, remembering the advice Whalen had given him: *Defend yourself, and try to turn the necromancer's own powers against him. Attack only when you must.* He thought about what he was about to face, but after a moment of hesitation, he shook his head. He had come this far and to hesitate now would be both foolish and deadly. Without waiting any longer to think or worry about what might happen, he threw open the door to the hiding place of the necromancer.

"Ah, you've come at last," said an ancient-looking dwarf sitting at a table.

"Silence!" a second voice screamed.

Nethrom's body went rigid, every muscle suddenly contracting. It looked as if the old dwarf had stopped breathing, and his face was pale. Alex looked around the room, searching for the source of the second voice, but there was no one else he could see. Slowly, Nethrom started to breathe, but each breath was clearly a struggle to draw in and force out.

"I should have realized that you would be in the one place I never thought to look," the second voice said from Nethrom's mouth.

"I think it best to be where I'm not expected," said Alex calmly.

"Cursed crystal—I should have known it would show me nothing of value," Nethrom said as he pushed his chair away from the table and slowly stood up. It seemed like he was trying to remember how to breathe, to remember how his body moved. "Still, it has some powers that are useful."

Alex glanced at the crystal on the desk, realizing that it was the same as the crystal he had once recovered for the Oracle of the White Tower.

"The crystal will not willingly work for evil."

"Most things won't, but I manage just the same."

"You admit you're evil, then," said Alex, surprised by the simple confession.

"Why not? I have lived too long to deceive myself, and I care not what others think," said Nethrom.

"Then you know why I have come," said Alex, moving a little farther into the room.

"To test your strength against me, of course," answered Nethrom, laughing slyly. "To call me to account for what I have done."

"And to free those you have enslaved with your power," Alex added.

"Noble tasks, though foolish," said Nethrom. "And all for nothing, really. What need have we to fight—two great powers in a land of small people? Surely we can settle any disputes without resorting to violence."

"Are you willing to give up your evil?"

"Are you willing to give up your life?"

"We give up when we are dead, and even then the struggle will often go on," Alex answered.

"You speak of Set and his miners. They are a small matter. One I could easily do without," said Nethrom carelessly. "My powers do not rely on my servants, and they do not bend simply because wizards wish them to."

"Have you strayed so far from wisdom, Nethrom?" Alex questioned.

"That is not my name," shouted the dwarf, a pained look crossing his face. "Nethrom was nothing—a fool caught up in his learning. I am Mog, the ancient one, the destroyer of souls."

"I see," said Alex. "And yet you have not been able to destroy Nethrom. He still fights against you. Why else would you lock yourself in this dungeon?"

"His efforts are meaningless," Mog answered angrily, picking up a short staff made of black stone. "I have taken his body and his power. All he can now do is play the fly, buzzing in circles but having no sting."

"Yet you fear him," said Alex as he took another step forward.

"Fear is for the weak," Mog spat back. "I fear nothing in this world, least of all a half-witted dwarf."

"Then I must destroy you," said Alex, raising his staff.

"You can try, but you will fail, as others have failed."

Before Alex could move, he felt himself swept away from the dark chamber where he faced the necromancer. He blinked to clear his eyes of the dark mist that seemed to flow around him, and he looked up at the imposing figure of Mog.

"Behold, boy, my true form," Mog called loudly.

For a moment Alex couldn't breathe. Nethrom's body grew into a giant and his head turned into something insectlike. His eyes glowed an evil green, and long, dripping fangs extended from his mouth. He was more terrible than Alex had thought possible, yet there was something inside Alex that made him feel pity rather than fear.

"Let me show you the power you face now," Mog growled. "Let me give you a sample of what I am and what I can do."

Flames leaped up around as Alex as far as he could see. The entire world seemed to be engulfed in a giant ball of flame, and for a moment Alex was afraid he would burn with it, but, strangely, the flames had no effect on him. He could feel the flames around him, but they were simply warm and felt like a summer breeze.

"You hide your pain well, boy," Mog called, looking down at Alex. "I know the pain of the flames. There is no need for you to hold your tongue."

Alex did not answer the creature, but watched as the necromancer began to move through the flames. Alex realized that the flames and the entire world around him was nothing more than an illusion created by Mog.

"Perhaps something else will pain you even more," Mog sneered.

The flames vanished as he spoke, replaced by thousands of lightning bolts which shattered the rocky ground where they struck. Alex felt several of the bolts strike him, but there was no power in them. He knew then that nothing Mog did in the pretend world could possibly harm him.

"You cast an interesting illusion," said Alex, catching one of the lightning bolts in his hand. "For a moment, I almost thought it was real."

"Real enough," said Mog, still sneering at Alex. "Whatever I create here, I can create in the world. Whatever pain you feel here will be nothing compared to the unending pain you will feel when I am through with you."

"Then why show me this foolishness?" Alex questioned, carelessly tossing the lightning bolt aside. "If you are so mighty, why waste my time with mere illusion?"

"To give you a chance, boy," answered Mog, his voice shaking with anger. "I am not cruel, and I do not destroy without a reason. Join me and share my power. Together we could do so much."

"You would do only evil," said Alex, waving his staff. Mog's imagined world vanished. "You can't create anything new; you can only call back what once was."

"You are a fool," said Mog from Nethrom's body. "A brave fool, perhaps, but a fool just the same."

"I will give you one chance to depart. Leave Nethrom and return to the darkness from whence you came," said Alex, lifting his staff.

Mog roared in reply, raising his own staff in a sweeping motion and spreading fire over the floor around Alex. Alex felt the heat of the flames and knew that this time the fire was real, yet he did not move nor did he try to counter the spell.

"Feel the heat of dragon fire, boy!" Mog laughed. "Begin to feel the pain that I will inflict upon you."

Reaching out, Alex took hold of the fire. It seemed almost alive in his hand. Mog had cast a spell of dragon fire, but he did not know that Alex was both a dragon lord and part dragon. The fire would obey *him*, not Mog. Alex pulled the fire together in his hand and swung it at Mog like a whip.

Mog screamed in surprise and pain as the flames struck him, throwing him back against the far wall of the chamber.

Alex coiled the flames for a second strike, but Mog spun away before he could land another blow.

"I see you've mastered fire," Mog said. "An impressive feat for any wizard, I'll not deny it. But I have other weapons—other, more deadly, ways of dealing with you."

Mog spun his staff quickly and an ice-cold blast of air hit Alex, pushing him back toward the wall. The cold tore at him, burning his bare hands and face as the air rushed over him. He felt strangely tired, and for a moment all he could think about was sleep. Shaking his head, Alex cleared his thoughts, and, raising his own staff, he turned away Mog's spell. One wall of the chamber went white with ice as the spell hit it. Mog raised his staff once more.

Alex was quicker this time, and he cast a spell of his own, a binding spell that would keep Mog from moving. He needed time to think, to warm his cold, numb hands, and to clear his mind. Fighting off Mog's spells was slowly draining his power, and he wondered how long he could keep it up.

Mog struggled against Alex's spell, but he was unable to break it. After several seconds he stood still, and Alex knew that Mog was gathering his own power to break the binding. Focusing his thoughts on the spell, Alex struggled to keep the binding in place, and for a brief moment he thought he'd succeeded, but then with a loud snapping sound, Mog broke free. The creature staggered slightly and leaned against the table, catching his breath.

Alex leaned against his staff, breathing hard after his effort to keep the binding spell in place. In the back of his mind, the wild, reckless feelings that he had been trying to understand for the last few months began to stir.

Mog moved suddenly, sending a blast of bloodred light at Alex.

The light hit Alex in the chest, throwing him against the cavern wall and knocking the breath out of him. He looked up to see the effort on the creature's face, the pain that it was costing him to keep the spell in place. Alex, however, didn't feel any pain; the true-silver mail he was wearing under his shirt had deflected the spell from him and sent it back to Mog.

"Curse you!" Mog shouted, breaking the spell. "That spell has killed more powerful wizards than you."

"Yet I remain," said Alex, pushing himself away from the wall.

"Not for long."

A blast of green light hit Alex like a hammer, driving him to his knees. There was no pain in this light, but it was full of feelings. His mind spun as memories he had thought all but forgotten returned to him. All of his darkest thoughts, his fears, and his sorrows seemed to gather around him like a mist as Mog continued to dig them out of Alex's own past.

Alex felt himself weakening little by little, unable to resist Mog's spell.

Mog pressed his advantage, forcing Alex's thoughts further back in time, drawing out the worst things that had ever happened to him.

Alex fell to the ground, his body suddenly too heavy for him to hold up. Darkness filled his mind with the memories and feelings Mog was forcing out of him. Alex knew the battle was lost. He would not be able to break Mog's spell; he would be destroyed. It was pointless to go on, pointless to resist the darkness.

Fight! a voice shouted in the back of Alex's brain. *Reach out and take the power that is waiting for you to claim it.*

It was a voice Alex had heard before, a voice that had told him what he needed to know when he'd fought other evils. This was his O'Gash, his sixth sense. Alex lifted his head and tried to focus on his enemy, but something hit him like a massive fist, driving him back to the floor.

Alex's deepest sorrow flooded into his mind. He was alone in a dimly lit room, standing in front of a coffin, a coffin that had only just been closed. Mog's spell began to lift the lid to reveal what lay inside, but Alex already knew what he would see: the pale face of his own mother, dead when Alex was only seven years old.

His mind raced with fear and with sorrow and with a desire Alex had never felt before. His body shook as he realized that he *wanted* the coffin lid to lift; he *wanted* to use the dark magic to call his mother back to the world of the living. More than anything, Alex wanted his mother to answer the questions that plagued him. Why had she never explained what his father had been? Why had she taken Alex to a world that held little magic? Why had she never told him about the family that should have been his?

He looked down on his mother's coffin and rage replaced his sorrow.

It will do no good, the O'Gash said calmly. *She had her own reasons, and she did what she did because she loved you. Calling back the dead is not the answer you are looking for.*

"Use the magic!" Mog's voice screamed from nowhere. "Rip the truth from those who have deceived you."

The coffin began to shake, its lid slowly opening. Alex closed his eyes, not wanting to see what was happening, but he could still hear the creaking of the coffin lid. With all the strength he had left, Alex lifted his right hand and reached out for something that had been waiting for him all of his life.

"Do it!" Mog shouted in excitement. "Take hold of the darkness, and live forever!"

"No," Alex growled in a voice that shook the mountain around him.

The reckless, wild power of the dragon surged through him as he fought off the despair. The flames of power rose up, filling Alex's whole body. He got back to his feet, and Mog's spell burned away like paper. A blast of golden light shot from Alex's staff, throwing Mog across the room into a shelf full of books. Mog looked up, startled and afraid, as a second blast hit him in the chest. His stone staff shattered into a million pieces.

Mog fell to his hands and knees, struggling to get back to his feet.

Alex moved forward, the reckless power changing him as he walked. When he stood over the broken body of Nethrom, he looked like a man made of golden flames.

"Dragon," said Mog in an awed whisper before collapsing to the floor.

A piercing scream filled the ancient chamber where Alex stood, and the dark shadow of Mog slowly lifted from the body of Nethrom. The shadow hovered for a moment as if trying to take shape, but Alex brushed it away with a wave of his hand, and it vanished without another sound.

Slowly, the feeling of reckless power began to slip away, and Alex found himself kneeling beside Nethrom's body. He was cold and worn out; he felt like he had just been sick. He gulped in the cool, damp air of the cavern, wiping sweat off his face with his sleeve.

After what felt like a long time, Nethrom stirred, his eyes opening slightly to look at Alex.

"You came," said Nethrom weakly. "You saved me from my own foolish mistake."

"I did what I had to do," Alex said softly.

"Thank you," Nethrom whispered. "Thank you for freeing me and my people."

"How did you find this place? How did you know it was here?" Alex asked.

"The order," Nethrom managed to whisper. "The order of Malgor."

Alex did not have time to ask anything more as Nethrom's eyes slipped out of focus and he let out his final breath.

CHAPTER NINETEEN
RETURN FROM DARKNESS

You have done well, young one, Salinor spoke in Alex's mind. *Now you must return to your friends. You have been too long in the darkness of the mountain.*

"I'm so tired," said Alex, looking around as he tried to find the dragon.

You must go, Salinor repeated. *You can rest later.*

"As you wish," answered Alex, struggling to get up.

When he opened his eyes, Alex wasn't sure if he was awake or dreaming. Darkness was all around him, and only the cold stone floor beneath him reminded him of where he was. Slowly he got to his feet, using his staff to help him stand. His head spun, and he stumbled sideways, bumping into something solid.

It was all he could do to conjure a single faint weir light, its dim glow reflected back to him by the crystal on Nethrom's table. Without thinking, Alex reached out and took the crystal, but he was too tired to put it inside his magic bag. Instead, he held it close to him with his free hand and pushed himself away from the table with his other hand.

It was difficult for Alex to find his way out of the room.

He was dizzy, and the feeble light he'd conjured did little to illuminate the path. He managed to close the door to Nethrom's prison behind him and then staggered across the chamber where he'd faced the golem. He felt like the weight of the mountain was pressing down on him.

The great cavern where he'd met the dwarf king, Set, was empty, and Alex hoped that that meant the king and his long-dead people had finally found their rest. As he made his way slowly across the wide floor, the darkness continued to press in on him, but he knew he had to go on, to return to his friends.

Pausing at the bottom of the cliff to rest, Alex looked up. He could not see very far in the darkness, but he felt a sudden surge of energy. He had to hurry. The darkness was growing heavier, and he could feel it all around him, trying to hold him where he was. More than once he had to stop and rest on the long climb to the top of the cliff, but each time he stopped, he felt the same urge to hurry push him forward. He longed for the feel of the wind on his face, but the air in the cave was deathly still.

By the time Alex reached the first chamber he'd entered, he was barely moving. His feet slid across the stone floor, and each movement took all the strength he could find. Only a strange light in the chamber drew him on, and when he stepped into the light, he had to blink to focus his eyes.

In the center of the chamber was a circle of torches. The jewels that had once been bats had been gathered into a great pile, and on the top of the pile sat the broken crown of Set. It had once been a beautiful crown of true silver, inlayed with gold and precious stones, and on its top was a star sapphire as large as an egg. The sapphire had been cut in half along with the crown, and Alex felt a great sorrow that such a beautiful object had been destroyed.

He thought he would leave the gems where they were, not having the energy to put them into his magic bag, but he had promised Set he would return the crown to Thorgood. He took a deep breath, and was pleased to discover that when he simply thought, *treasure room,* Set's crown, along with the entire pile of jewels, vanished into his magic bag.

Alex closed his eyes, trying to gather the strength to go on. It seemed only a moment later when he opened his eyes again, but the torches had almost gone out, and he realized he'd been standing still for a very long time. He felt stiff and found it difficult to move, but the sudden, loud crashing sound of stone falling on stone in the tunnel behind him told him that he had to move quickly.

Daylight shining into the mouth of the cave gave Alex hope, and he moved as quickly as he could to reach it. A cold breeze blew across his face as he left the cave, and he wiped away the tears that the bright light brought to his eyes. A huge weight seemed to lift from him as he stepped into the icy snow, and the cold, clean air woke him as if from a deep sleep. He crunched his way through the snow, moving away from the cave of the necromancer. Alex paused to look back just before he turned round the bend in the path. He felt the mountain shake, and as he watched, the cave crumbled into an unrecognizable pile of stones.

It was only then that Alex realized that he had been holding the mountain in check. It had been the weight of the mountain that had been pressing down on him, trying to cover the dark caverns below, and it had been his own unconscious will that had held it back. The realization shocked him, but he was too tired and weak to worry about it too much. If he had held back the mountain without knowing it, well, that was fine. At least he'd managed to get out before the caves had collapsed on top of him.

Alex started down the path once more, but it was slow going. The snow was deep, and he was still weak. After he'd walked a little more than a mile, he sat down in the snow to rest. He ate some dried meat from his magic bag and drank a great deal of water. He didn't remember water ever tasting so good before, or the air smelling so fresh. When he began to feel the cold bite of winter, he got up and started down the mountain again.

He thought about changing into a bird or a breeze, but the transformation spell seemed too difficult. Besides, he wasn't sure he would be strong enough to change back to himself when he reached Neplee.

Alex made his way slowly through the untouched snow of the Lost Mountains on foot. He was careful not to slip as he went along; the last thing he wanted right now was to roll down an icy mountainside and be covered with snow.

When the sun began to sink in the west, Alex began looking for a place to spend the night. He knew the clear sky would make the night much colder than the day had been. Normally, he could withstand the cold in the form of a tree, or he would conjure a fire to keep himself warm. He still felt too tired to change his shape, though, and he wasn't sure he could sustain a fire all through the night. Instead he found a sheltered spot close to some trees where a old pine had fallen. After resting for several minutes, he was able to ignite a small pile of branches with the inferno spell he knew so well, and he was grateful for the warmth the fire offered.

The night was long and cold, but even though Alex was terribly tired, he did not sleep. Instead he spent the time thinking about what had happened in the darkness below the mountain. An incredible amount of power had flowed through him when he needed it, a power he had not known was possible. It had come to him, filling him with both a wild recklessness and a joy he could not describe in words.

Then there was Mog's final word before he fled from Nethrom's body.

"Dragon," Alex finally said to himself in the darkness.

That was the name Mog had given him, the name Salinor had suggested that Alex would one day take, and the name he had been afraid of since he had first felt its power. Now that the reckless power had rescued him from despair, and, in a way, had become part of him, Alex knew why he was so weak. When he had released the power of the dragon and forced himself away from it, it had drained him. He also knew that the power was still there, waiting for him to call on it, or for some need to force it out of him. He knew that he would have to learn more about this power. But he could only do that if he took the shape of the dragon.

"Not yet," said Alex to the blowing wind. "Not yet."

He also thought about Nethrom's final words, his answer to the question Alex had asked: *The order of Malgor.* Alex's thoughts ran through his mind like the winter wind, and he was unable to hold on to them for long.

In the cold hour before dawn, Alex built up his fire and cooked some food. He wasn't really hungry, but he knew he should eat. He didn't know how long he had been in the mountains. He could remember the two days it took to reach the necromancer, but he had no idea how long he'd been in the dark caverns under the mountain, asleep. It felt like a long time, but that might have been because he'd woken in darkness.

When the sun rose, he was ready to move again. For a moment, Alex considered taking a form other than his own so he could return to Neplee more quickly. He felt stronger, but still he hesitated. A part of him wanted to take the shape of the dragon, the shape that was at least part of what he was. But he knew that taking the dragon form now would be foolish; he wasn't sure what changes it would make in him, and he wasn't even sure he would ever return to his friends if he took that shape now.

Instead he struggled through the snow on foot, slipping and falling several times as he went. He had no path to follow, but he knew he had to go down to get out of the mountains. He made good time in the beginning, but as the day wore on, he began to stumble more and more. The paths he chose through the trees often ended in snowdrifts that were taller than he was, and the cold mountain air was draining his body of heat.

Finally, when the sun was dropping behind the mountains once more, Alex came to a huge drift of snow. It looked as if all the snow on one side of the mountain had slipped into the valley, blocking his path completely. He walked along the drift away from the mountain, only to find his path blocked by a raging river full of ice. There was no way to move forward and no place he could take shelter for the night.

"Very well," said Alex to the shadows gathering around him. "I will change, but not to the dragon form. I'm not ready for that. Not yet."

Taking a moment to gather his thoughts, Alex took the shape of an eagle. Lifting his arms—now wings—he rose from the frozen ground with little effort. The cold wind whipped around him, but his new feathers kept him warm. He circled once above the river and then soared higher into the sky, becoming familiar with his new shape.

Flying, Alex discovered, was wonderful, even better than being a breeze. The mountains slipped away behind him as he glided on the wind, catching the last rays of the setting sun. His eagle eyes could see every detail of the land below him, even the small white rabbits that ran across the snow-covered meadows.

When the first stars came out, Alex flew lower, trying to stay out of the wind that blew across the mountaintops. He could feel the warm air of the day rising along the mountainsides, and he tried to stay as close to that as possible. He also tried to fly quickly, which was easy to do in the eagle's body. Neplee was not far away, and he felt a sudden urge to get there, an urge that did not come from fear or worry, but from his desire to see his friends.

As the moon rose into the sky, Alex spotted the dwarf

city in the distance. Bright torches had been lit beside the city gates, which had been left partway open. Diving down to get a better look, Alex saw that several heavily wrapped dwarfs were tending the torches, and he realized that they had been lit to guide him back from the mountains.

For a moment Alex considered taking his own form at the gate and receiving the welcome of the dwarfs. He knew how happy Turlock would be now that the curse had been lifted and the necromancer was gone. He could imagine his friends' happy faces and their questions about what he had done and how he had managed to defeat Mog.

It was that thought that made up Alex's mind for him. He was tired and wanted to rest before answering any questions. He decided to stay in eagle form for the night, resting in the trees nearby until morning. When morning came, he would change to himself and, rested, greet his friends and the happy dwarfs who waited for him.

Alex found a giant pine to settle in for the night, not far from the gates of the city. He folded his wings close to him, though he wasn't at all cold. Then he closed his eyes, and without really falling asleep, he rested.

As he rested, his mind took flight once more as the eagle, and the feeling of freedom that the form gave him made him happy. He let his dream self fly over the mountains and across the open plains, soaring in the warm sunlight. It was a pleasant, restful dream, and when his dream self returned before dawn, he felt better than he had in a long time.

Opening the eagle's eyes, Alex saw that the torches were still burning at the city gates. Several dwarfs were already working to clear away the snow that had blown around the gates during the night.

The day was just growing light when Alex saw Arconn step lightly onto the snow and start off toward the mountains. He passed the pine Alex was sitting in, and Alex called to him, forgetting that the eagle had no true voice. Arconn paused to look around and then he hurried on. Alex saw the determined look on Arconn's face, and he realized his friend was going into the mountains to look for him. He called out once more and took flight, not wanting Arconn to go too far before he could catch up and change back to himself.

Arconn moved fast over the frozen snow, and Alex was glad he had not changed back to his own form before trying to follow. He had to flap his wings hard to overtake his friend because there was no morning wind to help him. When he reached Arconn, Alex called once more, circling and coming to rest on the ground in front of the elf.

"What is this?" said Arconn in surprise.

Alex returned to his own shape. "It is what you are looking for, and what would have found you this morning, if you hadn't started off so early."

"Alex!" Arconn yelled in surprise and delight, rushing forward and throwing his arms around his friend. "We've been so worried about you. Turlock has kept the city gates open for the past week, hoping the light would help guide you back."

"The past week?" Alex questioned. "How long have I been gone? It seems that today would only be the fifth or sixth day since I left Neplee."

"You've been gone fourteen days, Alex," said Arconn. "Kat

told us that you'd succeeded in defeating the evil on the evening of the second day, and we've been expecting you ever since then. We never thought it would take you so long to return after you'd found and defeated the necromancer so quickly."

"I slept for a long time," Alex said. "I was asleep beneath the mountains for ten days, and then Salinor woke me."

"Salinor?" Arconn questioned.

"Forgive me, I spoke without thinking," Alex answered, shocked that he'd spoken the dragon's name out loud. "I should not have said his name. Please, forget what I said."

"But there is no need," Arconn said. "It is a name I know from long ago. I told you once that I knew a dragon—a dragon that was not evil, do you remember?"

"Yes, I remember," Alex answered, thinking back. "That was before I really believed in dragons, when I knew almost nothing of them."

"Yes," said Arconn. "And now I find that you've met the same dragon that I once did. You know him by the same name that I know him by, the name that I have never spoken to another living soul."

"And I should not have spoken it now," Alex said dejectedly. "I simply forgot to keep his name secret, and it is only a lucky chance that you are the one who heard it."

"Hardly luck," said Arconn seriously. "Ever since we left the Isle of Bones, I have wanted to tell you about Salinor. I felt something pushing me to tell you his name, some desire to share it with you that I could not understand."

"So you think he meant for us to know? Did Salinor want

us to talk about him to each other? Or at least know that we both had met the same dragon?"

"I am certain of it, though I cannot guess why," said Arconn. "The ways of dragons are difficult to understand, and Salinor is perhaps the most difficult, as he is the oldest dragon of all."

"Then we should not try to reason out his motives, at least not here and now," Alex added with a laugh. "We should return to the city so the rest of our company can stop worrying."

"Yes, that would be best," agreed Arconn. "Will you change shape again, or do you prefer to walk in the snow?"

"It would be quicker if I changed, but the walk is not a long one, and I'd like to talk a little before we rejoin the others," said Alex.

They turned and started off toward the dwarf city, Arconn walking across the top of the snow and Alex crunching along beside him. As they went, they talked about Salinor and the ways of dragons, though Alex did not mention anything that Salinor had told him about his true nature or his family. He thought it best to keep that information a secret, at least for the time being.

Alex did ask Arconn if he was also a dragon lord since he knew Salinor's true name.

Arconn laughed and said that only wizards could be dragon lords. "He told me his name because he knew I would not have power over him," Arconn said as he helped Alex through a snowdrift. "The name has power, that is true, but only a wizard can use it to control the dragon."

When they were close to the city gates, Alex heard a loud

yell. The dwarf guards had spotted them coming and were calling into the city to let Lord Turlock know that Alex had returned.

Arconn tried to help Alex hurry through the snow, but it was too deep for Alex to move quickly.

The guards all dropped to one knee as Alex reached the city gates, bowing their heads in gratitude and respect. Alex smiled, but was unsure what to say to them. He had not expected such a reaction to his victory and had not thought about how the dwarfs of Neplee would receive him.

Turlock reached the gates as Alex and Arconn passed through them, and before Alex said a word, Turlock also dropped to one knee. "Hail, great wizard, master of the dead."

"No," Alex said sternly. "I am no master of the dead and never will be. Please, Lord Turlock, rise and greet me as a friend."

Turlock got to his feet, obviously regretting what he'd said.

Alex smiled at him and took his hand in friendship, pulling him close as he shook it. He leaned forward so he could whisper in Turlock's ear. "Forgive my sharpness, but I will not be called a master of the dead."

"I spoke without thinking," said Turlock, embracing Alex like a brother. "It will not happen again, my friend."

Thrang and the others arrived as Alex and Turlock broke apart, and Alex was almost knocked over as his friends rushed forward to embrace him.

"I see you didn't have to look very far," Thrang said to Arconn once the dwarf had let go of Alex.

"No farther than the front gate, really," said Arconn with

a laugh. "Though Alex could have saved himself some walking if he'd come into the city last night when he actually arrived."

"Last night?" Turlock questioned.

"I thought it best to let you all rest until daylight before making my entrance," Alex explained.

"As if we've slept at all," Nellus said, slapping Alex on the shoulder.

"I slept." Barnabus laughed. "Though it's been difficult with Thrang storming around in his worry."

"I was not storming around," Thrang said defensively. "Though I have been worried, I won't deny it."

"And now some of your worries are over," Alex said, putting his arm around Thrang's shoulders. "Though I daresay you'll find new ones to replace them."

Everyone laughed at Alex's comment, even Thrang. When they stopped laughing, the questions began as everyone, especially Lord Turlock, wanted to know what had happened in the mountains.

"Am I to have no rest?" Alex asked with a smile. "At least let's go into the city and find a warm room before I tell the tale."

"An excellent idea," Turlock said. "And I'll arrange for your breakfast to be brought to you, if that's all right, and you can tell us your story while we are together."

"You are most kind," said Alex, bowing to Turlock.

"And if you don't mind too much," Turlock went on, raising his eyebrows, "I would like some of the lords of Neplee to be there as well. They should hear the story themselves, so they will know the great deed you have done for us."

"As you wish," said Alex, allowing himself to be guided into the city by Turlock.

Turlock led Alex and his friends to a large hall near the throne room. When they entered, Turlock quickly ordered some of the dwarfs to bring hot food to the tables and the others to summon the lords of Neplee. It was obvious that word of Alex's return had spread, and Alex hoped he had not caused too much trouble by being gone so long in the mountains. When the dwarfs had all gathered and Alex was seated with his friends, Turlock rose and began to speak.

"My friends. Lords and masters of Neplee, the curse that has been on our city for so long has passed. We are free once more. Once more, we can take pride in our city and our works. For this, we must give thanks to Master Taylor."

There was a general clamor of agreement as the assembled dwarfs cheered and began to chant Alex's name. Turlock beamed at Alex, and then held up his hands for quiet.

"Master Taylor will tell us the story of his deeds," Turlock went on. "Though perhaps he would prefer to eat his breakfast first."

"Not at all," said Alex. "Though the food is tempting, I will tell you my story first. There will be time for food later."

The room grew still and all eyes were on Alex. He could hear the deep, steady breathing of those gathered in the room, and he took strength from them as he began to tell the tale.

Alex told them everything—or almost everything—that had happened in the mountains. He was careful not to mention Salinor's call to wake him, or the crown of Set, which he now carried in his magic bag. He did pause to thank Volo, who was in the room, for the help he had given him in preparing to face the necromancer.

"So it worked, then," Volo said happily. "I had my doubts, though you seemed so certain."

"Yes, my friend, it worked," Alex answered. "It is a secret long forgotten by most, and I will share it with all of you now."

Alex unbuttoned his shirt as he spoke, pulling it back to reveal the true-silver chain mail shirt that Volo had helped him make. There was a gasp of astonishment as the light reflected off the silver, and the eyes of the dwarfs grew large in wonder.

"True silver," Alex said. "Not only beautiful and strong, but magical as well. True silver will always resist dark magic, and if made into armor such as this, it will reflect curses back at the one who sent them."

"You used Nethrom's own power against him?" Thrain questioned.

"In a way," Alex answered as he buttoned his shirt. "You see, Nethrom was not really the necromancer. He was not the evil one, though it was because of Nethrom that the evil came. When Nethrom died, he had been freed from the evil that had held him captive for so long."

"Then we have another reason to thank you," said Turlock. "You have taken the stain from Nethrom's name. We can re-member him as the good and decent dwarf he once was, and not as the evil he became."

Alex finished his story with his arrival at the city gates. When he was done, the dwarfs all cheered and bowed to Alex as if he were a king. Alex smiled and asked them to rise. He did not want to be rude, but he was concerned that the dwarfs of Neplee might think he had done more than he really had.

"You are kind and generous, Master Taylor," Turlock said, rising with the rest of the dwarfs. "We know you are a good man and will not willingly accept all of the honors that we would give you, so I will offer you this oath and ask all here to swear with me. If ever you have need—for treasure, workers, warriors, or simply a place to rest—the city of Neplee will be yours to command. This I swear as a lord of Neplee. How say you, lords of Neplee?"

"We swear it shall be so," the other dwarfs answered in one voice. "We bind ourselves, our families, and all that we shall ever have to this oath. We will answer the call of Master Taylor, in this life or the next."

"Thank you, my friends," Alex said, bowing his head. "I hope there will never be a need for me to call upon your oath, but I thank you for your vow."

The dwarfs all pressed forward to shake Alex's hands. Alex smiled and bowed to them, but he was beginning to feel tired. He had not slept properly in a long time, and he felt that sleep was what he needed more than anything right now.

"You are tired from your ordeal," Turlock said, noticing the look on Alex's face. "Go with your company; they will lead you to your rest. Tonight there will be a feast such as Neplee has never seen, and you will be the guest of honor."

"You are most kind, Lord Turlock," said Alex. "A day's rest will do me good, and I would not miss such a feast for a mountain of pure gold."

Turlock bowed once more as Thrang and Arconn came

forward to stand on either side of Alex. The crowd of dwarfs parted to let the company pass, but even the street outside the hall was crowded with hundreds of dwarfs. Alex smiled. It seemed that every dwarf in Neplee was there, wanting to see him, though most seemed too shy to meet his gaze.

When they reached their rooms, Alex thought he would go straight to bed, but Thrang pulled him toward the fire and motioned for him to take a chair.

"I've known you long enough to know when you leave out part of a story," Thrang said, taking the chair next to Alex. "The dwarf who spoke to you in the caves—did he give you his name?"

"He did," Alex answered. "Let me ask you a question, one that will answer your own. Can you tell me the story of a dwarf king named Set?"

"Set?" Thrang repeated, his eyes growing wide. "Set was an early king of the dwarf realm. He was a great king, and a defender of his people. The stories about him are many and long, but basically they all say that some evil came into Thraxon during his rule, and that Set went out to fight against it. Set did not return from the battle, but the evil vanished as well. The stories claim that Set defeated the evil, but that he paid for his victory with his own life."

"I see," said Alex.

"Was Set the dwarf you met in the caves?" Thrang questioned.

"Yes," Alex answered. "He seemed to know I was coming, but I was unable to find out how he knew." Alex hesitated, considering how much more he should say. "He asked me to take something to his heir."

"Enough," Thrang said, turning his eyes away from Alex and gazing into the fire. "I know enough to guess what he asked you to take, and I will not ask you for details now. We will not speak of this again until we return to Benorg. Thorgood should be present to hear all that you have to say and answer any questions you might have for him."

"As you wish," said Alex. "I also took some other things from the cave, gems that should be divided between us."

"Anything you took from the cave is yours alone," Thrang said quickly. "You may do with it as you think best. Whatever you do, though, keep your word to Set."

"I will do as you wish, my friend," said Alex, getting up. "Now I think I will sleep. Wake me in time for the feast, if I do not wake by myself."

Alex left Thrang staring to the fire and moved toward his room, but Kat caught his eye as he walked past. She sat alone at one of the tables in the back of the room. Smiling, Alex sat down next to her.

"You wish to ask me something," Alex said. It was not a question.

"You can see my thoughts more clearly than I can," said Kat.

"No, but I can guess at them now."

"Your battle with the necromancer—was it as close a thing as it seemed to be?"

"For a time it was very close," Alex answered. "But that is not what you really wish to know."

"No, it's not."

"Do you wish me to remove the spell I placed upon you?"

"Do you think seeing the truth will be too much for me?" Kat asked, looking him in the eye.

"No. You should see the truth if you are ready, and I think you are," Alex answered.

"Then show me," Kat pleaded.

Alex nodded. He stood up, touching Kat's forehead with his hand as he rose. He felt the spell he'd put on her begin to lift, but he removed it slowly so she would not be suddenly overcome.

Kat watched him for a moment and then turned away, her eyes filling with tears.

"Do not be too hard on yourself," Alex said in a low voice, bending toward Kat so only she could hear him. "Do not hate the gift you have because evil tried to use you. Learn from what has happened so you can prevent such things from happening again."

Kat did not answer him, but blindly caught his hand with her own. She pulled it to her lips and gently kissed it before letting go.

Alex glanced around, making sure that the others had not seen Kat's gesture. He was surprised by Kat's action and unsure of what she might have meant by it. He patted Kat on the shoulder, and, feeling tired beyond words, he went to find his bed.

CHAPTER TWENTY

TO THE GOLDEN ROCKS

------◆------

Alex and his friends remained in Neplee as winter slowly changed to spring. The city had become more like the other dwarf cities Alex had visited in the past, and everywhere he went he was greeted with bows and smiles. Turlock had officially named him a lord of Neplee, a title all the dwarfs took seriously. Even Thrang addressed him as lord, at least when they were out in public.

There were feasts and parties almost every night, and Alex soon longed for the quiet, simple life of the open road. The fact that all of the attention was to honor him and what he had done for Neplee meant he could not miss a single feast, no matter how much he would have liked to. He knew that the dwarfs meant well, and he loved them for their kindness, but he needed to be alone and think about what had happened to him.

Sometimes, when it all became too much and Alex thought he couldn't face one more party, he would leave the city for at least part of the day. Taking the shape of an eagle or sometimes the wind, he was free to roam the lands around Neplee.

He had sent a message to Whalen telling him what had

happened in the necromancer's cave and exactly how he'd managed to defeat Mog. He did not, however, tell Whalen about what Salinor had said. Something kept Alex from sharing the dragon's words, even with Whalen.

Whalen had been shocked to learn the necromancer's name, and he had gone into great detail about the stories and myths he'd heard concerning an evil spirit named Mog.

"I have no doubt now that some of the stories and myths are true," Whalen had written in his letter to Alex. "And once more, I am impressed by your abilities."

Finally the snows began to melt, and the smells of spring filled the air. Alex's companions were almost as eager as he was to be back on the road, and they were all excited to continue their adventure. The dwarfs of Neplee knew that Alex's time in the city was growing short, and they made great efforts to have as many feasts as possible before the adventurers left the city.

Alex had spent a lot of time thinking over the winter, and he had finally decided that the crown of Set should be remade. One night, after yet another feast, Alex went to his room and slipped into his magic bag. He collected the broken crown from the treasure room and then quickly went into his father's bag, hoping that his smitty friends would be able to help him.

"Bobkin, Belkin," Alex called as he entered the workshop. "I know it's late, but I need your help."

"Coming, Master Alex," Bobkin's voice answered.

Alex heard the hidden door open, and he was about to light some of the lamps in the dimly lit shop when he stopped short.

"What can we do for you?" Bobkin questioned, hurrying toward Alex with Belkin and Dobkin following close behind.

"Um, what?" Alex said, his attention fixed on Dobkin. "I need you to . . . Why is Dobkin glowing?"

"Oh, well, yes," said Belkin. "He does that sometimes, but it doesn't seem to bother him."

"That's not normal, is it?" Alex questioned.

"No, not normal at all," said Bobkin. "You had some tasks you needed our help with?"

"How often does Dobkin glow?" Alex asked, waving his hand and bringing light to the workshop.

"Every new moon," said Belkin.

"That would mean . . . Of course!" said Alex, setting the broken halves of Set's crown on the worktable. "I know what's happened to him."

"He was hit on the head," said Bobkin.

"No, he was hexed," said Alex. "Someone has tried to control him, but they didn't do a very good job. Every new moon the spell is renewed, which is why he glows."

"Are you sure?" Belkin questioned. "I mean, who would hex a smitty?"

"I don't know," said Alex. "But I'm sure I can remove the spell, and once I do Dobkin will be himself again."

"If you could help Dobkin, we would be even more in your debt," said Bobkin.

"Dobkin," said Alex. "Look at me."

The glowing smitty staggered forward, and his head bobbed about as if he was drunk. His eyes looked unfocused.

"Dobkin," said Alex, snapping his fingers to get the smitty's attention.

He looked up at the sound and his face slowly broke into a smile. "Dobkin!" Dobkin shouted.

"This shouldn't take long," said Alex. He lifted his right hand, extending his index finger.

Dobkin's eyes followed Alex's finger, and his head shifted to follow it as Alex moved his finger up and down and from side to side. Finally Alex reached out and tapped the smitty on the head. Dobkin instantly stopped glowing.

"That should do it," said Alex. "Of course, he'll need to sleep, but he should be his old self when he wakes up in the morning."

"Oh, that *is* good news," said Belkin happily. "You're sure it was a hex?"

"I'm sure."

"Well, if that's settled, tell us what you need our help with," said Bobkin, his eyes darting to the broken crown behind Alex.

"I need your help repairing this crown," said Alex as he turned back to the table.

Bobkin hurried to climb onto the tabletop. "Oh, this was a nice piece at one time. Well made, dwarven design, and . . ."

"And?" Alex questioned.

"It had some magic in it once," said Belkin, standing beside Bobkin. "I can't see what the magic was for, but it was definitely there."

"Is there any way to find out what the magic was?" Alex questioned.

"Maybe," said Bobkin. "We'll need to study it for a bit. How soon will you need it repaired?"

"Oh, there's no rush," said Alex. "I imagine it will be several months before I need it, and if you can discover what magic was in it in the meantime, that would be helpful."

"Well, if Dobkin is himself again in the morning, it shouldn't be too hard," said Belkin. "Dobkin has a knack for spotting magic and figuring out how it works. We might need you to work the magic, Master Alex, but at the very least we should be able to tell you what it was and why it was there."

"Excellent," said Alex. "I'll leave the crown with you, then. Feel free to use whatever you need to repair it."

"It doesn't look like it will take much," said Belkin in a thoughtful tone.

"The sapphire might be a problem," said Bobkin.

"Gems aren't something we usually repair," said Belkin.

"You have my permission to search the treasure room in this bag and in my other bag for a replacement," said Alex.

"Very good, Master Alex," said Bobkin with a bow.

"I'll come back in a day or two to check on Dobkin," said Alex. "And don't work too hard on the crown. Like I said, I won't need it for a few months at least."

"As you wish," Bobkin and Belkin said together.

Alex climbed into his bed knowing that the smittys would make the crown as good as new, possibly even better. He felt good about his decision to have the crown repaired, and he felt even better that he'd discovered and removed the hex that had been placed on Dobkin. He wondered again who would put a hex on a smitty, but the thought was soon lost as he fell asleep.

Before the snows had completely melted, Turlock sent several dwarfs to find horses for Alex and his companions, as there were few animals left in the city. Thrang began preparing for their departure, buying things he thought they might need along the way and stocking everyone's bags with food.

"Turlock doesn't know how far away Gal Tock is, and I doubt any other dwarf does. We should be prepared for a long road," Thrang said as he sorted packages one night.

"I've spent some time in the libraries," Arconn added. "All of the maps stop just south of the Lost Mountains, so there is no knowing what lies ahead of us."

"There are no dwarf cities farther south?" Thrain questioned.

"Oh, yes, there are several," said Thrang. "And even some to the west as well. The dwarfs of Thraxon have spread far and wide, and there's no telling where you might find a dwarf village or city."

"Is there some reason all the dwarf cities are not known to King Thorgood?" Alex questioned.

"Thorgood's capital is in the north," Thrang answered thoughtfully. "It has been a long time since any of the northern kings have sent messengers this far south."

"Why is that?" Barnabus asked as he stored the parcels Thrang had given him.

"There's no reason, at least none you could name," Thrang said, shifting in his seat.

"What is it that you can't put your finger on?" Alex asked, beginning to worry that trouble lay ahead of them.

"I only know what the legends say," Thrang answered. "The king of the dwarf realm has lived in Benorg for nearly three thousand years, so if some of the cities in the far south have forgotten him or found a new king, well . . . I suppose that's only natural."

"So it is possible that the dwarfs of the south will not recognize Thorgood as the king," Alex said thoughtfully. "In fact, they may not be too friendly with us once they learn we are on a quest for Thorgood."

"It is possible," said Thrang, returning to his sorting. "But if we don't speak of our goal—or Thorgood's name or title—there is nothing to worry about."

"A title Thorgood finds difficult to keep without the crown of the ancient kings," Alex said in a low voice so only Thrang could hear him.

Thrang didn't answer but nodded his agreement to Alex's statement. Alex thought about Thrang's words as he stored his own parcels in his bag, realizing just how important Set's request had been. Set knew that Thorgood was his heir, but there would be almost no way of proving it to some other king who ruled in the south of Thraxon. Suddenly, Alex remembered something else—something Mr. Clutter had told him before he had joined this adventure. Alex filed the thought away, determined to think about it more later.

That night, Turlock held a grand feast, and every dwarf family in Neplee presented a gift of some kind to Alex. Alex accepted their gifts with thanks and bows, but he thought most of the families could not afford the gifts they were giving. Yet, he knew that he could not refuse any of the gifts without losing honor. Still he worried, and after the feast ended, he asked Turlock for a private word.

"Your city has been very generous to me," Alex said once he and Turlock had entered Turlock's private room.

"No less than you deserve, my friend," said Turlock. "You've done us a great service and made it possible for us to prosper once again."

"Yes," Alex agreed. "But I fear that some of your people have given more than they should have."

"I see," said Turlock, taking a step closer to Alex. "And you fear they will suffer hardship because of their gifts to you."

"As I said, your city has been very generous."

"And I see you know enough of dwarfs to know that you cannot give back the gifts that have been given," Turlock said thoughtfully.

"I would not insult your people, Turlock. I have another solution in mind."

"What is that, Lord Taylor? Say what you wish, I will not be offended."

Alex took out his magic bag and spoke softly into the top of it. The air in the room stirred slightly as the huge pile of gems he had taken from the necromancer's cave appeared on the chamber floor.

"I wish you to use this wealth to help your people," Alex said. "I took it from the mountains, so it rightfully belongs to your city."

"I—" Turlock began but stopped, looking at the pile in

front of him. "You are too good to us. I cannot accept all of this, not even for my people."

"Yet you know that many of them will need your help," Alex pressed.

"Yes, they will, but I don't think they will need this much help," Turlock answered with a weak smile. "Leave a third of this wealth. That will be more than enough to help the needy of this city."

"You are wise and kind, and perhaps too generous," said Alex. "I will leave half, but you must promise me two things."

"Whatever you ask of me, I will do," Turlock answered firmly.

"First, no one can know that I left this wealth with you, at least it can't be generally known. You'll have to explain things to the lords of Neplee, but I'm sure they will understand my wishes."

"It will be as you wish. And the second promise?"

"That you use this wealth only to help those who are truly in need," Alex said, holding Turlock's eyes with his own. "You are not to give any of these gems to those who don't work or don't try to provide for themselves. You understand my meaning."

"Yes," Turlock answered with a bow. "It will be as you ask."

"Then I will leave you for tonight, my friend," said Alex. "And we will say farewell in the morning."

"You are forgetting something," Turlock said as Alex turned toward the door. "You are to take half of this with you, remember?"

"Yes, of course," Alex answered, laughing at himself. "You

know, there was a time when such treasure would seem like all the wealth in the world to me. Now it seems a small thing, something that is easy to forget."

"Your wealth is greater than gems or gold," said Turlock. "You have the love of friends, and their hopes for you."

Alex smiled and nodded. He spoke once again into the top of his magic bag. The air moved slightly and the pile between Alex and Turlock grew smaller. Alex nodded once more to Turlock before he left the room, slowly making his way back to his friends and then to his room to sleep one last night in Neplee.

Their departure the next morning was both a happy and a sad event. Every dwarf in the city lined the road to the main gates, and those who couldn't find a spot along the way crowded around and outside the city gates. Turlock waited at the gates to wish them farewell, reminding Alex one more time that if he was ever in need, the city of Neplee would come to his assistance.

"Farewell, my friends," Alex called as Thrang led them away from the city. "May your city prosper in peace."

There was a loud cheer in reply, and then the dwarfs began to sing an old traveling song.

"It is meant to bring us luck," Thrang said by way of explanation. "It is an old song, and some people say there is magic in it."

"Magic?" Kat questioned.

"I don't know if that is true, but it's well meant," Thrang said happily.

They rode across the open lands, their horses' hooves

crunching loudly through the last few inches of snow that remained on the ground. The air was pleasantly cool, and they could smell the promise of spring in it.

"The open air is wonderful," Nellus called from behind Alex. "The dwarf city was a good place to spend the winter, but I'm happy to be in the open again."

"As am I," Barnabus agreed. "We did too much sitting around in Neplee. I fear we've all grown soft from the kindness of the dwarfs."

"Then you'll have to harden in a hurry," said Thrang. "I fear our quest for Albrek's tomb is far from over."

"The dwarfs of the Lost Mountains didn't know where Albrek had gone," Kat said softly. "If they ever knew, they have forgotten long ago."

"And we are running out of places to look," Alex added.

"That's not true," Thrang said with a grunting laugh. "There are lots of places we can look; we're just running out of places where we know we should look."

"Growing tired of the adventure already?" Arconn joked with a glance at Alex.

Alex laughed and shook his head. He was partly amazed at what they had already accomplished on this adventure and partly troubled by what he had learned along the way. More than anything else, however, he was worried about taking the form of the dragon. Salinor had warned him that it might be difficult for him to return to his human form once he had made the change, or, at least, he had hinted that it might be difficult. Alex didn't want to risk it, and he didn't want to run into anything that might tempt him to use his new power. He took comfort in knowing that he had faced and defeated the necromancer without taking the dragon's shape, even though he had used some of the dragon's power to do it. For his own reasons he hoped he would have time to prepare himself before making the change.

Alex pushed his worries to the back of his mind as they continued riding south. It was a sunny day, and the land was pleasant to look at.

They camped that night near a small stream, and though it seemed unlikely they would meet trouble, Thrang insisted they keep a watch.

"We don't know what lies ahead of us, so we might as well prepare for the worst," Thrang said sternly.

"Hopefully nothing as bad as what's behind us," Thrain said.

"It has been an exciting first adventure for you so far," said Alex.

"Much more than I ever expected," Thrain agreed. "I'd heard stories about first adventures, and most of them seemed very dull. Your first adventure was full of excitement, but you were a wizard-in-training then."

"Yes, that's true," agreed Alex. "Though I don't think my first adventure was as dangerous as this one has been."

"Easy to say that now." Arconn smiled at Alex. "Your past adventure is over and you made it home safely."

"That is also true," Alex agreed. "But we've met more dangerous things on this adventure than we did on that one."

"Oh?" Arconn questioned. "That time we faced a three-legged troll, an oracle, bandits, wraiths, the dark shadow, and a dragon. This time it was a nagas, the hellerash, and a necro-mancer."

"You count the oracle as dangerous, but not the dragon on the Isle of Bones?" Alex questioned. "And you have forgotten to mention Bane."

"Oracles can be more dangerous than most other things," Arconn answered with a smile. "And the dragon on the Isle of Bones proved to be friendly—or at least not dangerous. As for Bane, I'm not sure."

"All right," Alex said, waving away Arconn's argument. "Thrain has had an exciting first adventure so far, but I hope that most of the excitement is over."

"As do I," Thrang agreed, taking a seat beside the fire. "We've been lucky so far, and I hope we don't need too much more luck to finish this adventure."

"I wouldn't call it luck," Arconn said with a nod in Alex's direction.

"No, I suppose not," agreed Thrang.

They ate in silence, as everyone was tired from the long day's ride. As the others went to bed, Alex remained by the fire alone, assuming his customary first watch. Staring at the glowing coals of the fire, he thought about the crystal he had taken from Nethrom's table. The crystal was the same as the one he had recovered for the Oracle, Iownan. He thought about the crystal and the empty tower by the Eastern Sea for a long time.

When his watch was over, Alex woke Thrain, but he did not go to his tent to sleep. Returning to the fire, he continued to think about the crystal, the tower, and the oracle that was to come. He wished he could make sense of it, but he didn't know much about the empty tower or the legends surrounding it. He watched the fire for a long time. Slowly he felt his mind drifting away, returning to the hidden Isle of Bones.

"So, you come again, young one," Salinor said softly.

"I wanted to thank you for waking me when I was under the mountain," said Alex.

"And to ask more questions of me," Salinor said with a smile.

"Yes."

"The crystal you took from the cave is the tool of seers and oracles," Salinor said calmly. "Yes, you could make it work, but you don't really need it."

"Should I give it to Kat? Is she to become the Oracle of the Empty Tower?"

"I do not know," Salinor said slowly, as if he were thinking about Alex's questions. "I know she could use the crystal, if she chooses to. I also know that the oracle must reach the tower soon or it will be lost. Also, only a dragon can take the true oracle to the tower—that much of the legend is true."

"Then I must take the shape of the dragon if Kat is to be the oracle?" Alex questioned, his heart racing.

"Perhaps," Salinor answered. "You still fear to take the shape?"

"I fear I will be lost."

"Yet it is your true shape, or at least one of your true shapes," Salinor said kindly. "You are so different from a dragon and yet so much the same. I cannot tell you what to do, but I can tell you this: you will never find your full power or become all that you can be until you accept both of your true forms."

"I know. What I don't know is if I am strong enough to do it. What if I become lost in the dragon shape? What if the power is too much for me to control?"

"Then you will break," Salinor answered. "As the Oracle of the White Tower once told you."

"Did she know?" Alex questioned, remembering everything that Iownan had told him. "Did she know what I was, or what I might become?"

"She may have guessed, but I don't think she knew," Salinor answered. "She knows a great deal, but even her powers are limited. I believe she told you as much as you needed to know at the time."

"Yes," Alex agreed. "I suppose even you don't know everything."

"I know many things," said Salinor. "But everything is quite a lot, and I have not lived long enough to know everything."

After a moment, Alex decided that Kat should have the crystal, even if he never took the shape of the dragon.

"You have my thanks, ancient one," Alex said. "You have given me much to think about, but the path ahead already seems less dim."

"If there is light on the path, it comes from you," Salinor said softly.

Alex's mind was already racing back through the darkness to his body. He heard Arconn call his name and he opened his eyes. "Was I gone long?"

"You were here all night," Thrang said, looking confused.

"Only my body was here," said Alex, getting up and stretching his legs. "My mind has traveled far, but my body is hungry."

"Then have some breakfast," Barnabus said, holding out a plate for Alex. "The rest of us have already eaten. Arconn said we shouldn't disturb you until we were ready to go."

"I'm sorry," Alex said as he took the plate from Barnabus. "You should have called me as soon as breakfast was ready."

"Not a problem," Thrang said, taking a seat next to Alex. "We're all a little stiff this morning. It won't hurt us to stretch for a while before climbing back into our saddles."

"We'd all be better off if we had some more of that dwarf remedy of yours," Nellus said.

"One sip each," Thrang said, holding out his silver flask for Alex. "More than that and you might go back to sleep."

"I wouldn't mind a bit more sleep myself," Barnabus laughed.

"There is something I need to do before we leave," Alex said, handing the flask back to Thrang and setting aside his plate. "And I need you all to witness it."

"Oh, what is that?" Thrang questioned.

Alex turned to Kat. "Kat, I won't insist that you take this, but I will offer it to you just the same."

"Take what?" Kat questioned.

Alex spoke into his magic bag and retrieved the crystal he had taken from Nethrom's table. As he held it up, the crystal caught the morning light and blazed like a ball of fire in his hand.

"An oracle's crystal," Kat said, stepping back from Alex, her eyes wide in wonder. "How did . . . Why would . . . I don't—"

"You are a seer," Alex said, getting to his feet. "You may even be more than a seer. You can use this crystal if you will, that much I know. I offer it to you now, freely and without condition."

"But, I . . ." Kat stammered.

"You are what you are," said Alex. "Who can say what you may become?"

"The tower," Kat said, holding Alex's eyes with her own.

"Perhaps."

"Very well, I will accept this gift you offer. I will try to use it wisely and for good." Kat took the crystal from his hand.

Alex turned to the company. "Will you all witness that Katrina Dayyed has accepted this crystal?" he questioned loudly.

"We will," the others answered as one.

"Then I think it is time we got moving," Alex said. "There's no telling how far the golden rocks are from here."

"Yes," Thrang agreed, shaking the stunned look off his face. "Let's get moving."

They rode south, taking their time and stopping for their regular midday meal. Kat remained silent as they went, and Alex thought he could understand at least some of her feelings. She was struggling with the idea of what her future might hold, just as he was struggling with his. The only difference was that everyone knew what Kat was thinking, and only Alex knew his own fears.

Two days later, Kat asked Alex for a private word. They

had already made camp, and Alex suggested he and Kat gather some extra wood for the fire.

"There's plenty here," Thrang started to say but trailed off when he saw the look on Alex's face. "Yes, that's a good idea. Spring is slow in coming, and some extra wood might be useful."

As Alex and Kat walked away from the campsite, Alex could feel the others watching them. He knew they all wondered what the two of them would be talking about, but he also knew they would not ask. In fact, the others seemed willing to accept Kat as a true oracle already, which was something that seemed to annoy Kat a great deal.

"You've given me a great honor," Kat said after a long silence. "You've formed my destiny around me like a cage."

"I . . . I'm sorry. I did not mean to," Alex said, surprised by Kat's words. "If you do not want the crystal, then do not use it. Hold it safe for another if that is your wish."

"It's not your fault," Kat said, her voice shaking slightly. "I suppose I should have expected something like this."

"Why?" Alex questioned, truly puzzled.

"When I was very young, a real oracle came to my village," Kat said in a low tone. "The oracle told me that I would be an adventurer, but . . ."

"But that you might become something more," Alex finished for her.

"He told me about being a seer, about seeing things that others could not. He also told me to beware of the sea. He said the sound of the sea would capture my heart, and once I heard it, I would never be the same."

"You've heard the Eastern Sea of Thraxon, and now your heart is there."

"The empty tower fills my dreams," Kat said, shaking her head. "Ever since that day when you stopped me at the gate."

"Do you think you are the oracle that was prophecied to come?"

"I don't know. I don't see how I can be. I'm a seer, and a good one, but an oracle is something more."

"And I am a wizard, though I never thought I would be," said Alex. "You know, when I went on my first adventure, I didn't even believe in magic. I didn't know anything about dwarfs or elves or oracles. It all seemed like a dream, or even some huge mistake."

"You didn't know?" Kat questioned in surprise. "How could you not know? You are a great wizard. How could you not know what you are?"

"Who really knows what they are or what they may become? We learn about ourselves as we do things. We discover what we are as we move through life. If we don't like what we see, we try to change. That is how we grow, that is how we become all that we can be."

"But what if I am not strong enough? What if I can't do what is needed?"

Alex heard echoes of his own questions in Kat's voice, his own doubts and fears.

"I asked the same questions of the Oracle Iownan once," Alex said. "I asked what if I was not strong enough to be a wizard. Do you know what she told me?"

"No."

"She said if I was not strong enough, I would break."

"That seems a very direct answer from an oracle," Kat said, a slight smile curling her lips.

"Iownan was kind to me, and she answered me as openly as she could."

"So I must try to do what is needed, and if I am not strong enough, I will break," Kat said softly.

"I will tell you this," Alex said as he turned and started back toward the camp. "I do not think you will break."

"Then at least I will have hope," said Kat.

When Alex and Kat returned to camp without any firewood, the others simply accepted the fact that their friend the wizard had talked with their friend the new oracle, and what was said did not concern them.

They continued their journey the next day and the next, always moving south, but never seeing anything that might be the golden rocks. After another week of riding, the Lost Mountains had almost vanished behind them, and the world seemed to open into a wide grass-covered plain in front of them. After the second week, they could see a single mountain in the distance, but even Arconn could not guess at how far away it was.

"We will ride toward that mountain," Thrang said in a decisive tone. "If ever a mountain called to a dwarf's heart, that one does."

The next day it started to rain, and the mountain was lost from sight.

"Spring rains, moving north," Arconn commented as they rode south. "I would guess they will last for several days."

"Weeks perhaps," Thrang said in a slightly grumpy tone. "The spring rains of Thraxon can sometimes last for a month or more."

"Then we will all be well watered before the sun comes out again," Barnabus said.

"We may all be drowned," Nellus added, pulling up his hood a little.

"How will we see the golden rocks if the sun isn't shining?" Thrain questioned.

Nobody answered, but they were all thinking about it. Of course, they knew the golden rocks were more myth than anything, but a little sunshine would help them to find such rocks, if they really existed.

A week later, as they continued to ride south through the rain, Kat suddenly stopped her horse. Alex paused as well, feeling something powerful move above them in the clouds. None of the others seemed to notice anything, but they stopped and looked from Kat to Alex and back again.

"Something big," Kat said, turning her face toward the rain clouds. "Something powerful."

"I felt it as well," Alex said. "Though it didn't feel evil, if that's the word."

"No, not evil," Kat agreed. "Yet powerful and possibly dangerous. We should try to move more quickly. We will need to reach the cover of the mountain before the rains stop."

"And if the rains stop before we reach the mountain, then what?" Thrang questioned.

"Then we will see what moves above us," Kat answered, her eyes still fixed on the sky.

"Must be part elf," Thrang grumbled, urging his horse forward.

For another week they rode as quickly as they could. When they camped, they only made small fires, allowing the rain to put them out as soon as Barnabus was finished cooking.

Alex remained alert, trying to feel whatever it was that had passed above them, but there was nothing. Finally, late on the eighth day, they came to the mountain.

"There is an entrance to the east of us," Kat said, pointing.

"Are you sure?" Thrang questioned. "Have you seen what lies in the mountain?"

"Yes," Kat answered. "Or I should say, I have seen *some* of what lies in the mountain. We have reached our goal, but I fear we will find sorrow here."

Thrang didn't ask any more questions, but nudged his horse forward. They all followed him through the gathering darkness, and suddenly they found themselves on a well-made road.

"This is dwarf work," Thrang said as he looked at the road. "Albrek's people must have made this road."

"Then it will lead to their city," Arconn said in a hopeful tone.

They all rode forward, eager to reach the dwarf city. It was almost completely dark when they reached the city gates, and they were shocked when they saw that the gates were nothing more than a pile of shattered stones.

"What could have done this?" Thrang asked. "The gates must have been three feet of solid stone, yet they lie broken like old wood."

"Whatever did it was powerful," Alex said. He looked up at the sky. "I think we might be safer inside the gates; the clouds are starting to break up."

"Has what you felt before returned?" Arconn questioned.

"I don't feel it now, but I would be happier inside the mountain than out here in the open," Alex answered.

"Yes, let's get inside," Thrang said, climbing off his horse. "We'll take the horses in as well, and find a place to make camp."

The others dismounted, leading their horses into the darkness. Alex conjured weir lights to show them the way, but the lights did little to make the dwarf cavern look inviting.

"It would seem that there are no dwarfs left here," Nellus said as they unsaddled their horses.

"And there haven't been any for some time," Arconn added. "There is a great deal of dust on the floor."

"Such a city should not be empty," Nellus said. "Something terrible must have happened here."

"Perhaps," said Alex. "I suspect the dwarfs were here for a long time because even dwarfs could not have built such large gates quickly."

"It would take months, even if they had worked on them night and day," Thrang agreed. "It is a mystery, but not the first one we've found on this adventure." He turned to Kat. "Kat, what do you see in this city?"

"The dwarfs of the Golden Mountain have either fled or died," Kat said in a trancelike tone. "Only their memories remain. Tomorrow, I will lead you to Albrek's tomb, but now I must rest."

"Very well," Thrang said with a bow. "We should all rest. Whoever has the watch should wake everyone if they hear or feel anything strange."

They all agreed and moved a little deeper into the cavern. There was a sad and lonely feeling in the empty city, and a sorrow seemed to have settled on them all.

Alex stood for a while, looking into the darkness outside. He stared at the ruined gates, wondering what could have destroyed them so completely. So many questions, and once again, he didn't have the answers he needed.

CHAPTER TWENTY-ONE

ALBREK'S TOMB

W hen morning arrived, the rising sun blazed
into the cave where they were sleeping,
waking them all at the same time. Without
speaking, they walked back to the ruined gates. Looking out
across the open plain, it was easy to see the truth of where they
were.

"The rocks all shine like gold," Thrang said softly. "Even
those in shadow seem to shine."

"The rain and the sunlight combine to make it look this
way," Arconn said. "A wondrous sight from a very sad city."

Kat stepped up next to Thrang, a troubled look on her
face. "I will take you to Albrek's tomb now. The Ring of
Searching is there, waiting to be claimed."

Thrang bowed, surprise and eagerness on his face.

Kat led the company deeper into the city. Alex conjured
weir lights, sending them ahead so the path was well lit, but
there was little of interest to be seen.

Alex knew something was bothering Kat, but she was silent
as they walked through the city.

Kat led them without hesitation, as if she knew the city

well. They walked down long corridors, through huge open chambers, and past large empty halls. There was no sign of dwarfs or any other living thing. Alex began to feel nervous, but he couldn't explain why so he kept his worries to himself.

Finally they came to a wide stairway leading down, the steps covered in thick dust. Kat walked quietly down the steps, turning at the bottom to follow another corridor that led to more steps. Once again, Kat turned down a corridor at the bottom of the steps, and again it led to more steps. There was even more dust here, deep in the dwarf city, and their footsteps sounded muffled as they walked.

After six corridors and six stairways, they reached a huge stone door. A silver ring hung in the middle of the door with several dwarf runes carved on it. Thrang hurried forward and brushed the letters softly with his hands.

"Here lies Albrek, lord of the south," Thrang said as he read the runes.

"The tomb of Albrek," Kat said in a sad tone. "He tried so hard to make a success here, but in the end, he failed."

"Help me," Thrang said as he began pulling on the silver ring.

Nellus and Barnabus both came forward to help Thrang, and slowly the stone door began to move. Alex stood by Kat, watching as the door opened. He wondered if Thrang had even heard what Kat had said. When the stone door had been moved far enough to allow them to enter, Alex sent the weir lights in ahead of his friends. Thrang hurried after the lights, eager to find what they had all been looking for.

The chamber was large and round. Bookshelves and

weapons covered the walls, and in the center of the chamber stood a huge stone sarcophagus covered with runes.

Thrang moved forward and once more brushed the dust away from the runes with his hands. For several minutes he was silent, then he spoke in a slightly shaky voice.

"Albrek's Tomb," Thrang said. "He died before his people were destroyed by an enemy they could not fight, but his monument does not say who or what that enemy was."

"Perhaps these books will tell us," Arconn suggested, moving toward the shelves along the wall.

"And the ring?" Nellus questioned.

"There," Kat said, pointing toward one side of the chamber. "It is with his weapons."

"You should take it, Thrang," Alex said, following Arconn toward the books. "Put it in your bag for safekeeping, and then help us search these books for some answers."

"Yes, yes, of course," Thrang said as he hurried to the pile of weapons. "Ah, yes, here it is. The Ring of Searching, just as Thorgood described it."

"Put it away for now," Alex said softly. "We need to learn what enemy destroyed Albrek's people. If we know what it is, we might be able to escape this city. If we don't know what it is, we're all in great danger."

Thrang put the ring in his magic bag and then joined Alex and Arconn by the bookshelf. The books were arranged chronologically, so Thrang pulled a book off the bottom shelf first.

"Brighten your lights a little, if you please," Thrang said to Alex, opening the book.

Alex changed the weir lights from yellow to white and then

looked over Thrang's shoulder at the book. The pages were in perfect condition, but Alex had trouble reading the runes as quickly as Thrang flipped through the book.

"Ah, here it is," Thrang said at last, leaning closer to the book. "It says that dwarfs have been attacked outside the city."

"Outside the city?" Barnabus questioned.

"Let me read," said Thrang, waving his hand so the others wouldn't ask any questions.

Thrang bent so close to the book that Alex could hardly see the pages. Instead of trying to read along with Thrang, he stood back and looked at the rest of the books on the shelf. For what seemed like a long time, Thrang said nothing. When he finally snapped the book shut, everyone jumped.

"A thunderbird," Thrang said softly. "The book says that a thunderbird destroyed Albrek's people and laid waste to the city."

"I've never heard of such a bird," Nellus said.

"Nor have I," Barnabus added.

"Thunderbirds are just a story," Thrain said nervously. "Something mothers use to scare their children into obeying."

"Some people think they are legends," Arconn said. "Others say that such birds did exist at one time."

"Kat and I both felt something large and powerful fly over us on our way here," Alex pointed out.

"Will someone please explain to me what a thunderbird is?" Nellus questioned in a pleading tone.

"The thunderbirds were an ancient race of magical, giant birds," Arconn explained.

"So what's so terrible about a giant bird?" Barnabus asked.

"Thunderbirds are birds of prey," Thrang answered. "They hunt and kill whatever they like. Some stories say that a single thunderbird could carry off a horse and rider with one claw and a full-grown cow with the other."

"Oh," Barnabus managed to reply.

"But thunderbirds never stay in one place too long, because if they do, they soon eat everything that is there," Arconn said.

"They might stay in one area if there's a large supply of food," said Thrang. "The book says that the thunderbird carried off dwarfs from this city whenever they went outside of the mountain. It says they tried to fight off the bird, but it became enraged and attacked the city. That was when Albrek's heir died, though the book doesn't say specifically that he was killed by the bird."

"What else does the book say?" Alex questioned, trying to remember anything he might have read about thunderbirds.

"Only that the remaining dwarfs were planning to escape," said Thrang. "They were going to wait for a cloudy day, then head across the plain."

"None of them made it," Kat said sadly. "Not a single dwarf made it across the plain."

"But that all happened years ago," Nellus said. "The thunderbird wouldn't still be here, would it?"

"I wouldn't think so," Arconn said. "Once there was no more food, the bird would have moved on."

"Unless it *couldn't* move on," said Alex.

"Couldn't move on? What do you mean?" Thrang questioned.

"It might have laid an egg," said Alex. "And thunderbird eggs take a very, very long time to hatch."

"What is the date of the last entry in the book?" Arconn questioned.

"Just over a hundred years ago," Thrang answered. "Surely the egg would have hatched by now."

"That's true," said Alex. "But even if the egg hatched, I have no idea how long it takes a young thunderbird to learn to fly."

"But you can fight it off with magic," Thrain said. "Or hide us so the thunderbird can't see us."

"Thunderbirds have powerful magic of their own," said Alex. "I'm not sure I can fight it off using magic, and I'm not sure that any illusion I create will deceive it."

"Then we're stuck here?" Thrang questioned. "We have to remain in this dead city or be taken as prey by the thunderbird?"

"We made it to the city when it was raining," Nellus said. "Perhaps we will simply have to wait until the rains return."

"That will be too long," Kat said in despair.

"Much too long," Thrang agreed.

"Then what do we do?" Barnabus questioned.

"First, we go back to the gates," said Thrang. "Then we will decide what can be done."

They all moved out of the chamber, pausing long enough to push the stone door back into place, and then followed Kat back through the empty city. As they walked, Alex racked his brain, trying to think of some way to protect them from the thunderbird. His magic books had mentioned them from time to time, but the information was incomplete.

"Why are they called thunderbirds?" Alex questioned.

"They can make thunder with their wings," Thrain answered. "They can make strong winds as well—strong enough to blow down trees."

"And it is said that they can shoot lightning bolts from their eyes," Arconn added. "Or possibly from their beaks, depending on which stories you believe."

"That's all very well, but we have no real proof that a thunderbird is still in the area," Thrang said.

"It is near," Kat said softly, her voice cracking slightly. "Hope may be lost."

"Don't say that," said Thrang. "If we have to wait for the rains, we will, but perhaps we can find some other way of leaving the city first."

When they reached the city gates, it was almost noon. Alex and the others stood in the shadows just inside the city, looking out across the open plain for a few minutes before anyone spoke.

"Well?" Thrang questioned. "Any ideas?"

"Let me try something," said Alex, shifting his staff in his hand. "I'll create the illusion of men on horseback. If the thunderbird is close, it should attack them."

"We should be ready to flee into the caves," Arconn suggested. "When the thunderbird finds that it has been deceived, it might come here looking for the source of the trick."

"A wise idea," Thrang agreed.

Alex nodded and then focused his thoughts on the illusion

he wanted to create. He heard the others gasp in surprise as his illusion took shape in front of them and seven riders made their way out into the sunlight.

"They look so real," Barnabus said. "I can hear them moving as they go."

"It has to be real enough to tempt the thunderbird," said Alex.

They watched as the figures Alex had created out of thin air moved away from them.

After a long moment, Thrang cleared his throat, but just as he opened his mouth to speak, a huge shadow moved across the open fields.

Alex looked up to see a golden bird diving out of the sky.

"Amazing," Arconn commented. "So beautiful."

"And deadly," Thrang added.

But long before the bird reached the illusion, it broke off its attack, shooting back into the sky at an incredible speed.

"It saw through the illusion," Alex said. "Let's try this instead."

He immediately transformed a large rock from the ruined city gates into a living, breathing stag. The stag looked at them for a moment, and then bounded away across the plain.

"I didn't know you could do that," Arconn said.

"It's something I learned on my last adventure," said Alex. "Though I've never conjured a stag before."

"And this one won't last long," said Nellus.

Once again, the thunderbird attacked. This time the giant bird did not break its dive, but quickly snatched the stag from the ground in one huge claw. Watching the bird rise into the air, Alex wondered how many stags he would need to create to give him and his friends enough time to safely cross the plains.

"A pity," Arconn said. "It was a beautiful stag."

"But we learned an important lesson," Thrang added. "We can't outrun that bird on our horses, and I don't suppose Alex can create enough stags to keep it busy while we cross the plains."

"I could try, but I'm not sure it would always go for the stags," said Alex.

"You haven't tried using magic against it," Thrain pointed out.

"No, I haven't," said Alex. "I'm not sure how well magic will work."

"You must try," Thrang insisted. "We need to know if your magic can drive off the bird. If not, I'm not sure I'm willing to chance the open plain, even if you created hundreds of stags to keep the bird busy."

"Very well," Alex agreed. "The bird will be much closer to us this time, so you might want to move back a little."

As the others stepped back, Alex transformed a large rock into a fat cow. The cow looked at him, confused, and then slowly started off toward the grassy plain. Once more the thunderbird appeared, only this time it hovered just outside the broken gates. As the bird caught the cow in its golden claw, Alex cast a binding spell, trying to freeze the bird to the ground. For a moment, it looked as if the spell had worked. The thunderbird gave a terrible cry of rage as it tried to lift off with the cow but could not. Alex watched in fascination, but then, realizing what was about to happen, he turned toward the cave.

"Run!" Alex shouted.

The others were slow to understand what he meant, but they soon saw what Alex had seen. The thunderbird, enraged by Alex's spell, had turned to look directly at the cave where they were all standing.

They had barely gone ten feet when a lightning bolt hit the wall of the cavern. A shower of rocks flew off the wall, and Alex and his friends dove to the ground and covered their heads. A second bolt of lighting hit the opposite wall, and a second shower of broken stone rained down on them.

Alex got to his feet quickly and tried to stop the third bolt of lightning with his magic. His spell only deflected the bolt, which hit the mountain above the city gates instead. Knowing how useless his magic was against the thunderbird, Alex removed the binding spell he had cast. The thunderous beating of the giant wings almost blew Alex off his feet, and then the bird was gone.

"It appears that my magic will do us little good," Alex said, leaning against his staff.

"Then we are trapped here," Thrang said, standing up. "At least until the rains come."

"It is too late," said Kat, sounding close to tears.

"I wonder where the bird goes," Thrain said, moving closer to the ruined gates.

"Stay back," Alex warned, but he was too late.

A huge golden claw reached in and snatched Thrain out of the tunnel. Alex turned quickly to restrain the others from rushing out after Thrain. He wondered what he could possibly do to save his friend.

"We have to do something," Thrang said angrily. "We can't just let that bird eat him."

"There is only one creature I can think of that has a chance against that bird," said Alex, his mind fixing on what he had to do. "I will go after Thrain. The rest of you wait here, well back from the gates."

"What creature?" Arconn questioned.

"Watch and see," Alex answered, turning and running toward the sunlight.

When the first rays of light touched Alex, he changed. He was filled with a wild, reckless joy, but his mind stayed fixed on the task at hand. With almost no effort at all, he leaped into the air, his massive wings lifting him higher as his dragon eyes searched for the thunderbird. He spotted it in a second, circling to land on the mountain behind him. Alex let out a deafening roar to attract the bird's attention, and then sped straight at it, ready for battle.

The thunderbird cried back, accepting his challenge. It spun away from the mountains, still clutching the struggling Thrain in its golden claw. Lightning flashed from the bird's eyes, hitting one of Alex's almost thirty-foot-long wings, but it had no effect. Alex felt like laughing at the feeble attack. Instead of laughing, though, he sent a jet of flame toward the giant bird, forcing it to turn sharply in midair. Alex roared again, frustrated at having missed his target and forgetting that the flames could have killed Thrain.

The thunderbird climbed higher in the sky, beating its wings wildly to create a forceful wind. Alex saw that the bird was trying to use the wind to drive him toward the ground, but the wind was nothing to a dragon—it felt like a gentle breeze. Alex climbed higher in pursuit of his enemy.

The thunderbird broke away once more, flying with all its speed to the north. Alex followed with ease, closing the gap between himself and his enemy. When he thought he was close enough, he sent another jet of fire at the bird, this time hitting its tail. The thunderbird screamed in pain and let Thrain drop from its talons.

For a moment Alex hesitated, wanting to continue the battle. He heard Thrain scream in fear as he fell, and the fear of his friend spurred him into action. He dove after the falling dwarf with blinding speed, gently catching Thrain in his own enormous claw that gleamed with true silver. He could feel Thrain thrashing wildly, terrified but very much alive. He realized that carrying Thrain with him would be too dangerous. He swooped down to the ruined city gates, opened his claw to let Thrain escape, and then returned his gaze to the sky, searching once more for the thunderbird.

The thunderbird was flying south, low to the ground as if hiding.

Alex turned quickly to follow, his desire to destroy his enemy growing. As he left the mountain behind, Alex saw that the land had come to an end and the bird was soaring over the open sea, rising slightly as it flew. The sun shined off the golden bird, reminding Alex just how beautiful his enemy was. He allowed himself to consider the beauty of the thunderbird for a moment, and he slowed his pursuit, but only slightly.

From a distance, he watched the thunderbird skimming over the waves toward a small island several miles from shore.

When the thunderbird circled, Alex thought it was turning for another attack, but instead the bird simply landed on the island, as if waiting for him. Alex was puzzled but not worried. If the thunderbird wanted to face him on an island, that was fine; he would destroy it just as easily one way or the other.

As he circled the island, Alex saw that the thunderbird was sitting on its nest. Alex had been correct. The bird had laid an egg and had come back to that egg in a last, desperate hope of protecting it. Alex knew he could destroy the bird and its egg easily, but for some reason he did not attack. He circled the island once more and then brought his own massive armored body to rest not too far from the thunderbird's nest.

"Change back," the thunderbird called out in a strange voice. "Take back your natural form."

It was a spell meant to change him. Once again Alex felt like laughing; the thunderbird was trying to change him into something he was not. He was a dragon, a dragon with impenetrable true-silver armor, claws that could crush the hardest stone like soft dirt, and a whiplike tail that could shatter the best defenses of any enemy he faced. This was the only form he needed, and the only one he wanted.

"You waste your time," Alex said to the thunderbird. "This is my natural form."

"You are two," the bird said in surprise. "You are both man and dragon."

"Dragon is enough," Alex answered.

"No, you must be both or neither," answered the bird. "You cannot be whole unless you accept both of your true shapes."

The bird's words reminded Alex of Salinor's words. The dragon's voice suddenly filled his mind, telling him that the bird spoke the truth. He was confused and hesitated, trying to understand, trying to remember what he was before he had become a dragon. The sunlight sparkled on the waves around him, and in an instant, he remembered everything.

"Yes, I must be both or neither," said Alex.

"Will you destroy me now, dragon?" the thunderbird questioned.

"I do not wish to," Alex answered. "But I can't allow you to attack my friends."

"You attacked me. You tried to bind me to the earth," the bird said in a fierce tone.

"And you destroyed the city of dwarfs that once lived in the mountain," Alex answered.

"Only for food," said the thunderbird. "I killed only for food, not for sport."

"Was there nothing else for you to eat? Nothing but dwarfs?"

"At first the sea was full and many wild herds of animals covered the plain. But soon the sea grew empty, and the herds fled from the plain."

"And you had to feed your young," Alex said, noticing for the first time the baby thunderbird tucked under its mother's wing.

"The dwarfs were nearly gone when the egg hatched. I've had to hunt farther and farther away, and my child is always hungry."

"Perhaps I can help you," said Alex. "I can fill the sea with life once more, but I will require a price."

"What price?" the thunderbird questioned. "Why would you help me? You have nearly destroyed me."

"You are not evil—you did only what you had to do," Alex said. "I will change the rocks into great fish and seals and whales. But you must promise never to fly north of this place again. Neither you nor any member of your race must ever fly north."

"You would fill the seas for me?"

"Do you promise?"

"Yes, I give my sacred word that it shall be as you ask," the thunderbird answered.

"Very well, I accept," said Alex.

The thunderbird bowed its golden head, and Alex turned to look out at the sea. He took a deep breath of the salty air and considered what he would do. He moved to the shore of the island, looking for what he needed as he went. The shore was rocky, and there were dozens of large, broken boulders just offshore. He thought about what would be needed, then he magically looked into the sea and saw that everything was already there. The thunderbird had eaten the large fish—the whales and the sea mammals—but nothing smaller.

Focusing his thoughts, Alex worked the magic, changing the dozens of offshore rocks into great whales. He knew that many of them would die to feed the thunderbird and its chick, but some would live, enough to ensure that there would always be whales here. Pleased with his work, he changed the rocks along the shore into a vast herd of sea lions. Their noise filled the air as they scattered into the sea. Finally, he changed another group of rocks into giant sea turtles—bigger than any sea turtles he had ever seen—and the last group of rocks into large fish. When he was done working his magic, he turned back to the thunderbird.

"You are more than I imagined, and for your kindness, my clan will always be in your debt," the thunderbird said, bowing its head again. "You have my promise, great one."

"Live well," said Alex. "Take what is needed and nothing more. Remember your promise, and warn your clan not to go north of this place or I will return and destroy them."

"It will be as you say," the thunderbird answered.

Alex rose from the island and skimmed across the sea, looking down at his own reflection in the waters. It was both strange and wonderful to see his own blue-green eyes looking back at him from the face of an enormous dragon of true silver. The dragon form was truly his own now, and he laughed at the thought that he had been so afraid to take such a wondrous shape.

Thank you, Salinor, Alex thought as he flew back toward the mountain. *Thank you for explaining what I am.*

I didn't do that, Salinor's voice replied inside his mind. *I only showed you what you might become.*

Alex laughed at Salinor's words, and he could hear Salinor laughing as well. He knew that Salinor understood exactly what he was feeling, so he simply flew on, enjoying himself as any dragon would.

CHAPTER TWENTY-TWO

THE DRAGON RETURNS

W hen Alex returned to the ruined gates of the dwarf city, his friends were nowhere to be seen. He dropped down to the ground and changed back into his human form. He felt wonderful—better than he could ever remember—and he knew the power of the dragon would be with him always.

Alex wondered why he had been so afraid to take the dragon form, but then he heard his friends talking in the darkness. It was obvious they hadn't heard him return, and he paused to listen to them.

"He is a danger to himself and to us," Barnabus said.

"He did not attack us when he returned with Thrain," said Arconn in a reasonable tone. "He brought Thrain back, shaken but unhurt."

"Yet he did not reply to our calls," Nellus countered. "He acted as if he couldn't hear us at all."

"And then he flew off after the thunderbird," Thrang added. "He was hot to continue the battle."

"You're sure that thing was Alex?" Thrain questioned in a shaky voice.

"It was Alex," Kat said calmly.

"*Was,*" Barnabus said loudly. "The longer he remains a dragon, the less of our friend will remain. Arconn, you know more about such things than any of us. How long can Alex keep that shape and not lose himself?"

"That depends on how strong he is," Arconn answered. "I've known wizards to take different shapes for days and even weeks, but I must admit, it is often difficult for them to return to themselves. And the dragon shape is the most dangerous form there is for a wizard."

"Alex has been gone for almost an hour," Barnabus said. "I begin to doubt he will ever return to us."

"He will return," Kat said in a confident tone.

"You seem so sure," Thrang said to Kat, his own voice shaking slightly. "Did you foresee this change? Do you know why he chose to become a dragon?"

"I am not an oracle," said Kat. "And now I may never be one."

"But you know something," Arconn said.

"I guess at many things, but I do not know," Kat said softly. "I believe Alex is safe, and that he will return to us as himself."

"More like the dragon—ready to destroy us when we step out of this cave," Barnabus said.

"No, I don't believe that," said Arconn.

"Perhaps the person we have traveled with isn't really Alex," Thrain said softly. "Maybe he's still on the Isle of Bones, and the dragon there took his place with us."

"Don't say such things," Thrang snapped angrily. "We'll wait until morning. If Alex has not returned by then—"

"Why wait until morning?" questioned Alex, moving forward toward his friends.

Alex could see his friends were both relieved and afraid. He understood their fear, because it was something he had also felt.

"You have no need to fear," Alex said. "I am your friend, not the dragon from the Isle of Bones."

"I didn't mean—" Thrain began.

"No harm is done," Alex interrupted. "I repeat, I am myself. And we are free to leave whenever we like."

"So you destroyed the thunderbird?" Arconn questioned.

"No, I did not," said Alex. "I struck a bargain with it. No thunderbird will ever trouble this land again."

"You were in the dragon form for a long time," Thrang said slowly. "Are you sure you're all right? Perhaps you would like to rest awhile."

"I'm fine," said Alex. He turned to Arconn. "You are right to say that changing one's own shape is dangerous, but the dragon shape holds no danger for me."

"Then," Barnabus began and paused, "then are you a dragon? Pretending to be a man?"

"No." Alex laughed. "I am a man *and* a dragon. I am both, and I can take either shape without fear of losing myself."

"That is not possible," Nellus said.

"And how would you know what is and is not possible?" Alex questioned. "You cannot see far enough into the past to know the truth. Not even Arconn can see that far into the past."

"No, I can't," agreed Arconn. "But I have heard legends, stories of ancient times that suggested men and dragons were once the same race. We elves never believed them."

"Yes, some men were once dragons," Alex said. "But that was long ago, and almost no one remembers that time now."

"I suspect the dragon on the Isle of Bones remembers," Arconn said, nodding his understanding.

"Yes, he remembers," said Alex. "He is the oldest living thing in the known lands. He is the guardian of the past, and he remembers."

"So you are both man and dragon?" Thrang repeated, shaking his head as he tried to understand.

"I am," said Alex. "And I must ask that none of you share this information with anyone. I doubt anyone would believe such a story, but it would be best if few people knew the truth."

"Yes, of course," said Thrang. "I, for one, will never tell this tale."

Alex looked at each of his companions one at a time, and they all swore in turn that they would keep Alex's secret. Alex turned to Kat last, but even as she promised not to tell what she knew, Alex saw a great sorrow inside her. He remembered Kat saying that it was too late—but too late for what?

"Kat," Alex said softly. "What did you mean when you said that you may never become an oracle?"

"Can't you guess?" Kat answered, tears filling her eyes. "The empty tower by the sea."

"The tower you once tried to enter, but I stopped you," said Alex.

"It will vanish into the evening mist in three days' time," Kat said sadly. "It is too late for me to enter. Too late to find out if I was meant to be the Oracle of the Empty Tower."

"It's too late when you are dead and not before," said Alex, his mind racing for some way to get Kat back to the tower in less than three days. It came to him so suddenly that he started to laugh.

"What?" Thrang questioned. "What's so funny?"

"The prophesy," Alex answered. "The dragon will bring the oracle—it is so simple."

"Of course," said Arconn. "As the dragon, you can reach the tower in a day or less. Then Kat can become the oracle before the tower vanishes."

"You would do that for me?" Kat questioned, a look of disbelief on her face.

"I told you that once we'd found what we were looking for I would help you any way I could," said Alex. "We have the Ring of Searching, so now we must get you back to the tower before it's too late."

"What about the rest of us?" Thrang questioned. "You can't carry all of us and our horses."

"Turn the horses loose on the plain; they will be safe there. The rest of you can all ride on my back," Alex answered.

"You will need to travel very fast," Arconn said. "We may not be able to hold on."

"Tie ropes to me and to yourselves," said Alex. "Then none of you will fall off, and we can move as fast as possible."

"Can't we ride?" Thrain asked in a shaky voice. "Can't you take Kat to the tower while the rest of us ride north again? I mean, well, I did promise Fivra that I'd try to go with him to see an oracle when we got back."

"Would you miss what is coming?" Alex questioned. "Oracles are not made every day. This will be something worth seeing, even if you have to ride on a dragon's back to get there."

"Besides, you can't go running off to an oracle with Fivra until you are released from this adventure," Thrang said sternly to Thrain. "It was a foolish promise, and one you'll find hard to keep."

"What about the treasure we left in Kazad-Syn?" Nellus asked.

"We can collect that on the way," Alex said with a wave of his hand. "I can take us close to the city and then change from a dragon into a bird to reach Thorson and collect our treasure. If you like, Thrang, I can even change you into a bird and you can go with me."

"But—" Thrain began, a look of fear on his face.

"No buts," Thrang said firmly. "Alex's plan is a good one. We will ride the dragon to the tower."

"As you wish," said Thrain in a dejected tone.

"There is no need to fear," Alex said, putting his hand on Thrain's shoulder. "I did not let you fall when the thunderbird dropped you, and I will not let you fall now."

"I know," said Thrain, his voice shaking. "It's just that . . ."

"I know," said Alex before Thrain could go on. "I have felt the fear as well. But there is nothing to fear now. Trust me, you will be safe."

Thrain nodded and slowly looked up into Alex's face. Alex gave him an encouraging smile. Thrain smiled back weakly and then hurried to collect his gear from the tunnel floor.

It was well after noon by the time they were ready to go. Their freed horses wandered across the grassy plain, and all of Alex's friends had strong ropes tied around them that they would attach to Alex once he had changed.

"With your permission," Alex said to Thrang, with a bow.

"Yes, of course," Thrang answered, returning the bow.

The change, now that Alex had time to think about it, was incredible. It didn't require any great magical effort, only a simple acceptance of what he was. He let his mind reach out, and felt the magic filling him, almost flooding into the space around him and connecting him with everything that made the land of Thraxon. His heart raced with simple joy as once again he became the dragon.

He lowered himself to the ground and stretched out his massive true-silver leg to form a step so his friends could climb onto his back, and then waited for Thrang to call out that they were ready. At Thrang's call, he leaped into the air, circling the mountain as he climbed into the afternoon sky. When he was as high as the highest peak of the mountain, he turned north and shot back across the plain that had taken them weeks to cross.

The sun sank in the west and the first stars came out, and still Alex flew north. His dragon eyes could see everything below him clearly, and he changed his course slightly as they approached Neplee. He didn't want to be seen by the dwarfs,

405

because he knew the sight of a dragon would terrify them for days to come.

They flew through the night, and though they were still miles from Kazad-Syn, Alex could clearly see the city in the darkness. Once again he changed direction slightly and flew lower so the mountains would hide him from any dwarfs who might be watching the sky. He flew as close to the city as he dared, looking for a spot to land. High on the mountainside, he found a hidden valley and quietly glided down into it. There was still snow on the ground, but the air was warm, and they were well hidden from the city below.

Once his friends had climbed off his back, Alex returned to his own shape. He felt wonderful, rested, and ready for anything. His friends, however, looked tired and worn-out, ready for sleep. Even Arconn looked tired, which was odd for the elf. Alex let them rest while he gathered wood for a fire. After he had stacked a large pile of wood and started a fire, he turned to Thrang.

"Do you wish to come with me?" Alex questioned.

"I think I should," said Thrang. "I doubt Thorson would let you take the treasure if you simply turned up asking for it. And I know he wouldn't be able to stop you from taking it if your mind was set on it."

"Then I should ask, which bird is the most loved in Kazad-Syn?"

"Many birds are loved, but the raven is the most respected."

"Very well, we will travel as ravens. I should warn you that taking the shape of a bird is thrilling. You will keep your mind, but you will be tempted by the freedom of flight. Try to stay focused on our task. I will not let you fly too far from me, and I will change you back to your natural shape when we reach Thorson."

"Very well," Thrang agreed. "The rest of you should rest and eat. We shouldn't be gone too long."

The others nodded, and Alex tapped Thrang once on the shoulder with his staff. Thrang immediately changed into a raven. He croaked loudly and took flight. Smiling at Thrang's sudden energy, Alex changed himself and flew quickly after his friend. He wasn't worried about Thrang flying away, because he had magically bound Thrang to him when he'd changed him.

The night air was refreshing as they traveled down the side of the mountain toward Kazad-Syn. Alex could smell the city as he flew, but he could see very little. Raven eyes were not as keen as dragon eyes, and he had to concentrate to find his way to Thorson's house.

Thrang seemed to know exactly where he was going, however, and when Alex saw him dive into Thorson's garden he followed close behind.

"What is this?" Thorson questioned, looking puzzled as a raven landed on his table. "No raven is so friendly with a stranger."

"He is no stranger," said Alex, taking his own shape as he touched down beside the table.

"By the ancients, Alex! How did you get here?" Thorson jumped up, knocking over his chair. His eyes were wide with wonder as he looked from Alex to the raven on the table and back again.

"Return," Alex commanded, changing Thrang back to his normal self.

The table tipped over with a crash, and Thrang staggered to his feet.

"You could have waited until I was off the table," Thrang grumbled.

"You could have landed someplace else," said Alex.

"Thrang?" Thorson questioned in disbelief. "You've learned to change shape?"

"Don't be stupid," said Thrang. "Alex changed me so we could come and talk to you."

"Are you in trouble? Are your friends trapped somewhere? Should I call the family to arms?"

"No, no, no," said Thrang, grabbing Thorson by the shoulders. "Everything is fine, but we're in a hurry. We only stopped in the city to collect the treasure we left with you. I don't have time to explain everything, and I don't know where I'd begin if I did have time."

"Yes, of course," said Thorson as he clutched Thrang's hand. "Have you heard the news?"

"What news?" Thrang questioned.

"Stories have come from the Lost Mountains," Thorson answered, motioning them to follow him. "The details are sketchy, but they said a great evil has been destroyed there."

"That is true," said Thrang. "Alex has done a great service for the dwarfs of the Lost Mountains, and he has been named a lord of their city."

"A man named lord of a dwarf city?" Thorson said in surprise. "That is something unheard of."

"Alex is one of the greatest wizards there ever has been," said Thrang as if that explained everything. They started down the stairs that led to the lower chambers.

"You are too kind," said Alex from behind the two dwarfs.

"Not at all," Thrang answered. "I don't know a lot about wizards, but I think you've done more in your short career as a wizard than most other wizards do in a lifetime."

"Perhaps," Alex allowed, hoping that Thrang would change the subject.

"Here we are," Thorson said as they came to the door of the lower chamber. "Sorted, just as you asked."

"You've done us a great service, brother," said Thrang. "I would offer to pay you, but I know you wouldn't accept."

"And you are correct." Thorson laughed. "It is an honor to have served you, and to be honest, a great pleasure to sort this treasure for you."

Thorson unlocked the door and threw it open, but the room beyond the door was dark. Laughing at his own forgetfulness, Thorson turned to get a lamp.

"No need," Alex said, conjuring up the familiar weir lights.

"Ah, a wonderful spell," said Thorson, watching the weir lights dart into the room. "I wish I could learn to do that."

"Your magic is worse than mine," Thrang said with a laugh.

"And we don't have time for me to teach either of you now," Alex said, catching Thrang's eye.

"Yes, we do need to hurry," said Thrang. "The others are waiting, and we still have a long way to go."

"You will spend the night at least," Thorson objected.

"No, we must go," said Thrang. "Alex, you are better than I am at storing things quickly. Will you place all of this in your bag and hold it until we can divide it properly in Darvish?"

"Darvish?" Thorson questioned. "Why are you going to Darvish? You've already been there once."

"I don't think I should say," Thrang said slowly, looking at Alex for help.

"Tell him why, but not how," said Alex as he turned his attention to the room full of treasure.

"The empty tower will vanish it two days' time," said Thrang. "We're taking the new oracle to the tower before it fades forever."

"But that's at least a week of hard riding," said Thorson. "Even as a raven, you'll be hard-pressed to reach the tower before it's gone."

"We'll be there before it fades," said Thrang. "Don't ask questions that I can't answer, brother."

"As you wish," said Thorson with a bow.

Alex stored the treasure in his bag and stood beside Thrang once more.

"If you have the time, Thorson, you may want to set out for Benorg," Alex said with a smile. "We will be going there after we leave Darvish."

"So you've found it?" Thorson said happily. "You've found what you were looking for?"

"And more," Thrang answered.

"We will be in Darvish at least a week," Alex said. "After that, we will be returning to Benorg."

"A week?" Thrang questioned.

"I believe that is the normal celebration time when a new oracle comes to power," Alex explained.

"And this oracle travels with you?" Thorson questioned.

"Yes," Thrang said with a laugh. "She's been with us all along, only we didn't realize it."

"Kat is the oracle?" Thorson said in surprise. "I . . . I don't know what to say."

"Then say nothing," Alex suggested. "It is not our place to judge oracles or decide who should be an oracle. It is best to simply accept them and what they say."

"Yes, of course," Thorson said with another bow.

"Come now, Thrang. We must go," said Alex, starting up the stairs.

Thorson walked along quietly as they made their way back to the garden. The chair and table were still lying on the ground, and Alex and Thrang helped Thorson set them back in place. Thrang hugged Thorson good-bye, and once again Alex touched him with his staff. The raven that was Thrang flew up and circled the house, waiting for Alex to join him.

"Come to Benorg, if you can," said Alex. "The party there will be a thing to remember."

"Yes, I will," said Thorson happily.

Without saying anything more, Alex changed himself into a raven, flying up to meet Thrang over the house. He could see Thorson watching them with a look of wonder on his face, before he was lost from sight.

Alex and Thrang flew close, climbing slowly back into the mountains where the rest of their company was waiting. It was not a difficult flight, but by the time they saw the campfire, Alex could tell that Thrang was growing tired.

"Alex," Arconn exclaimed as Alex changed back to himself in front of the elf, "I wish you wouldn't do that. Or at least give me some warning."

"Sorry," Alex said with a laugh. "It's easy to forget such things. Now, where has Thrang gotten to?"

Thrang squawked loudly as he hopped in the snow next to the tents that had been set up. Alex turned to look at him and, at the same time, broke the spell that had changed Thrang into a bird.

"A pleasant enough way to travel," Thrang said stiffly. "More tiring than horseback, but pleasant just the same."

"You make an excellent raven," Alex said. "Now, I think you should rest with the others. We still have a long way to go, but I don't think we will start too early."

"Early would be better than late," Thrang said as he yawned. "Less likely to be seen, and we need to get to Darvish quickly."

"There is time," said Alex. "And I doubt we will be seen. Even if we are, it fits into the legend, so there's no need to worry."

"Yes, of course," said Thrang, walking slowly to his tent. "Wake me for breakfast, then."

Alex smiled as Thrang walked away, and then turned back to the fire and Arconn. Arconn looked as if he wanted to ask a hundred questions but didn't know where to begin. Alex took a chair from his magic bag and sat down next to the fire.

"What is it you want to know?" Alex asked.

"Nothing and everything," Arconn said with a smile.

"That is easy and difficult," Alex said and started to laugh.

"How long have you known? I mean, how long have you known that you could take the dragon form without losing yourself?"

"I wasn't sure until today," said Alex. "I almost lost myself when I went after the thunderbird, but then the bird spoke to me."

"What did it say?"

"It tried to magically change me back to my true form. It didn't know that I was both man and dragon, and it thought it could force me back into the shape of a man."

"But the spell didn't work," Arconn said.

"No, but it made me think. At the time, I thought I was only a dragon and I couldn't remember what I was before," said Alex. "When I thought about it, though, I remembered what I was. The memory was enough to allow me to see my true self as both man and dragon."

"I am glad you did not lose yourself," said Arconn.

"So am I," Alex agreed. "But I must admit, I would rather be lost as a dragon than as any other living thing."

"Even a man?"

"Yes, even a man."

Arconn fell silent, and Alex allowed himself to rest in front of the fire. He wasn't tired at all, but he needed to relax his mind. Several things were happening all at once in Thraxon, and he seemed to be in the middle of all of them. Not only had they recovered the Ring of Searching, which had been their goal all along, but he was about to take Kat to the empty tower, where he hoped she would be able to enter and become the oracle. Then there was the crown of Set, which Alex needed to return to King Thorgood. Thrang probably knew what Thorgood had promised, but Alex knew he didn't want to talk about it until Thorgood was present.

Apart from everything else, there was also his link to Salinor and the other dragons. There was the evil spirit, Mog, which he had defeated in Nethrom's cave, and there was the hidden conspiracy Bane had talked about. These were all important, but Alex didn't know why exactly. It was like some huge puzzle, and he didn't know what the picture would be when he put all the pieces together.

"At the speed you flew yesterday, we should reach Darvish before noon," Thrang said to Alex over breakfast. "That leaves a full day and a half before the tower fades."

"We won't reach the tower today," Alex said softly.

"Why not?" Arconn questioned. "Surely there is no reason to delay."

"No real reason," Alex said with a smile. "But part of being an oracle is what people think."

"And you don't think the people of Darvish will accept me as an oracle if I arrive today?" Kat asked.

"I think they will accept you, but that's not enough," Alex answered. "There needs to be a legend, something impressive that will be passed down from generation to generation. You realize that you will live for a very long time as the Oracle of the Empty Tower."

"Yes, I've been thinking about that," said Kat. "I think that is the part I fear the most."

"Fear?" Thrang questioned.

"Perhaps *fear* is not the right word, but it is the only word that seems to fit," Kat said, shaking her head. "I think Arconn must know what I mean. After all, he has lived for a long time."

"You don't want to see your friends grow old and die," Arconn said in a kindly tone. "You don't want to see those you care about fade, only to be replaced by others you do not know."

"Yes," Kat said, staring into the fire. "Men live a short time, dwarfs a little longer. Only elves and oracles seem to go on for ages."

"And wizards and dragons," Nellus said, glancing at Alex.

"*Some* wizards and *some* dragons," Alex corrected. "Still, I can understand Kat's fear because I have felt it too."

"There are sorrows, that is true," Arconn said thoughtfully. "We lose those who are close to us, and we are sad when they are gone. Still, there is the joy of life and the knowledge that those we love are never really gone, as long as we remember them."

"Wise words, but they offer little comfort," said Kat.

"If you do not wish to go to Darvish, we will not go," Alex said softly.

"No, I must go," said Kat in a determined tone. "I just hope it will be worth it."

The others did not speak, mostly because they didn't know what to say. How could any of them tell what the future held? How could they know if Kat would find being the Oracle of the Empty Tower worth the effort and the sacrifice?

Alex realized for the first time how similar his life was to Kat's. He would probably live a long time as a wizard; Whalen had told him as much. How would he feel when his friends—the people who had taught him so much and been with him on his adventures—grew old and died? It was difficult to think about, but he knew it would happen.

"We should be going," Alex said after several minutes of silence.

"I thought you said we wouldn't reach Darvish today," said Thrang.

"We won't, but the dragon will," Alex answered. "We'll let the people of Darvish see the dragon today so the crowds can gather for tomorrow."

"And then you'll take us all to the city?" Thrain questioned.

"No, I will take only Kat," Alex answered. "I will find a place close to the city for us to camp. Then tomorrow, before dawn, the rest of you will walk to the city. I will join you in the crowd later. After all, I don't want to change into my human form in front of the crowd."

"And I will be left alone to try to enter the tower," Kat said sadly.

"You will enter the tower and become the oracle," Alex said confidently. "After I deliver you to the tower, you will dismiss me as if I were your servant. That will help build your legend and reputation. I will fly away and vanish from the city, returning as a bird and meeting the others in the waiting crowds."

"Very well," said Kat. "I see the wisdom of your plan. I just hope I can enter the empty tower without going mad."

"You *will* be the oracle," Alex said again.

"How can you be so certain?" Kat questioned.

"Why else would you be traveling with a dragon?" Alex laughed.

CHAPTER TWENTY-THREE
THE ORACLE RETURNS

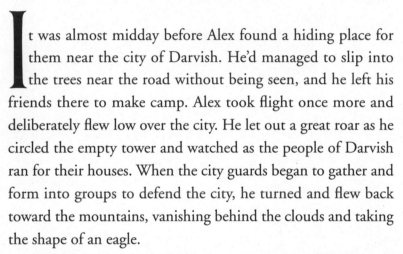

It was almost midday before Alex found a hiding place for them near the city of Darvish. He'd managed to slip into the trees near the road without being seen, and he left his friends there to make camp. Alex took flight once more and deliberately flew low over the city. He let out a great roar as he circled the empty tower and watched as the people of Darvish ran for their houses. When the city guards began to gather and form into groups to defend the city, he turned and flew back toward the mountains, vanishing behind the clouds and taking the shape of an eagle.

"An impressive show," Arconn said as Alex changed back into himself by the campfire. "The people in the city must have been terrified."

"Perhaps," said Alex with a wicked smile. "We'll give them a few hours to shake off their fear and remember the legends about the tower."

"Do you suppose all legends come true like this?" Barnabus asked as he handed Alex a plate of food. "Crafty wizards doing things so the people will believe?"

"I don't know," Alex answered. "I think most legends come

true because people believe in them and want them to come true, with or without the help of wizards."

"I think most come true because they are meant to," Arconn said. "I've been around for a long time, and I've seen and heard many legends. All the legends that have come true have done so more by luck than anything else."

"Perhaps," Thrang said. "Though I don't really believe in luck or chance. I think there is something more—something we haven't found a name for yet."

"Whatever it is, I'm glad you are all here with me," Kat said with a weak smile. "I don't think I could do this alone."

Later that day, Alex flew back over the city of Darvish, but this time the people did not run and hide as they had before. Once again he circled the tower, and once again he roared, but the city guards did not assemble to fight him. The people watched him, pointing and whispering to one another as he flew off toward the mountains.

When Alex returned for the third time, the sun was setting. He wasn't surprised to see that several people had gathered in the large square next to the empty tower. They looked up at him as he circled the tower, and he could tell that they wanted him to land. They all wanted, more than anything else in the world, for the dragon to deliver the oracle to the tower.

"The city looks ready for your arrival," Alex said to Kat when he returned to their camp. "People are already gathering near the tower."

"Yes, your plan is working perfectly," said Kat. "I hope it doesn't fail tomorrow when I try to enter the tower."

"It won't," Alex said reassuringly. "I'm sure you can enter the tower, and I think you know you can as well."

"Perhaps," said Kat with a slight smile.

None of them felt much like sleeping that night, but they all tried. Alex felt no need for sleep, having spent most of the day in the dragon's shape. He sat beside the fire with Arconn, watching the stars move across the sky. It was well before sunrise when Thrang roused the rest of them, and they all prepared to go to the city.

"We'll see you at the tower," Thrang said, bowing to Kat. "May fortune smile on you this day."

"You are most kind, my friends. I am in your debt," Kat answered with a bow of her own.

As the others left, Alex turned to Kat. She looked a little nervous, and perhaps a little pale, and her clothes looked worn from the long journey.

"I don't think you should enter your tower looking like that," Alex said, trying and failing to frown.

"No, I suppose not," said Kat, smiling weakly. "But I don't have anything an oracle would wear."

"With your permission," said Alex, bowing slightly and raising his staff.

He touched Kat lightly on top of her head with his staff and a ball of white light covered her for a moment. As the light faded, Kat looked down at the long silver-white gown that Alex had created for her.

"It . . . it's so beautiful," Kat said, tears filling her eyes. "I've never owned a gown as fine as this."

"It seems correct for the occasion," said Alex. "Your friends

420

may always remember you as Kat, but from this day on, you will be Katrina, the Oracle of the Empty Tower."

"Yes, and I owe it all to you, my friend," said Kat.

"You owe me only your friendship," said Alex. "You are an oracle—or will be before this day is over. You are in no one's debt, and all that you owe anyone is the truth."

"I will remember your words," said Kat. "And I will have to learn to hide the truth with words."

"It will come to you in time, I think," said Alex.

Alex and Kat sat quietly, waiting for the sun to rise and their friends to reach the city. Finally, Alex stood and walked away from the fire, preparing to take his dragon form. Kat stood back and watched, a fierce and determined look on her face.

As the dragon, Alex lowered himself and stretched out his leg so Kat could easily climb onto his back. He took flight gently, knowing that Kat would not be tied to him as she had been on their speedy journey from the south.

The square near the empty tower was full of people when Alex flew over the city, and all of the faces were looking up at him. He easily spotted his friends in the crowd, standing close to the tower gate. Alex circled the tower once, and then gently glided down to a large area that had been kept clear of people, apparently so he would have a place to land.

Alex lowered himself and stretched out his leg so Kat could climb down. The square sounded like it was full of bees as Kat, in her new gown, climbed off the dragon and looked up at the tower. Alex was pleased to see the surprised looks on his friend's faces. They had obviously not thought about what Kat would be wearing.

"Go, my friend," said Kat, turning back to Alex. "If I need you again, I will call."

Alex bowed his dragon's head to Kat and leaped back into the air. He saw that Kat stood watching him go, and the people in the square all watched as well. He flew up around the tower, roaring as he went. He sped away toward the mountains before the echo of his cry had faded from the city.

It took only a few minutes for Alex to reach the mountains, and as soon as he passed over them, he changed into a falcon. Like an arrow, he shot back over the mountains and toward the city. It was slower than dragon's flight, but fast enough. When he reached the main square, Kat was speaking to Kathnar, the old man who had first told Alex and Arconn about the tower.

Alex settled on Arconn's shoulder as if he belonged there. Arconn looked a little surprised, but he did not call out or draw attention to Alex. When Alex felt certain that his arrival as a falcon had not been noticed, he worked a little more magic. A shadow seemed to cover the empty space beside Arconn, and anyone who happened to be looking at the shadow suddenly felt the need to rub their eyes. In the blink of an eye, Alex returned to his own shape, standing next to Arconn as if he had always been there.

"Kathnar seems unwilling to accept her," Arconn said in a lowered voice. "He seems determined to prevent her from entering the tower."

"That's odd," said Alex. "He seemed so eager for the oracle to arrive when we were here before."

"Yes," Arconn agreed. "Now he seems like a man about to lose his power."

"And perhaps he is," said Alex thoughtfully. "He's been the guardian of the tower his entire life. That responsibility is something he will have to give up now that the oracle has come."

"You don't think Kat would throw him out, do you?" Arconn questioned.

"No, but Kathnar has no way of knowing that," Alex answered. "All he knows is that his world is about to change, and he isn't happy about it."

"Should we do something?" Arconn questioned.

"Not yet," Alex answered, taking a step back. "I think I know how to persuade the stubborn Kathnar."

Alex's hand moved slightly as he cast a spell on a group of people close by. He listened to them talking for a moment and heard their words quickly being repeated by others in the crowd. He turned to Arconn with a smile on his face.

"What did you do?" Arconn questioned.

"Listen to the crowd," Alex answered.

"What does that old fool think he's doing?" a woman behind them said loudly.

"He has no right to keep her from the tower," a man to one side of them said in an angry tone.

"The dragon brought her; she must be the oracle of the legend," someone in front of them said loudly.

It took only a few minutes for the words to spread across the square, and less than a minute more for people to begin calling for Kathnar to move out of the way. Alex was surprised at the crowd's growing anger as they began to chant together, "Let her pass. Let her pass."

"This could be trouble," Arconn said nervously.

Alex didn't have time to answer. Kat turned to face the crowd, holding up her hands for silence. As if by magic, the chanting stopped, and the people grew still, waiting to hear what Kat would say.

"Good people of Darvish, calm yourselves," Kat began. "Kathnar is the Keeper of the Empty Tower, and he has served long and well. Do not be angry with him for doing what he must. I am certain that he will not bar me from the tower. He only wishes to do his duty for you, and for the true oracle of the tower. I am the true oracle, and with Kathnar's permission, I will prove it."

The people broke into wild cheers when Kat finished speaking. Kathnar looked dumbfounded and completely lost. Kat moved forward and spoke softly to Kathnar, and then walked past him toward the gate of the empty tower. She never paused or slowed her pace, and soon she was lost from sight.

Kathnar turned to look at the tower gate. He dropped to one knee, waiting for Kat to return.

"Well, she's done it," said Thrang, turning around. "Oh, Alex—how long have you been here?"

"Long enough," said Alex with a laugh.

Kat soon returned to the tower gate, smiling as the crowd went wild with cheers around her. Alex watched as Kathnar acknowledged Kat as the true oracle and asked her forgiveness for his doubts. Kat nodded and took Kathnar's arm, leading him back toward the tower that was now her home.

"Well, that's that, then," Thrang said happily. "I suppose we should try to find a place to spend the night."

"Several nights, I would guess," Nellus said. "Alex said the celebrations would last for seven days."

"And after that we will need to aquire some horses," Barnabus reminded them. "It's a long walk to Benorg from here."

"I doubt we'll find anyone running their inns or selling horses for some time yet," Alex said with a laugh. "It seems the whole city is here, so we might as well take our time and enjoy ourselves."

Alex and his friends headed for the shady spot below the tower where Arconn and Alex had sat so many months before. They relaxed and watched as people milled about the tower, talking and planning the upcoming celebrations. They had not been there long, however, when Kathnar came hurrying toward them.

"Lords," Kathnar began with a bow. "The lady of the tower asks that you join her. She wishes you to be her honored guests for the days of celebration."

"The lady honors us, and we will do as she asks," Thrang said with a smile.

Once again, Kathnar bowed to them before leading them toward the tower gate. While they were walking, Thrang spoke quietly to the company.

"Kat is no longer the adventurer who traveled with us. She is now the Oracle of the Empty Tower, so remember to address her correctly and show the proper respect."

They all agreed as Kathnar led them through the courtyard

outside of the tower and to a large house that stood on the far side.

"This house has not been used in many years," Kathnar said in an apologetic tone. "We are still making things ready. I hope you will not be greatly troubled by this."

"You are most kind," said Thrang with a bow. "I'm sure we will be fine."

"If you have need of anything, ask any of the servants of the tower," Kathnar went on. "The lady asks that you join her for the evening meal. Someone will come for you then."

"As the lady wishes," said Thrang, and the entire company bowed.

Kathnar returned their bows and then departed. Alex and his friends entered the house and saw several people rushing about, trying to make things ready for them. It was a large house and richly decorated, but Alex could see that it had not been used for a long time, and that it would need more than cleaning before it was restored.

"It is fortunate that we collected our treasure from Thorson," Alex said. "Kat will need it to restore things to their proper order."

"The lady of the tower, you mean," Thrang said with a smile. "And yes, it appears that these rooms have been neglected for a long time."

"It's only her first day as an oracle," Arconn reminded them. "I'm sure things will be put in order quickly."

They made themselves comfortable in the house and found the bedrooms that had been prepared for them. They each removed their weapons and their magic bags, as was the custom when visiting an oracle, and then gathered in one of the large sitting rooms.

"We're hardly dressed for dinner with an oracle," Nellus said, looking down at his worn boots.

"Speaking of which, where did Kat get that beautiful gown she was wearing?" Thrang questioned, his eyes fixed on Alex.

"I couldn't let her arrive in worn travel clothes," Alex said with a smile. "It wouldn't look right."

"I don't suppose you could do something similar for the rest of us?" Thrang asked as he stroked his beard.

"I suppose I'll have to do something," Alex answered with a laugh. "You all look a bit worn, and it won't do to visit the oracle with you looking like this."

"You should talk." Arconn laughed. "Your clothes are as worn as any of ours."

"Yes, I suppose they are," Alex agreed, looking down at his own clothes. "I think a good wash is in order before we worry about clothes. I wonder if there is tub of hot water in this house."

When Thrang asked one of the servants about taking a bath, the servant led them to another room. The tub of water they were expecting was actually the size of a small swimming pool. The servant apologized that the water was not as hot as it should be.

"If you like, I can start heating water now, but it will be hours before enough is ready for you to bathe in," the young man said.

"That won't be necessary," said Alex. "Being a wizard means never having to take a cold bath."

Alex waved his staff over the pool, which instantly began to steam. The young servant looked at Alex in amazement, too shocked to say anything at all.

"The oracle has many friends," Alex said when he noticed the young man staring at him. "And I'm sure you have other work to do."

"Yes, master," the young man said with a bow.

"You'll scare him to death," said Arconn after the servant had left. "It's obvious that he's never seen a wizard before."

"And speaking of wizards," Thrang interrupted. "Why are you still carrying your staff? You know the custom of leaving weapons on your bed."

"I know the custom," said Alex. "A wizard's staff is not a weapon unless you are an enemy. I carry it now as a symbol of what I am and as a sign of respect for the oracle."

"Special privileges for wizards," Barnabus said as he slipped into the pool of steaming water. "And a good thing, too—the water is perfect."

When they had all washed, and the water was starting to cool once more, Alex conjured up a pile of dry, fluffy towels. After they had all slipped their old clothes back on, Alex had them stand in a line. Slowly he moved down the line of his friends, touching each of them with the end of his staff.

"These clothes are too fine," said Thrang, looking at himself in a mirror. "You've made us all look like great lords from distant lands."

"Which is exactly what you are," said Alex.

"And what about yourself?" Arconn questioned. "What change will you make to your own clothes?"

"I've been giving that some thought," said Alex. "Perhaps something like this . . ."

There was a flash of light around Alex, and his friends looked slightly stunned. Alex was suddenly wearing black pants, a bloodred shirt, and a long, dark blue cloak. He looked at himself in the mirror for a moment before speaking, unsure of his appearance.

"A bit much, I think," Alex said at last.

"You made such wonderful clothes for us, and this is what you choose for yourself?" Thrang questioned.

"It looks a little out of character," Arconn said.

"Yes, you're right," Alex agreed. "Let's try this instead."

There was another flash of light, and Alex's clothes changed into the soft white pants favored by elves. A soft leather belt circled his waist, fastened with a true-silver buckle. His white shirt was covered with a pale silver-gray robe. With his staff in his hand, he looked very much like a wizard, and Arconn nodded his approval of Alex's choice.

"Now we look like five lords and a wizard," Nellus said.

"Five lords and a wizard is what we are," said Alex.

When Kathnar appeared to lead them to dinner, his eyes widened in disbelief. Their fine, new clothes were stunning, and Kathnar had obviously never seen anything like them before.

"Lords," Kathnar began, his voice shaking slightly. "The lady of the tower asks that you come."

"We are at her service," said Thrang.

Kathnar led them to the tower, trying hard not to stare at them as they walked. They went up several flights of stairs and soon entered a large, brightly lit dining room. Kat sat in the large silver chair at the head of the table, looking a little pale and a little nervous. She smiled as they took their seats, and once Kathnar had left, she spoke.

"I see Alex has been practicing his craft."

"I wouldn't want tramps coming to your table," said Alex with a laugh.

"You would be welcome however you came," Kat answered. "But you do look better now than you did this morning."

"And you are now the Oracle of the Empty Tower," Thrang said. "We are honored to be your first guests."

"Yes," Kat said, her smile fading. "I hope this will not be the last time we dine together."

"As do we all, I'm sure," said Arconn.

Kat smiled and clapped her hands. Servants appeared with trays of food, which they placed on the table before quietly leaving the room. Kat watched them go, her smile fading again.

"They've been working all day," Kat said softly. "There are so few of them, and they try so hard."

"A meal fit for any king," said Thrang.

"Yes," Kat agreed. "Yet I don't know how many more such meals the tower can afford."

"Surely you remember the treasure we collected from Kazad-Syn?" Thrang said with a shocked look on his face. "We will divide it as soon as you wish. That should be more than enough to pay the tower's expenses for many years to come."

"Yes, of course, you are correct," said Kat, her smile returning.

"And there is the reward promised by Thorgood for the return of the ring," Alex added.

"And all good patrons of the tower will make gifts," Arconn went on. "It is not uncommon for lords and kings to make very generous gifts."

"All that you say is true," Kat said. "Yet I worry still."

"Let your worries rest," Alex said softly. "There are more important things to think about right now."

"The days of celebration," Kat said, nodding her head. "Yes, the preparations have been going on all day. I almost wish I could skip them."

"We will be there with you," Thrang said.

"And that will be enough," said Kat. "Forgive me. This should be a happy feast, not a time for me to worry. Let's forget all of that for now. As Alex says, there are more important things to think of."

Kat tried hard to look happy as they ate their meal, and she even asked Arconn to tell the story of Alex's first adventure once again. When Arconn finished the story, with some input from Thrang, Kat laughed and clapped her hands with the rest of them. Alex, however, could see that something more than money and celebrations were troubling her, but he didn't think he should say anything in front of the others.

Kat said good night, and Kathnar arrived at the door to show them the way out of the tower. As the others made their way to bed, Alex remained in the sitting room. After a few minutes of silence, he walked out to the courtyard, and, leaning on his staff, he looked up at the tower.

"Lord Taylor?" a soft voice questioned from behind him.

Alex turned to find a young woman standing in the shadows. She was extremely nervous, and she was clutching her hands as if afraid.

"I am Alexander Taylor."

"The lady of the tower said I might find you here," the young woman said softly. "She told me to ask you to join her."

"And where does the lady wish me to meet her?" Alex questioned.

"At the top of the tower," the young woman answered. "I would show you the way, but . . . but I don't know it. The lady said you would find your own way, but I don't know how you can."

"The lady knows me," said Alex. "Do not be troubled, I will join the lady as she asks."

"My lord," the young woman managed to say. She bowed and hurried away.

Alex watched her go, and when she was out of sight, he changed himself into an eagle. His wings lifted him with little effort, and he was soon circling the top of the empty tower.

Kat was there, looking out toward the sea. Alex glided down softly, returning to his own shape as he landed beside her on the tower.

"I'm always amazed when you do that," Kat said with a smile.

"And you couldn't resist having me do it now."

"A small pleasure in the middle of dark times," Kat answered softly.

"What darkness do you foresee? You've become the Oracle of the Empty Tower—what more do you wish?"

"Peace."

"I knew it was more than money that troubled you," said Alex.

"The lords and kings of Thraxon will soon know there is an oracle here," Kat said in a soft voice. "They will come or send messengers. Some of them will want answers that I might not have. Others will want to take control of the tower and make the oracle their servant. Even good King Thorgood will be tempted by this."

"You do not know your full power yet," said Alex. "Inside the walls of this tower, your power cannot be challenged, except by some great evil. Here, your word is law. Even I would not dare challenge you here."

"Only because you are good and kind," said Kat in a mournful tone. "Others may not have such an honorable soul."

Alex shrugged. "In the city of Darvish, you will have great power, more than kings or lords. Perhaps even as much as a great wizard."

"You seem so sure."

"I am certain of what I say," Alex said firmly.

"And if wars are started by men attempting to control Darvish and the tower?" Kat questioned.

"I will do what I can for you, as I promised, but it is your job to prevent the wars that might come," Alex answered.

"Already the weight of being the oracle is so heavy."

"It will become less in time, and I can give you two power-ful allies to call on if you are ever in need."

"Two?" Kat questioned.

"I will make sure that Thorgood and the dwarf realm will always stand at your side," Alex answered. "Thorgood has made a great promise for the return of something I carry, something that was lost long ago. I will give it back to him only if he promises to always be an ally to the Oracle of the Empty Tower. And I will place a spell on the object so that if the dwarf kings ever turn against the tower, it will be lost once more."

"That is a powerful promise indeed," Kat said with a weak smile.

"And I will give you more," Alex went on. "If ever you need me, send for me. I will come if I am able. If I cannot come, I will send help. If you cannot wait for me or for the help I send, there is one close at hand who will be at your call."

"The dragon on the Isle of Bones?" Kat questioned. "How can you bind him to me? You are the dragon lord; he has no reason to serve me."

"He will come at your call because I wish him to," said Alex in a definite tone. "I will give you the words to speak, but I warn you to speak them only at your greatest need."

Alex leaned close to Kat and whispered in her ear. When he pulled away, he looked into her eyes to make sure she had understood everything he had said. Kat nodded her under-standing but said nothing. For a long time the two of them stood in silence at the top of the tower, looking deep into each other's thoughts. Just before sunrise, Kat turned away, pale and shaking from the effort.

"Rest while you can," Alex said softly. "The days of celebration are about to begin, but that will be a small thing after this night."

"I owe you everything," said Kat, just as she had before.

"Everything and nothing at all," Alex answered. "Now rest, my friend, we will say our good-byes when the days of celebrations are over."

Alex didn't wait for Kat to reply. He stepped to the edge of the tower and took the form of an eagle. He caught the morning wind and soared up into the dark sky, gliding like a shadow over the city. He knew that Kat understood him, and that she would understand him better as the days went by. He also knew she was far more powerful than she thought. She would somehow find a way to prevent war from coming to Thraxon.

CHAPTER TWENTY-FOUR
THE CROWN OF SET

Two days after the celebrations for the oracle's arrival ended, Alex and his friends prepared to leave Darvish. Barnabus and Nellus had found six horses, and Thrang had released Kat from the adventurer's bargain so she could remain in Darvish as the oracle. Alex spent the hours before dawn in the tower with Kat, helping her to understand her new powers. When the sun touched the top of the tower, Kat and Alex entered the courtyard where the rest of the company was waiting for them.

"So, it is time to say farewell," said Kat with a smile. "And I have no gifts to give you in parting."

"You have already given us a great gift, lady," said Thrang. "You have honored us as your guests during the days of celebration. Few have ever been so honored, and we are all in your debt."

"Then ride on to your reward, my friends," said Kat. "And know that you all will be welcome here whenever you choose to come."

"And may we find our way here often in happiness," Thrang answered as he bowed.

Alex and the others also bowed to Kat before they climbed into their saddles. With a final bow, they rode out of the courtyard and into the city of Darvish. Alex knew how much Kat wanted to be riding with them, but he also knew that she was happy with the choice she had made.

"So the tower has an oracle," said Thrang as he led them through the city. "That is something I never thought to see in my days."

"I never thought I would call an oracle friend," Nellus said as he rode beside Alex. "Though I never thought I'd call a wizard a friend either."

They began talking about their adventure as they rode out of the city gates and back toward the mountains. It would take them at least two weeks to reach Benorg, perhaps longer, but the weather was good, and spring was spreading quickly across the north of Thraxon.

Their journey was pleasant, and they made good time along the road to Benorg. They passed groups of dwarfs going east from time to time, and all of them asked questions about the new Oracle of the Empty Tower. Thrang answered their questions carefully, not wanting them to know that Kat had once been a member of their company. Thrain asked Thrang why he didn't tell people that they knew the oracle, and Thrang laughed when he answered.

"It seems a little bigheaded to claim the oracle's friendship so openly," Thrang said. "After all, not many people ever know an oracle as well as we know the lady of the tower."

"But she is our friend, and she was part of our company," Thrain persisted.

"And that is nobody's business," Thrang answered in a stern tone. "You still have a lot to learn about what should and should not be said openly. I would think being around Alex and Arconn, you might have learned something."

"But they both say a great deal," Thrain complained.

"They say only what they want you to hear," Thrang corrected him. "It seems like a lot to you, but it is little compared to what they could say."

Thrain looked puzzled, but both Alex and Arconn smiled. Nellus and Barnabus both found the exchange funny, but refrained from teasing Thrain.

Spring was well underway when Alex and his friends finally reached Benorg, and the city had transformed into something that looked like a giant garden. Thrang had been talking more and more the closer they got to the city, but Alex noticed that he would sometimes look troubled. He knew Thrang was worried about the return of the crown of Set. Thorgood had made some great promise in exchange for the crown's return, a promise that Thrang didn't want to discuss unless Thorgood was present.

They rode into the city just after noon and were greeted warmly once again. The streets were full of dwarfs going about their business. It wasn't long before a messenger from Thorgood arrived, welcoming them in Thorgood's name and asking them to follow him to the king. The messenger, however, did not ride ahead as he normally would do. Instead, he fell back and rode beside Thrang as they went through the city.

"Your brother, Thorson, arrived two days ago," the messenger said. "He told us that you would be here shortly and that we should watch for you."

"Where is Thorson staying?" Thrang questioned. "I would like to talk with him."

"The king has asked Thorson and his company to stay at the palace. I'm sure you will have time to speak with him there," the messenger answered. "And there is other news. Thorson hinted that you might know something about it."

"What news is that?" Thrang questioned.

"There are stories that a dragon was seen in Darvish," said the messenger. "The rumors are that the dragon brought an oracle to the empty tower, and that the tower is no longer empty."

"That is true," said Thrang in a lowered voice. "But such things should be discussed with Thorgood, as he will want to know the whole story."

"Yes, of course," the messenger said quickly. "I meant no harm."

The messenger, obviously thinking he'd said too much, bowed to Thrang and moved ahead of the company. After a moment, Alex moved forward so he could speak with Thrang quietly.

"What story do you intend to tell Thorgood?" Alex questioned.

"The true one, of course," Thrang answered in surprise. "What do you think I would tell the king?"

"I mean, how much of the truth do you intend to tell him?" Alex pressed. "Remember, you have sworn to remain silent about some things."

"I remember," said Thrang. "I don't know why you wish to keep it a secret, but I will not go back on my word. It will make the story more difficult to tell, and I think Thorgood may guess what I leave out."

"He may," Alex allowed. "But it would be best for his guesses to remain guesses. The time may come when I choose to tell him the whole truth, but I alone will make that decision."

"As you wish," said Thrang. "A wizard's ways are not to be questioned."

"And a dwarf's tongue will always hold true," said Alex with a smile.

"You have learned a great deal about dwarfs," Arconn said from Thrang's other side. "I didn't know you had read the great dwarf poets."

"Only some of them," said Alex, still smiling. "I've not learned enough about dwarfs to love all of their poetry—at least not yet."

Thrang and Arconn both laughed, and Alex slowed his horse slightly to return to his place. He managed to get back in line just as they entered the courtyard of Thorgood's palace, where the king himself was waiting for them.

"Thrang," Thorgood called. "Thorson told us you would be coming. I take it you've found success on your adventure."

"We have, my lord," Thrang answered as he dismounted and bowed to the king.

"Wonderful," said Thorgood. "This is the best news of all, but . . . one of your company appears to be missing. Thorson did not say you would bring sad news."

"And we do not," said Thrang. "But perhaps the story should wait until the lords of Thraxon can be gathered."

"Yes, that would be best," said Thorgood after a moment. "For now, I will thank you and the members of your company that are with you. I've had rooms prepared for all of you. Tonight we will feast, and then you can tell the story of your adventure."

"You are most kind, great king," said Thrang as he and the rest of the company bowed.

Alex knew Thorgood didn't want to wait to hear the story of their adventure, but being a good king, he knew he had to. So instead of asking questions and talking to them as he had done on their previous visit, he had servants lead them to their rooms and ordered that they were not to be bothered.

"Once he hears our story, he will guess that Kat is the new oracle," Thrang said when they were alone.

"And what action will he take?" Arconn questioned. "After all, it is not often that a new oracle appears. He may feel that Kat is in his debt, as it was the adventure he paid for that brought her to the empty tower."

"I've known Thorgood for many years, but I don't know what he will do now," Thrang said slowly. "Kat becoming the oracle was unexpected, and it might cause trouble."

"Not from Thorgood," said Alex. "Perhaps the lords of

the dwarf realm will see things differently, but I don't think Thorgood will start any trouble."

"New oracles are often the center of trouble," said Arconn, sounding worried. "I've seen several come and a few go. In most cases, there is confusion and some kind of trouble."

"Yes, I believe you're right," Alex agreed after some thought. "Kat saw trouble coming after she became the oracle. I've promised to help her in any way I can."

"Well, that should be enough to prevent any real trouble," Nellus said with a smile. "After all, most kings will bow to the wishes of a wizard."

"Most wise kings would," Barnabus added. "Yet not all kings are so wise."

"You don't think Kat is in danger, do you?" Thrain questioned in a worried tone. "If she needs help, I can send to Vargland for soldiers. I know my grandfather would send a small army to protect the empty tower."

"And risk war with the dwarf realm of Thraxon?" Thrang asked, shaking his head. "Don't be silly, Thrain, it is too great a risk. Your grandfather may rule in Vargland, but that is far away."

"I'm not worried about a war," Alex said thoughtfully. "And I think Thorgood will listen to reason. As for the lords of the dwarf realm, I think I can make them see reason as well."

"Yes," said Thrang, his eyes resting on Alex. "I'm sure the lords will do as you wish, but remember, the dwarf realm is not the only power in Thraxon."

"No, it's not," agreed Alex. "It is, however, one of the greatest powers, and there are few that would challenge it. If the dwarf realm is an ally of the tower, I doubt anyone will start any trouble. And I've also given the lady of the tower a powerful defender if she should ever need him."

"The dragon?" Arconn said in wonder.

"She may call upon him only in the hour of her greatest need," said Alex. "I hope that she never needs to call, but she knows how."

"Well then, there is little for us to worry about," Thrang said in relief. "We will tell our story to Thorgood and deliver the ring to him. He will keep his word and make the payments he has promised. Once that is done, our company's business in Benorg will be finished."

"But you live here," Nellus said. "You can't pretend that Kat being the oracle won't affect you."

"I'm sure there will be a lot of talk, but if anything, it will improve my standing in Thraxon," Thrang said with a smile. He glanced at Alex. "And I think there is some other business that must be dealt with before we return to Telous."

"Yes," said Alex. "I would be honored if you would arrange a meeting, Thrang, with Thorgood and his lords. If you and I could speak with them, I think we might solve a great many problems before they actually become problems."

"As you wish," Thrang said with a bow. "I will speak to Thorgood tonight, after we return the Ring of Searching."

"Thank you," said Alex. "Now, I think we should all get cleaned up. We will be the honored guests of the king tonight, and we should look our best."

As Alex turned, he heard Thrang say softly to Thrain, "You

see, he said a great deal and you still don't know what he's talking about."

Alex smiled as he headed toward his room.

Once Alex and his friends had cleaned up from their journey, they didn't have to wait long before they were summoned to the great feast of King Thorgood.

Thrang looked happier than he had in a long time, and Alex could tell that his friend had already worked out the story of their adventure to the last detail. He was glad, because Thrang would have to leave out or make up several important parts of the story while he told it.

As Alex and his friends took their seats for the feast, Alex looked at the assembled dwarfs. Many of the dwarf lords looked as happy as Thorgood did, but a few looked troubled.

"My friends," Thorgood said once everyone was seated. "As many of you know, I asked my good friend Thrang Silversmith to set up an adventure some time ago. The details of this adventure I may now share with you all as Thrang and his company have returned to our fair city, and they have been successful in their quest."

There was a slight buzzing of conversation as the dwarfs in the great hall whispered to each other. Alex wondered how many of them had guessed what Thorgood had asked Thrang to do.

"As you all know, our mines have become less productive over the past several years, which has caused some difficulty for the kingdom," Thorgood explained. "I asked Thrang to find the one item that would solve this problem for us: the legendary Ring of Searching. Thrang has found the tomb of Albrek and retreived the ring, which has been lost for so many years. He and his company have done the dwarf realm of Thraxon a great service, and I am sure you will all wish to honor them."

Thorgood paused, allowing his words to sink in. Alex glanced around at the assembled dwarfs and saw that many of them looked both happy and excited.

"As the person who arranged for this adventure, it is my duty and privilege to declare the adventure a success," Thorgood said with a wide smile. "Thrang, if you would be so kind."

Thorgood motioned for Thrang to come forward, and Thrang slowly stood up and walked to where the king was standing. Bowing to the king, Thrang took the Ring of Searching from his magic bag, holding it high above his head so the assembled dwarfs could see it.

"Will you accept this ring as fulfillment of our bargain for this adventure?" Thrang questioned in a loud, clear voice.

"I will," Thorgood answered. "And I will fulfill the terms of our agreement to you and your company. This adventure is a success, and may all dwarfs honor you for what you have done."

Thrang knelt in front of the king and offered him the Ring of Searching. Thorgood took the ring from Thrang and motioned for two of his guards to come forward. The guards carried a large golden chest between them, which Thorgood opened, carefully setting the ring on the velvet lining. With the ceremony complete, Thorgood bowed to Thrang and thanked him for his service.

"And now, my friends, we feast!" Thorgood said in a loud

voice. "A feast to honor these great adventurers. And after we have eaten, Thrang will tell us the story of their adventure, and how they found the tomb of Albrek."

Thrang stood and bowed to the king before returning to his chair. As he walked across the hall, the dwarfs began to cheer loudly. Thrang stopped and bowed to all four sides of the room. When the cheering continued, Thrang motioned for the rest of the company to join him. The cheering grew so loud as Alex the others joined Thrang that it felt like the air was vibrating with the noise.

"The dwarfs of Thraxon honor you all," Thorgood shouted above the cheering. "You have done a great service for us, and we will never forget you."

The cheering ended only when Thorgood held up his hands to quiet his people.

The feast was a grand one, and it seemed to last for hours. The dwarfs who were serving made sure that Alex and his friends wanted for nothing, filling their goblets before they could empty them, and bringing fresh trays of food to the table whenever something ran low. Alex thought he would burst from eating so much, but the food was excellent.

As the feast was coming to an end, Thorgood motioned for Thrang to come forward once more. The lamps had been dimmed so that Thrang appeared to stand in a circle of light. Slowly at first, but with growing enthusiasm, Thrang began to tell the story of their adventure.

Alex listened as Thrang spoke, his eyes shifting from Thrang to King Thorgood and back again. He was surprised that Thrang did not change anything about their journey to the Isle of Bones, and he looked sad when he told the crowd about his confrontation with Alex. Alex noticed that Thorgood seemed to be watching him, but would look away whenever Alex looked directly at him.

Thrang was as good as his word, telling as much of their story as he could while leaving out some things that might bring too many questions. He hardly mentioned the dwarfs in Nethrom's cave, and he was careful to make it sound like Alex had summoned a dragon to chase away the thunderbird. He said the same summoned dragon had taken Alex and his friends back to Darvish and delivered the Oracle of the Empty Tower to her home.

Alex was a little surprised that Thrang did not name Kat as the oracle; in fact, he did not mention their stay at the tower at all. The fact that Kat was not with them would make it easy for Thorgood to guess she was the oracle, but most of the dwarfs in the room would not even think to ask questions.

"A wonderful tale," Thorgood said as Thrang finished. "I see now that we are more honored than I thought. It is not often that a king has a dragon lord as his guest."

Alex bowed his head slightly to Thorgood, which made the king smile.

"Now, I think our adventurers need their rest, as they have gone through a great deal to return here. I will, however, ask one last thing of them: that they remain in Benorg for as long as they can. I feel that one night's feast is not nearly enough to honor them properly."

Once again Alex and his friends stood and bowed to the

king, but Thrang made no promises about how long they would stay.

With the feast over and the story of their adventure told, Alex felt that nothing would be better than bed. As he and his friends stood to leave the hall with the king, the dwarfs in the hall began cheering again, but this time the adventurers simply waved to the crowd and followed Thorgood out of the hall and into a small chamber.

"I'm sorry for the ceremony, my friends," Thorgood said with a smile. "I know how much Thrang hates such things, and I can tell that the rest of you are uncomfortable with so much praise. Still, you've done a great service for me and my kingdom, and the lords of the realm expect ceremony."

"You are most kind, my lord," said Thrang. "Though you have already named this adventure a success, we are still at your service."

"Ah, then perhaps you will tell me the *whole* tale of your adventure," Thorgood said. "You are a good storyteller, Thrang, but I spotted a few holes in the story you told to-night."

"What was not said should not be said openly," Thrang answered. "Some things are best for your ears alone, while others I cannot say at all."

"No doubt, no doubt," said Thorgood, glancing at Alex.

"King Thorgood, Master Taylor has requested an audience with you and the lords of the dwarf realm," Thrang said. "There are parts of our adventure that will be of great interest to you, parts that have nothing to do with our quest for the ring."

"So I see," Thorgood said, stroking his beard. "I can guess part of this, at least. The seer who traveled with you has not returned, yet you make no mention of her being lost."

"She was not lost," said Thrang. "She led us to the ring, and without her aid we would have been much longer in our search."

"Yet she did not return with you to accept the honors due her," said Thorgood. "I am not so blind that I cannot see where she is. The empty tower has a new oracle—an oracle that you and your company delivered there with the help of a dragon."

"You see much," Thrang said softly.

"And you think I will have some claim on her, as she would not have come to the tower but for this adventure," Thorgood went on. "I must admit the thought crossed my mind."

"To make such a claim would be unwise," Thrang said quickly.

"You give good counsel, Thrang, and I believe you are correct in this as well," Thorgood said after a moment. "Yet I'm not sure all of our people will see it as you and I do."

"Perhaps I can help them see reason," said Alex, stepping forward.

"Oh, I don't doubt that," Thorgood said with a laugh. "Yet you will not always be here, and the memory of you may not be enough to keep all of the lords in line."

"There are other ways," Alex said in a low voice.

"Very well," said Thorgood. "Tomorrow morning, I will call the meeting you ask for. We will discuss the new oracle and anything else you may wish, and I hope that you are able to show the lords of Thraxon wisdom. I would hate to make an enemy of the oracle."

"You have our thanks, my lord," said Thrang, bowing.

"And you have mine, my friends," said Thorgood with a bow of his own.

Thrang led the company out of the main palace and back to their rooms. No one spoke until they were seated around the fireplace, and even then it took some time for Thrang to break the silence.

"I fear that some of the dwarf lords will see this as an opportunity to control the oracle," Thrang said.

"Surely they don't think they can control the oracle," said Arconn. "They cannot control what she says or who she agrees to talk to."

"Perhaps they think to control access to the oracle. They could demand a high price of anyone seeking her wisdom," Nellus said.

"Which would cause a great deal of anger in those who had to pay," Barnabus added.

"They wouldn't do that, would they?" said Thrain in a questioning voice, his eyes fixed on Thrang. "Oracles accept who they will. No one in Vargland would ever think of trying to control access to the White Tower."

"Perhaps not, but the White Tower seems to move, so only those who the oracle wishes to see can find it," said Arconn in a thoughtful tone. "I don't think the empty tower of Darvish can hide so well."

"No, it can't," said Alex. "But there is great power there,

and anyone who tried to control access to the tower would be a fool."

"You know this?" Thrang questioned.

"I felt the power that was there," said Alex. "It will take Kat some time to learn how to use that power, and to learn how far beyond the city of Darvish it extends, but she will."

"Then we must convince the dwarf lords not to try anything foolish," said Thrang, sounding worried. "Yet I don't see how we can."

"Don't you?" Alex questioned.

"You don't even know what Thorgood promised," Thrang said in a low voice. "We agreed not to speak of it until Thorgood was present."

"I know it was a great promise, and I can guess that whatever Thorgood promised, it will have little meaning for me," said Alex. "You and I will speak with Thorgood and his lords tomorrow, and we will see what sort of agreement we can reach."

"Not all of the lords will support Thorgood, no matter what he has promised," Thrang warned.

"They will support the true king of the dwarf realm, or they will lose face," said Alex. "And if the true king of the dwarf realm of Thraxon should break the oath I will ask him to take, then perhaps there will not be a true king in the dwarf realm of Thraxon."

"You are entering dangerous waters," Thrang warned.

"Perhaps," Alex answered. "Yet who better to meddle than a dragon lord?"

Thrang did not reply, and Alex didn't feel like answering

any more questions. There were things he needed to do before he met with Thorgood and his lords in the morning, and he knew that he would get little sleep, if any at all, tonight. He stood up and said good night to his friends, leaving them beside the fire without the answers they wanted.

———✦———

"You look as if you've been awake all night," Arconn said to Alex when he joined his friends for breakfast.

"I have been," Alex said with a tired smile.

"If you are too tired, I can ask the king to postpone our meeting," said Thrang.

"No, it would be best to do this as soon as possible," said Alex, taking his seat and reaching for the nearest platter of food.

Alex ate quickly, and then joined Thrang by the fire.

"Do you know what you will do today?" Thrang asked.

"Yes," Alex answered. "And I think the dwarf realm will be a better place for it."

"I hope you are right," Thrang said softly. "Whatever happens, I will stand by you."

"Thank you," said Alex, patting Thrang's shoulder. "Now, let's go speak with Thorgood and his lords. There are things that have gone on too long, and things that need to be stopped."

Thrang nodded as he turned back to the room and headed for the door. Alex walked quietly beside his friend across the courtyard toward the main palace. When they arrived,

Thorgood was already waiting for them, a nervous look on his face.

"The lords have gathered, but only with some grumbling," said Thorgood. "Be careful of what you say, my friends. Illius is in a foul mood and will try to twist your words to his advantage."

"Illius of Burnlap?" Alex questioned.

"Yes, how did you know that?" Thorgood asked in surprise.

"You can learn much if you pay attention," said Alex. "Do not worry, I will deal with Illius."

"I cannot allow you to harm any of my lords with your magic," Thorgood warned.

"I will not use magic against any of them," said Alex, bowing.

Thorgood nodded, then led the way into the chamber where the lords waited. Thrang looked worried, but Alex knew exactly what he would do and say.

"My lords," Thorgood began as they entered the chamber. "My honored guest, Master Taylor, has asked to meet with us all. He feels there are things that should be discussed with this council, which is why I have asked you all to come here this morning."

"*Demanded* we come would be closer," a thin and sickly looking dwarf to the right of the king said. "Forgive me, Lord Thorgood, but this is most uncommon. The council of lords seldom allows an outsider into this chamber."

"As Thrang told you last night, I was named a lord of the dwarf city of Neplee while on our adventure," said Alex in a pleasant tone.

"Yes, that is true," the sickly dwarf answered with a sneer. "But the southern cities are seldom represented here, and we have only Thrang's word that you were named a lord of Neplee."

"You doubt my word, Illius?" Thrang questioned angrily.

"Not at all, Lord Silversmith," Illius answered with a twisted smile. "Your stories of distant lands have thrilled us all for many years. I'm sure no one here would ever question your word."

"Enough of this," said Thorgood, sounding angry himself. "Master Taylor has been named a lord of Neplee, and furthermore, he is a wizard and a dragon lord. I think that is more than enough reason to let him enter this hall and speak to us."

"As you wish, my king," said Illius coldly as he returned to his seat.

"Very well," said Thorgood as he regained control of his emotions. "Master Taylor, will you tell us why you wanted to meet with us all?"

"There were two reasons that I asked for this meeting," said Alex as he bowed to Thorgood. "Now that I am here, though, I see there are even more reasons than I thought. However, I will begin with the first reason."

"And that would be?" Illius demanded loudly.

"That would be to inform you, King Thorgood, and your lords, that I have sworn to assist the new Oracle of the Empty Tower in any way she may require of me," said Alex, watching Illius out of the corner of his eye. "I have told the oracle to send for me if ever she is in need, and I, or my friends, would come to her assistance."

"A threat, then," said Illius in an angry tone. "You hide a threat in your words, wizard."

"I make no threats," Alex answered calmly. "I am simply informing you that I will aid the oracle if she is in need. Only those foolish enough to try to control the oracle—or control access to the oracle—need fear what I say. I'm sure King Thorgood has no such plans, and so there is no threat in what I've told you."

There was a general murmur of agreement at Alex's words, and Illius looked around angrily. It was obvious he wanted the dwarf lords to feel threatened by Alex, but they all seemed to understand and accept what he had said.

"Wizards are known for their cunning ways," Illius said in a sour tone. "My friends may not see through your words, but I do."

"Do you?" Alex questioned. "I doubt you see very much at all. Your eyes are fixed in one place, and you have failed to look around you."

"What do you mean by that?" Illius questioned, jumping to his feet.

"I mean that I found a new reason for this meeting the minute I heard your name," said Alex. "I heard your name before I ever came to this land or joined in the adventure to find the Ring of Searching."

"Where did you hear my name?" Illius questioned, his face going red. "In some wizard's trance? Or perhaps some dragon told it to you."

"No," Alex said. "I heard it in the adventure shop of Mr. Cornelius Clutter."

"What?" Illius shouted.

"Before I joined this adventure, I was visiting Mr. Clutter," Alex explained. "He was kind enough to tell me about some other adventures that needed members. One of those was to seek for the crown of Set, and the adventure was being paid for by one Illius of Burnlap."

"Lies!" Illius shouted. "You lie."

"That is something I do not do," said Alex coldly, his own anger growing. "If I did not respect Thorgood's wishes regarding the use of magic in this room, you would even now be babbling the truth about your secret adventure."

"It was not secret," Illius said quickly, looking away from Alex. "I was . . . I was going to seek the crown and present it to the king as a gift. I thought it would make a grand gift, that is all."

"And I suppose you never thought of keeping the crown for yourself, did you?" said Alex. "Never thought that the one who held the crown might be named the true king of the dwarf realm. Never considered the possibility that once you had the crown, you could claim to be the true heir of Set."

"No, I never . . ." Illius stammered. He had gone pale as Alex spoke. "It was to be a gift—I swear on my honor."

"You have no honor," Alex snapped. "You twist the words of others to suit yourself. You show no respect to your king when he asks you to attend a council meeting. In secret, you have planned to control the city of Darvish in order to force those who seek the oracle to pay you for the privilege. Yes, I see the truth, and I know where your soldiers are going. No wizard is so blind that he could not see what you are trying to do, Illius."

"Is this true, Illius?" Thorgood questioned, his eyes blazing with anger. "Have you sent soldiers to Darvish? Did you try to organize an adventure to find the crown of Set?"

"Yes," Illius spat back. "You old fool. You would let the opportunity of a lifetime slip away. We can control Darvish and make more in one year than we could in a hundred years of mining. You wasted time and money on a foolish quest for the Ring of Searching when true wealth lies at your doorstep."

"You dishonor us all," said Thorgood, shaking his head in sorrow. "Only a fool would try to control an oracle. If that was your only crime, it would be bad enough, but you have done more. You would seek to depose me and take the kingdom for yourself. Treason is in your heart, Illius, and you would do this whatever the cost to your people."

"The people mean nothing," Illius shouted, his face twisted with rage. "There are always people to do the bidding of the rich and powerful. You lavish wealth on the people, and they love you for it, but what good will it do you in the end?"

"Are you so blind?" Thorgood questioned. "Do you not see that the people make the king? The king does not make the people."

"Do to me what you will," Illius shouted. "I am dishonored by this foul youth, and my plans are made known. Yes, I am lost, but so are you, Thorgood. None of the dwarfs of this realm will ever accept you as king, not until you have the crown of Set, which you will never have. No adventurers would join the quest for the legendary crown, which can only mean that it is lost forever. Your kingdom will never be whole."

"And now you speak of the second reason I had for coming here today," said Alex. "Thorgood guessed that Thrang left out part of our adventure from his story when he told it last night. Now I will fill in that gap, as I alone was there when it happened."

"The cave of the necromancer, and the dwarfs you met," said Thorgood, his eyes wide with understanding.

"Yes," said Alex. "In the necromancer's cave, I spoke to the dwarf Set. He asked me to take his crown to his true heir in Benorg."

"No!" Illius screamed as if in agony. "The crown is lost forever. There is no true king."

"I carry the crown with me even now," Alex went on, ignoring Illius. "I am prepared to return it to you, King Thorgood, but first I must ask you something. What promise did you make? What did you promise in exchange for the return of the crown of Set?"

"Ah, the promise," Thorgood said with a nod. "It was a promise made by all the kings of the dwarf realm, and a promise I will not turn away from now. My lords all know the promise, which is simply this: one-half of all the wealth of the realm is to be given to the one who returns the crown of Set; or, if he wishes, one-half of the realm to rule as his own in the king's name."

"A great promise," said Alex thoughtfully. "More, perhaps, than any crown is worth."

"I am prepared to fulfill the promise," said Thorgood

proudly. "You need only say which you wish—half the wealth of my kingdom, or half of the kingdom to rule as your own."

"And if I should ask for something else?" Alex questioned.

"What else would you ask? You have only to name your price," Thorgood answered firmly.

"It's all a lie," Illius shouted as tears of rage ran down his face. "There is no crown. It is lost for all time."

"King Thorgood and lords of the dwarf realm of Thraxon," Alex spoke loudly enough to be heard over Illius. "In return for the crown of Set, I ask simply this—that you will swear to always be a friend to the Oracle of the Empty Tower. To aid her if she should call, to defend her if she is in need, and to always allow those seeking the oracle to pass through your realm freely."

"That is all you would ask for so great a prize as the crown?" Thorgood questioned in disbelief. "Nothing for yourself, or for your company?"

"That is what I have asked, and the only thing that I will accept," answered Alex.

"Then I swear as king of the dwarf realm, that we shall always be a true friend to the Oracle of the Empty Tower. I swear that we will aid her if she should call and defend her if she is in need. I swear we will do all that you ask and more," said Thorgood, his voice shaking with joy, and his eyes glistening with tears. "And I swear that your name will always be remembered in this kingdom with the greatest of honor."

"I will take you at your word, great king, the true heir of Set," said Alex as he reached for his magic bag. "And I will tell you something more. The crown of Set will remain with your people forever, unless they break the promises you have made this day. If ever the dwarfs of Thraxon turn against the oracle, the crown will be lost once more."

"So be it. How say you, lords of Thraxon?" Thorgood questioned.

"No, no, no, no," Illius shouted wildly. "It cannot be."

"We will keep the promises that have been made," all the dwarfs, except Illius, replied firmly.

Alex bowed to Thorgood, and speaking into his magic bag, he produced the beautiful crown of Set. Bobkin, Belkin, and Dobkin had done a wonderful job repairing it, and Dobkin had figured out what magic had been in the crown before it had been broken. Alex had renewed the old magic, and added a bit of his own. It was his magic that would keep the crown in the dwarf realm, and his magic that would make it vanish if the dwarfs broke their promise to him.

The true-silver crown shined and sparkled in the sunlit chamber, and Alex held the crown up for all the dwarfs to see. The star sapphire on top of the crown glowed faintly with the inner light of magic. Thorgood dropped to one knee in front of Alex, his eyes fixed on the crown.

"Will you honor me by placing it on my head?" Thorgood asked. "What more could any king ask than to be crowned by a true wizard and dragon lord."

"As you wish," said Alex with a bow. He gently placed the crown on Thorgood's head. "Rise, Thorgood, as the true king of the dwarf realm of Thraxon. And always remember the promises you have made this day."

"No!" Illius shrieked in agony. "It wasn't supposed to be this way. I was to be king! It was mine for the taking."

Thorgood got back to his feet, and the star sapphire in the crown seemed to come alive, shining like a flame from the top of the crown. The dwarf lords began to cheer wildly, but Illius fell silent, shaking with both rage and fear.

"Summon the guards," Thorgood commanded. "Illius must pay for his treason, as will all those who conspired with him."

"King Thorgood, I must speak," Alex said quickly. "I have spent the night searching your city, discovering the truth of what was being done. Illius is alone in his treason, and even the soldiers he sent to Darvish did not know why they had been sent. Illius told them it was by your wish that they were going and that they would receive instructions once they reached the city."

"No, he's lying," Illius shouted. "I have many allies, many followers who wish for me to be their king."

Thorgood ignored Illius's ranting. "I will send the swiftest riders after the soldiers at once so they will not trouble the oracle. Illius will be tried for his crimes, but I will not place his evil on the house of Burnlap. Now, my friend, if you have finished, I must ask you to leave us. You have given my lords and myself many things to discuss this day."

"As you wish, great king," Alex answered, bowing.

Alex left Thrang in the council chamber and followed the guards who were dragging the ranting Illius away. Illius was shouting commands that the guards ignored, and Alex thought that the dwarf might have lost his mind.

"I'll have my revenge on you, wizard. You've not won yet. I'll hunt you across the known lands and make you pay for this day," Illius shouted as the guards pulled him toward the dungeons.

"Be careful what you wish for, Illius," Alex replied coldly. "If you live long enough to come hunting me, you will find something much more deadly than a wizard waiting for you."

Alex turned away from his newest enemy and made his way back to the rooms where his friends were waiting. He was glad he had been able to restore the crown of Set to Thorgood, but he felt oddly sorry for Illius. Illius had not started out as an evil dwarf—no one ever started out evil—but he had let his love of power and riches destroy him.

Thrang returned to the company late that evening, looking worn out by the day's events. As he entered the common room, he greeted Alex and quietly thanked him for all he had done.

"I have been afraid for many years that someone might find the crown," Thrang said as they sat beside the fire. "If the wrong person had found the crown, the dwarf realm could have fallen into civil war."

"Then it is lucky that I found it," said Alex.

"Lucky?" Thrang questioned. "The longer I know you, the less I believe in luck."

"Well, all is right now," said Arconn. "How long will we remain in Benorg before returning to Telous?"

"Tired of the city already?" Thrang questioned.

"I could live here a hundred years and not grow tired of this city or its people," Arconn answered. "Yet the adventure is complete; our work in Thraxon is done."

"Yes, you are correct," said Thrang. "We will stay for ten days, anything less would be rude. Then we will return to Telous and conclude our adventure."

"Ten days of parties and stories? A high price to pay for success," Alex said with a laugh.

In the end, Alex and his friends stayed in Benorg for twelve days, and each day ended in a grand feast and a retelling of their adventure. Alex was pleased that Thrang told the same story as he had that first night and that nobody seemed to guess the truth about the dragon that had carried the oracle to the empty tower.

When they finally did leave the city, the streets were lined with dwarfs, and the company could hear the cheering long after they had left the main gates behind them. It was only when they were well away from the city that they began to talk of what the future held. Alex, of course, was planning to meet Whalen in Telous; he had already sent a message to tell his friend when he would be arriving. Arconn would be going to Vargland with Thrain to visit the elves who lived there. Barnabus and Nellus both planned to return to their own homes, and Thrang would wait in Telous for a company of dwarfs traveling from Vargland to Thraxon.

"Though perhaps I will ride with Arconn and Thrain into Vargland," Thrang said. "I can meet the trading company on the road."

"That would be nice," said Thrain. "I wish Fivra could come as well."

"Don't worry, I'm sure young Fivra will find an oracle to visit soon enough," Arconn said with a smile.

For a moment, Alex thought he might like to return to Vargland and visit his friends as well, but he knew that was not possible right now. Whalen had found a new home for him in Alusia, and he wanted to see it and start getting settled there. He also had a great deal to tell Whalen, things he had been unable to put into writing.

"I suppose you will be thinking about retiring again," Alex said to Thrang on their last night in Thraxon. "The payment for this last adventure will surely be enough to keep you comfortable for many years to come."

"It will indeed," said Thrang with a grunting laugh. "Yet I would miss the open road and the chance to be with good friends."

"And it would be too easy for his relatives to find him if he settled down." Arconn laughed.

It had been a pleasant night, and Alex didn't want it to end. It had been the same on his first two adventures: he was sad, knowing that he would soon be parted from his friends, but he was also happy because there was a good chance he would see them all again someday. There were always new adventures and new friends to come.

CHAPTER TWENTY-FIVE

A NEW HOME

———◆———

I t was almost noon when Alex and his friends arrived in Telous, and as always, the Golden Swan had plenty of food and drink ready for them. A message had arrived that morning for Alex, informing him that Whalen would be arriving the next day. So with nothing much to do after they had eaten, Alex and Arconn walked the streets until the sun was setting.

Their evening feast was as grand as any Alex had ever eaten at the Swan, and he was glad that Thrang did not make too long a speech at the end of it. They were all a little sad that Kat was not there with them, but Thrang was quick to point out that her absence was, in fact, a good thing. They finished their evening with a toast to the new Oracle of the Empty Tower and a wish that they might all travel together again someday.

Alex went to bed tired that night, and if he had dreams he could not remember them when he woke in the morning. The company met for breakfast, and then Thrang led them across the street to the building where they could donate to the Widows and Orphans fund. They could all afford to be extremely generous, not only because they had gathered a great deal of treasure on their adventure, but also because Thorgood had insisted on giving them an advance against the treasure he would owe them in the future.

"Thorgood will keep his word, but it was easier for him to pay us while we were in Thraxon," Thrang said with a smile. "I know you've all agreed to collect what the dwarf realm sends from here, but it will be costly to ship so much treasure to Telous."

"Perhaps we should have let Thorgood hold our wealth and simply collect it whenever we are passing through Thraxon," Arconn said with a smile.

"It would be good to return to Thraxon," Nellus added. "I, for one, would like to return often, if only to visit the oracle."

"A good idea," Barnabus said. "Several members of my family wish to visit an oracle, and it would be good to visit one I know."

"Do not wear your friendship with the oracle thin," Alex warned. "She may be our friend, but that holds no promise. As the oracle, she may not see the people you take to her."

"You don't really think she'd say no, do you?" Thrain questioned in concern.

"I don't think so, but we should not test her," Alex answered.

"And, as I told you before, Thrain, it is not wise to openly claim friendship with an oracle," Thrang added.

Thrain didn't reply, but Alex could see that the young dwarf was still confused about what he should and should not say openly. Alex remembered his own first adventure and how little he had understood or even believed. Now his world was completely different than the one he remembered. His life was divided between the world he knew before he'd accidentally walked into Mr. Clutter's shop, and the world he'd discovered after.

Alex and his friends gathered once more at the Swan for their midday meal so Thrang could officially end their adventure. It was a happy time, even though they would all soon be going their separate ways. Thrang recounted what they had done during their adventure, making a point of mentioning all the things Alex had done. Alex would have protested, but he knew Thrang too well, and he knew that it wouldn't do any good.

"And so, my friends," Thrang said as he stood to toast them. "We will call this adventure complete. And to quote another great adventurer, it has been a first-class adventure all around."

Alex and the others all gave a loud cheer and stood to toast with Thrang. And just like that the adventure was over, though no one seemed in a rush to leave the table. Alex asked Arconn and Thrain to take his best wishes to his friends in Vargland, which they both happily agreed to do. Then Nellus and Barnabus started to sing a traveling song, which made Alex wonder when his next adventure would begin.

As the song ended, the door to their private dining room opened, and Whalen Vankin stepped into the room.

"I thought it must be you," Whalen said with a smile. "I trust I'm not intruding."

"No, not at all," Thrang said quickly, getting to his feet and offering Whalen his own chair. "Our adventure has been concluded, and now we are simply a group of friends enjoying each another's company."

"Ah, you are most kind," said Whalen, taking the chair Thrang offered him. "You must be Thrang Silversmith; I've not had the pleasure of meeting you before."

"The pleasure is mine," Thrang answered with a bow. "I am honored you have joined us."

"To be numbered among such a group as this, it is I who am honored," said Whalen. "Now, perhaps my friend Alex will introduce you all to me, though I'm sure I know your names already."

"Yes, of course," Alex stammered.

Whalen seemed to know much more about Alex's friends beyond the details Alex had shared through his letters. Thrain blushed bright red when Whalen asked him about his family, and Nellus and Barnabus were both dumbfounded when Whalen was able to name people from their own lands that he knew. Arconn had met Whalen once before, but that had been many years ago.

"Still adventuring, then," Whalen said as he looked at the elf.

"As are you, my friend," said Arconn.

"It's not an easy job to quit," Whalen said with a laugh. "And it seems that I am needed more and more often, though I hope with Alex's help, I will be able to spend some time at home."

"I will be honored to assist in any way I can," Alex said, wondering if Whalen had already found a new adventure for him to join.

"I'm sure you will," Whalen said. "For now, however, I think you should come with me to Alusia. I've found a wonderful new home for you—if you're still interested, that is."

"I am," Alex answered. "Though it will seem odd, not returning to the place I've called home for so long."

"Oh, you can always go back," Whalen said, laughing. "Though the longer you stay away, the harder it will be for you to return. I almost never go back to the place where I grew up, even when I have the time. I suppose there are too many memories there, and too many things that I have chosen not to remember as well."

"You would honor us if you would join us for the evening meal," Thrang said, changing the subject.

"A kind offer that I must refuse," said Whalen. "I'm afraid I have other matters to attend to, and I'm only taking time out today to show Alex the home I've found for him."

"We will be leaving today?" Alex questioned.

"Yes, as soon as you are ready," answered Whalen. "I know you hate to leave your friends so quickly, but I am really very pressed for time."

"Is there something I can help you with?" Alex asked, surprised by Whalen's rush.

"No, no, nothing like that," said Whalen. "I've made promises to be places, and with one thing and another, well . . . let's just say I have time to take you to Alusia and then I must be off."

"As you wish," said Alex.

"I will leave you to say your good-byes, then. Gentlemen, it has been a great honor to meet you all. I wish you all good fortune, and I hope that I may have the pleasure of traveling with each of you one day."

"You are most kind," said Thrang.

Everyone in the room stood and bowed to Whalen as he moved out of the room, and then they turned to say good-bye to Alex. Alex had planned on saying his farewells the next morning, but Whalen was in a hurry, and as Alex still considered him to be his teacher, he thought it best to do as he was told.

"Until we meet again, my friend," Arconn said, pulling Alex into a hug.

"I hope that it will be soon," said Alex. "And when Thrang does finally retire, I'll have to make a special trip to Thraxon to visit him."

"Don't say that too loudly." Thrang laughed as he embraced Alex. "Thorgood will insist that I retire just so you'll return to his kingdom."

"What will I do without you?" Thrain questioned, his eyes bright with tears. "You've saved me so often, I'm getting used to having you there."

"You're going home in good hands," said Alex, nodding at Arconn. "And I'm sure you won't need to be saved very often in Vargland."

"You must come to my homeland one day," said Nellus as he shook Alex's hand.

"And mine as well," Barnabus added. "My family won't believe I actually know a wizard."

"I will try to come if I can," said Alex. "And if nothing else, perhaps we will travel together again someday."

After his good-byes, Alex turned to leave, pausing at the door to turn back one more time to smile at his friends. They raised their mugs to him in a toast, and Alex laughed and left them behind.

Whalen was waiting for Alex in front of the Golden Swan. He had already ordered Alex's horse saddled. The famous wizard was getting a great many looks from the people of the town.

"I'm sorry to drag you away so quickly," said Whalen in an apologetic tone when Alex came out of the front doors. "I wish we could spend the night, but I am running a little late. We must leave for Alusia now. It will take us at least two days to reach the home I've found for you, which should give us all the time we need to talk."

Alex smiled and climbed into his saddle, happy that Whalen seemed to understand how he was feeling. As they rode out of Telous, Alex tried to arrange his thoughts, considering what he should tell Whalen first. In the end, he decided to tell Whalen the story from the beginning, including all the things he hadn't told his friends.

They were a few miles outside of Telous when Alex finally began to talk. He found that the story was longer than he remembered it, longer than when Thrang had told it, and not nearly as exciting when he told it himself. Whalen didn't interrupt or ask questions as Alex talked, and when Alex finally finished, they were at the great arch.

"That's it," Alex said as Whalen climbed off his horse. "That's the whole story of what happened in Thraxon, and I still don't know what it all means."

Whalen nodded but didn't say anything. He seemed to be thinking about what Alex had said, and Alex thought that even Whalen might not know what to make of the story. How often had a wizard become a dragon lord? How many wizards had ever taken the dragon shape and survived? What had King Set meant when he said he had been waiting for Alex? There were too many questions and too few answers.

Alex unsaddled the horses while Whalen set up their camp. His mind was troubled by his unanswered questions, but he felt better now that he'd told Whalen everything. When he had finished taking care of the horses, Alex joined Whalen by the campfire, his eyes watching the flames as Whalen cooked their meal.

"Do you know how long it takes most wizards to become wizards?" Whalen asked suddenly.

"No," said Alex, surprised. "Several years, I'm sure, but I've never really thought about it."

"And do you know how much training most apprentices need before they are ready to even try to take a staff?" Whalen went on.

"No, I don't," said Alex.

"Most apprentices are in training for years," Whalen said. "A great many of them never learn enough to take a staff."

"But everyone knows there have never been very many wizards in the known lands," said Alex.

"Yet there are a fair number of people who can do magic of one kind or another," said Whalen. "Why do you think so few of them ever become wizards?"

"I don't know. Maybe they weren't able to find a wizard to train them."

"Yes, that is true for many of them," Whalen agreed. "Perhaps for others, the training is too difficult, or they are not patient enough to learn all that is required. Then, of course, they may not have enough magic in them to become wizards in the first place." Whalen shook his head and sighed. "I've accepted any and all who wanted to be trained and who were willing to learn. I've been alive for almost seven hundred years, Alex, and I've had countless apprentices. But only two have ever gone on to become wizards."

"What does this have to do with me?" Alex questioned.

"Ah, yes, what about you?" Whalen replied. "You used magic on your first adventure, before you understood it, before you became an apprentice. You were able to look into a dragon's eye and defeat him with your own power—something that most wizards would not dare try even after taking a staff. You've learned more magic on three adventures than most apprentices learn in a dozen years of study, and you've done it without a wizard there to teach you."

"I was lucky, and you've shown me the path I should take."

"I gave you some direction, but you found the path yourself," Whalen said with a smile. "You are something of a mystery, even to me. And I think your dragon friend was right—you are more than most wizards could ever hope to be."

"Don't say that," said Alex. "I'm just . . . I'm just lucky."

"Yes." Whalen laughed. "Lucky, and quick, and a wizard that is both a man and a dragon. Oh, there are legends and myths about wizards who could take the dragon shape without fear, but I think most of them are just stories, made up by people who didn't know better."

"So you think I am something else?" Alex questioned. "Not really a wizard, but something else completely?"

"You are a true wizard, Alex. That much I know for sure," Whalen answered in a kindly tone. "But it seems that you are also more than that, but all that you are, I cannot even guess."

"If you don't know, Master Whalen, who does?" Alex questioned in a defeated tone.

"Do not call me master," Whalen said in a kind but serious voice. "You have no master, my friend, and I doubt there is anything in the known lands that could become your master. As for what you are, I think only you can find that answer. And I believe you will, in time."

"Then I must continue searching for answers to my questions as I travel through the known lands," Alex said.

"And that makes you sad?" Whalen questioned.

"Yes. I thought you would know what I am and what I should do. You've always had the answers before."

"Most people, myself included, do not know what they are," said Whalen. "I know I am a wizard, an adventurer, and a man, but what am I really? That is a question I am still trying to answer, and I've been asking it for almost seven hundred years."

"But . . ." Alex began and stopped. "I don't understand."

"You are what you do," Whalen said. "You are what people think you are, and more importantly, what *you* think you are. If you think of yourself as a great hero, you will act like a great hero. If you think of yourself as a small thing—something that doesn't matter—well then, you won't matter."

"But I don't really think about myself," Alex protested. "I don't see myself as a hero or a wizard or anything like that."

"Do you see yourself as good or evil?" Whalen questioned.

"Good, of course."

"Friendly or not so friendly?"

"Friendly, I think."

"Hot-tempered or reasonable?"

"I try to be reasonable, but I sometimes lose my temper."

"You see many things about yourself already," Whalen said as he began filling bowls with stew. "And I wish I could say I see myself as a great cook, but I'm afraid the truth is that I'm only a fair cook."

Alex laughed and accepted the bowl. The stew was very good, in fact, and Alex thought about Whalen's words while he ate. Whalen may not have answered his questions as directly as he had hoped, but he had still given him some answers. Alex had never considered things the way Whalen put them, had never even thought about his own self-image. Now he thought about it for a long time, and he began to see that Whalen was as wise as ever.

They spent the rest of the evening in silence, Whalen watching the stars and Alex deep in thought.

———————

The next morning, they rode through the great arch into Alusia.

"What do you suppose Set meant when he said he had been waiting for me?" Alex asked as they rode along the well-worn trail.

"A wizard's deeds are often foretold," said Whalen in a thoughtful tone. "I've never sought out legends or prophesies in the hope of fulfilling them, but I have been looked for in places where I never thought I would go."

"So I shouldn't really worry about it," said Alex.

"Oh, I wouldn't worry," said Whalen. "Though you might want to find out about the prophecies later, after they've been fulfilled, so you know who made them and when. Unfortunately, I've found that most of the details that go with legends and prophesies are often lost, and only the waiting for things to come true can be remembered."

Alex thought for a long time before he asked his next question, hoping that Whalen would have a simple explanation for him.

"What about the books the dragon on the Isle of Bones gave me?" Alex asked.

"Ah, the dragon," said Whalen with a smile. "An ancient and wise creature, to be sure."

"But the books," Alex persisted after Whalen remained silent. "What are they? Where did they come from?"

"Yes, the books," Whalen said slowly. "I will warn you that you should keep them secret from everyone, and keep them safe. Never tell anyone you have one or more of them. If I had thought you might find one of these books on your own, I would have told you about them sooner."

"But what are they?" Alex asked, surprised by Whalen's warning.

"Ancient books of knowledge," said Whalen. "Never study them where others might see them, and never ever leave one lying about."

"Are they dangerous?" Alex asked.

"To people who have little or no magic, they are very dangerous. There are dangers even for wizards, but that comes from loving power too much," Whalen answered. "You see, the books will teach you things. As you study the pages, the letters will begin to take shape in your mind. Eventually it will be like a dream, and you will see and hear what the books have to say. I've seen one book that you could smell things in, but I don't know how common that is."

"You've seen books like these before?" Alex questioned.

"Yes, I have," said Whalen with a weak smile. "And your guess is correct—I have a few of them myself. Some of them are simple and will show you the history of the known lands, but some are full of power. Those that have power in them can teach you a great deal about magic. Others can even transfer their powers to you. Now you see why they could be dangerous to people who don't have any magic of their own."

"Yes, that make sense," said Alex.

They rode on for a time as Alex considered what Whalen had told him about the magic books. It seemed obvious that Salinor was protecting the books, keeping them safe. Why the dragon had chosen to give them to Alex was less clear, but Alex knew the dragon had his reasons.

"The dragon also talked about my family," Alex said carefully. "Do you know anything about them?"

"I do," Whalen said with a smile. "I didn't think you'd have time to ask old Clutter about them, so I did some digging on my own."

"And?" Alex asked in excitement. "Do you know where my family comes from? Do I have aunts and uncles and cousins?"

"Yes, I know where your family is from, or at least where it is from recently." Whalen laughed. "And yes, you have aunts and uncles and cousins and a great deal more. Your mother and father were related to almost every royal family in the known lands. Not just the human royal families either, but the elves and the dwarfs as well, though you might have to search a bit more to find those links."

"The royal families?" Alex questioned in amazement.

"Well, some of the relations are a bit distant, but still, you are related. I imagine most, if not all, of the royal families will want to do the family history for you. After all, it would be good for them to have a wizard in the family." Whalen looked at Alex. "But you should be careful with any information you learn about your family. From what little I know of your family, I would guess that not all of them are worthy of your assistance. I would suggest you learn all you can about any family members you meet before you help them."

Alex nodded his understanding.

"Not all kings are good or noble," Whalen reminded Alex. "I think you know what I mean, though you've not run into any really bad kings on your adventures so far."

"No, but I've seen men and dwarfs who wished to take

the place of a king," said Alex. "I imagine I'm related to some people like that since they had some claim to a royal bloodline."

"Oh, yes," said Whalen in a serious tone. "Bloodlines are important to most people, and most important to the royal houses."

"Will you tell me who I'm related to and how?" Alex questioned.

"Of course." Whalen laughed. "You don't think I learned all this for my own amusement, do you?"

Alex laughed at Whalen's reply and for the rest of the day, he listened closely as Whalen explained how Alex was related to the different royal families in the different lands. Their evening fire was burning low before Whalen had finished telling Alex all that he'd learned. Alex was amazed by how many relations he had, and the fact that Whalen seemed to know so much about all of them.

"Don't worry," Whalen said with a smile. "I've written it all down for you. I don't expect you to remember everything I've said, even if it is about your own family."

"I don't know how you remembered it all," said Alex.

"I've lived a long time, and I've learned to organize things in my mind," Whalen answered. "You've already learned to do this with some things, as you seem to have no trouble remembering magic spells."

"That seems almost natural," said Alex.

"Almost too natural sometimes? Almost too easy?" Whalen said as he watched Alex.

Alex nodded.

"Ah, your greatest fear," said Whalen in his kindest voice. "You fear that because it all comes so easily to you, that you will not appreciate or remember it when you need to."

"And that it might all slip away as easily as it came," Alex added.

"Yes, it is a common fear," said Whalen. "I've felt that fear myself, but very few things have ever slipped away without my knowing about it."

"So I should not worry about losing everything I've become?" Alex asked.

"What good does the worry do you?" Whalen asked in return. "If all your magic were to slip away tonight, would worrying about it help you?"

"No, I suppose it wouldn't."

"Then don't worry about things you can't control," Whalen said. "I doubt very much that your magic will ever slip away, and worrying about it won't make a bit difference one way or the other."

"It does seem a silly thing to worry about when you put it that way."

"Yes, and you have other things to think about. Tomorrow we will pass through the small town of Resprin. The home I've found for you is a few miles outside of the town."

"What kind of town is Resprin?" Alex questioned.

"Not large. The people of the town keep horses, and most of the horses belong to the king. I suppose that means that some of them are probably yours as well," said Whalen as he leaned back against his saddle. "They are good people, honest and fair in their dealings. I think you will like the town, and I hope you will like the house I've found."

"How far from Resprin do you live?" Alex questioned, rolling into his own blankets.

"Two days to the south," Whalen said sleepily. "There is another town called Albian, and my home is a few miles east of that town."

"I would like to see your house someday," Alex said as he closed his eyes.

"And I would like to see you in your dragon form," Whalen said through a yawn. "Perhaps tomorrow, if there isn't anyone near, you could show me your other self?"

"As you wish," said Alex and went to sleep.

The next morning after breakfast, Alex walked a little way from their campfire. He turned to look at Whalen and, then, after thinking for a moment, he laughed at himself.

"What?" Whalen questioned.

"The horses," Alex answered. "You had better put a calming spell on them, or we'll be walking the rest of the way to Resprin."

"Oh, yes," Whalen said with a laugh of his own.

Once Whalen had cast his spell, Alex relaxed his mind, accepting what he was. The magic filled the air around him, but it was different this time, more alive somehow. He paused to consider the magic, the connection to everything around him, and then he changed.

Yes, Salinor's voice said softly in his mind. *It is different in each land, but also the same.*

The connection to the land, it's . . . Alex trailed off.

It is something special. Something only dragons like ourselves can experience, said Salinor.

Dragons like ourselves? Alex questioned, knowing Salinor wasn't talking about all dragons, but something else.

We that are true silver, said Salinor. *We are . . .*

What?

In time. Salinor laughed. *You do not need to learn everything all at once, child.*

Alex wondered what Salinor meant, but he knew the ancient dragon was finished speaking. He would learn what he needed to know in time, and that was enough for now. He relaxed his mind, focusing his thoughts on his human form and letting the magical connection slip away.

"True silver," Whalen said in awe as soon as Alex was his human self once more. "You become a dragon of true silver."

"I know. I never really thought about it. Does it mean something?" Alex questioned.

"I'm not sure," Whalen answered slowly. "I've heard of legends that mention a dragon of true silver. I can't remember the exact wording, however, and I don't have time to look it up right now."

"But you will look?"

"Oh, yes, I'll look and let you know what I find," said Whalen. "You see, I don't remember everything, even if sometimes you think I do."

"Well, I remember that you are in a hurry," said Alex. "So we'd best be on our way."

"That is true, but before we go, I must swear an oath," said Whalen.

"What?"

"I, Whalen Vankin, swear by my staff that I will never tell anyone the secret that Alexander Taylor has shared with me this day," Whalen said quickly.

"Whalen, you don't need to swear by your staff," said Alex in surprise. "I'm sure the council will want to know, and—"

"Alex," Whalen interrupted. "Wizards should have some secrets that only they know. I think it would be best if you kept this part of yourself as secret as you can. Don't ask questions and don't ask for reasons because I don't have answers or reasons, just a feeling."

"As you wish," said Alex, accepting Whalen's advice.

Whalen nodded and removed his spell from their horses. They rode south and west, away from the main path they had been following the day before. As they crossed the grasslands of Alusia, they passed several large herds of horses, and Alex felt sad remembering the loss of his own horse, Shahree.

"There is one more thing we need to talk about," said Whalen after they'd gone several miles.

"The conspiracy Bane talked about," said Alex. "You didn't say anything about it in your letters."

"I didn't want to trouble you while you were in the middle of your adventure," Whalen replied. "But I believe Bane is right—there is something very wrong in the known lands. Nethrom's last words were an important bit of information, but not as conclusive as you might think. I've suspected for many years that part of the order of Malgor was involved."

"Should we warn the leaders of the order? Perhaps they

can find out who is working against them and deal with the problem," said Alex.

"Do you know the legend of the Gezbeth?" Whalen questioned suddenly.

"The Gezbeth? No, I've never heard of such a thing. What does that have to do with the conspiracy?"

"The Gezbeth is a legendary monster," said Whalen. "It is said that the monster had three heads and six arms, and that it ate everything it could get its hands on. Many brave warriors and soldiers died trying to defeat the monster, but none succeeded. Eventually an old man appeared and told the people the secret of the Gezbeth. You see, the monster had three hearts, and all three of them had to be destroyed at the same moment if the monster was to be killed."

"Whalen, what are you talking about?" Alex questioned.

"I think what we are fighting is something like the Gezbeth. A conspiracy that has more than one center—and more than one leader—but all working toward a single goal."

"And if we destroy only one center, the monster will simply grow a new center over time," said Alex, remembering his battle against the hydra outside the necromancer's cave.

"I believe we have already destroyed parts of this monster," said Whalen. "Your victory over the necromancer was a blow to their plans. I think the recent trouble here in Alusia might well have been another part of the plan. The trouble is, we don't know where the centers of the conspiracy are, and unless we can destroy them all, well . . ."

"You want to watch the people you think are involved,"

said Alex. "Perhaps they will lead us to other parts of the monster."

"Yes, that is our hope," said Whalen. "It's not just you and me, Alex. The rest of the council is involved, as well as many other people. We are watching and learning about our enemy. I hope that one day—and one day soon—we will discover what we need to know."

"And the conspiracy's goal?" Alex questioned. "Do you have any idea what this monster is trying to do?"

"No, not really," said Whalen in a defeated tone. "We're trying to piece it all together—looking for clues, listening to whispered stories—but we don't know what our enemy is trying to do. We don't know what their real goal is."

"Then I suppose we'll have to wait and watch," said Alex.

"Yes," said Whalen. "And you will be an important part of our watching, now that you know about the monster. As you travel, you will know what to look for and can report back to us what you have learned."

"I will try," said Alex. "I will try to find clues and answers, and I will hope that we can find the centers of power and destroy them before . . ."

"Before they destroy the rest of us," Whalen finished. "Yes, that is our greatest fear—that we will wait and watch too long and we will be unable to stop the monster when we finally discover what it is trying to do. For now, keep your eyes and ears open, and let me know about anything that seems suspicious."

"What if something happens to you?" Alex questioned.

"I have some letters of introduction I can send out," said Whalen. "It would be good for you to have contact with other members of the council, in any event. Then, if anything should happen to me, you'll have other people you can trust with the information you discover."

"A good plan," said Alex.

"I only hope it is good enough," said Whalen.

It wasn't quite noon when they came to a fair-sized house at the bottom of a large hill. The tall stone tower attached to one end of the house was at least twice as tall as the next highest part of the house. Behind the house was a barn, and a small stream ran alongside the house. Sitting on the front porch of the house was a tall, thin man. He stood up as Whalen and Alex approached and hurried into the yard to meet them.

"Master Vankin, Master Taylor," the man said with a bow. "I wasn't sure what time you would be arriving."

"You were kind to meet us, Jonathan," said Whalen with a smile. "Alex, this is Jonathan Tanner. Jonathan is the chief herdsman of Resprin, and as such, he is the king's representative in the town."

"A great pleasure," said Alex, bowing to Jonathan.

"The pleasure is mine," said Jonathan. "King Trion has sent word that I am to do whatever I can for you. I've heard the tales of your adventures with my friend Silvan Bregnest, and I am only too happy to do as Trion orders."

"You know Bregnest?" Alex questioned.

"There are few in this part of Alusia who do not know Bregnest," Jonathan said with a laugh. "He often rides to the towns on the king's business—or at least he does when he is not off on an adventure."

"I would very much like to see Bregnest again," Alex said.

"Let's take a look at the house first," said Whalen, reminding Alex of why they were there.

Jonathan took their horses for them and tied them to a rail beside the porch. He was happy to show Alex and Whalen around, and Alex was happy with what he saw in the house. There was plenty of room for him to store his things, but not so much room that he would feel lonely. There was even running water, piped into the house from a spring near the top of the hill behind the house, which Alex thought was very convenient. The rooms were large and friendly looking, and already furnished.

"Trion sent the furniture as a welcoming gift," Jonathan explained. "He hopes you will be staying in Alusia for many years to come."

"A kind gift," said Alex.

"Then you will take the house?" Jonathan questioned nervously.

"Let me think for a little while."

"Very well, Master Taylor."

"In the meantime, what is there to eat here, Jonathan?" Whalen asked.

"Oh, the pantry is full, Master Vankin," Jonathan answered. "I can prepare anything you may wish, or almost anything."

"An overstatement but kindly meant," Whalen said with a laugh. "Come, let's see to the pantry while my young friend does his thinking."

As Whalen and Jonathan went to the kitchen, Alex wandered out the front door to look at the grounds around the house once more. He walked around the tower toward the back of the house, not really looking at or for anything. He walked through the oak trees that grew behind the house, and when he came to the stream, he stopped. It was the perfect house and would be a wonderful place to live, but he felt sad for no reason he could name.

A sudden movement on the far side of the stream startled Alex, and he instantly brought up his staff to defend himself. He smiled when he saw the palomino horse on the far bank. He lowered his staff and called softly to the horse. It was a male horse, young and fairly large, with a mane as white as snow. Calling softly a second time, Alex remembered how much horses used to scare him. The horse seemed to study him for a moment, and then it walked slowly to him and nuzzled his shoulder.

"Well, my friend," Alex said softly. "What herd have you wandered away from?"

The horse whinnied in reply and pressed his head gently against Alex's shoulder. Alex was surprised by the strange show of affection, but he rubbed the horse's forehead gently just the same.

"Well, I suppose I should accept this house," Alex said softly. "It looks to be everything I've ever wanted or hoped for."

The horse bobbed its head up and down the same way Shahree had done sometimes when Alex had talked to her. Alex smiled at the memory and patted the horse's forehead again before he turned to go back and talk with Jonathan.

"Who's your friend?" Whalen questioned as Alex walked toward the front door.

Alex noticed that the palomino horse had followed him home. "He was drinking from the stream when I was out walking. He must have wandered away from one of the herds. Perhaps Jonathan will know where he belongs."

Whalen called Jonathan out of the house, but when Jonathan saw the horse at Alex's shoulder, the look on his face was something more than surprise.

"Do you know this horse?" Alex questioned.

"The herders call him Dar Losh. It means dragon fire in the common language," Jonathan said slowly. "He is . . . he is of the king's herd, though part of that herd belongs to you as well. I would have to search the records to make sure, but he's as likely to be one of your own horses as he is to be one of the king's."

"Why do you look so surprised to see him here?" Alex asked.

"No one has ever been able to handle him," Jonathan said. "He runs wild across the grasslands. We've tried to catch him in the past, but he can outrun any horse in the kingdom."

"Yet he seems friendly enough with Alex," Whalen said.

"He is," said Alex in a definite tone, turning to rub Dar Losh's neck. "He seems as tame as any horse I've ever seen."

"Tame to you," said Jonathan. "I swear no man has ever been able to catch him or befriend him as you have. Is this some magic? Have you put some spell on this horse to make him follow you?"

"No." Alex laughed. "I called to him from across the stream, and he came. I didn't know he was following me until Whalen pointed it out."

"Then I think you have found a very good friend," Whalen said thoughtfully. "What do you think, Jonathan? Would any other man be able to handle this horse?"

"No, I'm sure they would not," said Jonathan. "If Master Taylor wishes this horse for his own, I am authorized by the king to make it so."

"In that case," said Alex with a smile, "I accept Dragon Fire, or Dar Losh, as you call him, as my own horse. I also accept this house. How much is the king asking for it?"

"The king asks only that you keep it in peace," said Jonathan. "He said the house and the lands about it are to be yours for as long as you wish them to be."

"The king is most kind," said Alex. "I will accept Trion's goodwill and send a message of thanks to him as soon as I can."

"Very well," said Jonathan with a smile. "I welcome you to the lands of Resprin. If you need anything, please let me know."

"Thank you," said Alex. "And if I can be of service to the people of Resprin, or to King Trion, please let me know."

"You are most kind," said Jonathan with a bow. "And now, I must go about my duties. I must inform the citizens of Resprin that you have agreed to stay. I would not want them to be surprised by your presence."

"Thank you," Alex said again.

"Yes, thank you, Jonathan," Whalen added.

Jonathan bowed once more and left them, his eyes turning back to look at Dragon Fire and Alex several times before he rode out of sight.

"Your legend grows again," Whalen said. He looked at Alex's new horse. "He seems well named, does he not?"

"As if I'd chosen the name myself," said Alex, rubbing Dragon Fire's forehead again.

"Well, now that you are here and have accepted Trion's generous gift, I should be on my way."

"Already?" Alex asked in surprise. "I thought you'd stay the night at least."

"No, I've spent enough time here already. I must be going, but I'll leave you with one last piece of advice. Stay true to your friends, and stay true to yourself."

"That's two pieces of advice," Alex pointed out.

"Is it?" Whalen asked with a smile, and then rode away.

Alex watched Whalen until he was out of sight, and then he turned and looked at his new home. It was a beautiful house, really, and he felt happier than he could ever remember feeling before.

Dragon Fire nudged his shoulder gently. Alex absently rubbed the horse's nose and then turned to look at his new friend.

"Go," Alex said softly. "Run free across the land. I will call you when I need you."

Dragon Fire whinnied in response and galloped off across the grasslands. Alex watched him for a while, running like the wind across the low hills of Alusia. Finally he walked back to the house and went inside. It was time to get settled in, time to put things in order, and time to get ready for his next adventure, whenever it might come.

Discussion Questions

1. The first part of Alex's adventure is spent in the library and archives of Benorg. How can a library be a good place to start an adventure?

2. While traveling toward the Isle of Bones, Alex and his friends hear rumors about trouble on the road. Kat says that the trouble with rumors is that you never know what to believe. Have you ever heard a rumor that made you unsure what to believe? What did you do about it?

3. The dragon Salinor lost control and destroyed the dwarf on the Isle of Bones after they attacked him. Have you ever lost your temper and done something you felt sorry about? Is there anything special you do to keep from losing your temper?

4. When Kat first tries to enter the empty tower, Alex stops her and reminds her of her duty to the company. Have you ever had to give up something you wanted because you'd made a promise to someone else?

5. When Alex creates the monument for Shahree, he writes the words, "A True Friend" on it. Why do you think he chose those words? What do you think makes a "true friend"?

6. The dwarf Nethrom learned things that other people

had forgotten, but he wasn't willing to share what he learned. In the end, the secrets and his unwillingness to share his knowledge destroyed him. Why do you think that is? Have you ever kept a secret that has gotten you into trouble?

7. We learn that Nethrom isn't really evil, but he was being controlled by an evil spirit. Could something like that happen to real people? Could people have bad habits that, like the evil of the necromancer, control them?

8. After Alex gives Kat the oracle's crystal, she says that he has formed her destiny around her like a cage. What does she mean? Do you ever feel like people are building your future around you?

9. Near the end of the story, King Thorgood tells Illius, "The people make the king. The king does not make the people." What do you think he means by that? Who is more important—the king or the people?

10. While traveling to Alex's new home, Whalen Vankin tells Alex, "You are what you do." What do you think he means by that?

11. Whalen's final piece of advice to Alex is, "Stay true to your friends, and stay true to yourself." Alex says that it's two pieces of advice, but is it?